Ru

D0292729

Also by Syrie James

Historical Fiction
Jane Austen's First Love
The Missing Manuscript of Jane Austen
The Secret Diaries of Charlotte Brontë
Dracula, My Love
The Lost Memoirs of Jane Austen

Contemporary Romance
Songbird
Nocturne
Propositions

Young Adult Romance
Forbidden
Embolden

Runaway Heiress

A Dare to Defy Novel

Syrie James

AVONIMPULSE

An Imprint of HarperCollinsPublishers

RUNAWAY HEIRESS. Copyright © 2018 by Syrie James. All rights reserved. Printed in the United States of America. No part of this book may be used or reproduced in any manner whatsoever without written permission except in the case of brief quotations embodied in critical articles and reviews. For information, address Harper-Collins Publishers, 195 Broadway, New York, NY 10007.

Digital Edition JUNE 2018 ISBN: 978-0-06-284966-3

Print Edition ISBN: 978-0-06-284967-0

Cover photos: © Mary Chronis, VJ Dunraven Productions & PeriodImages.com (couple); © Akabei//iStock/Getty Images (garden); © Boonyachoat/ iStock/Getty Images (sky)

Avon Impulse and the Avon Impulse logo are registered trademarks of HarperCollins Publishers in the United States of America.

Avon and HarperCollins are registered trademarks of HarperCollins Publishers in the United States of America and other countries.

FIRST EDITION

18 19 20 21 22   HDC   10 9 8 7 6 5 4 3 2 1

For Bill, my real life romance hero

CHAPTER ONE

London, England
May 8, 1888

"One first-class ticket for Liverpool, please." Alexandra Atherton managed a smile for the ticket agent behind the window.

"One way or return?"

"One way." Alexandra anxiously made her way across the busy train station, hardly able to believe she was doing this: running away, dressed in her maid's old clothes, bound for Liverpool and the steamship that would take her home.

Her escape, she knew, would cause something of a scandal. Over the past few years, whenever her name or one of her sisters' names had cropped up in the press, it was always followed by "the American heiress," or "the daughter of multimillionaire banking tycoon Colis Atherton." As if they were not actual people in their own right.

Alexandra hated to feed the gossip, but after last night, what choice did she have?

She had left a note explaining where she'd gone and why,

which her maid Fiona was to "accidentally discover" later that afternoon. By then, it would be too late for her mother to prevent Alexandra from sailing. She just prayed that upon her reaching Liverpool, a berth would be available aboard the *Maritime*.

The train platform was alive with the clamor of movement and conversation. Gentlemen in black frock coats and ladies in elaborate plumed hats darted to and fro, checking the printed timetables, studying the large clock hanging from the rafters, purchasing apples from a vendor and papers from the newsstand. As Alexandra wove through the crowd, she heard a high-pitched voice at her elbow:

"Got a penny for a poor orphan?"

She paused. Before her stood a raggedly dressed, dirty little girl. Alexandra's heart went out to the creature, who gazed up at her with wide eyes, her hair all in a tangle.

Alexandra wondered how a penny could possibly be of any help to a child in such need. Withdrawing her coin purse from her reticule, she offered the child a shilling. "Here you go, little one." Suddenly, more children in similarly dirty clothing appeared and crowded around her.

"Mine!" cried a boy.

"No, mine!" cried another.

A grubby fist flashed out and snatched the shilling from Alexandra's grasp. She couldn't tell if it was the first girl who took it or one of the boys; indeed, she wasn't entirely sure *what* happened next. All Alexandra knew was that multitudes of small, filthy hands were striking at her as young voices erupted in raucous shouts. Her coin purse was suddenly wrenched from her grasp, and a second later her hand-bag was gone.

"Wait! Give it back!" Alexandra cried, as the flock of children fled. "Help! Stop those children! They've stolen my bag!"

No one made any move to help her. Alexandra pushed her way through the crowd, racing after the children, but the raga-muffin band vanished as quickly as it had appeared. At the end of the platform, she stopped to catch her breath. The whole incident, she saw now, had been cleverly played, the efforts of a pack of urchins who preyed on unsuspecting travelers.

She searched for a policeman (what did they call them here? Bobbies?), but realized that even if one materialized, she couldn't report the theft. She was dressed as a servant, in the act of running away.

Alexandra stood rooted to the spot, overwhelmed by a crushing sense of horror and disappointment as the depths of her predicament became clear to her. Her handbag was gone. It had held all her money as well as her train ticket. She hadn't been able to take anything else with her, and now had nothing left except the clothes on her back. Clearly, there would be no trip to Liverpool today, and no voyage to New York.

Tears stung Alexandra's eyes as she made her way back through the train station. What should she do now?

She considered the English girls she'd met over the past five weeks of the London Season, but realized they'd be no help. Not a single one had responded to Alexandra's attempts at friendship. They'd seemed to consider Alexandra too outgoing, too outspoken, and had eyed her with reserved and stony suspicion, as if she were there to deliberately steal away all the best men. The matrons Alexandra had met had all befriended her mother. Nor could she seek refuge from Rose Parker, a debutante from Chicago who'd landed her titled man the year before and was now the most miserable human being in creation, entirely under the thumb of her husband.

As Alexandra exited through the train station's high Doric portico, she wiped tears away. It was over. It was all over. Unless she wanted to starve on the street like the poor, ragged, toothless woman selling apples at the curb, Alexandra had no alternative but to go back to Brown's Hotel with her tail between her legs.

Even though it would spell her doom.

Even though her mother would surely lock Alexandra in their suite again until she agreed to marry Lord Shrewsbury.

Well, Alexandra told herself, as she hailed one of the waiting hansom cabs and climbed aboard, her ruse had worked this time. She would just have to think of something new and try again in a few days for another ship.

"Brown's Hotel," she instructed the cabbie through the trapdoor near the rear of the roof.

"That'll be a shilling." The man's tone conveyed his distrust of such a shabby customer.

Alexandra peered up at him through the tiny window behind her. "Sir, I've been the victim of a robbery. My handbag and all my money were stolen. I'll see to it, however, that you are paid upon arrival."

"Cash in advance, Yank, or there's no ride."

"Sir, my name is Alexandra Atherton. My father is a mul-timillionaire. If you will please take me to Brown's Hotel, I assure you that my mother will pay my fare."

"And who's your mother? America's first lady?" A brief, contemptuous laugh escaped his mouth. "There's plenty of folk who'll be happy to pay in advance, girl. Go on, step down."

Cheeks flaming, Alexandra climbed down from the vehicle. She tried every cab in sight, but it was always the same story: no fare, no ride. Alexandra was incensed and hu-miliated. She was an *heiress*. She'd attended college! She'd been the belle of the ball at numerous events of the London Season. Yet she was being treated harshly, simply due to the clothing she wore.

Alexandra realized she'd have to walk. How many miles lay between Euston Station and Brown's hotel? She had no idea. During the cab ride that morning, she'd been so ab-sorbed in her thoughts, she hadn't paid attention to their route.

Pausing at a corner, Alexandra asked a shoeshine man how to get to Brown's Hotel. His instructions were long-winded and delivered in a thick cockney accent. She was able to gather, though, that it was a journey of about two miles. Following his gesticulations, she began walking south.

It was a gray, cloudy spring morning with the threat of rain. Although Alexandra had always enjoyed long walks in the countryside growing up, she'd never been enamored of strolling in a city. The sidewalks of London were jammed with men and women rushing about their business, and the streets were clogged with traffic. Horse-drawn carriages of every size and description jockeyed for position with hansom cabs, men on high-wheel bicycles, and buses topped with crowds of people. The air, heavy with soot and smoke, was further befouled by the stench of horse dung and urine that covered the street and lay piled up in heaps at the curb. A boy of twelve or thirteen dodged among the vehicles, struggling to scoop the excrement into a bucket, but it was a futile battle.

Alexandra waited for an opening in the traffic, then raised her skirts and picked her way across the street. Thank goodness she'd worn her oldest, sturdiest pair of walking boots, the only shoes she possessed that wouldn't have looked out of place with the plain black cotton dress she wore. Even so, by the time she reached the opposite curb, she'd had to scrape off the filth that clung to her soles.

She plodded on, past a street locksmith's stall, a man towing a barrel organ on wheels, and a fancy wear dealer selling porcelain ornaments from a wheelbarrow. Sandwich-board men crowded the curb, wearing signs proclaiming such slogans as TRY DR. CLARKE'S TONIC AND HAIR RESTORER and DRINK COLA: IT QUENCHES THE THIRST AS NOTHING ELSE WILL.

Twice more, she stopped to ask for directions. Eventually, a clock on a bank building told Alexandra she'd been walking for two and a half hours, and she began to wonder if she'd made a wrong turn. She should have reached Brown's Hotel by now. At the very least, she should recognize something of the neighborhood. But nothing looked familiar. Instead of elegant white houses, she saw rows of redbrick buildings and streets lined with shops and pubs.

"Fresh muffins!" shouted a woman in a cheap dress and dirty apron who was selling bread and pastries beneath a makeshift tarp.

The aroma of freshly baked goods made Alexandra's mouth water. She hadn't eaten anything since dinner the night before, having planned to purchase something at the station. Although she'd never bought food off a city street cart in her life, she would have been happy to do so now, if only she had the money.

Alexandra's feet were beginning to hurt, and she was growing tired. She was more alarmed, however, by the darkening clouds and increasing chill in the air. Shivering, she noticed a chimney sweep leaning against a wall and approached him. "Is Brown's Hotel nearby?"

"Brown's Hotel?" The sweep scratched his head beneath his cap. "Well now, miss, if you're headed for Brown's Hotel, you'd best take a cab. It's a good three or four mile from here, and looks like rain any minute."

Alexandra's spirits fell. Three or four miles! Clearly, she'd wandered very far out of her way. "I have to walk," she replied with resignation. "Can you please point me in the right direction?"

He barked out a few instructions, then indicated an alley just up the street. "You can cut through that lane beyond the Horse 'n' Hound, it'll save you ten minutes."

Alexandra thanked him, and they moved off in opposite directions.

She turned into the narrow, refuse-strewn alley, and was halfway down it when a big man in a rough coat and cap emerged from a doorway and stopped directly in front of her.

"Well, well, well, what's the hurry, lassie?" he called out in a thickly accented voice which was slurred from drink.

A foul stench emanated from his body. Alexandra wrinkled her nose, more irritated than afraid of this unexpected disturbance. "I've already been robbed once this morning," she declared flatly, as she attempted to dodge around the man. "I have nothing left to give you."

He grabbed her forcefully by the arm, grinding her to a halt. "I wouldn't say nothing, lassie." With beady eyes, he studied her slowly from head to toe, then back up again, giving her a leer that exposed a mouthful of rotten teeth.

Alexandra's pulse now quickened with apprehension. "Please, let me go."

"Not until you gives us a kiss." He pressed his free hand to her back and yanked her against his chest.

"Don't!" Panic surged through her as she turned her face away, struggling to break free.

The man persisted, pressing fleshy lips against her neck. He reeked so strongly that Alexandra felt bile rise in her throat. Her arms were trapped, so she kicked at him, landing a good one against his shin. He roared in pain and fury. Still gripping her upper arm, he raised his other hand as if to slap her, when all at once the skies opened up and unleashed a sudden, cold, and very heavy rain.

Her attacker started in surprise, the unexpected downpour causing him to loosen his grip. Alexandra took advantage of the reprieve to free herself and fled back down the alley. The pelting rain came so fast and furious that in seconds, she was wet through.

At the lane's end, Alexandra burst onto the sidewalk—and plowed directly into someone. She heard the sound of breaking glass, glimpsed a man's startled face. Spinning in a half circle, she staggered backward into the street.

What occurred next came all in a whirl: the clatter of hooves. A horse's whinny. The sight of a vehicle bearing down on her. The world tilting as she dodged sideways. A sharp pain in her head.

And then she knew no more.

"**B**loody hell!"

Thomas Carlyle stared at his recent purchase, now smashed to bits on the sidewalk, the victim of a collision with a woman who'd raced out of the alley.

As he stood there, pelted by freezing rain, he saw the woman career into the street, directly into the path of an oncoming vehicle. He gasped in horror as the woman stumbled and fell to the ground, where she lay unmoving as the horse and carriage thundered past, narrowly missing her.

Was she dead? He hoped not—the carriage didn't appear to have touched her. A few people hurried by, huddled beneath their cloaks and umbrellas, paying no attention to the prone figure lying in the muck and mud.

He ought to do the same.

This is not your affair, an inner voice warned. He was cold and wet. He had work to do. He shouldn't get involved. But another, stronger voice insisted, *This is partly your fault.* If she—whoever she was—had not run smack into him, she might not have stumbled backward into the road.

Thomas spied a carriage rapidly headed in the young woman's direction. She could be crushed in the next instant. With no time for further deliberation, he darted into the street and scooped her up. Once he regained the safety of the curb, he stared down at the limp form in his arms, rain dotting his spectacles as he noted several things in rapid succession:

She was young and slender with long limbs and a pale complexion. Her black dress and worn boots marked her as a member of the working class. The bodice of that dress pulled tight across an ample bosom—a sight mere inches from his eyes, and from which he had difficulty averting his gaze.

Those breasts, he saw now, were moving gently up and down. *Thank heavens.* She was breathing. She was alive. But what on earth had happened, to cause her to run full tilt like that out of the alley, without looking where she was going?

Thomas peered down the alley from which she'd emerged. No one was there. He glanced back at the street to determine if she had dropped a handbag or any other item which might help identify her, but he saw nothing other than the sodden, trampled remains of a straw hat.

The rain was coming down in buckets, rapidly washing away the street muck that had clung to the young woman's hair and clothes. What was he supposed to do now? He considered dropping her off at the Horse and Hound, in the hope that someone would take pity on her. But no, that wouldn't be gentlemanly. Besides, she might need medical attention. He had no idea, though, if there was a doctor's surgery in the neighborhood.

He couldn't just stand there holding her in the pouring rain. He lived a block away. It seemed best to bring her there and let Mrs. Gill take over.

When he arrived at the redbrick townhouse, unable to reach the key in his pocket, Thomas gave the dark green door a few solid kicks. "Mrs. Gill! A little help, please!"

A moment later the door was flung open. His Irish landlady, her graying hair half hidden beneath a white cap, was all astonishment. "Mr. Carlyle! What on earth?"

"This young woman fell in the street," Thomas explained as he brushed past Mrs. Gill into the compact foyer. "She was nearly run over by a carriage and appears to be unconscious. Pray, allow me to bring her into your parlor."

"Of course," Mrs. Gill cried, skirts rustling as she bustled after him. "The poor thing! Who is she?"

"I have no idea. Forgive me," Thomas added as they entered the small, overstuffed room, where a fire was blazing in the hearth. "We are both drenched through and dripping all over your carpets."

"Just you stand by the fire and wait, Mr. Carlyle. I'll fetch towels and blankets before you set her down." Mrs. Gill disappeared into the back room.

Thomas moved to the hearth, grateful for its flickering warmth as he made a more comprehensive study of the woman in his arms. She looked to be in her early twenties, a few years younger than himself. She was pretty, her oval face and delicate features reminiscent of Romney's early paintings of Emma Hart. Her hair, too wet to determine its true shade, had come loose and hung in waves to her waist.

He guessed her to be a shop girl or seamstress, or perhaps a servant on her day off. As he gazed down at the lovely yet helpless form he was holding against his body, Thomas felt an unexpected spark of interest and compassion. He hoped she was going to be all right.

"Here we are." Mrs. Gill returned, her arms full of cottony fabric. She draped several towels over the sofa, and Thomas laid the insensible young woman down.

She was starting to shiver now, and so was he. Mrs. Gill removed the girl's gloves and dabbed at her with a towel, then tucked a blanket over her, while Thomas dried off his own face and hair and wiped his spectacles clean.

"You'd best take off that wet coat, Mr. Carlyle," Mrs. Gill advised, "lest you catch a chill."

He obliged, shrugging out of the sodden garment, which she took and hung over the fire screen. "Now what? Shall I fetch a doctor?"

"Let's give her a minute. She's young and healthy-looking, no doubt she'll wake up soon enough. A doctor would cost a pretty penny, which you and I can ill-afford."

Thomas flinched at this assessment. He had never told Mrs. Gill—nor any of his clients in town, for that matter— who he really was. If anyone knew, he would be treated differently; he certainly wouldn't be able to stay here any longer, or to continue his work. But what she'd said was true. His fi-

nances *were* in a bad way. Ever since he was a child and aware
of such things, he'd had the vague impression that money,
for his family, was a problem. Now that he was twenty-eight
years old and faced with all the sordid facts, his sense of mortification over the situation was acute.

A soft moan issued from the direction of the sofa, interrupting his thoughts. Glancing over, he saw that the
young woman was moving restlessly beneath the blanket—
hopefully, a sign that she would soon wake up.

CHAPTER TWO

Alexandra was running down a garden path, tall hedgerows looming on either side. Her head ached, an incessant throb that echoed the hammering of her feet. What was she running from? She couldn't remember.

A group of young ladies in evening gowns suddenly glided into her path.

"What sort of girl marries a man thousands of miles away from home?" intoned the first lady in an upper-crust English accent.

"An American girl with a heart of ice," replied the other from behind her fan.

They both sent withering glances in Alexandra's direction. Her heart seized with indignation. Before she could formulate a reply, her mother stalked up, eyes glittering with anger and ambition.

"You *will* marry him, Alexandra! How else are your father and I to earn a spot in Mrs. Astor's Four Hundred?"

Suddenly, her mother vanished, replaced by two well-dressed Englishmen smoking cigars. The first was Viscount Shrewsbury: middle-aged, red-faced, and so obese, the buttons of his waistcoat looked fit to burst.

"I am looking forward to dipping my wick into *that* one." Lord Shrewsbury tapped ash from his cigar as he darted a covert grin at Alexandra.

"And looking forward to getting your hands on all that money," declared the second gentleman with a dark laugh.

Her stomach churning, Alexandra tried to dart around the two men. But as the second man disappeared, Shrewsbury dropped his cigar and blocked her path. "No need to be shy, Miss Atherton." Before Alexandra could blink, one of his beefy hands pulled her to him, and the other fondled her breast through her low-cut gown. Then his mouth clamped down on hers as his tongue thrust deeply into her throat.

Alexandra pushed him away with a choking gasp of horror. He tasted like a chimney laced with something stale and foul. "Sir, you forget yourself!"

"I forget nothing." Lord Shrewsbury smirked. "We are soon to be wed. I am simply sampling the merchandise." He grabbed her again. Alexandra tried to scream, but no sound emerged from her throat.

A woman's voice now seemed to come out of nowhere: "I think she's coming round."

Alexandra opened her eyes, heart pounding, her mind whirling in a fog of dazed confusion. Her first coherent thought was a jolt of immense relief. *She'd just been dreaming. She wasn't in that garden with Lord Shrewsbury, not anymore.*

But where was she? Why did her head ache? And why did she feel so cold, grimy, and wet?

Alexandra took in her surroundings. She was lying on a sofa beneath a coarse blanket in a small, unfamiliar parlor.

The furnishings were simple and looked as if they'd seen better days. Two windows draped by heavy, faded curtains looked out on a brick wall. It was pouring down rain outside. A kind-faced, middle-aged woman in a white cap loomed nearby, smiling.

"There! She's with us." Her lilting accent was decidedly Irish.

"Pray, do not be alarmed," came another voice, a male voice, with an English accent as rich as clotted cream.

A tall gentleman approached the sofa. He had a long, lean frame. His hair, cropped shorter than the current fashion, was wheat blond shot through with gold, as was his neatly trimmed mustache. As he crouched down beside her, she noticed that the collar of his white shirt was frayed.

"Welcome back, miss." His eyes, behind wire-rimmed spectacles, were the warmest, most captivating shade of chocolate brown she'd ever seen. "You fell in the street. I brought you to the lodging house where I am staying. This is my landlady, Mrs. Gill. How do you feel?"

Alexandra wanted to say that her head hurt and she ached in several other places as well, but her lips wouldn't formulate a reply.

"Can you tell me your name?" he persisted.

Her name? A memory presented itself: she was a young girl, playing in a garden with two other girls. "Lexie," she murmured softly.

"My name is Carlyle. Do you remember what happened to you?"

Alexandra tried to think, despite the dull pounding

inside her temple. The man—what was his name, Carlyle?—said she'd fallen in the street. She vaguely remembered that now. It had been raining. A carriage was bearing down on her. She'd stumbled, must have hit her head and passed out. Another memory surfaced: she'd collided with a man on the sidewalk—*this man*.

Before that, she'd been running down an alley, like the one in her dream, trying to escape.

Escape. With a sudden flash of clarity, the realization of who she was and everything that had happened to her came back in a rush: the events in the garden last night, the escape from the hotel that morning, the children who'd robbed her, her exhausting trek across London, the villain in the alley.

"Yes, I remember," she replied slowly. "I was accosted by a drunk in an alley. Then I was almost run over by a horse and carriage."

Mr. Carlyle abruptly stood, the warmth he'd formerly displayed disappearing. "You're *American*." He frowned down at her in surprise, pronouncing the last word with un-disguised disdain.

Her nationality didn't seem to bother Mrs. Gill, who gave a short, delighted laugh. "American! Well now, who would have guessed?"

"I *am* American," Alexandra remarked, adding with an attempt at humor, "but don't worry, it's not contagious."

Mr. Carlyle didn't even crack a smile, just took a step back and lapsed into silence. Alexandra had the sense that he was done with her. Why? She wondered if he was one of those people who thought all Americans were vulgar and obnoxious. Well, it didn't matter. She wouldn't stick around where she wasn't wanted. "How long have I been out?"

"About ten minutes or so is all," Mrs. Gill answered. "Does your head hurt, dearie?"

"Yes. But I guess that's to be expected. Thank you both so much for your help. Now I ought to be on my way." Alexandra flung back the blanket and tried to stand, but her head began to pound so violently, she had to grab the back of the sofa to keep from falling.

"You're not ready to go anywhere just yet," Mrs. Gill insisted. "You just sit back down, Lexie, there's a good girl."

Alexandra did as she was bidden. "Thank you." It was strange to hear this woman call her Lexie—no one ever used that nickname except her sisters.

"Is there a friend or family member whom we might contact, to let them know you are here?" Mr. Carlyle seemed anxious to get rid of her.

The mention of family caused a brief flash of guilt to warm Alexandra's cheeks. Hours ago, she would have been discovered missing from her hotel room. Her mother would be livid. But if Fiona had played her part and delivered Alexandra's note, her mother would presume Alexandra to be in Liverpool by now, boarding the steamship *Maritime*.

It suddenly occurred to Alexandra that the accident might have proved to be a good thing. Mrs. Gill seemed like a sympathetic woman. If Alexandra could just stay here for the night, it would buy her time to think, to figure out where to go next and what to do.

"What's your surname?" Mr. Carlyle asked impatiently.

Alexandra hesitated. If she told these people who she was, they'd surely contact her mother, who would storm down here like the seven Furies and drag Alexandra back to the hotel, force her to marry that horrid man. If, on the other hand, Alexandra kept her identity a secret . . .

Honesty, Benjamin Franklin had once written, was the best policy. It was a point of honor for Alexandra that she'd never lied to anyone. People didn't always want to hear the truth; she'd lost friends because of it. Still, she'd clung to the principle, believing that life was simpler if you stuck to the facts. It pained her to even *think* of deceiving this kind woman who'd taken her in, and this man who'd most likely saved her life.

But she couldn't go back to her mother. She just *couldn't*.

Alexandra swallowed hard. Maybe she could just *bend the truth* a little.

"My name is Lexie Watson," she said, blurting out the first surname that popped into her head, inspired by a story by Arthur Conan Doyle, published the previous December. "I'm afraid I have no friends in England, nor any family to turn to."

"None?" Mrs. Gill was aghast.

Alexandra shook her head.

"An employer, then?" Mr. Carlyle prodded. "What brought you to London? Who do you work for?"

So, he presumed her to be a member of the working class. She had no wish to dissuade him of the notion; it seemed like an excellent cover. "I'm not employed at present." Entirely true.

"What did you do before?" Mrs. Gill asked.

Now that she'd started down this road, there was no turning back. Willing the pain in her head to go away, Alexandra thought fast. She needed a story that would fit with the clothes she was wearing. She considered saying that she was a lady's maid like Fiona, but doubted she could portray someone of that profession or social standing with conviction.

And the less lying, the better.

In the Poughkeepsie neighborhood where she grew up, Alexandra used to read to children who were sick, and at the library. She'd also helped to organize summertime fetes for young people. "I worked with children."

"Oh, you're a governess, then?" Mrs. Gill nodded. "I suppose you came overseas on holiday with one of those wealthy American couples? I hear they bring their entire staff with them to watch over their children, while they traipse all over Europe and God knows where looking at monuments and such."

Alexandra cast her eyes downward, hoping her silence evoked affirmation.

"Well, what happened?" Mrs. Gill went on. "After bringing you all this way, why on earth did they let you go?"

Here, Alexandra could also stick to the truth. "Last night, at a party, a gentleman of high rank tried to force himself on me."

"Dear me!" cried Mrs. Gill.

"Tried to force himself . . . ?" Mr. Carlyle's brow furrowed with reprehension.

Alexandra blushed fiercely at the memory of Lord Shrewsbury's assault. "When I reported what happened, the gentleman's side was taken. Circumstances deteriorated, and I had to leave."

The reserve Mr. Carlyle had exhibited earlier began to fade, replaced by a hint of empathy. "I see."

"So they didn't believe you." Mrs. Gill sniffed with disgust. "It doesn't surprise me; highborn folk like that always take the man's side in such things."

"I wandered the streets for hours." So far, except for her last name, Alexandra hadn't uttered a single lie—and she was determined to keep it that way. "A band of urchins stole my few belongings. Then I was attacked by a drunk in an alley. I was trying to escape from him when I ran into you, Mr. Carlyle." It was strange to think that for twenty-four years, she'd led such a sheltered, pampered existence . . . and now, in the space of less than twenty-four hours, she'd been robbed, physically assaulted by two different men, and nearly trampled to death by a horse and carriage.

"Good heavens! What an awful time you've had, Miss Watson."

Mr. Carlyle frowned. "Do you truly have no one in London whom we might call?"

"No. If you hadn't helped me, I don't know what would have happened. I'm in your debt, sir. Once again: I thank you." Alexandra attempted to stand, but her head began to spin again and she had to plunk back down. "Oh. I'm sorry."

"No need to be sorry." Mrs. Gill patted Alexandra's shoulder. "You hit your head and were senseless, and that's nothing to make light of. Why, I had an uncle who bumped his noggin and went right back to work the same day, then dropped dead the next morning! No! I won't hear of you going anywhere—and where would you go in any case, not knowing a soul in London, and without a penny to your name? You're just going to have to stay the night."

Success! Alexandra thought.

Mr. Carlyle's expression, however, implied that he wasn't thrilled by this idea. He excused himself to go change out of his wet clothes, and Alexandra heard his footsteps as he hurried up the stairs.

An hour or so later, when she felt strong enough to stand and walk, Mrs. Gill invited Alexandra to accompany her to the kitchen.

"Mr. Carlyle seems to be annoyed with me," Alexandra commented as she followed Mrs. Gill down a narrow hall to the back of the house, presuming that she was to be offered an early dinner. "Have I offended him somehow?"

"Don't worry yourself about him, dearie. He's a strange one, for all that he's so handsome, and the best tenant I've ever had."

"Strange in what way?"

"Well, for one thing, he's so quiet. Normally, I'd be grateful for that in a tenant. But just now, when he brought you home, that's the most I've heard him say in one sitting since the day we met. All right then, here we are."

The kitchen was old and cluttered but clean, with a fire blazing in a large grate. Several pots were boiling on the stove, and the aromas of cooked beef and hot broth filled the room. A girl in a stained apron sat at a table, peeling potatoes.

"Here's some soap and towels," Mrs. Gill announced, handing said items to Alexandra, "and a clean nightdress. It belongs to Mary, but should fit you all right."

Soap and towels? Nightdress? That's when Alexandra spotted a sizeable tin tub by the fire, half filled with water. She froze in dismay. Alexandra was dying to wash the street grime from her hair and body, but did Mrs. Gill truly expect her to bathe here, *in the kitchen*, in front of the scullery maid?

Her thoughts darted to the extravagant bathroom at her family's new mansion on Fifth Avenue—the polished marble floor and walls, the luxurious claw-foot tub, the gleaming porcelain sink, the gold-plated fixtures. Every hotel she'd ever stayed in on the continent and in London had been first class. Even the modest bathroom she'd grown up with in their house in Poughkeepsie, with its tile floor and exposed pipes, had been palatial in comparison to this.

"My lodgers are obliged to use the public baths," Mrs. Gill explained, as if noticing Alexandra's hesitation, "but they're closed now. After falling in the road, I thought you'd be glad of a wash on the premises, as I do."

"I am," Alexandra said slowly, glancing at the maid.

"Mary!" Mrs. Gill cried sharply, pulling the curtains shut on the windows. "Leave the potatoes and be gone with you. Let's give this young lady some privacy, shall we?"

"Yes ma'am." The maid wiped her hands on her apron and scooted out the door.

"If you give me your dress, I'll brush it clean as best I can," Mrs. Gill offered.

"That's very kind of you." Alexandra removed her dress and handed it over.

"I put a pitcher by the tub for rinsing. You enjoy a good soak now. I'll be in the front parlor when you've finished."

"Thank you."

Mrs. Gill left the room and shut the door.

Alexandra set her shoes on the hearth, then slipped out of her undergarments, unsure what to do with them. She'd always had a maid to take care of such things. Noticing her gloves hanging over the fire screen, she followed suit, hanging her wet petticoat, drawers, stockings, chemise, and corset in a similar fashion.

What have I gotten myself into? she wondered as, naked and shivering, she stepped into the tub and sat down. She had now descended to the lowest of the low: bathing in the kitchen of a London boardinghouse.

It's only a temporary inconvenience, she reminded herself against the dull pain that still throbbed inside her head. She'd find a way out of this mess, and soon. As she lathered up her hair and body with the bar of hard castile soap, and dipped the pitcher into the bathwater to rinse herself, she was just grateful to be warm again, and to feel clean.

Thomas cursed inwardly as he bounded down the stairs. His landlady was a kind woman. Far too kind. It was bad enough that Miss Watson would be staying the night—most likely in the room directly down the hall from his. But knowing Mrs. Gill, it was entirely possible that she'd let this penniless vagabond stay for weeks on end, until she figured out what to do with herself.

He couldn't let that happen. Being around this Miss Watson for even a single day would be a constant reminder of all that he had suffered and lost.

He'd thought that was behind him, that he'd gotten over it, had moved on.

Clearly not.

The two women looked nothing alike, although both were admittedly beautiful. But their American accents were the same, their voices eerily similar: a husky, melodious contralto he had once thought endearing. The moment Miss Watson had opened her mouth, all the bad memories had come crashing back, a stab to the gut.

Somehow, he told himself as he marched down the hall to the rear of the house, he had to make it clear to Mrs. Gill that the young woman must leave in the morning, even if it meant *he* had to pay for her to lodge elsewhere.

Turning the handle on the kitchen door, he pushed it open, expecting to find Mrs. Gill.

He froze in the doorway. Mrs. Gill was not within.

Instead, he beheld a vision of supreme loveliness.

Chapter Three

Miss Watson, naked and glowing, was sitting in a bathtub before the blazing hearth.

Thomas knew he had no right to be seeing this. He should leave, *this instant*. Instead, he stood on the threshold, drinking in the sight of her, a perusal which would be forever after imprinted on his brain.

She looked like something out of a painting by Botticelli. Firelight glimmered on ivory skin and round, perfect breasts with luscious pink nipples. Her head was tilted back, her eyes were closed, and her lips were curved in a smile of serene contentment as she slowly emptied a pitcher of water over herself. Rivulets streamed over her long hair and down the lush curves of her body. Beneath the water, he glimpsed her crossed legs and a hint of the dark patch that lay between.

Damnation. His reaction was almost primeval. Heat consumed his face. His mouth went dry. His heart pounded like a hammer. All the blood in his veins thrummed through his body and arousal flared up within him.

His conscience bore down on him as he struggled to regain his wits. He should not be staring at her like some despicable Peeping Tom. He had no right invading her privacy, had seen far more than was proper or decent.

Thank heavens her eyes were still closed, and she didn't appear to have sensed his presence. Backing away, Thomas quietly shut the door.

Alexandra thought she heard a sound. Was it the door? With a flash of unease, she set down the empty pitcher, wiped moisture from her eyes, and opened them—but the door was shut, and there was no one else in the room.

Alexandra stood and toweled off, shivering. She put on the nightgown, grateful that Mrs. Gill had also left her a shawl of pale gray wool to wrap around her shoulders.

She found the landlady asleep in the front parlor, her knitting in her lap.

"And how was your bath?" Mrs. Gill asked, awakening and heaving her plump form out of her chair.

"Very nice, thank you." Alexandra never would have guessed that a bath in a tin tub in a kitchen could prove to be so revitalizing.

She followed Mrs. Gill up the stairs to a small bedroom where another fire burned in a tiny fireplace. The furnishings were simple: a bed, a dresser, a small corner table, a chair. The carpets were as threadbare as those in the hall, and the wooden floor equally scuffed.

"My rooms on the top floor are all let," Mrs. Gill explained. "I hope this will do for the night."

"It's great. Thank you so much, Mrs. Gill."

Alexandra dried her hair by the fire and drank the bowl of soup and dose of aspirin Mrs. Gill brought up on a tray.

"I hope you feel better in the morning, dearie," Mrs. Gill said as she cleared away the tray.

Alexandra climbed into bed and lay back against the pillow, weariness descending on her like a cloud. The night before, she'd been so tense she hadn't slept a wink, and her long walk through the London streets, not to mention the bump on the head, had done her in.

"You've gone to so much trouble on my behalf, Mrs. Gill," she murmured. "I don't know how to thank you."

"You just did." Mrs. Gill turned down the light with a warm smile. "You get a good rest now, Miss Watson. Tomorrow is another day."

When Alexandra opened her eyes the next morning, to her relief, her headache was gone. A glance at a bedside clock revealed it to be half past eleven. Dear Lord, she'd slept nearly half the day away! As she sat up in bed and remembered where she was, the anxiety over her situation came flooding back.

Her desperate attempt to run away had gone disastrously awry. In one fell swoop, she'd removed herself from all familiar comforts and privileges and was stuck in a frightening limbo, dependent on the kindness of strangers. As good-hearted as Mrs. Gill was, she likely expected Alexandra to depart that very morning.

Which meant she was going to have to figure out her next move, and quickly.

Rising, Alexandra discovered a pitcher of water and a basin atop the dresser, along with a hairbrush and a dish containing hair pins. All of her clothes lay on the corner chair, dry and neatly pressed, and the black dress had been brushed clean.

Such kindness, Alexandra thought.

A stab of guilt pierced through her. How could she ever repay Mrs. Gill? Judging by her modest home, Mrs. Gill wasn't a wealthy woman. She depended on the income of boarders like Mr. Carlyle to make a living. Yet she'd given Alexandra shelter and cleaned her clothes without asking a thing in return.

What had Alexandra done to deserve it? Nothing, other than to arrive on the doorstep unconscious. Then she'd given a false name and, hoping to gain Mrs. Gill's pity and hospitality, had allowed that good woman to draw erroneous conclusions about her.

It wasn't right.

Maybe she ought to come clean. Tell Mrs. Gill and Mr. Carlyle who she really was. Go back to Brown's hotel, to her real life. That's all it would take: a simple admission, and she would be Alexandra Atherton again, dining in five-star hotels, bathing in marble bathrooms, and not beholden to total strangers.

Instead, she'd be beholden to her mother.

She'd have to marry Lord Shrewsbury.

No, no, Alexandra's mind screamed. *Anything but that.*

"We'll start with you, Alexandra," her mother had gloated when she first brought up this London Season nonsense, "then introduce Madeleine and Kathryn, one at a time. *That* will open every door to New York society for your father and myself!"

Alexandra had tried to do her part, hoping she'd meet someone she could respect and perhaps love, and make her mother's dream come true. But the past five weeks had been a real eye opener. The gentlemen she'd met talked of nothing but hunting and horses. They complained about being in debt, but did nothing about it. Compared to the men Alexandra knew in New York, who were ambitious and worked hard for a living, British noblemen seemed dull and lazy. She couldn't bear the thought of spending her life buried in the country on some crumbling English estate with such a man in exchange for the dubious prestige of a title. Especially Lord Shrewsbury. Just thinking about him make her skin crawl.

As she freshened up and got dressed, Alexandra considered what to do. She still wanted to go home. She wanted to go back to school. Her mother had forced her and her sisters to leave college to prepare for this title-hunting madness. Madeleine and Kathryn were back at Vassar now, waiting their turn for a Season, and Alexandra wanted to join them. If her father refused to pay for another year's tuition, Alexandra determined that *she'd* make it happen. There must be someone who'd be willing to give her a loan. Her parents might try to force Alexandra to marry someone else someday, but she wouldn't do it. She'd support herself if need be. How, she didn't know—she'd cross that bridge when she came to it.

In the meantime, she had to figure out how to *get* home.

A second-class ticket on a steamship would cost ten pounds. Could she wire her father and ask him to send money? No, he'd just alert her mother to Alexandra's whereabouts, and tell her to do whatever her mother wanted.

The irony of her situation wasn't lost on her. Once, ten pounds would have been such a paltry sum. All her life, whenever Alexandra had needed money, her mother or father had given it to her. She'd never worried about where her next meal was coming from, or given a thought to how much that meal might cost. Even as a child, when her father had earned a comparatively modest living as the owner of the local bank, there'd been enough money for anything she or her sisters wanted—a new sled and skates in winter, Bavarian china tea sets for their dolls in summer, the newest fashions in spring and fall. And ever since her father had become obscenely rich, there'd been an endless well of money at their disposal.

Now, she was cut off, entirely on her own.

To the average person, she knew, ten pounds was a great deal of money. How was she going to get her hands on it?

With a sigh, Alexandra buttoned up the bodice of her black cotton dress, studying her reflection in the small looking glass. The dress was truly ugly, such a step down from the exquisite gowns she'd been wearing recently, created especially for her by Frederick Worth in Paris.

She quickly chastised herself for the thought. At least the dress wasn't wet or dirty anymore. For that she was extremely grateful.

Picking up the brush from the dresser, Alexandra tugged it through the tangles of her long hair, perplexed as to how to style it. She'd never done her own hair before. Even while at Vassar College, she and her sisters had lived at their family home in Poughkeepsie and commuted to classes, relying on servants to take care of their every need. During the Season, an expensive French hairdresser had curled and woven Alexandra's locks into elaborate styles, while she'd sat reading magazines or novels. She had no idea how to do this on her own.

Her fingers were clumsy as she struggled to pin her hair up into a simple bun at the back of her head. It took several tries to get it looking halfway presentable. She still wasn't satisfied with her efforts, but there was a light tap at the door. Alexandra answered it to find Mrs. Gill holding a tray.

"Ah, at last you're up! I was getting worried, and didn't want to wait any longer. Did you sleep well? I hope your headache is gone?"

"Yes to both questions." Alexandra stood back to allow Mrs. Gill entry. "Thanks so much, Mrs. Gill, for drying out all my clothes and cleaning my dress."

"It's the least I could do, after what you've been through." Mrs. Gill set down a tray holding a cup of tea and a dish covered by a metal dome. "I've got a hot breakfast for you, for all that it's after noon. Mr. Carlyle was finished with his newspaper so I brought it along, in case you wanted something to read."

Glancing at the newspaper, Alexandra caught sight of a small headline announcing an article to be found in the society pages: *American Heiress Leaves Country.* Involuntarily, she let out a gasp.

"What is it, Miss Watson?"

Alexandra's mind raced. She wondered if the article was about her, and if Mrs. Gill suspected who Alexandra was. A brief glance at the landlady calmed her fears; the woman was merely gazing at her with concern. "It's nothing. I'm just hungry. This smells wonderful."

"My tenants do seem to like my cooking. Well, enjoy your breakfast, Miss Watson. Set the tray on the table in the hall when you've finished, and Mary will fetch it. When you're up to it, we can discuss what's to be done with you."

"Thank you." As soon as the door closed behind Mrs. Gill, Alexandra dropped into the chair, flicked open the newspaper to the society pages, and began to read:

American Heiress Leaves Country
No Word for Peer Fiancé
Returning to New York aboard Maritime

American heiress Alexandra Atherton, 24, who dangled her charms and fortune before the elite of London society in the first five weeks of the Season hoping to exchange cash for a coronet, has reportedly left London and is en route to New York.

Miss Atherton is the daughter of American millionaire and banking tycoon Colis Atherton. Considered by many as a featured prize this season, her dowry was said to be $1 million, the equivalent of £200,000.

The heiress reportedly received two proposals of marriage before her abrupt departure from these shores. The first offer, this reporter was told, came a fortnight ago

from the Baron Reginald Waterbeach-Stokes but was refused, suggesting that Miss Atherton may have set her
sights on landing a higher-ranking peer.

That appeared to be the case, as Miss Atherton's engagement to Viscount Shrewsbury was reported yesterday in this newspaper.

Such transatlantic alliances have become increasingly
common of late, featuring title-seeking young American
women whose fortunes provide a much-needed injection
into the estates of cash-strapped British peers.

Not everyone, however, is enamoured of the trend.
Some feel that this influx of Americans threatens the
British way of life, and dilutes the blood of the peerage
by producing heirs that are half-American—a people
who, little more than a hundred years ago, declared their
freedom from our country via a violent war.

Other views are more personal. One debutante this
season was recently overheard commenting: "What
chance does a British girl have against these wealthy,
social-climbing Americans, who can afford elaborate
jewels and endless new dresses from France? If they
continue to shuttle across the Atlantic and invade our
Season, who will be left for us to marry?"

Alexandra Atherton has apparently shuttled across the
Atlantic in the opposite direction, without a chaperone,
and with no word for her fiancé.

According to our source at Scotland Yard, the young
lady's mother, Mrs. Josephine Atherton, discovered her
daughter missing from their rooms at Brown's Hotel yes-

terday morning. Fearing that Miss Atherton had been abducted, Mrs. Atherton immediately informed the authorities, who began an investigation.

A few hours later, Mrs. Atherton insisted that they call off the search. A letter had apparently been discovered explaining her daughter's whereabouts. Miss Atherton, it seems, made her way to Liverpool, where she boarded the steamship *Maritime*, bound for New York.

The reason for Miss Atherton's departure is unknown. It remains equally unclear whether or not a union between Atherton and Lord Shrewsbury will now take place.

Viscount Shrewsbury and Colis Atherton could not be reached for comment.

Alexandra flung the newspaper down on the table with annoyance. To describe her as someone who'd "dangled her charms and fortune before the elite" was unfair. She hadn't come to London by choice. She'd never wanted to "exchange cash for a coronet." It had all been her mother's idea.

The thing that really raised Alexandra's hackles, though, was that from reading this article, no one would know how vile Lord Shrewsbury was. He'd been after Alexandra's money and had tried to take physical liberties with her. She'd never even accepted his proposal; her mother had arranged it behind her back. This article lay all the blame at Alexandra's feet, making her seem like a spoiled princess. And there was nothing she could do about it.

Alexandra's irritation was momentarily diverted by the

aromas rising from the food tray. She realized she was famished. Lifting the dome, she discovered a full English breakfast: eggs, bacon, grilled tomato, browned mushrooms, and a slice of buttered toast.

Alexandra picked up the fork and dug into the meal, savoring every bite.

As she ate, Alexandra mulled over her situation. Her mother thought Alexandra was on board the *Maritime*. Presumably, her father would send someone to fetch her when the ship docked in New York in ten days. Which gave Alexandra ten days to come up with a new plan.

Her best bet, she decided, would be to try to stay here until she had money and a safe place to go. This gave her three immediate objectives. Somehow, she had to

1. Extend her stay at the lodging house.

2. Figure out a way to recompense Mrs. Gill for room and board.

3. Acquire the money for passage to New York.

How was she going to accomplish all that?

Could she find a job? Alexandra had never worked a day in her life. Who would hire her, and to do what?

Still stewing over this dilemma, Alexandra left the room with her empty breakfast tray. Moving down the hall, she noticed that the door to a room across the way was slightly ajar, and a pungent odor emanated from inside.

She paused in surprise, recognizing the smell: it was oil paint.

Her curiosity aroused, Alexandra set the breakfast tray on the hall table and knocked lightly on the door. "Hello?"

No answer. Unable to restrain herself, Alexandra quietly pushed the door open.

The spacious sitting room clearly served as an art studio. No one was there. The two large windows were open, filling the room with light and admitting a slight breeze. All the tools of the oil painter's trade were scattered about: brushes, paints, palettes. A privacy screen stood next to a rack of clothing. The sofa was piled high with books and props. Against one wall, a cream-colored backdrop hung from floor to ceiling. An inner doorway led to an adjoining chamber, where she spied a bed.

The most arresting focal points of the room, however, were two large portraits painted in oils, standing on easels. Drawn like a moth to a flame, Alexandra crossed the room to study them more closely.

The first painting—a gentleman in fine clothing— appeared to be completed. It had been rendered with such mastery and attention to detail, Alexandra couldn't take her eyes off it. The subject's expression was so real and captivating, she felt as if he lived and breathed. The portrait was signed in the bottom right corner: *T. Carlyle.*

So, this was Mr. Carlyle's room. Mrs. Gill had mentioned something about him keeping to himself and just doing his work. Now Alexandra knew what he did for a living. She had always admired artists, oil painters in particular. A thrill ran up her spine, to think that the man who'd rescued her—had carried her in, unconscious, from the street—was a portrait-ist. And what a tremendous talent he was!

She turned to examine the second portrait. It was far

along, but unfinished. It featured a tall, slender woman in a spectacular white satin evening gown. Alexandra guessed the subject to be in her late twenties. Small pink roses adorned the young woman's upswept dark hair. Her dress was embellished by a glimmering silver sash that crossed over her chest just beneath the bustline, and billowed in stiff folds at the shoulder. The pale skin of her face and chest appeared almost luminescent. The subject's arms and hands were as yet only hastily sketched in, as was part of the sash, and the background was still incomplete.

"What are you doing in here?" a male voice called out crossly.

Alexandra started with surprise and whirled to find Mr. Carlyle behind her, carrying a small package wrapped in brown paper. "Sorry, I didn't mean to snoop, Mr. Carlyle. I was walking by and smelled paint. The door was open, and I just had to look."

"Well, you have looked. Now please leave."

Alexandra frowned. Why was he so angry? He was even taller than she'd remembered—he must be well over six feet. And she hadn't really noticed yesterday how handsome he was. Straight nose. High cheekbones. Noble chin. His charcoal gray tweed suit, well cut but old, strained over his broad chest and wide shoulders while emphasizing his trim waist and hips. All of which might have made an appealing picture, if his forehead hadn't been creased practically in half, and his mouth beneath his trim golden mustache hadn't been curled up in a glower.

"I'll go," Alexandra said quickly, "but first I just wanted to say . . . these portraits are beautiful. You're very talented."

"You need not feel obligated to pay me compliments." He nodded dismissively toward the door. His accent, so cultured and refined, seemed somewhat at odds with his shabby clothes.

"I didn't say it because I feel obligated. It's the truth. The details are exquisite. The portrait of the gentleman reminds me of Frans Hals's *Laughing Cavalier*."

He darted her a brief, surprised glance as she went on, "Your subjects seem so lifelike, I feel as though you captured their personalities in paint."

He seemed moved by Alexandra's words. "You are very kind."

His short blond hair was brushed back from his forehead, above wire-rimmed glasses that framed beautiful eyes the color of milk chocolate. Alexandra felt a sudden frisson vibrate through her, and couldn't tear her gaze away. "Are these commissions?" she asked, struggling to keep the conversation going.

"Yes." Mr. Carlyle set his package down on a table and tore off the wrapping, revealing a glass jar containing a clear liquid labeled LINSEED OIL.

A sudden memory surfaced in Alexandra's mind. "Yesterday, before I plowed into you, were you carrying a jar of linseed oil?"

He nodded.

"And *this* jar is the replacement for the one that gave up its life on that sidewalk in the pouring rain?"

His lips twitched briefly, reluctantly. "Yes." He shrugged out of his coat and hung it over the back of a chair.

"I'm so sorry. Whatever that jar cost, I'll pay for it."

He glanced at her skeptically. "You haven't any money."

"True, but I'm determined to get some. Once I make up my mind to do something, it usually gets done."

"I see." A new expression flitted across Mr. Carlyle's face: a blend of doubt, amusement, and a begrudging hint of approval.

Alexandra felt a slight easing of the tension in the room, which came as a relief. As she tried to think what to say next, he unfastened the cuffs of his white shirt and began rolling up his sleeves.

"Miss Watson. It occurs to me that I have been remiss."

She was so distracted by the sight of his forearms, which were lightly dusted with golden hair and far more well-muscled and tanned than she would have expected for a painter, that she was only half aware of her response. "Remiss? How so?"

"I should have long since inquired as to your state of health. I hope you are feeling better this morning?"

Alexandra struggled to regain her wits. Even if he was a poor painter and as surly as a tiger, it seemed that beneath the surface lay impeccable manners. "That's quite a formal way to say, 'Sorry, how're you doing?'" she blurted.

Now he couldn't prevent a smile, however brief. "We English pride ourselves on formality."

"So I've noticed."

"And?" he persisted. In an imperfect imitation of her accent, he said, "How're you doing?"

His attempt to recreate a flat, American tone was so amusing, she laughed. "Heaps better, thank you."

"I am glad to hear it. I further hope that you did not find the smell of the oil paint in the hall too unpleasant? I sometimes forget to lock my door, and when I just pull it to, the latch does not always catch."

"The smell wasn't unpleasant at all. It beckoned me in. I'm an art enthusiast myself. I studied art history, among other things, at Vassar."

"Vassar?" He didn't appear to have heard of the place.

"It's one of the first colleges to open to women in the United States."

"Ah." His eyebrows raised. "I imagine such an education is useful, when it comes to your charges?"

"My charges?"

"The children you care for."

Alexandra felt blood rush to her cheeks. She'd forgotten that he presumed her to be a governess. "Yes, of course." She was going to have to stay on her toes, and be careful about what she said. "Well, I should let you get back to your work, Mr. Carlyle. I hope you'll forgive me for stealing into your rooms uninvited. I didn't mean to upset you."

"It was not your fault. My being upset, I mean. I was startled to find you here, but my irritation was due to another source."

"Oh?"

He took an envelope from his coat pocket and gestured toward the unfinished portrait on the easel. "My subject, Mrs. Arabella Norton, has just informed me that she is leaving town and will be unable to come in for the last few sittings. 'It is so nearly done,' she says, 'surely you can do the last bits without me.'" He tossed the envelope onto a table with a frown. "She insists that the painting be completed and delivered when she returns to London in a fortnight."

"Can you do it?"

"I can try. I could do the final varnishing at her house, and let it dry there. But it is a great disservice to the portrait. Without a live model, I cannot finish the arms and hands with any accuracy. And the sash has to be in place, to get the shadows right on the skin."

Alexandra glanced at the portrait, then at the rack of clothing across the room. An idea began to take shape in her mind: a way to solve Mr. Carlyle's dilemma, which might also fix one of her biggest problems.

"What if *I* stand in for Mrs. Norton?"

CHAPTER FOUR

Mr. Carlyle looked at Alexandra as if she'd lost her mind. "*You* think to pose for Mrs. Norton's portrait?"

"Why not? It's almost finished. You just need to do the arms, hands, and sash."

"I do not think—"

"It could work," she interrupted. "I seem to be about her size and coloring. That white gown on the rack—is it hers?"

He nodded.

"We could see if it fits. How long would you need me to model, to finish the portrait?"

He thought about it. "Three sittings, I should guess."

"I have the time."

"No, this is madness." But he paused, reluctantly considering her proposal. "Have you ever sat for a portrait before?"

"Several times, as a child. I—" Alexandra stopped herself. *Careful, careful.* She was supposedly a governess. Having attended schools all her life, she'd never had a governess herself, except for the ghastly year she and her sisters had spent in training with Madame Dubois, imported from France to "finish" them in preparation for entrée into English society.

One of her favorite novels, *Jane Eyre*, was about a governess. Other than that, the only thing Alexandra knew about governesses was what she'd read: that they were generally well-educated, middle-or upper-class women who'd come upon hard times and had to support themselves.

"In my youth," she went on, struggling for words that were true, "my family was well off. It is only recently that my circumstances changed."

"I see." He looked uncomfortable now. "Forgive me, I did not mean to pry. I only meant that sitting can be a tedious process. I wanted to make sure you knew what you were volunteering for."

"Oh, I'm not volunteering, Mr. Carlyle."

He looked at her. "I beg your pardon?"

"I didn't mean to imply that I'd do this for free. I thought we could make it a sort of business arrangement. You need a model. I need room and board."

"You must be joking."

"Not at all. In exchange for three sittings, all you have to do is persuade Mrs. Gill to let me stay on for . . . a week, and pay her whatever is fair and reasonable. And I'm hoping there might be a little cash in it for me, as well?"

He let go a short, harsh laugh. It wasn't a pleasant sound. "You are quite the American girl, aren't you, Miss Watson?"

Alexandra didn't like the way he was suddenly looking at her, as if she were a bug he wanted to squash. "What do you mean?"

"So opportunistic. Thinking of no one but yourself. Out to see how much you can get."

He looked so disgusted, Alexandra couldn't help asking,

"What do you have against Americans, Mr. Carlyle? What did an American ever do to you?"

He flinched at that, and she regretted saying it. Before she could attempt to apologize, however, he said stonily, "You have a lot of nerve, waltzing into my studio uninvited, then trying to negotiate your way into extending your stay at this house. With a few inquiries, Miss Watson, I can surely find an experienced female model who will suit my needs."

"Fine," Alexandra retorted. She knew she wasn't helping her cause by showing her temper, but she couldn't let him have the last word. "Forgive me for intruding into your private sanctum and making a suggestion you find so offensive. But I wasn't just thinking of myself. I thought it was a way we could help each other. I was also thinking about Mrs. Gill. I don't want to impose any longer without paying her, that's all."

A moment passed in which they stared at each other heatedly as tension crackled through the air. Then Alexandra whirled and started for the door.

"Wait."

She paused, looking back at him.

He blew out a long breath. "I may not appreciate your method, Miss Watson, but I admire your spirit and your sense of honor. I suppose we could give it a try, see if the dress fits. However, *if* it works out, and I am not saying it will, all I can offer to pay in exchange for your modeling services is room and board for three days. There will not be any. . . . how did you put it? 'Cash in it for you'?"

Alexandra shrugged and gave him a smile. She had

achieved her aim: she'd bought herself some time. "That's okay. I had to try, didn't I?"

It was the cheekiness of it, Thomas thought, as he set up his brushes at the small oval table by the easel. That's what bothered him. Her cheekiness.

Well, that was one of the things.

If he had just stood his ground, insisted that he could get on perfectly well without her standing in for his missing client, Miss Watson might have been obliged then and there to take her leave from this establishment. Which would have been better for him, all around.

Ever since he saw . . . what he had seen . . . the night before, he had been unable to remove the image from his brain. The memory had kept him awake half the night, making his blood simmer. Knowing that she was sleeping just down the hall had not made things any easier. Even now, wanton thoughts continued to surface in his mind.

It had been far too long since he'd had a woman in his bed—that was the problem. It explained why he felt such a visceral attraction to this woman. But it was merely a physical response, that was all. He did not know her. And he did not care to know her.

He had no interest whatsoever in pursuing a relationship with a woman. Women could not be counted on. They professed their love, and then left you flat. He had learned *that* the hard way. Never again would he risk his heart. There were other outlets to satisfy a man's physical urges. If he did ever choose to engage in a dalliance with a woman simply for pleasure, it would certainly not be with a governess, however appealing she might be.

He had hoped that when he returned from his errand this morning, Mrs. Gill would have given Miss Watson her walking papers. That she would be gone from his life.

No such luck.

Now, he thought, frowning as he mixed a small portion of linseed oil and turpentine in a glass jar, he was going to be cooped up with her for three separate sittings in his studio. Three days in which he was going to have to stare at her for two long hours, and paint the very flesh that his hands ached to touch.

What had he been thinking when he agreed to this? He felt as if he had made a deal with the devil. But the deal had been made. He'd gone down and spoken with Mrs. Gill, who had happily agreed to let Miss Watson stay on for a few days—and why not, it was at *his* expense. Now, at this very moment, Miss Watson was behind the privacy screen, changing into Mrs. Norton's gown.

He was anxious to get this portrait done and delivered. It had given him no pleasure to paint it, any more than the others he had been commissioned to create over the past few months. It was aggravating to be obliged to fall back, in this covert manner, on an art he had been so determined to give up. It often felt as though he were painting by rote. *Stand here if you please. Mix paints. Pick up brush. Apply to canvas.* But it was work, and God knows he needed the money.

He was just going to have to make the best of this unwelcome situation. Three days. By that time, he should be done with the essential parts of the portrait, and Miss Watson would have hopefully made other arrangements for herself.

Squeezing a dab of white paint onto his palette, he called out, "How are you doing back there?"

"Okay."

Okay. He gritted his teeth. It was one of those uniquely American terms which just served to remind him of a certain someone else. "Does it fit?"

"Pretty well, I think."

A rustle announced Miss Watson's emergence from behind the privacy screen. Thomas looked up and caught his breath. Although Mrs. Norton had looked well in the white gown, on Miss Watson it was simply spellbinding. The folds of the white satin skirt billowed sumptuously around her, emphasizing her tiny waist. Her bare arms were slender and utterly feminine. The bodice was so low cut and fit so snugly, her breasts seemed to be bursting from its confines.

"I managed to get it fastened. Thank goodness the hooks are on the side. I have no idea how to wrap this sash, though." She stepped forward, the coiled length of silvery fabric in her outstretched hands.

Thomas struggled to modulate his respiration into something approaching normalcy. *Why did she have to be so stunning?* "Allow me to assist you," he said quietly, gesturing to the backdrop before the easel. "If you would kindly step over here."

She joined him in the designated spot. Retrieving his box of straight pins, Thomas moved closer and wrapped the first part of the stiff, shiny sash around her waist, then began pinning it in place so that it billowed above her shoulder. As he worked, he was intensely aware of their proximity.

They were standing almost as close as if they were dancing a waltz. She was half a head shorter than he, and he inhaled the clean scent of soap from her hair and skin. Today was the first time he had seen her hair dry. It was a glorious shade of burnt sienna, one of his favorite colors of the palette. She had pulled it back into a rather inexpert bun, and several curling tendrils had already dared to escape.

She glanced up at him, and for a moment their gazes met and held. Her eyes were a startling shade of deep blue, like bluebells in a shaft of sunlight.

He quickly lowered his gaze, only to find himself staring at her lips. They were parted slightly and eminently inviting. He glanced lower still. With each breath she took, her breasts rose and fell. The bodice looked close to splitting its seams at any moment, an event which would cause those perfect globes to spill out mere inches from his view.

Oh, if only they would.

Concentrate, you fool. Heat rose to his face and his heart drummed as he continued pinning the sash in place. *Whose brilliant idea was the sash, anyway? Couldn't he have simply painted Mrs. Norton in the gown?*

Alexandra's heart pounded. She'd expected this to be a simple matter of posing for a portrait. That it would require no more than standing still for a couple of hours a day while wearing a particular gown.

She hadn't counted on feeling . . . what she was feeling.

Admittedly, other than Lord Shrewsbury's disgusting kiss (which Alexandra would prefer to banish forever from her mind), she had virtually no experience with men. She'd danced with dozens of strangers, but that hardly counted, nor did the brief embrace she'd once shared at age sixteen with a farm boy she'd met on vacation. The dancing and that one chaste kiss had been exciting at the time, and had left a lasting impression.

Never before, however, had Alexandra felt a magnetic pull similar to the one she was now experiencing. As Mr. Carlyle's hands pressed against her body through the layers of her clothing to pin and adjust the sash, each touch sent a jolt up her spine. He was standing so near that she could feel the warmth emanating from his body. He smelled tantalizing, like linen and soap and cologne and something totally, indefinably male.

She felt a tingle reverberate through her body as she took in the width of his shoulders, the way his white shirt strained against his broad chest, the way the wiry muscles in his gently tanned forearms moved as he worked with the pins. How, she wondered, had his skin achieved that lightly sun-kissed tone?

Her attention was drawn to his lips. They were full and well formed, set tersely in a face she considered to be classically handsome. She found herself wondering what it would be like to be kissed by those lips—then silently censured herself for such thoughts. At the same time, a sudden, strange warmth bloomed deep in her belly.

From the heightened color on Mr. Carlyle's face, and the slight alteration in his voice and respiration, Alexandra wondered if he was experiencing a similar discomposure.

"That will do," Thomas barked when he was finished with the sash. Crouching down, he smoothed out the train of her gown along the floor. *Get your mind out of the gutter. She is just another model. A female body to paint, and nothing more.*

Miss Watson cleared her throat. "How do you want me to stand?"

"Tall and straight, with your arms at your sides."

"Like this?"

He stood and looked her over with a frown. "Not quite." He reached out, pausing before making contact. "May I?"

"Of course." She flushed.

Thomas quickly and unceremoniously adjusted the angle of her body and arms to match that of the subject in the painting. "Now curl your fingers slightly."

She curled them.

"That's not quite it." He was obliged to take her hands in his and arrange her fingers into the required position. This skin-to-skin contact sent another curl of desire threading through him. "Hold that position," he instructed gruffly, retreating to his easel, where he took a deep breath to steady himself.

He had worked with dozens of models at the academy in Italy, and had painted countless portraits. Never before had he been so vitally aware of his subject. What was it about this woman that was different? She stood before him with her head held high, as if born to the part, looking every bit as noble as a duchess.

Not something he would have expected from a governess.

Adding a smidgeon of crimson to the white on his palette, he mixed the oil paints with a brush to create one of the requisite shades of pale pink for Miss Watson's skin. Achieving the desired color, he began to paint.

The clock ticked in the silent room as he divided his attention between the subject and the canvas. Thankfully, his body was once more under control. But every time their eyes inadvertently connected, he felt as though an invisible charge sizzled through the air between them.

Twenty minutes in, he paused to give Miss Watson a resting period, for which she seemed grateful. He spent the time mixing his paints, while she sat decorously on a chair. Then she resumed her stance. This time, to his relief, she managed to place herself in the proper position without assistance. He got back to work. Although he was determined to keep his face impassive, the enterprise was anything but tranquil.

To paint her hands and her arms, he had to stare at them.

Her breasts, so lovely and so very much in view, were very close to her arms.

Painting her skin only made him want to touch it again.

Bloody hell. Thomas shook his head slightly to clear it. If he didn't get ahold of himself, he might go mad.

Alexandra stood still, holding the pose. According to the clock on the mantel, this second phase had so far lasted five minutes, although it felt like five hours. All this time, other than when he'd insisted she take a break, not a word had passed between them.

The hot and bothered feeling had dissipated. If *he* was still feeling hot and bothered, he certainly gave no indication of it. As he painted her, he stood tall and straight before the easel, his facial features composed, his attention entirely on his work. In his faded white shirt, with his neat mustache and wire-rimmed glasses, he looked every inch the intellectual, bohemian artist.

Alexandra exhaled and closed her eyes. Clearly, the unprecedented frisson of attraction she'd felt pass between them earlier was just a thing of the moment for him. He must have painted dozens of women. Some might have even been nude. Alexandra was nothing special to him. He regarded her as an artistic subject, nothing more.

And why shouldn't he think of her that way? Alexandra was merely his *modèle du jour*. She was, she told herself, reacting like a ridiculous schoolgirl. And it *was* ridiculous. She had no business being attracted to Mr. Carlyle—a poor painter who lived in rented rooms. She was standing here with one purpose only: to earn her board and keep until she could find a way to get home to New York and back to school. She'd soon leave this place and never see Mr. Carlyle again. For some reason, the notion was accompanied by a tiny pang of disappointment.

"Miss Watson?"

Mr. Carlyle's voice came at her out of a fog. Who, she wondered idly, was Miss Watson? One of the servants?

"Miss Watson?" he repeated more insistently.

Alexandra opened her eyes. Mr. Carlyle was looking directly at her. She stifled a startled gasp, recalling that Miss Watson was the name she'd given him. "Yes?"

"Have I overtired you? Would you like to rest again for a few minutes?"

"No! I'm fine. Really. I was just woolgathering."

"All right, then. You may relax your fingers now, but please keep your body in the same position. I am going to work on the sash."

There, Thomas thought. That was better. He was painting fabric, not her creamy, porcelain skin. The room still seemed to flicker with an unseen energy, however.

Conversation, that was what was needed. He rarely spoke to his clients, but with her, he needed something to divert his mind. "Where are you from, Miss Watson?"

"New York."

"City, or state?"

"Both. I grew up in Poughkeepsie, a town in Upstate New York. The last two years, I've lived in New York City."

"That seems unusual for a governess."

She hesitated. "How so?"

"English governesses are generally employed by families

in the country, who have no access to good schools. Yet you were employed in the city?"

She paused before answering. "The very wealthy in New York are often particular. They don't all consider the local schools as good enough for their sons and daughters."

"Indeed? Yet I have read that there are some superb schools in New York City."

"True."

"You must be an excellent governess, for your employers to choose you to educate their children over a more formal institution." He didn't know why he was pushing the subject; it was almost as if by goading her, he hoped to mitigate this lure of attraction that refused to dissipate.

Miss Watson's cheeks grew pink again. "A governess has far fewer pupils under her care than a teacher in a school. It's more like one-on-one instruction, isn't it? Maybe that's the appeal." For some reason she looked uncomfortable.

"Forgive me. I meant what I said as a compliment, not a criticism."

"Then I will take it as such."

He dipped his brush and returned it to the canvas. "Tell me about Vassar. What did you study?"

"Literature, Greek, Latin, French, Italian, philosophy, political economy, history, music, mathematics, physics, geography—the curriculum offers greater diversity than any other women's college in America."

He was taken aback, and deeply impressed. "Well done, you. I have to say, you are the first woman I have ever met who has been to college."

"Really? The first?"

"Few women in England have the opportunity or the desire to pursue higher education."

She frowned. "I read that two women's colleges were recently established at Oxford, but the enrollment is tiny. Only ten or twelve students, I believe. It's a shame. Attending college was one of the highlights of my life."

"One of mine, as well." As he worked, the familiarity of the motions took over and he finally felt himself begin to relax.

"Where did you study?"

"Oxford. And the Accademia di Belle Arti di Firenze."

"Oh! I adore Florence. It's heaven for art lovers. It must have been wonderful to study there."

"You've been to Florence?" He was surprised.

She hesitated again. "It was some years ago. I used to travel abroad frequently with my mother and sisters, before. . . ."

She seemed too embarrassed to finish the sentence. She'd mentioned that her family was once well off. He wondered what had happened to change that, to force her into working to support herself. He certainly was not about to ask. "While in Florence, did you see Botticelli's *Birth of Venus* at the Uffizi?"

"I did. It's brilliant. Venus looks so shy, standing on a half shell with the wind blowing through her hair."

"*Winds* plural," he corrected.

"That's right! They are personified, and blowing roses at her."

"They say the model for the painting was a married noblewoman whom Botticelli loved from afar but could never have."

"I didn't know that." Miss Watson looked intrigued. "Did Botticelli ever marry?"

"Never."

"Good for him."

His eyebrows lifted. "Most women, I believe, would think it sad to learn that a man remained forever unattached."

"I'm not most women."

"I am beginning to realize that."

Silence stretched between them. He kept painting. She kept her pose. Then she said, "I hope I'm still standing the way you want?"

"You are perfect." As he uttered the words, he was aware of their dual meaning, and hoped she did not discern it. She was indeed perfection. Physical perfection. But beyond that, their conversation had revealed a glimpse of the woman within, who he was finding more fascinating by the minute.

When the portrait session ended at four o'clock, Alexandra returned to her room and sank down on her bed with relief.

She hadn't realized until that moment how exhausted she was. It wasn't just standing and holding that pose for so long that had been tiring. It was keeping up this pretense of being Miss Watson. It had been difficult to answer all his questions honestly, but somehow she'd managed. Although a little voice in the back of her head kept castigating her: *It's still lying. Lying by omission. Lying by misdirection.*

She'd almost given herself away with that mention of Florence. And there was the moment when he'd called her Miss Watson, and she hadn't responded. *That* couldn't happen again.

She couldn't stay here forever, either. She'd only bought herself three days. Was it time enough to figure out how to earn the money for a ticket to New York? Alexandra sighed, too tired to think about it. Stretching out on the bed, she instantly fell asleep.

CHAPTER FIVE

When Alexandra awoke some hours later, it was growing dark. The clock told her it was a quarter past eight, and she was hungry.

Venturing down the hall, Alexandra saw a light shining under the closed door to Mr. Carlyle's room. As she made her way downstairs, she wondered what he was doing. They'd chatted amiably on and off while he worked on the portrait. She'd enjoyed the experience, despite the tension of pretending to be someone she wasn't, and the simmering attraction she couldn't seem to shake. Session two was to take place the following morning at eleven o'clock. She realized she was looking forward to it.

She found Mrs. Gill in the front parlor, knitting by the fire.

"Ah! There you are, Miss Watson. I saw you sleeping and didn't want to wake you. Are you hungry?"

"Starving."

Mrs. Gill stood, taking her knitting with her. "You missed supper, but I put something aside for you just in case."

They retreated to the kitchen, where Mrs. Gill served Alexandra tea and a slice of beef-and-kidney pie. It wasn't the sort of fare Alexandra was accustomed to, but the pie had a crisp crust and was full of carrots, peas, onions, tender meat, and flavorful brown gravy.

"This is delicious," Alexandra said in between bites. "Thank you."

"You're very welcome." Mrs. Gill sat in a rocking chair by the fire and resumed knitting. "So, how did it go with Mr. Carlyle and his painting?"

"Fine. Thank you again for letting me stay on like this. I really appreciate it."

"Don't thank me. It's Mr. Carlyle who's paying. To my way of thinking, it's a sensible arrangement that benefits all parties."

"I'm glad you agree." It was only with extreme reluctance that Mr. Carlyle had agreed to let her pose for him. Mrs. Gill had said he rarely spoke a word to her. Yet after that first silence during the portrait session, he'd opened up to Alexandra, and she'd glimpsed a hint of a charming man. "Mrs. Gill, how long have you known Mr. Carlyle?"

"About a year and half or so, I guess. This is the second time he's stayed with me. Three months only the last time, then he packed up and went home."

"So he doesn't live here full time?"

"No, he only comes to town to paint portraits."

"Where's he from?"

"Somewhere in Cornwall, he says."

"Cornwall? That's far away to the south, isn't it?"

"It's the southernmost county in England. I've heard it's charming, though I've never been."

"Neither have I. Well, I can see why people in town hire Mr. Carlyle to paint their portraits. He's a remarkable artist."

"He is that. I have a word with his customers every now and again, those that come here to have their portraits done, anyway. Everyone says he's got a real gift. But to tell you the truth, I still don't know what to make of him."

"Why is that?"

"Well, for one thing, his temper is so changeable. He's often in a foul mood for no reason I can see. And all he does is work."

Alexandra had noticed his moods, but they'd been fleeting. "Isn't his work ethic a testament to his drive and talent? I admire a man who works hard."

"I agree, Miss Watson. The thing is, I always thought folks in the art world stuck together. You know, artists visiting other artists, chatting about their work and such, and carrying on scandalously with young models." She brought a hand to her mouth to cover a short laugh. "Not that I approve of any scandalous behavior, mind you. But Mr. Carlyle isn't like that at all. I've not seen but two women walk up those stairs in all the time I've known him, and they were married ladies he was painting, who came with their chaperones. He doesn't seem to have any friends at all. He doesn't belong to a club, and rarely goes out to eat."

Alexandra finished her last bite of pie and sipped her tea. Although still an enigma, Mr. Carlyle sounded like a good man. "Maybe he's just shy." But even as she said it, the words didn't ring true. Mr. Carlyle didn't seem shy. He was more the brooding type.

"He never spends a penny on anything but art supplies, from what I can tell. He just paints and sells his paintings. What kind of a man is that?"

"A lonely man, I think."

"He is that," Mrs. Gill said again. "He's lucky I had a room for him again when he came to town this year. He can't afford to pay for the full year, and I can't keep a room empty for him in the months in between."

Alexandra suddenly felt guilty that she'd asked him to pay for her to stay on at Mrs. Gill's, considering he was on such a tight budget. She frowned, remembering that it had only bought her two more days.

The landlady seemed to read Alexandra's thoughts. "Well, now. Let's talk about you, Miss Watson. Have you any idea what you'll do next?"

Alexandra sighed. "What I *want* is to go home to New York. But I have no way to pay for it."

"How much is the passage?"

"A second-class ticket costs ten pounds."

"Oh my! That's a lot of money. You'll have to find another job, and soon."

"As what?"

"Why, I'd start with your profession, of course. Look for work as a governess."

Alexandra set down her teacup. A governess?

She recalled that Charlotte Brontë, the author of *Jane Eyre*, had worked as a governess, and infused that novel with the indignities she'd experienced. Well, Alexandra thought, she could endure a few indignities, if it meant she didn't have to marry Lord Shrewsbury, and could earn her passage back to New York.

But was she qualified for such a job? What did governesses do? She presumed they were responsible for teaching young boys and girls the basic subjects. Surely, she could come up with a plan to teach the children of the landed gentry or aristocracy, couldn't she?

She had no idea how to go about seeking such a position, though. She asked Mrs. Gill, "What do you suggest? I mean, it might be different here than in the States. What's the best way to get a governess job in London?"

"I expect you'd best sign up with an agency that specializes in placing domestics. I can help you find one."

The next morning, Alexandra rose early, pleased to see sunshine peeking through the clouds outside her bedroom window.

After breakfast, she walked the three blocks to the employment agency Mrs. Gill had suggested. She felt slightly naked going out without a hat, but as she did not possess one, she had little choice. She found the agency waiting room full of ladies of all ages and descriptions, their expressions ranging from glum to hopeful.

Alexandra gave her name as "Lexie Watson," then sat down on a hard bench, taking the only empty space available. For nearly two hours, she anxiously watched the clock tick the minutes by, knowing that she was due in Mr. Carlyle's studio at eleven o'clock.

At a quarter to eleven, she was finally called into a small, musty office, where a businesslike woman behind a cluttered desk introduced herself as Mrs. Farthing.

"Take a seat," the woman said, dipping her pen into an ink pot. "Your name is Lexie Watson?"

"Yes."

The woman scribbled the name down on a form. "What position are you seeking, Miss Watson?"

"I'd like to work as a governess."

Mrs. Farthing's eyes widened as they met Alexandra's. "Are you from America, Miss Watson?"

"I am."

"How interesting. Why are you seeking employment in England?"

Alexandra paused, deciding it wouldn't be a good idea to admit that she was just trying to earn her passage home. "It's a beautiful country. I came for a visit, but thought I'd stay. And I'd like to start working as soon as possible."

"These things take time to arrange, Miss Watson."

"How much time?"

"Generally, it takes about three weeks for us to gather the information we need, exchange correspondence, and match you with an appropriate employer."

"Three weeks?" Alexandra was alarmed. "I can't wait that long."

"Let's get started, shall we, and see where we are. Tell me about your experience as a governess."

Alexandra opened her mouth, prepared to make something up, or just to repeat the story Mrs. Gill had supposed about her. But somehow, she couldn't bring herself to lie. "I was educated at Vassar College in New York. I've read to children who were sick, and at libraries. I love children."

Mrs. Farthing looked at her again. "Do I take it that you've never actually served as a governess?"

"No. But I'll be good at it."

"You said you attended college?"

"Yes."

"That is most unusual. Do you have a certificate or transcripts to authenticate your education?"

"Not with me."

The woman gave her a doubtful look. Alexandra began to feel a ripple of discomfort creep up her spine.

"Do you have references of any kind that you can offer?"

"References? No."

Mrs. Farthing put down her pen, her mouth tight as she pointed to a stack of paperwork on her desk. "Miss Watson. I'm sorry. While I respect your desire for employment, I have dozens of experienced young ladies seeking these positions whose references are impeccable. I'm afraid you will have no chance of competing with them."

Alexandra's heart sank. "But I need a job, Mrs. Farthing. I'm out of money, and in two days, I'll have nowhere to live. What am I supposed to do?"

Folding her hands, Mrs. Farthing leaned across the desk, saying gently, "You seem like a decent young lady. If you need employment that urgently, you might check in the shops in the neighborhood to see if anyone is hiring. Shopkeepers might not care so much about references and experience."

Alexandra, downhearted, raced the three blocks back to Mrs. Gill's boardinghouse, where she blew into Mr. Carlyle's studio and apologized for being ten minutes late.

"Is everything all right?" Mr. Carlyle asked, as he set up his paints and brushes.

"Fine, I was just out looking for a job."

She'd hoped that today, she'd be able to be in the same room with him without a repeat of that earlier, heart-skittering attraction. But the moment she saw him, she felt the same jolt to her senses. Something, however, seemed different about him today, although she couldn't put her finger on what.

As she moved behind the screen and changed into the white gown, she told him about her job-seeking venture. "Unfortunately, it was a waste of time."

"I am sorry to hear that." His sympathy sounded genuine.

"I'm not giving up. I'm going to check in the shops this afternoon."

"I hope you have better luck."

"Thank you." When she'd finished changing and came out to stand before the backdrop, she asked, "What happened to the sash? I didn't see it back there."

"I do not need you to wear the sash today. I found another way to reconstruct it." Mr. Carlyle gestured toward a table, where he'd recreated the billowing sash in the portrait by mounting it on a small, temporary scaffold of what looked like bottles, books, sticks, and other pieces of wood.

"How creative." Alexandra hadn't realized until this

moment that she'd been looking forward to him pinning her into the sash again, and was sorry it wouldn't be repeated. At the same time, she wondered if he came up with this new arrangement specifically to avoid another such encounter.

She resumed her stance. The portrait session began. Mr. Carlyle was concentrating so hard that for ten long minutes he didn't say a word. When she could stand the quiet no longer, Alexandra cleared her throat and said brightly, "Mr. Carlyle. Mrs. Gill tells me you're from Cornwall?"

"Yes."

"I've heard Cornwall is beautiful."

"It is."

"It must be a wonderful place to paint."

"For some, I imagine it can be." He didn't smile as he said it.

She wondered why. "Do your parents live in Cornwall?"

"My parents passed away some years ago."

"I'm sorry."

"Thank you." That was all he offered. He didn't seem to want to talk about his parents any more than she wished to discuss hers. Another few minutes ticked by. Finally, he said, "Tell me about your family."

She hesitated. How much could she say without giving herself away? "I have two younger sisters."

"So do I." He frowned, as if he hadn't meant to share that. "Do your sisters live in New York?"

"They do."

He dipped his brush, continued painting. "What are they like?"

Alexandra couldn't hold back a smile. "How much time do you have?"

"I am all ears, Miss Watson."

Surely, she could talk about her sisters without mentioning their real identities or financial status. "Well. They're both beautiful and smart. Sometimes they frustrate and infuriate me, but at the same time, I adore them. We're as close as sisters can be. I haven't seen them in ages and I miss them terribly."

"Oh? How long have you been away? I had the impression you arrived overseas a short while ago, with your former employers."

Alexandra bit her lip. Why had she said that? How to answer without lying? She paused, flustered. "I've actually been away from home for some time. We were in France for a while before coming here."

"I see."

She was struggling for something else to say, determined to direct the conversation away from herself, when her gaze came to rest on his face. She suddenly realized what was different about him today. "Mr. Carlyle. You're not wearing your eyeglasses."

His hand froze. A blush rose to his cheeks. He set down his brush, retrieved his spectacles, put them on, and resumed his position by the easel. "No wonder you looked a bit fuzzy this morning," he commented with a tight smile. "I tend to be absentminded when I work. Thankfully, my prescription is slight."

It was a reasonable enough explanation, but he now

seemed preoccupied and a bit uncomfortable. After that, Alexandra's every attempt to engage him in conversation was met with brief and often monosyllabic replies. The session dragged on, as he worked and Alexandra tried not to fidget. At one thirty, Mr. Carlyle declared them finished for the day.

"You did well, thank you," he said when she emerged from behind the screen, dressed again in her own clothes.

A glance at the portrait revealed that he'd made great progress. Alexandra felt a tingle of wonder and satisfaction as she noted the new parts he'd added to Mrs. Norton's arms and hands, knowing that they were actually based on herself.

They agreed to meet the next morning at the same time. At which point Alexandra left the house in search of employment.

She called into every shop and lunchroom that looked the least bit promising, whether or not there was a Help Wanted sign in the window. At each stop, she was met with a smile until her American accent was discovered. Confusion followed. Why, everyone wanted to know, did an American woman want to work in a London shop? Wasn't she in town on holiday? All the Americans they'd ever met were customers with plenty of money to spend.

Having failed so miserably at her attempt to land a governess position by telling the truth, Alexandra resorted to brief, mostly fictitious explanations of her circumstances: she'd come overseas on vacation but had run out of money. She was a lady's maid who'd lost her job. She'd worked in a dress shop or bakery or greengrocer in New York but had always dreamed of living in London. She even tried the tale Mrs. Gill had inferred, about being a governess who'd been let go. But no one offered her a job. They were polite, they were sorry, but they didn't have any openings just now.

After four hours, Alexandra's spirits were completely deflated. She was heading back to the lodging house when she came upon a stationery stop, and decided to give it one more try.

She was approaching the door when, through the window, she noticed two well-dressed young women inside, completing a purchase. As they turned for the door, Alexandra froze with shock. She recognized the women. They were debutantes Alexandra had met during the Season. One of them was Lady Minnie Dewsbury, in Alexandra's estimation, one of the most pompous, disagreeable, and indiscreet young women in England.

Shielding her face with one hand, Alexandra rushed away. If Lady Dewsbury recognized her, she'd surely inform Alexandra's mother, if not the whole of London society, that Alexandra was still in town.

She ran almost the entire five blocks back to Mrs. Gill's, cursing the corset that made it so difficult to breathe. What a fool she'd been to walk about so cavalierly, looking for a job! It had never occurred to her that she might encounter anyone she knew. But the truth was, she'd met hundreds of people during her brief involvement in the London Season. As an American heiress with a fortune, she'd been a visible presence at every single affair. Even dressed as she was, someone might recognize her. And what if it had been her mother coming out of that shop!

Alexandra arrived at the boardinghouse with a painful stitch in her side. She sank down on her bed, utterly discouraged. As if it wasn't bad enough that no one would hire her, now it seemed unsafe to even go out looking.

What on earth was she going to do?

That night, Alexandra dreamt that she was trudging down a London street, looking in shop windows for Help Wanted signs, when her mother and Lord Shrewsbury suddenly appeared before her.

"Grab her!" cried her mother, the feathers in her hat dancing as she and the viscount forced Alexandra into a waiting carriage. The vehicle immediately took off at a rapid pace.

"Where are we going?" Alexandra cried frantically.

"To church of course," replied Lord Shrewsbury with a sardonic smile. "It is our wedding day."

"No!" Alexandra tried desperately to reach past her mother for the door handle. "Let me out! Let me out!"

Alexandra awoke in a panic, perspiring profusely. The nightmare still lingered, weighing heavily on her mind, when she appeared at Mr. Carlyle's studio at the appointed hour.

His door was open. She went in and crossed the room, preoccupied. This was her last sitting. Tomorrow, she'd be out on the street. She'd have no alternative but to go back to her mother. She was halfway to the rack of clothing at the back of the studio, when she noticed Mr. Carlyle pacing back and forth, looking as anxious and distraught as she felt. Pausing, Alexandra asked, "Is something wrong?"

"You might say that." His tone was bitter.

She noticed an open letter in his hand. "What happened?"

He waved the letter as he paced. "I have just returned from the post office, and received some bad news."

"Is there any way I can help?"

"What?" he muttered distractedly.

"I just asked if I can help."

"You?" He uttered the single word in disbelief, as if she'd just suggested that she might be the next queen of England.

Insulted by his tone, she replied in a huff, "Excuse me. I was just trying to be polite."

He stopped in his tracks and stared at her sharply, as if an idea was just occurring to him. After a long moment, during which a range of conflicting expressions crossed his face, he said tentatively, "You are looking for work, are you not, Miss Watson?"

Whatever she'd been expecting him to say next, it wasn't that. "Yes I am. Why?"

"Well then. Perhaps there *is* a way you can help me. A way in which we can, once again, help each other."

"I'm sorry. I don't follow."

"I would like to offer you a position, Miss Watson. As governess to my sisters in Cornwall."

Chapter Six

Miss Watson stared at him. "You want me to be your sisters' governess?"

Thomas nodded, waving the letter in his hand. "My housekeeper writes to say that the governess has quit and the girls are running wild. She begs me to return to Cornwall at once with a replacement."

It was an inconvenience that could not have come at a worse time. He needed to stay in London another couple of months, to finish his current works and drum up more commissions. But he had to remedy this situation before it got truly out of hand.

When he'd first read the letter, he had been all at sixes and sevens. A qualified governess was difficult to find and even harder to keep, especially where he lived. He'd never had much luck with the employment agencies in London, and it would take weeks to advertise and locate someone on his own.

The answer to his dilemma, however, was staring him in the face. In the brief time in which they'd been acquainted, Miss Watson had proven herself to be intelligent and reliable. He no longer flinched every time she spoke. She had a lively personality and was extremely well educated. She had attended college, for God's sake. She had younger sisters of her own.

What more could he ask for in a governess?

What you could ask for, a small voice insisted in the back of his head, *is a woman who doesn't make you want to shag her every time you look at her.*

The past two days, it had been an exercise in frustration and restraint to be cooped up with her in this studio, painting her perfect flesh. Knowing exactly what she looked like beneath that all-too-revealing white satin gown. Wishing, with every passing second, that he had the nerve and the right to stride across the room, take her into his arms, and kiss her until they were both breathless.

To take her home to Polperran House? It would be madness.

It will not be a problem, he countered silently. He would simply keep his distance from her. He had never spent any time with the previous governesses, after all. What did he have to lose by trying her out?

"Normally, I would ask for references," he informed Miss Watson, "but it would take far too long to write and hear back from America. And I don't suppose there is any point in speaking to your previous employers, after what occurred?"

"No." She colored at that. In fact, she seemed to be taken aback by the whole idea.

"Forgive me. I realize that you know next to nothing about me, which may affect your ability to make a decision. Feel free to ask any questions you might have. I will do my best to answer."

She glanced at him. "Why did the last governess leave?"

"My housekeeper did not say."

"How old are your sisters?"

"Fifteen and twelve."

"What are their names?"

"Julia and Lillie."

"Are they difficult?"

"Not at all." That wasn't exactly true, but would the truth persuade her to take the job? "They just need a firm hand, someone to harness their energy in the proper direction."

"Couldn't they attend a local school?"

Perhaps she was unfamiliar with the English education system. "The local school only takes boys and girls up to age twelve."

She paused, taking that in. "Where do you live in Cornwall?"

"About thirty miles south of Plymouth."

That seemed to mean nothing to her. "Do you live in a town, or the country?"

"The country."

"Would I have my own room?"

An absurd question. But then, he reminded himself, she must think him to be an impoverished artist, the part he had worked so hard to play. The impoverished part was certainly close enough to the truth, but as to the rest . . . well. It was a misconception he was not about to rectify while under Mrs. Gill's roof. "Yes. You will have your own room."

If she accepted the post, he owed her a more complete

explanation as to who he was. He just hoped she wouldn't pry too deeply into the matter until they'd left town.

"How much does the position pay?"

"I am sorry, I should have said. The post comes with a salary of forty pounds per annum. Naturally, room and board are provided."

Miss Watson seemed to process that, as if the number were important. "Would we leave for Cornwall at once?"

"The day after tomorrow. I have to finish Mrs. Norton's portrait, fill in the background and such. While it dries, I can escort you to Cornwall, but I will be obliged to return to London soon after."

"I see." She appeared undecided.

"Do you have any further questions?" he persisted, feeling anxious now. "Do you need more time? Or can you tell me now whether or not you will accept?"

This turn of events was so unexpected, Alexandra hardly knew what to think.

The idea that Mr. Carlyle was offering her such a position came as a shock. He'd said his parents were both dead. Apparently, he was obliged to take care of his sisters. But from what she'd gleaned about him from Mrs. Gill, he was a man so poor, he could barely afford the rooms he rented several months a year while in town, plying his trade. How could he afford to employ a governess?

On the one hand, Alexandra realized, the offer was a lifesaver. She needed a place to go, the farther away from

London, the better. There'd be no chance of her mother or anyone else she knew stumbling upon her in faraway Cornwall. It would give her the opportunity to see more of the English countryside, which she'd so admired on previous trips. And with the salary Mr. Carlyle was offering—if she saved every penny—in three months, Alexandra could afford a second class ticket on a steamship to New York.

What other means did she have to acquire that money? None.

She'd already convinced herself that, despite her lack of specific experience, she could do a reasonable job as a governess. But *should* she do it?

Accepting this position would mean going somewhere completely unknown with a man of only very recent acquaintance. What did she know about Mr. Carlyle, other than that he was a brilliant painter? Well, she knew he was a man of modest means, who no doubt lived in a modest house. According to Mrs. Gill, he was also a quiet, responsible, hardworking man who kept to himself. All admirable qualities. Not everything about him was admirable, of course. For some reason, he had a chip on his shoulder about Americans. Did she really want to work for a man who seemed to dislike people of her nationality?

Did she have any choice?

There was another, more critical, stumbling block: Alexandra found Mr. Carlyle extremely attractive. Too attractive for her own good. If he was going to be her employer, there could be no relationship of any kind between them, beyond polite civility. Not that she wanted any other kind of relationship! Certainly not. She had no desire, she reminded herself fiercely, to get involved with him or any other man. She just wanted to go home.

The heart, however, did not always listen to the head.

Alexandra couldn't forget the rush of feelings that had come over her that first day in this studio. Or how she'd felt—how she *still* felt—every time she looked at him. Sometimes, she had to remind herself to breathe. What would it be like, being around him every day in his house in the country?

But then, how often would she actually *be* around him? Governesses spent all of their time with their pupils, didn't they? And he wouldn't be staying in Cornwall, anyway; he was just going to escort her there, then return to London. By the time he came to Cornwall for good, she'd probably be leaving.

"I'm interested in the position," Alexandra announced, her eyes flicking up to meet Mr. Carlyle's expectant glance.

"Wonderful," he responded with a relieved smile.

"But I should be honest with you." If she couldn't be honest about *everything*, this was the least she could do. "I can take the job for a limited time, only three months. My object is to earn enough money to sail home to New York."

His smile fled. "I see."

"If you prefer to offer the job to someone else, who can commit to a longer term of employment, I'd understand. It might be better for your sisters."

After a moment's reflection, he shook his head. "I understand your circumstances. Three months will have to do. This solves my immediate dilemma, and gives me plenty of time to find your replacement."

"All right, then. Now, we must discuss the problem of clothes."

"Clothes?"

"Yes. Unfortunately, everything I had in the world has been left behind or stolen."

He appeared confounded. "A servant's wardrobe is her own affair. I have never provided clothing for a governess."

Alexandra didn't realize that's the way these things worked. Thinking fast, she continued, "I would have been happy to provide for myself, if things were different. But as things stand, if I'm to take the job, I can't be expected to wear this one dress every single day."

His brows furrowed. "What would you need, exactly?"

"One full change of clothing at the very least: a new dress, undergarments, stockings, a nightgown, hat, shawl. I'll need a handbag, handkerchiefs, another pair of shoes—"

"I get the picture," he interrupted, holding up his hands. After a brief deliberation, he added, "Your shoes will have to do. I am sure we can find you a handbag, handkerchiefs, nightdress, and a hat at my house. As for the rest, I can purchase fabric. I presume you sew?"

The question threw her for a loop. She groped for a reply, then said slowly, "I am competent at needlework, of course, but I was never taught anything beyond basic embroidery, having had dressmakers until . . . recently."

"I see." He considered, frowning. "Well, there is a woman down the street who makes gowns for my sisters. You may have one dress made up and whatever . . . undergarments you require. I will arrange to have them delivered. You may also purchase a shawl and stockings. May I suggest that you choose nothing too fancy, as the cost will be docked from your salary."

"Docked from my salary?" Alexandra stared at him. "That's hardly fair."

"From where I stand, it is perfectly fair, if not generous. You are a governess without references. I have no idea if your services will suit. Should you decide to bolt after a day or a fortnight, your clothing will surely go with you. I am offering to pay for it in advance, in the hopes that our arrangement will work out."

Alexandra hesitated. If her salary was docked for new clothing, it would take even longer to earn shipboard passage. Still, she needed clothes. And the job. She did a few mental calculations. "All right. I'll take the job. But for a salary of fifty pounds per year."

His mouth dropped open. "Fifty pounds? That is out of the question. The salary I offered is generous and non-negotiable."

"Every business deal is negotiable, Mr. Carlyle. And this is business, don't you agree? You need a governess, and fast. You're asking me to travel to a place I've never been, to care for two young ladies I've never met. I have no idea if the job will suit. If I want to leave, it's a long way from Cornwall to London. The way I see it, I'm taking a big risk in accepting your offer."

He returned her stare, saying nothing for several seconds. Then, unexpectedly, he laughed. It was the first time Alexandra had heard him laugh. The hearty, delightful sound came from deep within his chest, and she couldn't help laughing in return.

Holding out his hand, he said, "You drive a hard bargain, Miss Watson."

She shook his hand, an action which caused a tingle to run up the length of her arm. "I might say the same about you, Mr. Carlyle."

After the final sitting that afternoon, Mr. Carlyle sent Alexandra off with a note to the dressmaker's, where she was fitted for a new dress and undergarments.

As summer was approaching, she ordered a dress of high-quality cotton in a pretty shade of pale blue, in a style the seamstress assured her was appropriate for a governess. It was the plainest garment Alexandra had ever bought, but at least the color would be more cheerful than the black dress she was wearing. She also stopped in at a shop and, with money Mr. Carlyle had given her as an advance on her salary, purchased stockings and an inexpensive shawl of light wool.

Mrs. Gill was delighted to learn of Alexandra's employment opportunity. She lent her a small black bonnet for her journey, which Mr. Carlyle agreed to bring back on his return to town. Alexandra warily checked the London newspapers, relieved to discover no more articles about her. She began to feel an obligation, however, to let her parents know something of her circumstances.

On the morning of their departure, Alexandra dashed into the post office and sent the following telegram to her father:

TO: MR. COLIS P. ATHERTON
650 FIFTH AVENUE NEW YORK CITY

NOT ABOARD MARITIME. CANNOT MARRY
SHREWSBURY. AM SAFE. DON'T WORRY. FOR-
GIVE ME. ALL MY LOVE TO MADDIE AND
KATHRYN.

    ALEXANDRA

Alexandra also posted a letter to be delivered to Brown's Hotel:

Dear Mother,

Forgive me if my abrupt departure caused you worry. Unfortunately, I was unable to achieve my aim to board the Maritime—but I didn't dare return to you, knowing your grand ambitions for me.

I've tried hard to do everything you wanted. But as I tried so desperately to explain, I cannot and will not marry Shrewsbury. It is criminal to ask me to throw my life away on a union that would be a disaster, just to buy a title. There are far better uses for Father's money. Let us find one.

I pray that you and Father will come to understand my point of view. By the time you receive this, I will have left London. Don't worry, I'm perfectly safe, and will be well cared for. Please give my deepest love to Father, Maddie, and Kathryn when you see them. I remain,

    Your daughter,
    Alexandra

When Alexandra and Mr. Carlyle boarded their first-class carriage on the train, they found it occupied by two prim-looking elderly ladies. Alexandra sat down on the opposite velvet-upholstered bench. Mr. Carlyle sat beside her, placing his hat on the seat between them.

The journey, he told her, would take about nine hours—seven by train to Bolton, a small station some ways beyond Plymouth, where they would disembark and travel another two hours by coach to Longford.

"Longford?" she asked. "Is that the name of your nearest town?"

"It's more of a village. I live just beyond it."

A few minutes later, a shrill whistle blew, and the train lurched forward. Mr. Carlyle took out a book from his valise and began to read. Alexandra always brought a book or two with her when she traveled, and it felt odd sitting there without something of her own to read.

The rhythmic sounds and movement of the train were a lulling staccato as they made their way out of the city. She was happy to say good-bye to London, but also apprehensive. She was off to an entirely new life, with no precise idea where she was going or what she'd be doing there. She told herself it was an adventure—the kind of adventure she used to long for as a child—and prayed she wasn't making a terrible mistake.

Alexandra's gaze shifted to the man seated beside her. Sunlight streamed in through the window, illuminating the highlights in his golden hair. One long, lean leg was crossed above the other, and his wide shoulders and upper arms strained against the seams of his charcoal gray coat, the same rather shabby garment he always wore.

Her gaze came to rest on Mr. Carlyle's hands, which held the book he was reading. She recalled the way those hands had made her tingle just by grazing against her in his studio, a memory that made butterflies dance in her stomach.

Stop it, Alexandra. Mr. Carlyle had always behaved in the most upright manner where she was concerned. He was now her employer. He didn't have any feelings for her beyond that which were proper and respectable, and for that, she was grateful. She was on her way to Cornwall to do a job, which she would do to the best of her ability. When she'd earned the money she required, she'd leave and never see him again.

It was to be a long train ride, however, and it would seem even longer if they didn't converse with each other. Since he didn't seem to have any plans in that direction, she decided to take the bull by the horns.

Glancing at his book, Alexandra commented, "*Great Expectations.* An excellent choice."

He glanced up. "You've read it?"

"Several times. It might not be considered Dickens's defining novel, but I think it's his best."

"I agree." He closed the volume, removed his eyeglasses, and placed them in his coat pocket. "I've read it several times myself."

He smiled, something she'd so rarely seen him do. It took her by surprise. She'd thought him a handsome man before, but when he smiled, it lit up his face in a most arresting way, prompting her to smile in return.

A lively discussion followed in which they dissected the novel in detail, a conversation which he seemed to enjoy as much as she did.

"I feel bad now that I did not bring you something to read," he said eventually, offering her his book. "You are welcome to this, if you do not mind yet another perusal."

Alexandra laughed. "Thank you. But this is a part of England I've never seen. I'll be happy to just take in the view."

He nodded, and after a moment went back to reading.

The elderly ladies sitting opposite were gently dozing. As the train rumbled along, Alexandra took in the beauty and tranquility of the landscape. The sky was cornflower blue, embellished by puffy white clouds. Wide green meadows spread as far as the eye could see, dotted with grazing sheep. They passed village after village with rows of quaint houses, many topped by thatched roofs and fronted by neat, colorful gardens. In the distance, Alexandra glimpsed the rooftops of small towns and ancient church spires. And the trees! They passed trees more enormous than any she'd ever seen, some of which she guessed to be over a thousand years old.

Alexandra had traveled a great deal with her family. She had seen untamed, expansive vistas in the American West, and the galleries and monuments of Europe. But nothing had filled her with quite as deep a sense of pleasure as the pastoral views outside her window. Maybe it was all the British literature she'd been reading since she was a child. Somehow, this countryside felt comforting and familiar, like a page out of a beloved storybook.

Even though this train was hurtling down the track, transporting her to a place she had never been.

With a man she hardly knew.

CHAPTER SEVEN

The ladies sitting across from them exited the train at Salisbury, and were replaced by two gentlemen who immediately became immersed in their newspapers. Halfway through the trip, Alexandra and Mr. Carlyle ate the ham-and-cheese sandwiches Mrs. Gill had sent along.

Alexandra spent part of the time thinking about Madeleine and Kathryn. It was months now since she'd seen her sisters, and she missed them dreadfully. They had rarely been separated before. She wondered what they would think when they learned of her decision to flee the London Season. Would they chastise her or congratulate her?

She wondered, too, about Mr. Carlyle's sisters: what they were they like, and whether or not they would welcome the arrival of a new governess. When they passed Exeter, Alexandra, growing sleepy from the motion of the train and hoping that renewed conversation would keep her awake, decided to broach the subject.

"Mr. Carlyle, I wonder if you could give me a little information about what to expect when we reach Cornwall."

His lips suddenly pressed together, and he darted a glance at the gentlemen sharing the carriage. "What to expect?"

"Yes. Can you tell me something about your sisters?"

"They are typical girls, I suppose," was his oblique reply.

"What do you mean, typical?"

He shrugged slightly. "Julia, the eldest, is never satisfied with anything. Lillie is quiet. She keeps to herself."

That wasn't much to go on. "What are their interests and pursuits?"

"I have no idea. You will find out soon enough."

She frowned. Did he really know so little about his sisters, or was he being deliberately evasive? "What about your parents?"

"As I believe I said, they are no longer with us."

"I know, but . . . what did your father do?"

"Do?" Mr. Carlyle frowned and said bitterly, "My father never did much except drink, gamble, spend money like water, and chase after women. Not surprisingly, my mother was a very unhappy woman. She passed away when I was sixteen, giving birth to Lillie." As soon as the words escaped his mouth, his forehead creased with obvious regret and he glanced away. "Forgive me, I should not have said that."

"I'm glad you told me." Alexandra's heart went out to him and his sisters. "It helps me to know something of the family I'm working for. I'm just so sorry. That's far too young to lose one's mother."

"I believe any age is too young to lose one's mother. At least I knew her. Julia and Lillie have no memory of her at all."

Alexandra thought about her own mother. They hadn't gotten along in years, but she had pleasant memories from early childhood, before her mother was overtaken by social ambition. She wondered what it would be like to grow up with no memory of one's mother at all. "When did your father die? If you don't mind my asking?"

"Three years ago."

"I'm sorry," she said again.

"You and Julia would be alone in that sentiment," was his curt reply, before returning to his book.

The subject was clearly closed.

The carriage and driver were waiting for them when they stepped off the train at Bolton.

Thomas was embarrassed, as always, by the condition of the brougham, particularly by the shabbiness of its interior. When he ushered Miss Watson inside, however, she appeared to be too weary to notice.

"How long did you say, until we reach our destination?" she inquired.

"About two hours."

She sank down onto the single cushioned bench and gazed out the window. "It's so beautiful here."

Thomas sat next to her. "There is nothing remarkable in the scenery at Bolton."

"Oh but there is! The meadows seem to go on forever. And it's so green." She laid her head back against the seat, causing the small black flowered hat that sheltered the coils of her sienna hair to go slightly askew. "I want to see everything," she murmured sleepily, "but we got up so early, and it's so warm. If I nod off, I hope you'll forgive me?"

"I will." Thomas tapped the roof. The vehicle lurched forward, slowly leaving the tiny railway station and making its way down the dusty road. He sat tensely, his hands resting on his knees.

Two hours.

It had been easy enough to keep a certain distance between himself and Miss Watson on the train. But in the confines of the small brougham carriage, it was impossible. By necessity, she was seated immediately beside him, so near that their shoulders were almost touching. So near, that with every inhalation he could smell the pleasant, light fragrance of her hair and skin.

Two hours. How was a man supposed to stand it?

This was, he realized, the worst idea he'd ever had. What had he been thinking, bringing her to Cornwall, where the very sight of her would be a daily exercise in frustration?

She wasn't just beautiful, this woman. She wasn't just smart—a woman who understood art and could match him, detail for detail, in a discussion about literature, challenging him with thought-provoking ideas that didn't simply agree with his own. She was also clever. She'd gotten him to increase her salary, before even proving herself capable in the position for which she had been hired. In effect, with that raise, she had gotten *him* to pay for the new clothes he had insisted *she* pay for herself.

Clever.

If only she could have been the nervous, quiet, withdrawn type, like the two previous governesses. Or an aging, self-involved battle-ax, like the two before that. There had been no danger of him being attracted to any of *those* women.

This woman had far too many qualities that he liked.

He had no business liking the governess. Or being attracted to the governess.

His friends at Oxford had often joked about it. Tupping the serving staff was a common thing, to be expected. They had all done it. Certainly Thomas's father had had no compunctions about taking his pleasure whenever and with whomever he saw fit, often causing the end of that young lady's career in service, and in one case Thomas knew of, her life.

Thomas had vowed to never so indulge himself. He had developed a code of ethics, and he had stuck with it. Even during his two years in Italy, he had stuck to his principles. There had been plenty of other women who were willing and available yet experienced enough not only to take care of themselves, but also to teach him a thing or two. It had been quite an education.

Two years ago, when he first started painting portraits in town, he'd allowed himself to find release now and then with a dancer or a model. But such fleeting alliances had not proven satisfying, and there was always the risk of disease. Lately, while in London, he just applied himself to his work, by necessity keeping his head down and staying out of sight.

How long had it been now since he had been with a woman? He could not remember. There were times when abstinence made him as restless and surly as a bear. Even Mrs. Gill had commented once or twice upon his dark moods. But still, whether at home or in town, he had stuck inexorably to one resolve: *Hands off the serving staff.* Else what separated man from the beasts?

It was a resolve he had not questioned in many years.

Until Miss Watson stumbled in the road, and into his life.

He realized that he owed her an explanation of who he was, and what was to come. He had fully intended to fill her in when they boarded the train, but they had never been alone. He was not about to spill his guts with those two biddies or those top-hatted gentlemen to overhear it; he knew how far and how fast gossip could spread. Far better to wait for the privacy of his carriage.

Thomas took a deep breath. There was no time like the present. He might as well get it over with. "Miss Watson," he began quietly, turning to face her.

Miss Watson's eyes were closed and her head lay against the seat back, mere inches away. From the sound of her breathing, she was fast asleep.

He sighed. It would have to wait.

Or perhaps, he reasoned, it would be better to say nothing after all. At this late hour, what good would come of an admission? She would understand everything very soon.

Settling back against the seat himself, he stretched his legs out before him, thinking he might also try to nap. But when he closed his eyes, he remained all too aware of the woman beside him. All too aware of the body that lay beneath her high-collared, long-sleeved dress—the body he had seen naked in the bath. The breasts which he had been obliged to stare at for two hours a day, three days in succession, as they rose provocatively above the tight confines of that low-cut white gown.

The carriage lurched twice, interrupting his reverie. Thomas felt Miss Watson's head drop softly onto his shoulder. His eyes snapped open, as all his nerves seemed to leap into high awareness. Turning his head ever so slightly to face her, he watched the rise and fall of her chest as she slept.

Dear God. How he longed to touch her.

His hand hungered to venture forth, to settle on her waist. To feel, beneath his fingers and palm, the slender curves of her body, even if it was through her clothing.

He gazed down at her closed eyelids. The long, feathered eyelashes. The rosy lips that were slightly parted. Lips that were just inches from his own. How he longed to taste those lips. Just one kiss. One kiss to slake the lust that was running rampant through him.

In his mind, he visualized what it might be like to press his lips against hers. Did he dare? He wondered how she would respond. Whether her tongue would meet and tangle with his, or if she would slap him in dismay and push him away.

She stirred slightly and let out a low moan in her sleep.

Thomas jerked away and leaned back against the seat again, taking a long, deep breath. To calm himself. To restore his sanity. Only a rapacious cad would take advantage of a woman who was asleep. He had no business touching her or kissing her at *any* time, much less at a time like this. He needed her to take care of his sisters. Did he want her to quit before she had even begun at her post?

Alexandra awoke to find the carriage filled with the amber light of the late-afternoon sun.

She stretched and glanced at Mr. Carlyle, who was staring moodily out the window. "Have I been asleep long?"

"Two hours."

"Oh no, I've missed everything."

His eyes remained on the view outside. For some reason he seemed tense, irritable, distracted. Which she knew from past experience meant the less conversation, the better.

She peered out her own window. A small sign read WELCOME TO LONGFORD. She recalled him saying that he lived just outside Longford. They were nearly there.

The village consisted of a single main street bordered by narrow cottages of gray stone. Although picturesque, the place looked neglected. Many of the cottages had broken windowpanes, missing roof tiles, and fences in disrepair. It saddened Alexandra to see a place in such a state of dilapidation. But then, she hadn't expected Mr. Carlyle to live in glamorous environs.

They continued up the road about half a mile, past green fields and rolling hills, and then turned onto a narrow tree-lined lane. After winding through the woods for some minutes, they emerged into an open space with vast meadows on one side. On the other, a tree-shaded granite wall seemed to extend endlessly before them, interrupted by a castle-like structure of gray granite that looked like it dated to the sixteenth century.

To her surprise, the carriage stopped before this very

building. Three stories high, the edifice featured an arched entryway and mullioned windows, and was topped by battlements and turrets. The driver stepped down and opened a gigantic wrought-iron gate.

"What's this?" Alexandra asked.

"The gatehouse."

Thomas was acting so brusque and aloof, she didn't want to ask any of the many questions rattling in her brain. They drove on, winding through an expanse of trees carpeted by bracken and the profuse yellow blooms of gorse and broom. After traveling up a slight incline, the carriage followed the curving avenue downward again, bringing into view a massive, three-story house of gray slate and granite.

Alexandra had visited plenty of large houses on both sides of the Atlantic, and the mansion her parents had recently built on Fifth Avenue was very imposing. But this was one of the most immense and magnificent houses she'd ever seen. Similar in style and age to the ancient gatehouse, it featured countless windows and a forest of chimneys. It was built in a U shape, with a central tower-like entry in the main building flanked by ivy-covered wings that surrounded a gravel courtyard.

What was this place? She wondered if Mr. Carlyle had been hired to come here, to paint someone's portrait. As they drew nearer, Alexandra began to notice that the edifice wasn't quite as impressive as it had appeared at first glance. The huge granite bricks were green at the edges with moss. Ivy that had not been clipped in ages had flung itself over the walls and rooftops. Some of the mullioned windows on the upper floors had been boarded over, and several chimneys and sections of battlements showed signs of decay and neglect.

She realized that Mr. Carlyle was looking at her, as if trying to gauge her reaction. She was about to ask him whose house this was, when he quietly said, "I would be grateful, Miss Watson, if you would say nothing to anyone—at the house, in the village, or anywhere else—about my activities in London."

"Your activities? I don't understand."

"I prefer that it not be generally known that I paint when I am in town."

"Why?"

"You are a perceptive woman, Miss Watson. The answer will very soon become clear to you."

As the coach rattled into the courtyard, the great oaken door of the turreted entry tower was thrown open. Two people exited and stood at attention by the front steps: a white-haired man of regal posture in a black tailcoat, and a trim woman in a severe navy-blue dress. From another, lesser, door in the left wing appeared three more women: one was middle aged, in a faded dress, white cap, and apron; the other two were maids in uniform.

Servants, Alexandra realized, lined up to greet their master. A very small group of servants, considering the size of the house. All at once, a new idea began to form in Alexandra's mind, an idea so unexpected, she could hardly credit it as real.

A young lady who looked to be about fourteen or fifteen

years of age sullenly strolled out the front door and joined the lineup. Her burgundy-colored gown was well made and fashionable. Her expression made it obvious that she was there with reluctance.

Alexandra turned to the man beside her, who was staring straight ahead, his expression unreadable. "Is this place *yours?*"

He gave her a brief, unsmiling nod. "Welcome to Polperran House."

Chapter Eight

The carriage stopped. The driver hopped off, opened the door, and pulled down the step. "Welcome home, my lord," he said with a bow as he stepped aside.

My lord?

A confluence of emotions washed over Alexandra: amazement, awe, and at the same time, anger. The hollow feeling that she'd been tricked, lied to.

Mr. Carlyle was not an obscure, impoverished artist at all. He was not even a *mister*. He was a peer of the realm—of what rank she had yet to determine. Whatever his title, he was the master of Polperran House, which looked to be an ancient estate. He was the owner of this carriage, which she'd presumed to be hired. Owner of the village and all the woods they'd just driven through, and no doubt many thousands of acres more.

The man had totally misrepresented himself. The deception rankled.

She wondered if she should have guessed it—if she had missed some telltale clue. Looking back, she remembered thinking that his accent was more elegant than might be expected for a painter, but she'd just thought he was a quick learner, or maybe the younger son of a gentleman. A nobleman? It had never entered her mind. No, he'd played the part perfectly, all the way down to the shabby clothes. The question remained: Why?

Why didn't he want anyone to know he was a portrait artist? She thought all country lords owned fancy townhouses in Belgravia and Mayfair. Yet he had led her and Mrs. Gill, and who knows how many others, to think he was a commoner, renting rooms in a modest boardinghouse in a lesser neighborhood in London.

Exiting the carriage, Mr. Carlyle—or Lord whatever his name was—turned and raised a hand to assist Alexandra to alight. As she stepped down onto the gravel, gazing into the unapologetic eyes of her new employer, she hissed at him under her breath, "You said you were a poor painter."

"I am," he answered quietly. "But to be fair, I never said anything of the kind."

Alexandra opened her mouth to reply, then shut it again, realizing that she had formed her conclusions about him entirely on what she'd observed in London, and what she'd heard from Mrs. Gill. When he'd offered Alexandra the position, she should have asked more questions. A *lot* more questions.

Even so, she thought. *He lied to you by omission.*

The phrase was eerily familiar. Her anger began to dissipate, replaced by a dash of guilt. What right did she have to be angry with him, when she'd never been honest about who *she* was? She didn't even have a right to complain. She'd expected to live in a modest cottage of some sort for three months. This place was clearly a palace. If anything, she ought to see this as an interesting development.

As the driver closed the coach door behind them, she glimpsed a coronet and coat of arms painted on the side, something she'd been too exhausted to notice when they'd boarded the vehicle at the train station.

"Is your name even Carlyle?" she whispered, trying to rein in her annoyance.

"It is."

"What am I to call you?"

"Longford will do." He gestured for her to accompany him toward the lineup of servants, presumably to be introduced.

Alexandra was unfamiliar with the protocol for such a meeting. All her years of training in the social graces had taught her how an American heiress ought to behave, not a governess. She strained to recall something from the novels she'd read, or from the behavior of her odious finishing governess, Madame Dubois, but came up short. She didn't know if, when meeting other servants, a governess was supposed to curtsy, nod, or shake their hands. She decided to take her cue from them.

"Good afternoon." Mr. Carlyle greeted the assembled group. *No, no,* she mentally corrected herself. *Lord Longford.* It was going to take some time to get used to that. He seemed to be a different person here, standing taller, head held higher, his very speech infused with a more commanding air. "Pray, allow me to introduce you to the new governess. This is Miss Watson, from America."

Surprised expressions crossed every face at this pronouncement.

"America?" repeated the young girl dubiously. There was no doubt she was his sister. She had the same wheat-colored hair, the same long, thin nose, the same chocolate-brown eyes.

"Julia," Longford said, "may I present your new governess, Miss Watson. Miss Watson: my sister, Lady Julia Carlyle."

Julia eyed Alexandra with undisguised disdain. "How do you do."

How could the girl hate me already? Alexandra gave her a smile nevertheless. "I am well, thank you, and very pleased to meet you, Lady Julia."

An awkward silence fell. Lowering his voice, Longford told Alexandra, "Perhaps you are not familiar with the way it is done here. The servants call my sister Lady Julia, but as the governess, you may address her as the family does, as simply Julia."

Alexandra blushed at her mistake. "I see. Thank you."

"Where is Lillie?" Longford asked his sister.

"I have no idea," was Julia's curt reply.

Next up was the white-haired man in the black tailcoat, who Longford introduced as Mr. Hutchens, the butler.

"It is very good to have you back, my lord," Hutchens declared with a bow, before giving Alexandra a grave and dubious nod beneath bushy white eyebrows. "Miss Watson."

"Mr. Hutchens." Alexandra gravely nodded back.

The woman in the navy-blue dress, who had a ring of keys hanging from a chain at her waist, neatly styled brown hair, and a sharp-eyed, appraising look, was the housekeeper, Mrs. Mitchell. She looked to be in her late forties, and stood with her hands clasped before her, as ramrod straight as Mr. Hutchens. "It is a pleasure to meet you, Miss Watson," she stated formally.

"And you, Mrs. Mitchell," Alexandra responded in kind.

She met the other servants in turn: the cook, Mrs. Nettle; the coachman, John, who also served as footman and groom; and the maids: a petite girl named Susan and a tall, gangly brunette, Martha.

"I beg your pardon, Your Lordship," Mrs. Mitchell said, when these introductions were complete, "that Lillie isn't here to greet you. I've looked high and low for her all afternoon, but she's nowhere to be found."

"Do not worry yourself, Mrs. Mitchell. I am certain she will present herself when dinner is on the table."

"I'm afraid that won't be the case, Your Lordship. The dinner hour for the young ladies has already come and gone. I've had quite a time of it this past week since Miss Larsen left, I can tell you."

"Thank you for taking charge so admirably, as always, Mrs. Mitchell."

"It was my pleasure, Your Lordship."

Mr. Hutchens told John to bring the luggage upstairs. As John went to retrieve the single valise strapped to the carriage, Longford informed the butler: "Miss Watson has no luggage."

"No luggage?" Mr. Hutchens and Mrs. Mitchell repeated in unified surprise.

"Some things are being sent from London, and should arrive in about a week," Longford replied, giving no further explanation.

As the maids and cook curtsied and walked off toward what was, presumably, the servants' entrance, Longford led the way in through the great front door. Julia followed. The butler, housekeeper, and footman waited, a silent signal to Alexandra that she was to go next.

Pausing a moment before entering, Alexandra turned to Mrs. Mitchell and asked in a low tone, "Pardon me, but what is Mr.—I mean, His Lordship's title?"

"His title?" Mrs. Mitchell stared at her. "You mean he didn't tell you?"

"He neglected to fill me in on that particular detail."

"Why, he's Thomas Carlyle, the seventh Earl of Longford."

The entry hall of Polperran House opened into an enormous drawing room with a high open-beamed ceiling. As Alexandra took in the room with its fine architectural details, her first impression was that, although equal in size to the gilded drawing room at her parents' new house on Fifth Avenue, in other ways it was very different.

For one thing, it was hundreds of years old.

And there was nothing gilded about it.

A faded, decaying central rug covered the stone floor. Despite the fire burning in the huge marble-framed hearth, the room felt chilly. A sweeping oak staircase curved up to a gal-

lery on the upper level. The oak-paneled walls, in the room
and along the stairway, were hung with oil paintings, primar-
ily ancestral portraits of men and women from centuries long
past. From the faded markings on the walls, it appeared that
other pictures which had once hung there were no longer on
view. The furniture, although it looked to be of good quality,
was threadbare and outdated.

"I do not know why you brought her," Julia was saying to
her brother irritably. "I keep telling you, I am too old for a
governess."

"You are not too old. You are only fifteen."

"I was glad when Miss Larsen quit! I hated her. And this
one will be no different!"

"Julia," Longford responded sternly. "You will not speak
to me that way."

But Julia had already turned and fled up the stairs.

Longford turned to Alexandra with an apologetic shrug.
"She can be rather willful."

"That she can," agreed Mrs. Mitchell. "I have two nieces
who are Lady Julia's age, and they are all the same: they think
they know what's best for them, when really they don't have
the slightest idea."

Alexandra tried to smile. She could see that she had her
work cut out for her here, and she'd only met one of the sisters so far. While Mr. Hutchens and Mrs. Mitchell engaged
in conversation with Mr. Carlyle—*Lord Longford*, she corrected herself again—Alexandra made another survey of the
room.

It had a kind of graceful old-world elegance about it.

at five o'clock. As I mentioned, the girls have already dined today, so I'll have something brought up to your room shortly."

"So I won't be eating with the servants? Or with Lord Longford?"

"Dear Lord, no!" Mrs. Mitchell sounded astonished at the very idea. "I don't know how these things are done in America, Miss Watson, but I imagine you are an educated young lady of the middle or upper class?" She glanced questioningly at Alexandra, who nodded in confirmation. "Well then, you cannot dine with the servants. And His Lordship never dines with his sisters, let alone the governess. He generally takes his meals in his study."

Alexandra struggled to conceal her disappointment. It sounded like she wouldn't be seeing very much of *His Lordship*. And it was becoming more and more clear why he hadn't had much to say about his sisters. Apparently, he didn't spend much time with them.

Upon reaching the first floor, Mrs. Mitchell led the way down a corridor past numerous closed doors, finally pausing and opening one of them. "This is the schoolroom."

"You have a schoolroom?"

"The fifth earl had a large family. Twelve children, ten of them boys, who were educated at home until they came of age or went to university."

Alexandra glanced in from the threshold. The muted light of early evening shone in through the single window, illuminating a small chamber outfitted with two rows of desks with connected bench seats. A large blackboard rested on an

Her family's new home in New York City seemed cold and brash in comparison. Overall, though, the effect was that of a stylish grand dame holding her head high despite wearing shabby clothes.

My father never did much except drink, gamble, spend money like water, and chase after women. Longford's statement had even deeper impact now that Alexandra knew the full circumstances. Polperran was a fine old house that was deteriorating, and looked like it had been stripped of some of its saleable belongings. Like so many of the peers she'd met during the Season, Longford's fortune had clearly been compromised.

"Would you care for something to eat, Your Lordship?" Mrs. Mitchell's voice interrupted Alexandra's musings. She noticed that the butler had exited.

"I shall wait for supper," Longford replied. "I leave it to you, Mrs. Mitchell, to get Miss Watson settled."

"Of course, my lord."

"Miss Watson, you are in good hands. Mrs. Mitchell has been with us for—how long is it now?"

"Over thirty years, my lord. Since before you were born."

"And how lucky we are to have you at the helm," Longford replied sincerely. With a brief nod to Alexandra, he added, "If you will excuse me, I have much to attend to."

Mrs. Mitchell dipped a curtsy. Alexandra's training leapt to her aid, reminding her that she was a governess in the presence of a peer. She similarly curtsied as Longford turned and left the room through an adjoining door, leaving her alone with Mrs. Mitchell.

"Well, Miss Watson," commented Mrs. Mitchell, looking Alexandra up and down. "I must say, we've never had an American governess before."

"I've never worked in an English household before," Alexandra admitted.

"Then we shall both be testing new waters. May I show you to your room?"

"If you would, thank you." Alexandra started for the grand staircase, but Mrs. Mitchell was headed in another direction.

The housekeeper paused and glanced back at Alexandra. "You may use the main stairs whenever you're accompanying one of the children. Otherwise, it is preferred that you use the servants' stairs, as we do."

"I see." Alexandra's skin prickled with shame and annoyance. She was in unfamiliar territory and didn't much like it. The last time she could recall using the servants' stairs was when she was a child, playing hide-and-seek with her sisters.

"How old is this house?" Alexandra asked, as she followed the housekeeper through a rear door into a sizeable but dingy inner hall.

"The original part of the house dates back to the sixteenth century, before the first earl took residence. It has cellars, but no real basement, so the kitchens and servants' hall are on the ground floor. Many of the family rooms are upstairs on the first floor, where they have the best views."

The house, she noticed, had not been updated with gas lighting, unlike the houses she'd visited in town. "How many rooms are there?"

"Fifty-three, though not all of them are open nowadays."

"It must be difficult," Alexandra observed tactfully, "to manage so large a house with such a small staff."

"Oh it isn't easy, I'll grant you that. As I'm sure you can guess, we've had hard times of late, which call for harsh measures. We're down to two housemaids and one footman. We've managed to hold on to the scullery maid, one stable boy, and a gardener, thank the Lord, and a woman comes in from the village twice weekly to help clean. For years, Mr. Hutchens has served as both butler and valet, and I have a great many more responsibilities than I used to. But we get by. We live more simply these days, no house guests and no parties—there's just His Lordship and his sisters to think of. When he's in London, it's very quiet indeed. But I couldn't ask for a better master, he treats us well and fair."

Mrs. Mitchell led the way up a plain, narrow back staircase, continuing, "Now as to your duties. You are to begin tomorrow. The girls' schedule is as follows: Martha gets them up every morning. Breakfast is served in the nursery at eight thirty A.M. Lessons begin promptly at nine. The girls' bedtime is eight o'clock, after which you have your evenings free."

"Am I to be in charge that entire time?"

"Of course. Except for their afternoon rest time. Naturally, you'll have one Sunday off a month."

Alexandra's stomach seized. To be responsible for two girls all day long, every single day, with only one day off a month! It began to dawn on her that she hadn't thought this through very well.

"Luncheon is served in the nursery at noon, and dinner

easel. The faded blue walls were bare except for a map of England hanging from a peg. On a low table stood an old globe, several slates, and a small pile of dusty-looking books.

"You may use this room or the nursery for teaching French and such things—I leave that to your discretion."

French and such things? Alexandra thought it a strange way to describe the curriculum, but the opportunity to ask about it was lost, as Mrs. Mitchell moved rapidly down the hall and entered the next room.

"Here we are. This has always been the nanny's room, but as we have no young children at Polperran House now, it's where the governess sleeps."

The small room was one of the ugliest Alexandra had ever seen. A brass bed outfitted with a thin, faded quilt took up one corner. A cradle occupied another. A frightful wardrobe and dresser that looked hundreds of years old competed for space with two hard-looking chairs, a table, and a writing desk. Numerous small pictures crammed the walls—religious paintings, engravings from books, and ancient embroidery samplers.

The only two bright spots were the fireplace, with its wood mantel and sturdy screen, and a window seat that, framed by fraying draperies, looked out onto a large overgrown garden fronting an expansive green vista.

"I hope you'll find it comfortable," Mrs. Mitchell commented.

"I'm sure I will."

They peeked into the room immediately adjacent, which could be reached both via the hall and through a connecting door. The former night nursery, Mrs. Mitchell explained, it had been converted into a bedroom for Lillie.

Next door to that was the day nursery. Although as old and outdated as the rest of the house, it was a large, airy, light-filled chamber, and one of the nicest rooms Alexandra had seen thus far. Immense windows took up nearly the entire north wall, providing an impressive view of the verdant landscape. The floor was covered by a faded red rug embellished with a gold lattice pattern. An upright piano held yellowed sheets of music. In the center of the room stood a round table of scarred mahogany, outfitted with four chairs. A large, elegantly outfitted dollhouse stood proudly beside a toy box brimming over with wooden soldiers, dolls in frilly dresses, and other old toys.

This, Alexandra realized with a kind of fascination, was a room where Lord Longford must have passed many hours as a child.

"You will take your meals here with the girls," Mrs. Mitchell announced, "and may also use it for teaching, as you like. I'm sure you have a curriculum in mind, but the one thing His Lordship insists upon is that they practice the piano for at least an hour every day."

In fact, Alexandra didn't have any specific curriculum yet in mind, but she didn't want Mrs. Mitchell to know that. "Why did the last governess leave?" she heard herself blurt.

Mrs. Mitchell hesitated. "She said she missed her family, so she found a post closer to home." Returning to the former subject, she went on: "Now, as to afternoon activities for the girls. Fresh air is encouraged, but it goes without saying that they're not to leave the property at any time without permission from myself or His Lordship, and without you as escort. Lillie is not fond of horses, but Lady Julia likes to ride. The last governess didn't often allow it, but if you find time in your lesson plans, Lady Julia may take her horse out for an hour or two on the grounds, if the weather is fine."

"I see." It struck Alexandra as odd that Mrs. Mitchell referred to Julia as Lady Julia, but referred to the younger, mysteriously missing girl, as simply Lillie. Was it a slip of the tongue?

"I should add," Mrs. Mitchell went on briskly, "that the horses are for the family's use only."

Alexandra said nothing. Although her mother had imposed horseback riding lessons on her and her sisters, believing it was a necessary skill for a member of the British nobility, Alexandra hadn't taken to riding the way Madeleine and Kathryn had. Even so, she felt her hackles rise at this stipulation, which implied that she was somehow less worthy than the girls she was meant to teach.

The last room Mrs. Mitchell allowed Alexandra to peek into was Julia's bedroom, just around the corner. It was more luxuriously appointed than Lillie's, the wallpaper blooming with pink roses. Julia lay on the bed atop the pink satin comforter, looking at a magazine.

"Do you mind? I am reading." Julia glared at them in annoyance. "Close the door, would you?"

"Yes, my lady." Mrs. Mitchell shut the door with a sigh. "Well, Miss Watson," she commented as they moved back down the hall, "you must be tired after your journey. Would you like to rest, or shall I call for your dinner?"

Alexandra realized that, despite her nap in the carriage, she was indeed tired. It had been a long day. "Dinner would be very much appreciated, thank you. I think I'll go to bed shortly after."

"I'll have something sent up immediately." Reaching Alexandra's room, Mrs. Mitchell paused. "Normally, this is the moment where I'd say, 'I'll leave you to settle in.' But as you have nothing to unpack . . ."

"About that," Alexandra interjected. "I should probably explain: all my things were recently stolen. I have nothing but the clothes on my back. Even this hat is on loan from Lord Longford's landlady in London." As soon as she uttered the last phrase, Alexandra wondered if she'd made a blunder. Was it known that he rented rooms while in town? But Mrs. Mitchell didn't even blink.

"There's no need for explanations, Miss Watson. His Lordship has already given Mr. Hutchens and myself an overview of your circumstances, and requested that I make you as comfortable as possible."

"Did he?" That was thoughtful.

"I'll take a look in the servants' cupboard, to see if one of the maids who used to work here left behind a nightdress. I'll round up a few other things as well."

"Thank you."

Martha soon appeared with broth and sandwiches. By now, the sun had set, and the fireless room had grown chilly. Even the shawl Alexandra had bought in London wasn't enough to keep her warm. Finding an extra quilt in a drawer, she wrapped herself in it and ate by the light of a single candle at the corner table.

When she'd finished her meal, Mrs. Mitchell returned with a white cotton nightgown that, although plain and well-worn, looked clean. She also gave Alexandra three embroidered handkerchiefs, an old handbag, and a gold-rimmed hairbrush and comb, which she said had belonged to the late Countess of Longford.

Alexandra expressed her thanks, then said, "It's so cold. Is it possible to have a fire in my room?"

Mrs. Mitchell frowned. "His Lordship has requested that we only light fires in rooms as necessary. Since you're about to retire, I see no need. I'm sure two quilts on the bed will suffice." She turned for the door.

Such frugality! Alexandra wasn't accustomed to it. "Before you go, could we try to find Lillie? I'd love to meet her before I turn in for the night."

"There's no telling where Lillie might be hiding, Miss Watson. She's old enough to put herself to bed. You'll just have to wait until morning to meet her."

CHAPTER NINE

Anxiety combined with unfamiliar surroundings caused sleep to evade Alexandra for many long hours. It seemed that she'd finally just drifted off when she was startled back into consciousness by a loud wail.

She lay in bed for some minutes, listening. It soon became apparent that someone was crying. Bitterly. It was coming from the room next door.

Throwing back the covers, Alexandra rose and wrapped herself in her shawl. Treading cautiously in the darkness, she moved to the connecting door that led to Lillie's room, but found it locked. On the other side of the wall, Alexandra heard a sharp female voice, although she couldn't make out the words. The sobbing ended abruptly.

Alexandra issued out into the hall, where she met Mrs. Mitchell in her dressing gown and cap, carrying a candle. "Was that Lillie crying?"

"She just had one of her nightmares," Mrs. Mitchell stated matter-of-factly. "She's fine now. You may go back to bed." With that, she headed down the hall toward the back stairs.

Alexandra stood there, awash with curiosity. Lillie was

in her room at that very moment. The temptation to open her bedroom door and sneak a peek was almost irresistible. But Alexandra worried that such an intrusive step by a total stranger might frighten the girl more than the nightmare that had already disrupted her sleep.

Alexandra returned to her own room and climbed into bed, shivering beneath the quilts as she pondered the realities of her new circumstances.

She was employed by an earl who was evidently broke and leading a double life. She was to be in charge of a fifteen-year-old girl who'd hated her on sight, and a twelve-year-old girl who suffered from nightmares and was too shy to show her face. She was to live in an ancient, deteriorating house, in a kind of limbo—neither a servant nor a member of the family. Her wages were a pittance. Her wardrobe was stultifyingly plain.

What a mortifying descent from all that she'd known previously!

Worse—far worse—than any of the material discomforts was the knowledge that for three long months, she would have to continue pretending to be someone she was not. And for all that time, she would be separated from sisters.

Alexandra sighed as she lay back against her pillow. It wouldn't do any good to feel sorry for herself. One of her father's maxims suddenly came to mind: "The best cure for depression is hard work." That was the ticket. Tomorrow, she'd find out what the last governess was teaching, and come up with some kind of plan.

And hopefully, she'd meet the mysterious Lillie.

Alexandra was awakened by the sound of heavy draperies being thrust open.

"Good mornin', miss," Martha said, before quickly disappearing from the room.

Outside the window, the morning sky was a vibrant, cloudless blue. Alexandra rubbed her eyes and yawned.

She'd just been having a dream, which still hovered, web-like, at the corners of her consciousness. It was so lovely, she struggled to remember it. She'd been in a beautiful green park, strolling with a man. A faceless stranger, but someone she adored. They'd been having a pleasant conversation, talking and laughing.

He'd stopped and had gently drawn her close. Then he'd kissed her.

Not that Alexandra knew much about kisses. But her imagination had conjured up something delightful. In the dream, the man's lips had pressed against hers softly and tenderly. Something low and deep inside Alexandra warmed even now at the memory of it.

A sudden, new awareness made Alexandra gasp aloud. It wasn't a faceless stranger who'd kissed her. The man in her dream was Thomas Carlyle, the seventh Earl of Longford.

Alexandra's cheeks flooded with heat as she curled up in bed, sternly reprimanding herself. Why was her subconscious mind inventing romantic interludes between them? Such thoughts and dreams were unwelcome. She didn't want to be kissing anyone.

Yes, she was attracted to him—but the attraction was

certainly one-sided. They might have enjoyed a few conversations in town and on the train, but the closer they'd gotten to Polperran House, the more moody and aloof he'd become. He'd seemed relieved to turn her over to Mrs. Mitchell the moment they'd arrived.

Besides which, she worked for him now. She had to maintain a certain distance from him, remain professional. *Jane Eyre* notwithstanding, it was against some unwritten rule for a governess to become romantically involved with her employer.

Even though she wasn't really a governess. Even though she was an heiress to an immense fortune, which gave her a pedigree in her own right, considered by many as the American equivalent to an English noblewoman.

As Alexandra rose and got dressed, she pondered the problem. She'd taken this job with the best of intentions, but she was here under false pretenses. If only she could tell Longford who she really was, it would be such a weight off her conscience. It had been too risky to tell him in London. Instead of paying for her to stay at Mrs. Gill's, he would have surely sent her packing. But now that she was in Cornwall, hundreds of miles away from her mother's grasp, would it be safe to reveal her true identity?

She played out the scenario in her mind:

Your Lordship, I have something to tell you. My name's not really Lexie Watson, it's Alexandra Atherton. You may have read about me in the papers. I'm one of the heiresses to the Atherton fortune, the one who's gone missing. Yes, I've been lying to you since the day we met, sorry about that. I've never worked as a governess a day in my life, but thanks all the same for giving me the job, because I really need the money.

No, no. It was impossible.

She'd have to wait until she'd proven herself as a valued employee he could trust and couldn't do without. Then, maybe she could make him understand, and he'd be willing to keep her on for the three months she needed to earn the money to go home.

If she had any more dreams like that, however, three months was going to seem like a very long time.

A fire burned in the nursery hearth when Alexandra entered at 8:30 A.M. Julia was eating a bowl of porridge at the table, which was draped in white linen and set for two. Lillie was nowhere in sight.

"Good morning," Alexandra said as she sat down. Julia didn't respond. "Good morning, Julia," she tried again with a smile.

"Good morning," Julia shot back without raising her eyes, and without an ounce of warmth.

"Where's Lillie?"

"I don't know."

Alexandra rose, opened the adjoining door to Lillie's bedroom, and glanced in. The bed had been made, and the room was unoccupied.

What an odd state of affairs, Alexandra thought. Returning to her seat, Alexandra stared at her bowl of porridge. She hadn't eaten porridge since she was a girl, and hadn't liked it

even then. There wasn't even any sugar or fruit to make the
offering more palatable. Alexandra added milk to the bowl
and tried a spoonful. It was as tasteless as she remembered.
But it was food, and she was hungry, so she ate it.

The meal was consumed in silence, as Alexandra puzzled
over what to do about Lillie. Just as she finished, Martha appeared and began piling the breakfast dishes on a tray.

"Martha, I'm concerned about Lillie. She's not here, and
no place was set for her at breakfast."

"Oh, never you mind," Martha answered. "Lillie was up
and dressed at the crack of dawn. She et her porridge with us
in the servants' hall."

"Does she do that often?" Alexandra asked, surprised.

"Aye, miss."

"Can you tell me where I might find her now?"

"Oh, I wouldn't know, miss. I haven't seen hide nor hair
of Lillie since half past seven." Martha headed out the door
with her tray, just as Mrs. Mitchell entered.

"I thought I'd check and see if you have everything you
need, Miss Watson?" Mrs. Mitchell announced cheerfully.

"Actually, no. I seem to be short one pupil. And I checked
the schoolroom. The only books I could find were one on etiquette, a religious text, some children's morality books, and
old French primers."

Mrs. Mitchell looked at her. "Will you need more than
that?"

Alexandra returned her stare. "Well, yes. I—"

"The last few governesses found the books sufficient,"
Mrs. Mitchell interrupted. Indicating a mahogany hutch, she

continued, "Sewing and embroidery supplies are in that cupboard. There's sheet music in the piano bench. As for Lillie, I don't know what to tell you. That girl plagues my heart out. If I find her, I'll send her in. In the meantime, I suggest you proceed with lessons for Julia." Mrs. Mitchell took her leave.

No one seemed to be the least bit bothered by Lillie's absence or behavior. Alexandra was shocked. She'd been hired to teach two girls, and was determined to do so. Which brought up another point. What was she expected to teach?

Turning back to the other occupant of the table, Alexandra mustered her best smile and said, "Well, Julia. It looks like it's just the two of us. Can you give me an idea of what you were studying with your last governess?"

"The usual subjects on the schedule," Julia responded bluntly.

"Schedule?"

Julia pointed to the hutch. "Top right drawer."

Alexandra opened the indicated drawer. Inside, she found a piece of paper on which had been inscribed the following:

DAILY SCHEDULE OF INSTRUCTION

9 AM.: French
10 AM.: Manners and etiquette
11 AM.: Singing and dancing
12 noon: Luncheon
1 P.M.–3 P.M.: Fresh air and exercise
3 P.M.: Rest
4 P.M.: Piano practice (Julia)

Needlework (Lillie)

5 P.M.: Dinner

6 P.M.: Piano practice (Lillie)

Needlework (Julia)

7 P.M.: Supervised personal time

8 P.M: Bed

Alexandra stared at the list, dumbfounded. "Is this truly your entire curriculum? French, etiquette, music, and sewing?"

"Of course. I'm fifteen. I've already learned everything else I need to know from my preparatory governesses."

"Did you really?" Alexandra struggled to hold back a smile. "And what is a preparatory governess?"

A crease formed in Julia's forehead. "You mean you never had one?"

"No, I attended school."

Julia made a face, as if this meant Alexandra were irretrievably stupid. "A preparatory governess is for ages eight to twelve. After that, girls have a finishing governess."

Alexandra's heart sank. So, that was to be her job. She'd been hired as a finishing governess, like the detested Madame Dubois, who'd bored her and her sisters to tears during the longest and most frustrating year of her life. "Have you found this curriculum satisfying?"

Julia shrugged. "It is necessary, if I am to find a husband."

"A husband? Aren't you a bit young to be thinking of marriage?"

"No. I intend to be married the day I turn eighteen."

"I see. Do you already have the young man picked out?"

Julia's cheeks turned crimson, and she glanced away. "*No*."

Alexandra wondered if Julia had a crush on someone. "Well, you never know what the future holds. You may change your mind and not wish to marry so early, or at all."

"I will not change my mind. I am the daughter of an earl. I *must* marry. *You* do not know anything!"

"I know that in America, girls are encouraged to learn and grow and expand their minds well past the age of twelve." Alexandra paused. "Tell me: what books have you read?"

"I don't know."

"You can't recall the title of even one book?"

Julia shrugged again. "Miss Larsen said libraries made her sneeze. Miss Haverstock read aloud to us while we sewed, boring things about what happened to children who did not say their prayers. Sometimes Miss Treethorn made us read us aloud from books of poetry. Promise me you will not make us do *that*, Miss Watson."

"Okay, no poetry." It seemed that Julia had never been introduced to the delights of literature, and that she'd had a great many governesses who hadn't stayed long. With Julia's poor attitude, and Lillie not even present, Alexandra was beginning to understand why. "What do you like to do for pleasure, Julia?"

"I read the *Lady's Illustrated Magazine*."

"That's it?"

"There's nothing else to do, not since Papa and Grandmamma died."

It was a sad statement, and the first time Alexandra had

heard about a grandmother. "Did you know your grand-mamma well?"

"She lived with us until she died three years ago, right after Papa." Julia frowned as she drew invisible designs with her fingertip on the tabletop. "When I was little, Thomas used to go riding with me."

Alexandra reminded herself that Thomas was Lord Longford, Julia's brother. "Do you have any friends you could ride with?"

"I did. Helen Grayson. But Thomas won't let me see her anymore."

"Why not?"

"I don't know."

Alexandra tried another tactic. "Mrs. Mitchell mentioned that you have your own horse?"

Julia nodded, her eyes briefly flickering with a positive emotion. "Windermere. She rides like the wind. Riding is my favorite thing in the whole world. But Miss Larsen would only allow it once a week."

"Would you like to ride Windermere today?"

Julia glanced at Alexandra in wary surprise. "Yes."

"Well, if you apply yourself to your studies this morning, I believe we can make time in the schedule to allow you to ride this afternoon, and hopefully a few days a week after that."

"Do you mean it?"

"I do." Alexandra stood. "I think I'm up to speed now. Let's move into the schoolroom and start with the first subject on the agenda: French."

With the promise of a ride later that afternoon, Julia settled into her lessons with a degree of resigned submission, and the morning passed quickly.

Alexandra wished she could teach the young lady more than the assigned subjects, but for the first day, felt she ought to stick to the schedule. It turned out that, although Julia had no real aptitude for French, she had a fine singing voice. For her etiquette lesson, Alexandra instructed Julia on some of the finer points of letter writing.

All morning long, every time Alexandra heard a footstep in the hall, she glanced up, wondering if it might be Lord Longford stopping by the nursery or schoolroom to see how things were going. But he didn't appear. She hadn't had so much as a glimpse of him since her arrival the evening before.

Lillie still hadn't made an appearance when Martha brought up the lunch tray at noon, which turned out to be plain boiled mutton and an overcooked, tasteless vegetable.

At one o'clock, as promised, Alexandra allowed Julia to change into her riding habit and race off to the stables. With Julia dispatched, Alexandra's thoughts returned to Lillie. She wondered where the girl had been hiding all day, and why no one seemed to care. Alexandra felt guilty that the girl had missed an entire morning of instruction.

With a few unscheduled hours ahead of her, Alexandra decided to employ them in trying to find Lillie. No sooner had she left the nursery than she caught a glimpse of a young girl dashing around the farthest corner of the hall, long brown hair, pale pink skirts, and pink ribbons trailing behind her.

Chapter Ten

A lexandra raced after the mysterious figure, but when she turned the corner, the girl had vanished. Proceeding down the hall, Alexandra tried the door to various rooms, but all were locked. She soon came to a room that was open, and couldn't help entering to admire it.

It was a grand library, entirely paneled in oak, and fitted with tall bookcases stuffed with many thousands of old volumes. Alexandra was tempted to choose a book from the shelves, sit down in one of the wingback chairs by the hearth, and read. But she couldn't allow herself to be distracted from her mission. Lillie was not here; there were no conceivable hiding places in the library.

Alexandra continued on. Rounding a bend, she came upon another room so vast, it nearly took her breath away.

The long, paneled chamber was hung with so many portraits and other oil paintings, it could only be considered a gallery. It was of such size, however—it made up the entire east wing of the house—that it could easily be used as a ballroom. Alexandra strolled in, agog as she took in the features of the ancient but exquisite space. A superb white plasterwork ceiling curved overhead like the inside half of a barrel, illustrated with unusual beasts and scenes from the Old Testament.

Two gigantic marble fireplaces bisected long rows of immense windows, each of which was inset with a window seat covered in faded cushions and framed by heavy, red velvet draperies that hung to the floor. The furnishings, though shabby, could not take away from the magnificence of the overall setting and design of the room.

Alexandra's eyes were drawn to the drapes of a window seat at the farthest end of the gallery; they were fluttering, as if they'd just been hastily drawn shut from the inside. Alexandra's pulse thumped as she moved toward them.

She deliberated whether or not to say anything. Staring at the velvet curtains, Alexandra was reminded of a scene from one of her and Madeleine's favorite novels, where a little girl was similarly concealed in a window seat, reading a book. An idea came to her.

Quickly making her way back to the library, Alexandra scanned the titles to get some semblance of their method of organization. Unlike many libraries she'd seen in great houses, where the books were shelved by size and binding for a more uniform appearance, these books were for the most part shelved by subject. Most looked very old, and appeared to be well loved. She was delighted to discover a section devoted to novels.

She spotted a set of carved mahogany library steps standing three stairs high. Dragging the library stairs into position, Alexandra climbed up and studied the fiction titles until she found the novel she sought. It was a three-volume set, beautifully bound in burgundy leather. She hesitated, wondering if she should ask for permission before borrowing it.

But who would she ask? She hadn't seen Lord Longford since the evening before. She had no idea where Mrs. Mitchell was, and if she went in search of her, Lillie might be gone. Taking down the first volume, Alexandra returned to the gallery, to the drawn curtains behind which the little evader was hiding, and said in her friendliest voice, "Hello, Lillie. My name is Miss Watson. I'm your new governess. I'm sorry to have missed you today, and hope you'll join us this afternoon. In the meantime, I've brought you the first volume of a novel that was *my* favorite when I was your age. I hope you'll enjoy it as much as I do every time I reread it. There are three volumes in all. When you've finished the first, I'd be happy to give you Volume Two."

Alexandra parted the draperies just enough to thrust the book within. There was a pause; then she felt the book being pulled from her grasp. "Happy reading," Alexandra said, before turning and hastening back through the gallery.

Relieved that she'd found Lillie and had given her a worthy occupation, Alexandra decided to take a walk in the gardens.

On her way out of the gallery, her attention was caught by a portrait of a well-dressed man who looked to be in his early twenties. His attire suggested that it was a recent addition. The brass nameplate beneath the portrait read THOMAS CARLYLE, SEVENTH EARL OF LONGFORD. Alexandra's eyes widened. *This* was the present earl?

As she retrieved her hat and moved down the servants' staircase, Alexandra surmised that the portrait must have been painted three years ago, when Longford inherited the title. At first glance, she would never have guessed it was him. In the portrait, his hair was much longer, reaching his shoulders; he had no mustache; and he wasn't wearing glasses. Slight changes, but enough almost to make him appear to be a different man.

Leaving the house through a rear door, Alexandra found her way around the massive building to the walled gardens she'd spied from her bedroom window. What might once have been extensive flower beds were just long stretches of dirt featuring straggly, untended plants.

Beyond the garden walls, towering trees seemed to call to her. The afternoon sun warmed Alexandra's back and shoulders as she made her way across a vast green lawn, where sheep grazed in small clusters. She spotted a half dozen lambs, bouncing along after their mothers like wooly springs with feet, an enchanting sight that made her laugh. A gravel path wound into the shade of a grove, which was alive with birdsong. She'd never before heard such a chorus of bright, natural music, and although she couldn't name the birds she was hearing, every chirp and tweet filled her with delight.

Wandering on, Alexandra discovered embankments choked with weeds, through which wildflowers and the strangled remains of other plants strained to make their presence known. She recognized yellow jonquils, daffodils, and white narcissus, their scent floating about her like an incense. A seemingly endless series of paths beckoned, but

each one was fighting a battle against burgeoning undergrowth. She clambered up and down broken steps, discovered the ruined remains of a marble fountain, and peeked
into cracked, weedy urns and pots.

Despite the gardens' neglected state, Alexandra was entranced. Although several of the moss-and ivy-covered redbrick walls sagged dangerously, and some bricks had tumbled
to lie in heaps at their base, they were so old and picturesque,
they spoke of centuries gone by, and of all the people who'd
strolled that way.

To think that Lord Longford owned all of this! Her family's garden in Poughkeepsie had been small. Nothing much
had grown beyond grass and the hardiest of bushes. And
they'd no garden at all in New York City.

This reminder of home brought Alexandra to a standstill.
Although she was captivated by all that she was seeing and
thrilled to be experiencing it, she was suddenly filled with
such a deep longing for home, it made her chest ache. She
imagined the joy she'd feel if Madeleine and Kathryn were
to emerge from around the next bend of the path. What fun
they would have exploring these gardens together! It would
be so wonderful to be in their company again.

A tear leaked from one of Alexandra's eyes and she wiped
it away, blinking rapidly as she took a steadying breath. She
was only going to be here a few months, she reminded herself. She'd see her sisters soon enough. In the meantime, she
ought to enjoy the delights of this lovely place.

Moving on, Alexandra spotted an old man on a ladder
wearing a rumpled waistcoat and tweed cap, pruning an

enormous hedge. A task which, at the rate he was going, would take him days to complete.

"Hello," she called out. He looked to be at least eighty years old.

The old man glanced down at her and touched his cap. "Ye mus' be the new governess from Ameriker, I'm guessin'."

Alexandra smiled. News traveled fast, even among the groundskeeping staff. "Yes. I'm Miss Watson." The name still felt foreign on her tongue.

"Darrows," was his reply.

"These are beautiful gardens, Darrows. We have nothing like them in the United States, and certainly none so old."

"They be old enough, miss, fer certain. Go back centuries, these gardens do."

She recalled Mrs. Mitchell mentioning that they only had one gardener. If the entire job of caring for this place fell to this elderly man, it was no wonder it was in its present state. "It was nice meeting you, Darrows."

"And ye, miss."

Alexandra continued on, soon finding herself in front of an old blue wooden door that was set into a long brick wall and sagged halfway open on its hinges. On the other side, she glimpsed an inviting tangle of undergrowth. Curious, she passed through the opening and made her way along a path bordered by dense vegetation and overhung by leafy trees covered in pink flowers.

The farther in she went, the more tropical the setting became. Eventually she came to a break in the trees. Before her stretched a wide blue pool, surrounded by a grove of the same pink-flowered trees and other tropical-looking plants, including numerous tree ferns. Birds chirped. Insects buzzed. Green lily pads clustered in spots on the surface of the water, and reed-like plants at the water's edge were topped with buds of white, pink, and yellow flowers that threatened to burst into bloom.

"Oh," Alexandra murmured, reveling in the sweet, floral scent that filled the air. She would never have guessed that such a place existed on the estate. It was like a secret jungle garden.

At the same time, she became aware of movement from one of the flowering trees a few yards away. Despite the lack of a breeze, one of the branches was swaying and rattling. Below it, piles of leafy branches looked as if they'd been ripped from the tree itself.

Suddenly, the waving branch toppled to the ground with a crash, partially exposing a man who was standing beneath the canopy, wielding a pair of pruning shears. Well, Alexandra thought, it seemed that Polperran House had more than one gardener, after all.

A few more movements with the pruning shears, however, brought down another limb, and with it the revelation of the man responsible.

It was the Earl of Longford himself.

Alexandra's heart skittered despite herself. Beneath a jaunty felt hat, his face was smudged with dirt and glowed with sweat. Tight-fitting dark trousers emphasized the leanness of his hips and thighs. The sleeves of his dirty white shirt were rolled up past his elbows, once again exposing the sun-kissed muscular forearms that she had so admired when he'd painted her.

So this explained where his tanned coloring came from. It was because he worked out in the sun. But what was an earl doing trimming his own trees?

As she stood gaping, Longford turned and saw her. His eyes widened. "Miss Watson."

She had to remind herself that, even though he was dressed like a groundskeeper and was trimming a tree, he was an earl. She dipped a curtsy. "My lord."

Ducking beneath a low branch, he skirted around the piles of scattered limbs and crossed the bank toward her. She supposed it wasn't entirely proper for them to be alone together like this, in such a remote part of the gardens—but she'd never expected to see him here. The top two buttons of his shirt were undone, exposing the curly golden hair that covered his upper chest. Which was also glowing with perspiration. *Dear Lord.* Even dirty and sweaty, he was a specimen of exquisite masculine beauty.

Alexandra felt her cheeks flush as he approached, recalling the dream she'd had about him that morning. Thank goodness he couldn't guess what she was thinking. His own expression was equally difficult to interpret. As he looked her over, his eyes and the tilt of his mouth seemed to convey an odd mixture of frustration and pleasure. He commented under his breath, something that sounded like "If thoughts were a magnet."

"I beg your pardon?"

He shook his head slightly as if to clear it, then said more audibly, "You are quite the adventuress, Miss Watson, to have found this place."

Alexandra willed her heart to stop thumping as she groped for words. "How is it that a place so tropical exists in England?"

"This sort of garden is not uncommon in Cornwall. Our climate is typically warmer than the rest of the country."

"Well, it's beautiful. I feel like I'm in paradise."

"An apt description. I have loved this spot since I was a boy. I think I am the only person who comes here now."

She gestured toward the piles of broken branches on the ground. "I see you are pruning?"

"The rhododendrons require regular maintenance, or they take over."

"An unusual activity for an earl."

He frowned at her now. "You disapprove?"

"Not at all. I'm merely making an observation."

He took a long breath and blew it out in a huff. "I was holed up all morning in my study, going over the accounts of the estate. I can only take so much of that without going mad. I wanted to do something useful. Thus . . ." He nodded toward the trees.

"You made excellent progress. I'm sure Darrows will be impressed."

"You have met Darrows?"

"I have. He seems like a good fellow."

"Darrows is wonderful. He has worked for our family since he was a boy in short pants. His father was head gardener, and his grandfather before that. He is so old now, he really should retire. I can only afford one gardener, and I would be far better off hiring someone young, energetic, and fit, but . . ."

"But?"

"His wife and child are gone. He has nowhere else to go. Apparently, he wants to die standing on a ladder and clipping something, and who am I to tell him no?" He cast her a small, shrugging smile.

"It is kind of you to keep him."

"It makes him happy, gives him purpose. And it does not really matter in the long run, since the whole garden is going to rack and ruin anyway." He briefly removed his hat, raking his fingers through his hair as if to cool off his head. "So," he went on, changing the subject, "what brings you here, so far from the house? Have my sisters treated you so ill that you were obliged to escape?"

"No, I think Julia and I made a decent beginning with her studies today. She wanted so badly to go riding this afternoon, I allowed it. I'm mortified, though, that I have yet to meet Lillie! I think I found one of her hiding places, but was loath to force her to come out."

"Well, she is shy." He didn't sound concerned, or ask where the hiding place was.

Alexandra frowned. "Are you aware that Lillie often takes her meals in the kitchen with the staff?"

"Mrs. Mitchell mentioned something about it."

"Doesn't that bother you?"

"No."

"No one seems to know where she goes or cares what she does all day. She could be in danger for all we know."

"I doubt that, Miss Watson."

His lack of interest in his sister's welfare was infuriating. "You hired me to teach both of your sisters. How am I to do so, if Lillie doesn't show up?"

"Give it time. Surely you have run into this kind of thing before? First day on the job and all?"

"Well," Alexandra began, wishing she could tell him the truth: that she'd never run into this kind of thing before, because she'd never been a governess before, or had a *first day on the job* of any sort. "Not really."

"I used to hide from the governess on a daily basis when I was a boy." He flashed her a mischievous grin.

The merriment in his eyes was so infectious, it speared straight through Alexandra's indignance. She gave him a reluctant half smile in return. "You say that with pride."

"I think I spent half of my childhood in some far-flung, forgotten corner of the house, or in these gardens on my own. Supervised instruction is necessary, but a child also needs some alone time, do not you think?"

"Yes. But—"

"When Julia goes riding, Lillie may roam free as well, as long as they both return at a given time. It will be beneficial for all concerned."

"I'll keep that in mind. I just pray Lillie makes an appearance soon."

"I am sure she will."

"I wish I shared your confidence."

Removing his hat again, Longford wiped his perspiring forehead with the back of his forearm, an action that drew

Alexandra's attention to his eyes. A sudden realization struck her, bringing a memory with it. He must have noticed her looking at him strangely, because he said, "Is something wrong?"

"No. Yes. It's just that . . . you're not wearing eyeglasses."

He paused. "True."

"And you weren't wearing them yesterday, on the train."

"On the train?"

"Not long after we boarded, you removed your spectacles. Yet you spent most of the journey reading."

He flushed slightly but didn't comment.

"And there was that time in London when you were painting me, and forgot to put on your glasses." She thought about the portrait in the gallery, in which he was clean-shaven and long-haired, but not wearing glasses. All at once, the pieces of the puzzle fell into place. "You don't need eyeglasses at all, do you?"

Longford replied tersely, "No."

"The fake eyeglasses, your mustache, the short hair . . . is it so people in London won't recognize you?"

He smiled grimly. "You have figured me out, Miss Watson."

"But why? Why would you go to such lengths to disguise yourself?" Even as she asked the question, the answer finally occurred to her. "Oh," she said, now recalling something Madame Dubois had told her, and what she'd gleaned from people she'd met during the London Season. "*Oh*. I see. I understand."

Chapter Eleven

Thomas had known, of course, that Miss Watson would figure it out. It was only a matter of time.

More surprising, though, was the fact that she was standing here before him. After a nearly sleepless night, in which he'd been unable to banish the lovely Miss Watson from his mind, he had ventured here, to the farthest corner of his estate, to vent his frustration with physical labor.

It was the last place he had ever expected her to find him, and yet here she was. A vision of loveliness, her sienna hair sparkling in the sunlight beneath her bonnet, her luscious curves accentuated beneath the confines of that awful black dress. Thank God he'd agreed to buy her a new gown. The sooner it arrived, the better.

He crossed his arms over his chest and stared out over the sparkling blue pool, trying to keep his voice even, to ignore the longing that stretched his every nerve. She seemed to suspect the reason behind his little deception, but he felt he owed her a fuller explanation. "You have seen the condition of my house, Miss Watson, and the deplorable state of my gardens."

She nodded.

"As you have no doubt gleaned, my income is insufficient to maintain this vast property. My chimneys and rooftops are crumbling. The lighting and plumbing are decades out of date. The furnishings are ancient and threadbare. But how am I to acquire the money I need to repair and improve them? Any attempt to engage in an honest occupation—"

"Like painting portraits," Miss Watson interjected quietly.

"Like painting portraits *for hire*. God forbid we should in any way associate ourselves with the middle or lower classes by accepting *money* for a service rendered. That would be vulgar. That would be *unseemly*."

Miss Watson nodded again. "*That* would be considered *trade*."

Her expression was so perceptive and deeply felt, it cut straight through Thomas's wall of bitterness and made his heart turn over.

Reminding him once again of why he had gone to such lengths to avoid her all day.

It had been a means of self-preservation. He could not be around her, could not talk to her, without wanting to touch her. Even now, standing three feet away, discussing a subject that never failed to infuriate him, he longed to take her hand, pull her close, touch her cheek, discover if her skin was as soft as it appeared. And then kiss her.

He had hoped that whacking away at those trees would distract him, but it had been a futile exercise. His head had been full of her the entire time he was working. And then she'd found her way here. As if his thoughts were a magnet that had drawn her.

"It is the exact opposite of the way we do things in America." Miss Watson's voice cut through his thoughts. "There, men are rewarded for hard work. A man can earn enough in a single generation to rise from poverty to exceptional wealth, and be respected for it." She looked troubled suddenly, as she went on, "Yet even in America, the highest levels of society can be snobbish and exclusive toward the *nouveaux riches*."

"The great irony is, were I not the heir—had I been a second or third son—I would have been *obliged* to find a profession. From a short list of those occupations considered suitable for our class, that is."

"Portrait artist not being among them."

"Unfortunately, no." He sighed. "Recently, I had to sell some of my family's prized paintings and other collectibles to cover expenses. I couldn't bring myself to sell the books yet."

"The books! Oh, I hope you do not have to sell those."

"I hope so as well. At this point, though, it would require a king's ransom to make even a dent in the improvements my property requires. But I could not sit idly by and watch the place fall into utter disrepair. Two years ago, I decided I had to do *something*."

It felt strange to be discussing this with her. He hadn't opened himself up like this to anyone in years, and certainly never to an employee. But for some reason, he felt compelled to go on. "The portraits do not bring in much. But they help keep a few servants employed, make it possible for the tenants to go on about their lives. I hope that as my reputation grows, I can raise my fees, which will allow me to put a bit away towards my sisters' dowries."

"I admire your determination, and applaud your decision to circumvent convention. But aren't you afraid you'll run into someone you know in town?"

"I have spent very little time in London before now. There are hundreds of earls in this country, and Carlyle is a common name. There *is* the worry that I might run into an old acquaintance from school. Which is why I keep my head down when I am in town, take commissions by word of mouth, and rarely go out. So far, the mustache, glasses, and shorter hair seem to be working. I have found that no one looks too closely at the artist who paints their portrait."

An odd expression crossed her face. "People see what they expect to see."

"Exactly."

Her mind seemed to drift elsewhere for a moment. "When we arrived yesterday," she commented finally, "you said you don't even want anyone *here* to know about the portraits you paint in London."

"Servants talk. If they knew, word would get out, and could easily travel to town."

"I see. But you're so good at what you do. I hope you paint here as well, for pleasure?"

He felt his lips tighten. "If I had my way, Miss Watson, I would never pick up a brush again. I paint only because I have to. I no longer get any enjoyment from it."

"But—why?"

"I think I have said enough on that subject." Gesturing toward the pile of branches on the ground, he added, "And I have done enough damage for today. It will take Darrows a week to clean this up. May I accompany you back to the house?"

"Yes, thank you."

Thomas led the way back down the narrow path, pausing now and then to hold aside branches so Miss Watson might pass by.

"How long have things been so bad, financially?" she asked as they walked. "If you don't mind my asking?"

"I do not mind. It is common knowledge in these parts. It began with a fire about a hundred years ago that destroyed the entire west wing of the house. My great-grandfather could not afford to rebuild that wing, so it was removed."

"Oh! Is that why Polperran House is shaped like a U?"

"Yes. It used to be a square. Four wings around a central courtyard."

"Why is it called Polperran House?"

"It is an old Cornish name. *Pol* in Cornish means a pool, no doubt named after the very pond where you found me. *Perran* is the patron saint of tinners. Tin mining has long been a staple industry in Cornwall."

"So I've read. What a shame about the fire."

"It caused a great deal of interior damage to the adjoining wings. Untold sums were spent to repair and refurnish them. The family debt only increased after that. My grandfather and father were both given to too much drinking, and could never resist an evening at cards. Then there was the custom-made billiards table from Italy, the collections of French and Chinese porcelain, elaborate fountains in the gardens. The Longfords are proof positive that when you combine rampant overspending and gambling with an agricultural recession, you can run a family fortune into the ground in three generations."

"I'm so sorry. You deserved better."

"I do not know what I deserved." Thomas frowned. "I always had the sense, growing up, that my family had financial problems, although my father tried to hide it. My first proof was when, while I was at Oxford, he sold our London townhouse, which had been in the family for a hundred and fifty years."

"So that's why you stay at Mrs. Gill's in town."

"Yes. But it also served my purpose as an excellent cover." He shrugged, continuing, "In any case, I did not understand the true depth of our troubles until my father cut off my allowance and I was obliged to return from Italy."

"How long did you study in Italy?"

"Two years. The best two years of my life." They reached the blue door and continued walking side by side along the hard-packed dirt path, stepping over the tangled roots of trees and shrubs. "I was furious at first that my father had called me home from an enterprise I so enjoyed."

"I know exactly how you felt. I loved college, found it so challenging and intellectually stimulating, and then my mother forced me to leave so that—" She broke off, her face coloring.

"I presume you were called home from school for the same reason I was: lack of funds to continue?"

Miss Watson's gaze remained on the ground and her cheeks burned. It was a reminder of how little he knew about her. Clearly, she was a well-educated young woman of good social standing who had come down hard and fast in the world. Just as clearly, she was ashamed by it.

"Please do not be embarrassed about your financial circumstances, Miss Watson," he said gently. "You have heard my family's sad story. You are not alone." The path had become so narrow that they were nearly walking shoulder to shoulder. "I am sorry, though, that you were unable to finish your education. I know how painful that can be."

"Yes. You said you were upset when you first came home from Italy?"

"I was. Until my father explained the size of the financial hole into which we had descended. We could very well lose Polperran House, he said. I put it to him that I could help. I could try to earn something, by painting pictures and selling them. He laughed in my face. A man of our station, he insisted, could never engage in commercial enterprise. He *did* expect me to help, however—but he had something quite different in mind."

"What was that?"

"He commanded me to find an heiress as quickly as possible and marry her." He spat out the word *heiress* with more venom than he'd intended.

Miss Watson suddenly missed her footing, stumbling over a tree root. Instinctively, Thomas reached out to prevent her from falling. It all happened in an instant: he grabbed her, pulled her upright, and they were standing face to face, his right hand gripping her upper arm, his left wrapped around her waist, their bodies colliding.

Thomas's thoughts scattered to the wind. He could feel the rapid rise and fall of her chest as her breasts pressed against him, could hear her breath stutter. He found it difficult to breathe himself, could not take his eyes off her lips, which were just inches from his own. For the hundredth time, he wondered what it would feel like, taste like, to kiss those lips. Wondered if she would respond with a passion equal to that which burned inside of him. He had dreamed of a moment like this so many times over the past week, and here she was, in his arms, in the privacy of his garden, where no one could see.

Her bluebell eyes raised to his, and he met them squarely, reading there what appeared to be a mirror of his own rampant desire. At the same time, he detected a hint of fear and uncertainty. Which sobered him up quickly.

He had too much respect for Miss Watson to seduce her in a remote bower. Or anywhere else, for that matter. Swallowing hard, he released her and stepped back. "Forgive me."

"No, forgive me." Her voice trembled slightly. "I'm not usually so clumsy."

"The fault is mine. These paths have become quite treacherous. Let us proceed with caution."

They walked on for some minutes without speaking, as Thomas struggled to regain his composure. A glance at Miss Watson told him that she was similarly engaged.

He broke the silence. "What were we saying before?"

"Something," she answered quietly, "about your father wishing you to marry an heiress."

"Ah, yes."

"Many men in your position, or so I'm told, are eager to make a match that comes with a fortune."

"I have good reason to avoid such an arrangement."

"What reason?"

He paused. "For one thing, my own parents' example."

"Oh?"

"My father married for money. My mother came from a good Yorkshire family and had a substantial dowry. In short order, she produced me, the obligatory heir. But stuck here in the country, so far from her friends and family, she was lonely and homesick. My father was repeatedly unfaithful, leaving her for months at a time to go up to town. They came to despise each other. It is no wonder that it was another thirteen years before Julia came along. During all that time, not a day went by that I was not aware of the misery of their union. My father burned through every penny of my mother's money, and then . . ."

"And then?"

Thomas paused, a rush of feelings curling in his gut at the memory of his mother. He pushed it all away. He had no desire to think of her, or to go into all the details that followed. It would be like throwing salt in a wound. Besides, he reminded himself, Miss Watson—as charming and sensitive a listener as she was—was an employee. He had said too much already.

"And then she died," Thomas went on flatly. "Years later, with all the money gone, my father expected me to pay the price for his foolish behavior. And I . . ." Again, he censored himself. "In the end, let us just say that my eyes were opened.

My father passed away two days after my twenty-fifth birthday. I decided I would never make the same mistake he did. I would never marry for money."

"I understand. I feel as you do: that no one should be forced to marry against their own inclination, and certainly never just for money."

He nodded, frowning. "I cannot marry a poor woman, Miss Watson, for I cannot support her. At the same time, I have my pride. I will not take another man's money to pay back *my* family's generations of debt. Nor will I destroy my soul by attaching myself for life to someone I do not love, just to save a crumbling house and overgrown gardens."

She glanced at him. "What if you were to fall in love with a woman who happens to have money?"

"Love exists only in fairy tales, Miss Watson," Thomas insisted grimly. "In real life, it brings only pain and disappointment."

"So, are you saying you'll never marry at all?"

"That is the inevitable conclusion."

"Doesn't that put you in a rather difficult position?" She glanced at him with delicate innuendo.

"You mean, don't I need to sire an heir?"

"Isn't that what every nobleman needs?"

"When I die, Polperran House will go to my second cousin Reginald Carter. He is a solicitor with seven sons, and will no doubt be thrilled by the opportunity. In the meantime, I will do my best to keep the estate going for my sisters, what is left of my staff, and my tenants. End of story."

The path took them out of the grove and down a wide green incline studded with bleating sheep, bringing the house once more into sight before them.

As they walked, Alexandra's heart thudded in her chest. A few moments ago, when she'd stumbled into Longford's arms, she'd forgotten all her vows to remain calm and professional. She'd wanted more than anything for him to kiss her.

Get ahold of yourself, Alexandra reprimanded herself now with a frown. This was not the time nor the place for her to be having foolish crushes. She struggled to set all such thoughts aside, concentrating on the fact that in the past hour, she'd learned more about Lord Longford than she had in all the days she'd known him put together.

How difficult it must have been to have so much responsibility thrust upon him at such an early age. Alexandra's own parents spent most of their time apart, and had a relationship she considered to be cold and formal. Yet they'd built a life together which seemed to make them content. Knowing that Longford's mother and father had married for money, and that their son had borne witness to their misery, helped to explain so much.

She could understand his aversion to marriage, based on his parents' example, and even his being too proud to ever take another man's money. But that didn't explain the antipathy in his voice when he'd uttered the term *heiress.*

"Your charge has returned, Miss Watson." Longford's voice interrupted her reverie.

Alexandra caught sight of Julia riding past on a black steed toward the stables. Longford gave Alexandra a nod, as if he were about to say good-bye.

"Have you spoken to her today?" Alexandra asked quickly.

"Who? Julia? I have not."

"She'd love it if you did."

The idea seemed to surprise him. "Why?"

"She's your sister. She said you used to ride together."

"That was years ago, when she was a child."

"She seems to look back on it fondly. I think she misses your company."

"I cannot think why. She is fifteen years old. What would she have to say to me?"

"You'll never know if you don't talk to her."

He hesitated. "Well, I have a minute. I suppose I can say hello."

They strode to the stables, where Julia, fresh faced and glowing from her exertion, was turning over her horse to the groom. The place smelled of clean hay and manure. The stalls were empty except for two other horses, who filled the air with the sounds of rustling straw and chomping teeth.

When Longford greeted her, Julia's face lit up. She introduced her horse Windermere to Alexandra, and then chatted with her brother for a few minutes while Alexandra waited nearby.

"Are you busy tomorrow afternoon?" Julia asked her brother as they began walking back toward the house.

"I have tenants to see," he replied.

"What about the day after that?" Julia countered, a gentle plea in her eyes. "It has been so long since we went riding together."

Longford glanced at Alexandra, as if to say *See what you got me into.* She just gave him an encouraging look.

"All right," he conceded, nodding to his sister. "The day after tomorrow, we shall ride."

Julia beamed. It was just a horseback ride, but it pleased Alexandra to think that she'd been the gateway to this small reconnection between brother and sister.

The afternoon quickly faded away. During the rest hour, Alexandra checked the gallery to see if Lillie was still hiding there, but the window seat was empty.

Julia practiced the piano for an hour, an enterprise in which she was proficient but which gave her no apparent enjoyment. At five o'clock sharp, dinner was brought up to the nursery. Before partaking of anything herself, Alexandra hurried down to the kitchen to ask if anyone had seen Lillie.

"Oh aye, she's been and gone," said Mrs. Nettle, as she pulled a tray of hot rolls from the oven. "Never seen a body et their supper as fast as that girl did tonight. Fair inhaled it, she did, and flew out of here like a bird."

"Mrs. Nettle," Alexandra said, striving to keep calm, "this seems very irregular. I was told that Lillie is supposed to dine in the nursery with me and her sister."

"I wish you luck with that, miss." The cook set the hot

tray on the vast wooden center table and put down her hot pads. "I've never had any luck trying to tell Lillie what to do."

Here was yet another member of the staff who referred to the girl simply as Lillie. Longford had told Alexandra that although as a governess, she could call his sisters by their first names, the other servants were supposed to use the courtesy prefix *Lady*. She was beginning to think this wasn't a slip of the tongue, but a sign of disrespect.

"Do you know where Lillie goes all day, Mrs. Nettle?" Alexandra asked, perturbed.

"Not a clue. But she's strong and healthy. I don't worry about her none."

Neither does anyone else, it seems, Alexandra wanted to say, but she held her tongue.

Returning to the nursery, Alexandra joined Julia for dinner. After the light meal was cleared away, Alexandra checked the next item on the schedule and announced that it was time for needlework.

"I hate needlework," Julia complained, sinking into a chair as she plunked her sampler and a skein of red thread on the table. "It is so pointless."

"It was my least favorite subject growing up," Alexandra admitted.

"It was?"

"I preferred to read, write, do mathematical problems, pretty much anything other than embroidery, which just ends up sitting in a drawer or hanging on a wall. But it seems to be a subject required of young ladies. So, let's see what you have here."

Julia's sampler was a traditional rendering of the alphabet in red cross-stitch on white linen, with rows of upper- and lowercase letters, followed by the numbers one through ten. A start had been made below on the capital letters in cursive. "This is an excellent effort, Julia," Alexandra said honestly. "Your needlework is impressive."

"Well, it had to be. Miss Haverstock rapped our knuckles if we made an incorrect stitch. If Miss Treethorn didn't like the way a letter or number looked, she made us clip it out and do it all over again."

Alexandra looked at her. "How long have you been working on this sampler, Julia?"

"Since I was five, I think."

"You've spent your entire life working on this one piece of embroidery?" Alexandra was aghast.

"Yes."

"I don't blame you for being tired of it." Alexandra thought for a moment. A childhood memory presented itself, of a way that she, Madeleine, and Kathryn had added a measure of interest to this dreaded task. With a little smile, she said, "Do you have any other colors of thread besides red?"

Julia shrugged. "We have a whole box of thread."

"Would you mind fetching it?"

With a sigh, Julia sauntered to the cupboard and brought back a small metal tin, which contained packets of needles and thread in a rainbow of colors.

"Let's try something different, Julia. Let's make the next letter a different color."

"A different color?" Julia stared at Alexandra as if she'd

just suggested that they break into the Tower of London and steal the crown jewels. "We cannot do that."

"Why not?"

"Because the letters are supposed to be red."

"Says who? Who would it hurt if you added some color to that sampler? It's just an exercise, after all." Alexandra took a skein of royal blue thread from the tin box. "Let's do something crazy, Julia. Let's turn this thing into a work of art."

Frowning her reluctance, Julia slowly threaded a needle with the blue thread, then began working on an "H" in cursive. "This is stupid," she muttered as she worked, but a hint of amusement tugged at her lips.

The next hour was scheduled as "supervised personal time." Julia spent it thumbing through a magazine, while Alexandra made lessons plans for the next day. But the book of etiquette was ponderous, and the French verb conjugations didn't hold her attention. Her thoughts kept drifting back to Lord Longford, the time they'd spent talking together in the gardens, the way her heart had raced when he'd briefly held her in his arms.

The clock on the wall chimed a quarter to eight. In a few minutes, it would be the girls' bedtime. It was ridiculous, Alexandra thought, that she still hadn't met Lillie. The situation was out of hand.

She'd just decided to spend the rest of the evening in Lillie's bedroom, waiting for the errant girl to show up, when the nursery door burst open and the girl herself rushed in.

Chapter Twelve

Small and thin, the girl who could only be Lillie looked to be nine years old instead of twelve. She skidded to a halt a few feet away from the table where Alexandra and Julia sat. Her pink frock was imprinted with tiny blue flowers and reached just below her knees, revealing pale, skinny legs. Her long, curly brown hair was tied back with a pink ribbon. A sprinkling of freckles chased across her cheeks and nose, and her hazel eyes looked huge and wild as they stared unblinking at Alexandra.

"Where is it?" The question was abrupt and demanding, although her young voice trembled. She held a book in one hand.

Alexandra recognized the volume as the one she'd slipped behind the curtains of the window seat which Lillie had been occupying earlier that afternoon.

"Do you have it?" the girl further probed. She seemed to be bubbling over with nervous excitement and anticipation.

"Do I have what?" Alexandra could guess what Lillie was after, but wanted to hear it from the girl herself.

"Volume Two! You said there were three volumes, Miss Watson, and I could have the next one when I had finished the first."

Alexandra stood, pleased that her choice of book had been so well received. It was edifying as well to discover that Lillie not only remembered Alexandra's name, but was a fast and eager reader. She must have read nonstop to finish the entire first volume of *Jane Eyre* in the past seven hours.

"The other two volumes are in the library," Alexandra told her.

"Can we get them now?"

"It's bedtime. Let's wait until tomorrow."

"I cannot wait until tomorrow! I have to see what happens next!"

"Anticipation only increases the pleasure of an event."

Lillie stamped her foot as she rubbed one eye with her fist. "I do not want to anticipate my pleasure. I want to read it *now*."

"I understand. When I first read *Jane Eyre*, I could hardly put it down myself. But it's late, and apparently, you've already done a great deal of reading today." Alexandra raised her eyebrows meaningfully at Julia. "It's time for bed."

Julia rose from her chair without comment and headed for the nursery door, not bothering to acknowledge her sister.

"Good night, Julia," Alexandra called out.

"Good night," was Julia's crisp reply before she vanished from the room.

Alexandra sighed, hoping that in time, things would warm between her and Julia. Gently, she took Lillie's hand and led her into the adjoining bedroom. "By the way, it's nice to meet you, Lillie."

Lillie's only response was a yawn.

As Lillie undressed and washed up at her pitcher and

basin, she peppered Alexandra with questions about *Jane Eyre*. Alexandra did her best to answer, without giving away the upcoming twists in the plot. As she tucked the girl into bed, Alexandra asked, "Was it you who locked the door between our rooms last night?"

Lillie nodded.

"Why did you lock it?"

"I was afraid. I did not know you."

Alexandra gently caressed Lillie's silken head. "We know each other now. I hope to be good friends. And that you'll keep the door unlocked always."

"I will." With another yawn, Lillie turned and hugged her pillow.

"Lillie," Alexandra couldn't help asking, "will you tell me where you've been all day?"

"Reading," was Lillie's only reply as she closed her eyes. In seconds, she was fast asleep.

When Alexandra arrived in the nursery for breakfast the next morning, she was relieved to see both Julia and Lillie seated at the table, downing their porridge.

Lillie eagerly jumped up from her chair as Alexandra approached. "Can we get it now, Miss Watson?"

"If you're referring to a particular book," Alexandra answered, taking her seat, "we'll get to that in good time."

"When? You *promised*."

"I mean to keep that promise. But first, let's begin the day properly. Good morning, Julia. Good morning, Lillie.'"

The girls returned the sentiment, Julia only a bit less sullenly than the day before.

"Lillie," Alexandra said as she took a spoonful of the dreaded porridge, "I was very distressed yesterday when you disappeared."

"Why?"

"I was worried about you. You can't stay away all day like that."

Lillie shrugged. "Nobody cares what I do."

"I care. From now on, I expect you to spend your days and evenings with me, and take all your meals here in the nursery."

"When can I read *Jane Eyre?*" Lillie pouted.

"You may have some free time in the afternoon, and there's always rest hour."

"All right." Lillie rested her chin on one hand, her expression changing to heavenly bliss. "I cannot think when I have ever read anything so *thrilling*."

"Oh do be quiet!" Julia blurted. "It's only a *book*."

Alexandra, sensing that Julia felt left out, said, "Julia, would you like to read *Jane Eyre?* Or I could find another book especially for you from the library."

"No thank you." Julia tossed her head with indifference. But her expression indicated that she was more intrigued than she cared to admit.

The morning French lesson went well. Lillie proved to be adept with the language. When it came time for manners and etiquette, Alexandra found she didn't have the stomach for it, and decided to focus instead on geography.

"That is not on the schedule," Julia pointed out.

"It is today," was Alexandra's reply.

She began by asking them to locate particular countries on the globe. It became clear that their knowledge on the subject was limited. So, Alexandra devised a game in which the girls took turns spinning the globe, and with their eyes closed, touched a spot on it with their finger. Alexandra would then tell them something about the country pointed out—its people, history, climate, and landscape.

They warmed to the game quickly, showing real interest in every new place they discovered. Lillie was so enthralled that she moaned with disappointment when the hour was up.

"Can we do geography again tomorrow? Please?" Lillie asked.

"We can," Alexandra answered, turning to Julia. "Is that okay with you?"

Julia shrugged, but the half smile beneath her hooded eyes revealed that she was not at all opposed to the idea.

Lillie was incredibly shy when it came to singing, so Alexandra switched to dancing, which both girls preferred. She worked with them on their waltz steps by partnering with first one and then the other, while the odd girl out played the piano. The lesson ended with them all laughing and breathless.

After lunch, Alexandra retrieved Volume Two of *Jane Eyre* from the library, and Lillie eagerly stretched out on the long cushion of her window seat of choice, delving into the story. While Julia went riding, Alexandra strolled in the garden. She tried without success not to think about Lord

Longford, or how much she'd enjoyed their conversation in the gardens the day before. He'd said he was visiting tenants today. She hoped he'd finish early and she'd run into him again, but there was no sign of him.

The afternoon grew blustery and cold. Soon after she returned to the house, it began to rain. Julia came back from her ride damp but exhilarated. That afternoon, while an angry storm pelted the windowpanes of the nursery, they sat cozy and warm by the fire.

Lillie proved herself to be as competent on the piano as her sister, but just as disinterested. When it came time for needlework, and Alexandra brought out the tin of multicolored thread, Lillie thought it the most exciting idea in the world. She used bright yellow thread for the left side of a letter, and emerald green for the other. Although Julia continued to protest that the whole thing was stupid, Alexandra caught her pupil smiling to herself while she worked, as if what they were doing was delightfully mischievous. During the quiet hour before bed, Lillie was glued to her novel. Alexandra didn't miss the puzzled but envious glances that Julia, looking up from her magazine, sent her sister's way.

Once the girls were tucked into bed for the night, Alexandra was determined to find a book that would capture Julia's interest.

The sun had fully set now, the storm wailed, and the house was freezing. Wrapping herself in her shawl, Alexandra took the candle from her room to light the way down the corridor to the library, expecting to find the room dark and silent.

She entered and stopped short in surprise. Two oil lamps were lit. A fire was burning in the hearth.

And the Earl of Longford was seated in a wingback chair near the fireplace.

Her hand went to her chest, beneath which her heart was beating a mile a minute. He glanced at her, mirroring her surprise. A book was open on his lap, and a glass and decanter of amber liquid stood on the end table beside him. He looked elegant and refined in a dark suit, striped shirt, embroidered violet waistcoat, and black tie. It was the first time she'd seen him wearing clothes that weren't old or shabby, and the effect was dazzling.

"Forgive me, my lord." Alexandra curtsied. "I didn't mean to disturb you."

"You are not disturbing me." He set aside the book, his expression admitting that he was glad to see her.

The air between them seemed to flicker with some unseen force. She found her voice again. "I have come in search of a book. I hope you don't mind?"

"Not at all. You may borrow any book you like, anytime."

A slight shiver danced down her spine; whether it was from the frigid air in the room, or being in his presence, she wasn't certain.

"You are cold," he noticed. Gesturing toward a second wingback chair beside him, he added, "Please, come sit by the fire."

She hesitated, then moved to the chair he'd indicated. Rain pattered against the library windows, but the flames from the nearby hearth cocooned the area in which they sat with light and heat.

"Would you care for a brandy? I can get another glass."

"No thank you."

"On a cold, dark evening such as this, a brandy can warm the soul."

The fire's glow shone like twin beacons in his brown eyes, and brought out the highlights in his golden hair. "My father also likes his brandy," she murmured.

"Your father?" He regarded her with interest. "I believe you mentioned that your parents live in New York? Are they comfortable with you working overseas?"

Why did I mention my father? Alexandra chastised herself. Not wanting to lie, she answered, "I hope they are."

"Please feel free to write to them as often as you like. I am happy to provide letter-writing paper and the cost of postage."

"Thank you."

"What is your father's occupation, if I may ask?"

"He . . . works in the banking industry."

He paused, then said delicately, "A very volatile industry. Investments can go south with uncommon rapidity." The sympathy in his gaze made it clear he presumed this to be the reason for her present financial problems.

"They can indeed." A true statement, even if it didn't apply to Alexandra, or her father, whose investments over the past decade had born fruit exponentially. Desperate to change the subject, she went on, "By the way, I borrowed a book yesterday for Lillie. I used it to coax her out of hiding."

"What book was that?"

"*Jane Eyre.*"

"Ah, yes. Quite the gothic page-turner, as I recall. But is it not a bit advanced for Lillie?"

"Not at all. I first read it at age eleven, and she's twelve." She waited, but he said nothing further. "Aren't you the least bit curious *where* she was hiding?"

"Where was she hiding?"

"In a window seat in the gallery, behind the curtains. I suspect it's a favorite spot of hers."

"I had no idea."

"Today, she actually graced us with her presence, and joined us for lessons."

"Congratulations. It sounds as if you are making headway."

"We are."

"The book you came in search of tonight—is it for you?"

"No, for Julia."

"Julia?" He made a scoffing sound. "An optimistic gesture, Miss Watson."

"Why?"

"Julia never reads anything but fashion magazines."

The comment made Alexandra's dander rise. "Julia is a capable and intelligent girl. If she doesn't read books, it's because she's never been encouraged to do so."

"And you plan to encourage her?"

"I do," she said heatedly, sitting forward in her chair. "Julia mentioned the kinds of books her previous governesses have forced upon her and Lillie. All odious morality texts and childish drivel. The right novel could change her opinion on the subject forever. I hope to open up her mind, introduce her to the world of glorious stories that await."

A smile crept across his face. "Bravo, Miss Watson. Forgive me if I sounded dubious. If you can convince Julia of the merits of such a pursuit, I should be most gratified."

"Would you?" His expression was so good-natured, it gave Alexandra the courage to continue. "In that case, there is something else I wish to say. May I speak plainly?"

"Please."

"It's about the curriculum I'm apparently expected to teach."

"What about it?"

"Do you really want the girls to fritter away the best years of their youth engaged in nothing more edifying than embroidering samplers, conjugating French verbs, playing the piano, and dancing the waltz?"

"Is that not what girls of their age are supposed to be learning?"

"No! At least, not the only things. Yet that's the schedule of instruction I found in the nursery. Julia insists it's all that's required, that she needs nothing more because her goal is just to prepare for marriage."

"As the daughter of an earl, marriage is her future."

"I respect that. But there's no guarantee she or Lillie *will* marry. Even if they do, it would benefit them both *then* and *now* to learn more than these purely feminine pursuits. Don't you want them to have more interesting things to think and talk about than the latest fashions from Paris, what's to be on the dinner menu, or which glasses, forks, and spoons are to be used with which course?"

"What would you have them study?"

"At their age, I was immersed in a wealth of subjects: history, world events, reading, writing, mathematics, physical science, geography, and other languages, like Italian and German. Studies that fed my brain as well as my soul."

"That may be all well and good for an American girl, Miss Watson, but it's different in this country, particularly for girls like Julia and Lillie. They must be correctly prepared if they are to be proper wives and mothers, to run a household like Polperran. At least, the way Polperran used to be," he finished.

"I can prepare them. But I also want to empower and educate them. You run this estate, my lord, yet you went to Oxford. Why should boys learn all there is to know, but girls be kept in the dark? They ought to be equally challenged, or they'll grow up to be vacuous women, bored out of their skulls, knowing nothing more about the world than the tiny sphere in which they live. Only today, we had a lesson in geography. You should have seen the excitement in their eyes when I showed them where Turkey and India were on the globe, and described something of the people who live there, the foods they eat, and the types of animals they encounter! Julia was full of questions I couldn't answer, and I wished I had illustrations to show them. I need more books. And permission to teach more diverse and interesting subjects than those currently allowed."

Alexandra caught her breath, forcing herself to stop,

hoping she hadn't irritated him by her passionate diatribe. But glancing at his face, she saw only thoughtful introspection, along with a sparkle in his eyes suggesting he was more impressed than offended.

"I see the influence of your Vassar education in all of this, Miss Watson."

"I've been fortunate to be well educated. I'd like to see that privilege extended to girls of every age and station in life." She waited, her stomach tensing, wondering what his verdict would be.

"I admit," Longford said after a pause, "you make a compelling case. We have never had a governess qualified to teach the subjects you propose. As you are here, I suppose we ought to take advantage of it." He gave her a slow smile. "You may feel free to teach any subject you feel is of value and importance, Miss Watson."

Alexandra's heart leapt. "Thank you."

"For continuity's sake, I hope you will also give a modicum of time to the 'feminine pursuits,' as you call them." Looking around the room, he added, "The books you need—can you find them here in this library?"

"I will take a look. Most of the books I've seen, however, are rather old, and may not be suited to teaching young minds."

"Give me a list of what you require. I make no promises, but I can look for a few new schoolbooks when I return to London."

"Excellent." Alexandra was thrilled. It meant a great deal to her that he'd listened to what she had to say, and actually gave credence to her opinions. "Thank you again." She rose.

Disappointment flooded his face. "You are going so soon?"

It was flattering that he wished her to stay longer. She wished it, too. "It's getting late." Outside, the wind rustled through the trees, and rain still pummeled the house. "I should let you get back to your reading."

"I prefer your company to a book."

He stood and his eyes met hers. Alexandra read there admiration, respect, and something else. Something unexpected, that looked very much like *affection*. Her pulse quickened. It was a quality she'd never observed in the eyes of any man in the drawing rooms and ballrooms of New York or London. There, she'd been a cash cow, the human embodiment of her father's fortune. Here, stripped of the title of heiress, she was being seen and appreciated for the first time as *herself*. It warmed Alexandra's heart, meant more to her than she could have expressed.

"I'm flattered that you should say so."

"I do not say it to flatter you. As you once said to me in London: I say it because it is the truth."

Truth. There was that word again. Alexandra felt a hot rush of guilt rise to her cheeks, freshly aware of the truth that was missing from this conversation. She was perpetrating a fraud. Pretending to be an experienced governess. Allowing him to believe that she was impoverished and friendless. Her scheme was helping her to escape from an unthinkable fate. Still, she felt terrible.

If only she could tell him the truth. But if she dared to blurt it out at this moment, she knew all the warmth and admiration would instantly vanish from his eyes. He would, no doubt, be angry to learn of her deception. And he would send her back to London, to her mother.

Suddenly desperate to flee the room, she said quickly: "Thank you. But I really must go. I bid you good night."

"Wait. What about the book you came for?"

"Oh yes. I'll fetch it."

"May I be of assistance? What are you looking for?"

She started for the bookcase that had been her object when she first entered the library. "I'm looking for Miss Austen. And I know just where to find her."

He accompanied her as she crossed to the short flight of library stairs, waited while she climbed to the top step and retrieved the volume she sought. She turned to find him standing immediately below, reaching up a hand to her. She took hold of it. The strong press of his warm fingers against hers sent a jolt up her arm as she moved down the steps. In seconds, she stood before him at floor level, their bodies barely a foot apart. Her breath quickened at his nearness. He made no move to step back or to release her hand.

"What did you choose?"

She gave the book to him.

"Ah. *Pride and Prejudice*."

"It's a particular favorite."

He set the book down on a step of the ladder. "A favorite of mine as well." The way he was looking at her, it was unclear if he was referring to the book or her. "'I have been meditating,'" he said softly, quoting Austen, "'on the very great pleasure which a pair of fine eyes in the face of a pretty woman can bestow.'"

If Alexandra had been affected before by the affection in his gaze, what she read there now made her feel weak in the knees. It was the heat of desire, so combustible it threatened to set her on fire. Never had any man looked at her with the undisguised yearning she saw in Lord Longford's eyes.

"I . . ." she began, but could go no further. She trembled, felt her shawl slip from her shoulders to the floor.

Still clasping her right hand in his left, he reached up to cup her chin with his other hand, brushing his thumb gently across her cheek, an action that caused a zing of electricity to shoot through her. "I have tried to stay away from you, Miss Watson. But you always seem to find me. And now, I find I cannot help myself."

He lowered his face toward hers until his mouth was so close, she could feel the warmth of his breath against her own lips. He smelled wonderful and masculine: a hint of something woodsy combined with the sharp, fruity tang of brandy.

"I give you fair warning, in case you wish to fly away," he said, his voice deep and soft. "I am going to kiss you."

CHAPTER THIRTEEN

All rational thought fled from Alexandra's mind. She only knew one thing with certainty: she didn't want to fly away. She wanted his kiss, welcomed it. She waited, her heart pounding so hard and so loudly against her ribs, she wondered if he could hear it.

Lowering his hand from her cheek, he moved his lips closer still, until they brushed against hers briefly, with no more than the gossamer caress of a butterfly's wings. "Last warning," he murmured.

Alexandra had no idea how to kiss, but wanted, somehow, to remove all doubt from his mind. Instinctively, she began moving her mouth ever so softly against his.

It appeared to be all the response he required. Longford drew her to him with one hand, while the other hand slipped up to the back of her neck. Gently cradling her head, he pressed a series of small kisses against the sides of her mouth, her upper lip, and the lower one, then concentrated on her mouth as a whole. His soft, trim mustache gently tickled her. His lips were warm and smooth, and she felt the ardor that simmered behind them, waiting to be unleashed.

Alexandra returned the kisses, her breath quickening as

she raised one hand to sift through his silky hair, allowing the other to roam across the broad expanse of his back.

With increasing fervor, he feasted on her mouth. His tongue pressed against her lips, parting them as if seeking entry, an action that surprised her. She gave way, and he emitted a sudden groan as his mouth took hers, a sweet melding as his tongue slipped inside and tangled with her own, a new sensation that she reveled in.

His arms were all around her now, pressing against her back, stroking her hair. She felt a few pins come free from her tresses, heard them scatter on the wooden floor as strands of hair loosened around her face.

A low and throaty sound escaped her mouth as he pressed her up against the bookcase. Alexandra's heart throbbed, and sparks flew throughout her entire body. At the same time, the entire room seemed to glow, as if lit by a thousand candles. A corner of her mind wondered what had made that sudden gleam.

All at once, a crack of thunder rent the air, explanation for the lightning that had preceded it.

Longford paused and stiffened in her arms.

To Alexandra's crushing disappointment, he pulled back and released her. They stared at each other for a long moment, both of them struggling to catch their breath, the sound of the rain battering the windowpanes. She saw him swallow hard; then, to her dismay, saw the ardor in his eyes shift and change.

"Forgive me. I should not have kissed you like that. It was unbelievably inappropriate."

But I wanted you to, she longed to say. Her lips wouldn't form the words.

He stepped away, picked up her shawl from the floor, and handed it to her. "Again, forgive me. I hope we can forget my brief lack of self-control. That can never happen again."

Longford strode from the room, his footsteps echoing in the vast chamber until he vanished through the far door.

Later, lying in bed, Alexandra kept replaying in her mind the scorching kiss she'd shared with Longford. She'd never imagined such a kiss, had never dreamed anything could be so stimulating or so powerful.

She'd loved every second of that kiss, and would like nothing more than to kiss Lord Longford again. But whatever had just happened in the library, it was to be the only such moment they would ever share. Despite his attraction to her—and it was obvious now that he *was* attracted—he was too honorable to have a relationship with her, a woman in his employ.

She couldn't fault him for his convictions. They were commendable. And, she told herself, it was better this way. Fate alone had put her in this position. It was a charade that would soon end. In a few short months she'd be home again where she belonged, back at Vassar College, finishing her studies. She was going to make something out of her life, not be the wife of an English nobleman in far-off Cornwall.

Wife? Where had that thought come from? A single kiss was hardly a first step toward matrimony. She had no desire to marry, and as Longford had so firmly pointed out, neither did he.

As Alexandra tossed and turned on her pillow, however, one question kept haunting her:

After that kiss, how would she be able to look him in the eye?

When she arrived in the nursery the next morning, Alexandra presented Julia with the copy of *Pride and Prejudice*.

"What's this?" Julia asked.

"It's a novel about the unmarried daughters of a gentleman and his foolish wife as they look for love among the landed gentry."

That seemed to catch Julia's attention. "It is about *love?*"

"The heroine, Elizabeth Bennet, is remarkable. And there's a handsome hero, Mr. Darcy, who has to grow and change to be worthy of her love."

"Well, I suppose I could look it over."

Martha entered and set out bowls of porridge beneath their silver domes. As the girls took their seats, Julia announced: "Do not forget, Miss Watson. Thomas and I are going riding this afternoon."

"I'm afeared ye won't be havin' nary a ride with His Lordship this day, Lady Julia," Martha commented.

"Why not?"

"'Cause he's gone away to London."

"Gone to London?" Alexandra repeated. Disappointment surged through her like a tide.

"Left at first light, he did. Said he might not be back for months."

"Months!" Lillie cried. "But he was not to leave for days yet. Why did he go so soon?"

"I s'pose he got tired of dallyin' in the country," Martha surmised.

"This isn't fair," Julia complained. "He promised to ride with me. What does Thomas do in London, that he has to go so often and stay so long?"

"I'm sure whatever it is, it's important," Alexandra said quickly. With sympathy, she added, "I'm sorry you won't be able to ride with your brother today. I know how much you were looking forward to it."

"Now he will be away again for months," Lillie murmured dejectedly.

And it's all my fault, intoned a voice in the back of Alexandra's mind. She could guess exactly why Longford had chosen to leave sooner than intended. It was last night's kiss in the library, the memory of which brought sudden heat to her cheeks.

He'd run away, unable to face her.

As the week wore on, Alexandra deeply felt the void left by Longford's absence.

While working with the girls in the nursery and schoolroom, she found her mind constantly drifting to thoughts of him. Every time she ventured into the library, she couldn't help remembering the kiss they'd shared. She was surprised by how much she missed him.

Although Alexandra enjoyed the hours spent with Julia and Lillie, they were also a constant reminder of how much she missed her own sisters. Since she'd left New York, Alexandra had become accustomed to exchanging letters with Madeleine and Kathryn on a regular basis, yet it had been weeks now since they'd been in communication. Thinking about them brought a lump to her throat. They used to talk about everything, sharing and advising each other on even the smallest things in life.

Alexandra longed to tell her sisters about her escape from the hotel. She smiled, thinking how Kathryn would react, laughing and calling it a marvelous adventure. She wondered what they'd say if they knew Alexandra was working as a governess for a handsome earl at his country estate in Cornwall, how they'd react if she admitted they'd kissed. A kiss that had been far more wondrous than anything she'd ever imagined.

Alexandra and Madeleine had often bemoaned their lack of experience with the opposite sex, desperately curious as to what it'd be like to be intimate with a man. Kathryn, the most daring of the threesome, had kissed any number of boys—and men—and thoroughly enjoyed it. Now, Alexandra understood why.

She'd wanted to write to her sisters before leaving London, but hadn't had enough money for postage. If only she could write to them now. But it was impossible. The postmark would reveal her location. Her father might see it, might even read the letter. He'd tell her mother. In a village as small as Longford, it wouldn't be long before Alexandra was discovered.

She wondered if her mother was still in London, or if she'd started for home. Ten days had passed since the steamship *Maritime* left Liverpool. It would have docked in New York today. Did her parents tell the press she hadn't sailed on the *Maritime* after all? Or was a news-hungry public surprised to discover that Alexandra didn't arrive on board that ship?

Since the earl's departure, there had been no newspapers at Polperran House. Suddenly, Alexandra felt desperate for information about what was going on in the outside world.

One afternoon while Julia was riding and Lillie was reading, Alexandra walked to Longford village. It was a warm spring day. As she strolled down the road, she inhaled the fragrance of sun-warmed grass and wildflowers. The tiny village was virtually empty of people or traffic, the narrow main street with its small stone houses and shops as beleaguered-looking as she remembered, a testament to the strain of financial hardship that weighed it down.

At the post office, she bought a day-old London newspaper with a coin Mrs. Mitchell had been kind enough to give her.

"Ye must be the new governess at Polperran House, I expect?" the postmistress said with a curious smile.

"I am," Alexandra replied, amazed by the speed with which small town news spread. "Nice to meet you."

Alexandra stepped outside, sat down on a bench in the shade of a giant elm, and perused the newspaper hungrily. Although it was full of interesting news, there was nothing in the paper about her.

The next day, she repeated the exercise. This time, she found an article in the society pages that made her gasp.

American Heiress Alexandra Atherton
Gone to Switzerland

An earlier report that American heiress Alexandra Atherton departed the London Season for New York was apparently in error. Miss Atherton, the 24-year-old daughter of New York multimillionaire banking magnate Colis Atherton, reputedly came with a dowry of $1 million (£200,000), and was in London seeking to marry a title.

The heiress refused two offers of marriage before leaving the London scene very suddenly eleven days ago. In a letter discovered soon afterward by her mother, Mrs. Josephine Atherton, the vanished Miss Atherton explained that she was taking passage on the steamship *Maritime* and returning to New York.

However, it has now been ascertained that Miss Atherton never set foot on the *Maritime*, but rather, went to Switzerland for her health. Mrs. Atherton, out of respect for her daughter's privacy, has refused to reveal any details about the state of the young lady's health or the facility where she is staying, other than to say that she is expected to be out of the country for several months.

Fortune-hunting bachelors who were hoping to cash in on an Atherton fortune need not feel totally dismayed, however. Although Alexandra Atherton will apparently not be returning anytime soon, it has come to this newspaper's attention that there are two other Atherton girls of marriageable age, one of whom may be en route to London at this very moment, to be introduced in the last months of the Season.

Alexandra stared at the newspaper in shock and repugnance. Switzerland? For her health? What a preposterous lie!

She threw the newspaper into a rubbish bin and walked the mile back to Polperran House, her head spinning. So, her mother was still in London. Was it true that one of her sisters was coming to England to finish out the Season in Alexandra's stead? If so, her mother would surely send for Madeleine, the next in line. She wouldn't put it past her mother to have all of Alexandra's gowns made over to fit her younger sister, who was almost her size.

Alexandra's heart went out to Madeleine. Her sister was beautiful, smart, vibrant, and highly creative. She deserved the right to finish her college education and to choose her own husband in her own time, not to be subjected to the dictates of their mother, or the public onslaught that was the London Season.

Alexandra continued down the road, suddenly heartsick

and so homesick it made her chest ache. The unfairness of her circumstances tormented her with every step. She was living in a freezing-cold house that was stuck in the dark ages, without gas lighting or indoor plumbing. She was earning mere pennies, her days spent teaching two young girls, and her evenings alone. The servants only spoke to her if she approached them first. She had to be up early, take care of every personal detail herself, and only had a single dress to wear. The food on offer was tasteless and always the same. She was completely cut off from her sisters and family. Every hour of every day she was on edge, carefully watching everything she said, so as not to make a false step or give away her true identity. And the man she'd come to care about was conspicuously, deliberately absent.

Alexandra allowed herself a dash of self-pity. Until this moment, she hadn't truly appreciated the safe, peaceful, pampered life she used to lead, or fully valued her loving relationship with her sisters.

As she passed through the gates of Polperran House, however, and walked up the drive, taking in the ancient, imposing building beyond the avenue of trees, she reprimanded herself for her complaints. She was far better off than many people in the world. She was housed and fed, living in a beautiful part of the country, and teaching two girls who she believed desperately needed her attention.

She might be lonely. She might not see the Earl of Longford for many weeks, if ever again. But while she lived in his house, she would make a difference in the lives of his sisters. She would be the best governess she could be.

Julia, to her evident surprise, admitted that *Pride and Prejudice* was an interesting book, and Lillie was eager to discuss *Jane Eyre* at every available opportunity. Alexandra now had permission to expand the breadth of their education still more, beyond the reading of novels and the limited subjects that had comprised their curriculum.

She searched the Polperran House library and found many interesting volumes, but they were old, geared toward a sophisticated readership, and much of the information was out of date. In the absence of new schoolbooks, and no guarantee that they would ever come, Alexandra decided she must turn to her own devices, and create those materials and lesson plans herself.

They continued the geography sessions with the globe. To study physical science, Alexandra took the girls to the gardens, where they examined the way that plants and flowers grew and were pollinated by insects. Their French lessons were no longer dry recitations of verb conjugations, but rather, dialogs invented by the girls, which were then translated, memorized, and spoken aloud, often evoking bursts of hilarity. Julia's belligerent attitude began to thaw as she became increasingly interested in the new things she was being taught.

The game Alexandra invented for mathematics was the girls' favorite of all. She asked Julia and Lillie to gather articles of clothing, along with old toys and personal items such as combs, brushes, and shoes, which they spread out on tables and chairs in the nursery. Each object was carefully tagged with a price. The girls were given a budget, and, with pretend money they made themselves, went on a shopping expedition to buy whatever they could afford, taking turns playing shopper and shopkeeper. The activity not only provided many hours of enjoyment, but demonstrated to them a valid purpose for honing their mathematical skills.

Etiquette lessons were relegated to twice a week, needlework to once a week, and evenings spent either playing piano, discussing their books in progress, or reading aloud. Although Julia still fell into sulky moods at times, she seemed far happier than she'd been when Alexandra first arrived. Lillie no longer hid during the day, took all her meals in the nursery, and seemed to be settling into the new routine with enthusiasm.

One morning, they were in the middle of a French lesson, when Alexandra observed a finely dressed gentleman approaching the house on horseback. His hat was pulled too low for her to glimpse his face.

"Who's that?" Alexandra indicated the horseman below.

Julia glanced out. "Charles Grayson, the Earl of Saunders, eldest son of the Marquess of Trevelyan. I do not know *why* he still bothers to come. Even if Thomas were home, he would not see him."

The name Grayson sounded familiar. "Didn't you tell me you had a friend named Helen Grayson?"

"Yes, Lord Saunders is her brother."

"Is he a friend of *your* brother?"

"He used to be. He and Thomas went to school together. But now Thomas will not even speak to him."

"Why not?"

"I have no idea. They stopped speaking not long after Thomas returned from Italy, just before Papa died."

"I wish Thomas did not hate Lord Saunders," Lillie interjected with a frown. "It is so unfair that we cannot go to Trevelyan Manor anymore."

"Where is Trevelyan Manor?" Alexandra asked.

"About five miles away, on the coast," Julia explained.

"On the coast? How lovely." Alexandra hadn't realized that the sea was so close by.

"Anna was my best friend." Lillie's expression was woebegone.

"And Helen was mine. We used to do *everything* together." Julia let go a wistful sigh. "But no matter how much I beg, Thomas will not let us see them anymore."

"You do not just want to see Helen," Lillie commented matter-of-factly. "You want to see *James*."

Julia blushed fiercely. "That is not true."

"Yes it is. You *like* James."

"Who is James?" Alexandra asked, although she already suspected the answer.

"Lord Saunders's younger brother," Lillie replied.

"And I don't like him!" Julia retorted heatedly.

Alexandra thought it best to end the conversation, and they returned to their French lesson. Moments later, she saw the horseman trotting back in the direction from which he'd come.

The girls' account perturbed her. In this faraway county where there seemed to be few people of their own class, it was strange that the daughters of a marquess wouldn't be allowed to associate with the Carlyle girls, daughters of an earl. What had happened to cause such a deep discord between the two families?

CHAPTER FOURTEEN

That afternoon, a box was brought up to the nursery by the footman, addressed to Alexandra. To her delight, it contained her new light-blue gown and the underclothes she'd ordered from the dressmaker's in London.

"What a pretty color!" Lillie cried as Alexandra withdrew the new dress from its tissue-paper wrapping.

"It has no frills, pin tucks, or pleats," Julia countered with a frown, "and not a single inch of embroidery or lace."

"No more should it," pointed out Mrs. Mitchell, who was watching the proceedings with interest, "for it's the frock of a governess."

"Why do governesses always have to dress so plainly?" Julia complained.

"Because they spend their days in the schoolroom, young miss, not at a party."

Alexandra didn't care that the dress was plain. It was exactly what she'd ordered, the workmanship looked to be very fine, and she was thrilled to have a new gown to wear. "I think it's lovely. I just wish I had a hat to go with it. The only one I have is on loan, and trimmed in black."

"We might be able to do something about that," Mrs.

Mitchell remarked. "As I recall, Her Ladyship, God rest her soul, had a hat in that very shade of blue, in a style which is still in fashion. If you'd like, Miss Watson, we can take a look in the attic this evening."

After dinner, while the girls studied and practiced piano, Mrs. Mitchell led Alexandra up the servants' stairs to the top floor of the house, which she'd never seen.

En route, Alexandra took advantage of the moment to tackle an issue that had been bothering her. "Mrs. Mitchell, I've been wanting to ask you about the children's food."

"Food? What do you mean, food?"

"I mean the meals that we're served are very dull indeed."

"Well-cooked vegetables, plain bread, meal, and mutton, are the only foods necessary for growing children, Miss Watson. And milk, in Isabella Beeton's words, is 'the most complete of all articles of food.'"

Alexandra knew that Mrs. Beeton, an English journalist, had written an extensive guide to running the Victorian household with an emphasis on food and cooking, a tome which had become gospel in Britain. "I believe a more varied diet is necessary to the health of a child," Alexandra replied, as they passed through a door and continued up another dark, narrow stretch of stairs. "Couldn't you at least serve fresh fruit at breakfast?"

"Fresh fruit is an indulgence. It causes many *unpleasant* digestive ailments. If you like, I can arrange to send up a small dish of stewed rhubarb on occasion. But food in general is a means to teach children moderation and discipline."

Alexandra repressed a sigh; she was getting nowhere on this subject, so she said no more.

They reached a narrow landing at the top of the stairs and she followed Mrs. Mitchell through an old wooden door. The vast attic space seemed to stretch on forever. Beneath the low sloping ceiling and exposed beams, long rows of dormer windows shed muted light on endless collections of dust-covered things.

Boxes of every shape and size were stacked everywhere. Antiquated household items took up residence beside musty furniture that was either outdated or in need of repair. Several racks held clothing, both male and female, that seemed to date back for centuries. Alexandra even spotted a row of military uniforms. There were old chests, worn traveling cases, a rocking horse, holiday decorations, fencing equipment, and other sporting goods—far too much to take in at one glance.

Mrs. Mitchell rummaged through an enormous pile of hatboxes, then opened one. "Oh, how lovely." She took out a dramatic ladies' hat made of forest green velvet, trimmed with ostrich plumes and peacock feathers.

Alexandra studied the hat in fascination. "It looks like something Marie Antoinette would have worn."

"That it does, Miss Watson."

How thrilling it was, Alexandra thought, to know that some Longford ancestor had worn this very hat, and that other relations had worn all the sumptuous, faded gowns on the rack. How wonderful to live in a house with so much history!

As Mrs. Mitchell continued searching through the hats, Alexandra's attention was caught by a group of unframed paintings leaning against a nearby wall.

"What are these?" There looked to be at least two dozen canvases.

"That's His Lordship's artwork. What he did as a child and when he came home from school on holiday, plus all that he brought home from Italy."

Alexandra was intrigued. "At what age did Lord Longford begin studying art?"

"Oh, very young. Six or seven, as I recall. Such a good boy he was. Never gave a moment's trouble."

Alexandra crouched down to look through the artwork. It was easy to see which ones Longford had done in his early years. They were mainly watercolors, pastels, and sketchbooks of pencil drawings. They revealed a good sense of color and form, but were nowhere near as detailed as his later works. Those—numerous landscapes and portraits in oil, which she supposed to be from his Italian period—had been executed with a skill similar to the paintings she'd observed in his London studio.

Flipping through them, Alexandra came to an oil painting of an Italian garden and paused. A stunning work of art, it showcased tall cypresses guarding a maze of geometric hedges and topiaries, interspersed with beds of red poppies, purple lavender, rosemary, and other colorful flowers and herbs. A vigorous flowering vine created an arched bower over an inviting stone bench beside a sparkling, triple-tiered marble fountain. Beyond it, a path curved into the distance, disappearing over a rise that overlooked distant hills beneath an azure sky.

"This is wonderful." Alexandra had the uncanny sense that she could step right into the painting, and inhale the fragrance of all those blooms. "His Lordship is so talented."

"So I've always said. His mother was so proud, she hung his work all over the house for everyone to see. But he doesn't like to look at them anymore. He gave up art, moved all his pictures up here, not long after . . ." Mrs. Mitchell broke off.

"When did that happen? Was it right after he came home from Italy?"

Mrs. Mitchell glanced away. "It is not my business to say, Miss Watson."

Alexandra stood, too curious to let the matter drop. She recalled Julia mentioning that Longford, after his return from Italy, had stopped speaking to his friend from Trevelyan Manor. She wondered if the two events were connected. "I heard that Lord Longford was once good friends with the Earl of Saunders, but they fell out about that same time."

"Loose tongues are worse than wicked hands, Miss Watson. I will say nothing about that."

Alexandra repressed a frustrated sigh. It was such a shame that Longford's beautiful paintings were sitting in the attic, unseen and gathering dust. Something had caused him to relegate a pursuit he'd once openly loved to a reluctant enterprise he practiced only in secret and without enjoyment. But what?

Turning back to the stacks of hatboxes, Mrs. Mitchell lifted a lid and said, "Ah, here it is. The very hat I was looking for." She brought out a lovely confection trimmed in light blue satin and adorned with ribbons, lace, flowers, and leaves. "I remember when Her Ladyship wore this to a garden party." Her eyes misted over as she handed the hat to Alexandra. "This will go very well with your new gown."

"Yes, it will. Thank you, Mrs. Mitchell."

Later, in the privacy of her own room, Alexandra tried on the new dress. It fit perfectly, and the hat was a good match. Her pleasure in having a new *ensemble*, however, was overshadowed by her concern for Lord Longford, to whom her thoughts kept returning. He'd made it clear that he only painted portraits while in town for the money. Once, however, he'd loved art for the sake of art. He had painted wondrous landscapes and glowing portraits that deserved to be seen. Why had he given it up?

Her mind went back to the last moments she'd spent with him. In the library. The kiss. Six day had passed since he'd left Polperran House. Every day, she'd keenly felt his absence. When she'd strolled on the grounds, her footsteps always seemed to take her back to the secret garden behind the blue door, and the path they'd walked together. Every day, she'd hoped he might appear there, as if by magic. But of course he hadn't.

The nights had been even worse. For then, he entered her dreams. This night was no different. Alexandra woke several times with a start, trying to hold on to an ephemeral image, always of herself in his arms, his mouth on hers.

Thomas drummed his fingertips on the arms of his chair, staring out the window at the traffic on the London streets.

The past week had been an exercise in frustration. He had delivered the two completed portraits and met with a few customers to discuss new commissions. Normally, he would take any portrait work he could get on the spot, no matter how prosaic or uninspiring the candidate appeared. Work was work, and he needed the income. But although the prospective clients had promised to pay well, Thomas had not given them a definitive commitment.

If he accepted any new commissions, it would mean spending another month or two in town at the very least, paying for these rented rooms. There would be regular sittings, with time in between in which he would be forced to sit idle, waiting for the paint to dry. Time in which he would have nothing to do other than to think about Miss Watson. As he had been doing, every single day since their fateful meeting in the London street below.

He should never have kissed her. It had been entirely inappropriate. But more than that—it had been difficult enough, having glimpsed her in the bath, knowing that what lay beneath her modest governess clothing was the body of a goddess. Ever since, she had infiltrated his thoughts and fantasies.

And that kiss.

He had kissed many women in his life, but he had never felt anything quite like that kiss. She had been so tentative at first, suggesting an innocence that was both endearing and tantalizing, almost as if she had never been kissed before. And then she had responded to him. Ah, what a response. He had sensed hot embers burning beneath the surface of her skin, just waiting to burst into flame.

The same heat had burned within his own body. Now that he'd tasted her lips, he could think of nothing else.

He wondered if this is what it felt like to go insane. To want something so much, something you knew you could not have.

When he left Cornwall, he had told himself it was because he was obliged to return to work. But now that he had completed his obligations, he could no longer avoid the truth. He had run away, afraid he could no longer trust himself around her. Time and distance should have enabled him to cool down, to forget about her. But he could not forget. Over the past week, his mind had been full of her, every waking moment.

The nights had been no different. Miss Watson haunted his dreams. When he slept, she came to him, naked, gleaming, and wet, as if she had just stepped out of the bath. Sometimes, he would reach up to cover her breasts with his hands and knead them, then take her nipples in his mouth, suckling their sweetness. Other times, he was naked in bed beside her, making slow, passionate love to her. Every morning, he woke up gasping and so intensely aroused, he was on the brink of release.

He had considered seeking out a dancer or hiring a model for a few days' work. They were often very willing partners, and it had brought him relief in the past. But he did not want some nameless stranger in his bed. There was only one woman he wanted: Miss Lexie Watson. *Lexie.* He wondered if her Christian name was short for something. Alexis? Was that a common American name?

It was not just the beauty of her face and form that aroused him, that he yearned to touch and explore. He also yearned to simply be with her, to learn more about her.

Her accent had bothered him at first, that speech pattern full of contractions—*don't* instead of *do not*—so reminiscent of another time and another person. But, he realized, he had become accustomed to it. So accustomed that instead of dreading it, he'd found himself actually looking forward to hearing that voice echo along the halls at Polperran House. A voice that was so uniquely *her*.

He knew that kiss could never be repeated. But he could be content, couldn't he, with just seeing her, being in the same room with her? She challenged him. She kept him on his toes. He liked that. *That* was as arousing as all of his sexual fantasies of her. He wanted more of it.

Miss Watson was only going to be at Polperran House a short time—three months at most, she had said. He did not want to miss a single day of it.

He wanted to go home.

Alexandra tapped at Julia's door. "Julia? May I speak to you a moment?"

It was the rest hour. At Julia's hesitant, "Come in," Alexandra entered the girl's room to find her sitting atop her bed, quickly closing a fashion magazine and thrusting something under her covers.

"Do you want something?" Julia asked, her cheeks rosy.

"I wanted to ask about this evening. It's your turn to choose the selection to read aloud. Have you decided what it should be?"

"Yes. I was thinking a chapter from *Pride and Prejudice*. That one when Mr. Collins proposes to Lizzie."

Alexandra smiled. "Wonderful. Do you want to do the honors? Or take turns with Lillie?" Although the girls had been uncomfortable reading aloud at first, Alexandra had gently coached them until they found their courage. Now, after a week of practice, they seemed to enjoy the exercise as much as she did.

"I do not mind alternating with Lillie. She likes that story as much as I do."

"Very well, then. I'll tell her." Alexandra was about to leave, when Julia moved slightly, causing a pencil to slip out from beneath her covers and clatter to the floor.

Alexandra wondered why Julia had kept the pencil hidden. As the girl reached down to retrieve the pencil, the magazine she'd been holding fell open, revealing something else she'd been hiding: a tiny piece of paper on which she'd been sketching. Julia quickly flipped the magazine closed and held it to her chest.

"Julia. What are you drawing?"

"Nothing." Julia blushed fiercely, her eyes downcast.

"I'm fond of drawing myself, although I haven't done it in a while."

Reluctantly, Julia commented: "I do not really *draw*. I just copy pictures from the magazines."

"Can I see?"

"It is not very good."

"Let me be the judge of that."

Julia hesitantly withdrew the tiny sketch and offered it to Alexandra. "The fashions are so beautiful. I like to imagine that one day, when I am married, I will have gowns like these."

"I'm sure you will." Alexandra studied the drawing, a small but detailed sketch of a woman in a fashionable ensemble. "Julia: this is excellent."

"Do you think so?"

"I do. You are quite the artist. You have that ability in common with your brother."

"Thomas gave up art."

Before she could think how to reply, Julia went on:

"Lillie and I used to study drawing. Thomas made our governesses stop teaching it."

"Why?"

"He said it was a waste of time."

Alexandra frowned. "Art is never a waste of time." Did she dare to overrule one of Longford's edicts? She wondered if that would be going too far. But no: he gave her carte blanche to add anything to the curriculum she considered to be of value. "You needn't draw in secret, Julia. Let's add it back to the schedule."

Julia reacted as if Alexandra had just proclaimed that

Christmas was to be celebrated every day of the year. "Could we really, Miss Watson?"

"I have a bit of experience with the subject. We can have drawing lessons two or three times a week, if you like."

"Oh! That would be wonderful!" Then Julia's face clouded over. "But we have no materials. I have only this pencil, and I draw on whatever scraps I can find."

"Let's see what we can do about that."

Alexandra found Mrs. Mitchell at her desk in her tiny office near the kitchens.

"Mrs. Mitchell. How would I get hold of some art supplies?"

"Art supplies?" Mrs. Mitchell set down her pen and glanced up. "Whatever for?"

"Julia has a talent and an interest in drawing. I'd like to teach what I know on the subject. But we need sketchbooks and pencils."

Mrs. Mitchell looked dubious. "I don't know if His Lordship would approve."

"The earl told me, before he left, that I should feel free to teach anything I liked. Julia said they've had lessons in the past. I hoped there might be some old art supplies stashed away somewhere in the house."

"Not that I know of, Miss Watson. In any case, this is a subject best taken up directly with His Lordship."

"I should write to him in London, then?"

"No. You may ask him yourself. He is due to return this evening, around seven o'clock."

"'And now nothing remains for me but to assure you in the most animated language of the violence of my affection,'" Julia read aloud in a lively voice, filled with amusement.

Alexandra's eyes drifted to the clock on the nursery wall. The hour of seven had already come and gone. The minutes ticked by with glacial slowness as she sat with the girls, listening to them read from the pages of *Pride and Prejudice*.

Normally, she enjoyed this activity almost more than any other, but tonight she was having difficulty concentrating. Ever since Mrs. Mitchell had given her the news of Longford's impending arrival, she'd felt restless. She kept wanting to dash to the window and look out for an arriving carriage.

Longford had said he might be in town for several months. Alexandra knew he had work to do there. If he was coming back after only a week, what had made him change his mind? Her heart began a rapid dance as she contemplated seeing him again. Then she frowned, realizing that she might not see him at all. Polperran was a big house. After the kiss they'd shared, he might avoid her entirely.

Alexandra forced herself to concentrate on the matter at hand. Julia had handed the book to Lillie, who was playing up her part for all it was worth:

"'Upon my word, Sir, cried Elizabeth, your hope is rather an extraordinary one after my declaration. I do assure you that I am not one of those young ladies (if such young ladies there are) who are so daring as to risk their happiness on the chance of being asked a second time.'"

Julia and Alexandra laughed with delight. Alexandra was soon caught up in the performance, focusing all her attention on Lillie, who threw herself into the role of Mr. Collins, her sense of comic flair eliciting further bursts of laughter from her audience.

Sometime later, one of those laughs came from the doorway, and had a distinctly masculine ring to it. Alexandra's gaze darted in that direction, and she gasped in surprise.

The Earl of Longford was leaning against the doorjamb, his arms casually crossed as he watched them, his twinkling eyes and wide grin expressing his delight.

CHAPTER FIFTEEN

Julia and Lillie froze in astonishment.

"Thomas!" Julia seemed to be struggling to hide her happiness at seeing him.

Alexandra stood and curtsied. "My lord." She hoped her own expression didn't show just how pleased *she* was to see him. He seemed to still be dressed in his traveling clothes, the shabby gray suit he'd always worn while in London.

Longford strode into the room, smiling. "Pray, do not stop on my account." An awkward silence fell. He made no move to hug his sisters, nor did they rise from their chairs. He turned to Lillie. "Well done, Lillie. You captured Mr. Collins to a T."

Lillie's eyes were as wide as saucers, all her former shyness returned. She seemed incapable of a reply.

To Julia, he added, "You were excellent as well. I heard you from the hall. I had no idea you could read with such personality and flair, Julia."

Julia blushed and looked down at her hands.

Alexandra's cheeks also burned as she recalled what had happened the last time she'd been in his presence. She dared to lift her eyes to his, and caught him looking at her. For the briefest of seconds, their gazes touched. She couldn't read his expression. Was he aware of the riot of feelings within her chest, or that she'd spent the past week in embarrassed longing? Quickly, she tore her glance away.

"Why so quiet, everyone?" Longford demanded abruptly. "Are you not glad to see me?"

"Yes," Julia responded slowly. "Of course we are. But . . . you never come to the nursery."

"That is not true. I have come up here before."

"You have not," Julia insisted.

"Well, I am here now."

"Martha said you were not coming home for months," Julia further observed.

He made an irritated sound. "I changed my mind. I missed you. A brother can miss his sisters, can he not?" He seemed to be looking anywhere but at Alexandra.

Alexandra found her voice again. "It is nice to see you again, my lord. Welcome home."

"Thank you, Miss Watson." He gave her a brief smile, then changing the subject, said: "So. What have you all been up to since I was away?"

"Miss Watson has added new subjects to the schedule," Julia admitted.

"So I see," Longford commented. "What else, besides reading aloud from classic works?"

"Oh, heaps of things." Julia's enthusiasm mounted as she spoke. "Science, geography, mathematics. Miss Watson invented the most marvelous game." She went on to gushingly describe the shopping game.

"It was fun!" Lillie blurted, the first words she'd uttered since Longford entered the room.

"Was it? It certainly sounds imaginative." Longford glanced again at Alexandra, then added, "Well, I have interrupted what appeared to be a lovely moment. I will therefore take my leave. I wish you all a good evening." With a formal nod, he turned for the door.

"Your Lordship." Alexandra stepped forward, her words stopping him. "There is something I'd like to speak to you about, if I may?"

"Pray, what is it, Miss Watson?"

She lowered her voice. "I would rather discuss it in private, if you don't mind?"

His eyebrows lifted. "Very well. You may come to my study after the girls have gone to bed. Do you know where it is?"

Alexandra nodded. "I'll see you there."

At half past eight, Alexandra knocked at the half-open door of Longford's study.

"Come in," his deep voice intoned.

She entered. The chamber was both elegant and masculine. Longford sat facing the door, behind a carved walnut desk that would have looked at home in the palace of Louis XV. An elegant lamp on the desk, along with several candelabras, cast the room in a golden glow. Through the mullioned window at the back of the room, the vanished sun had painted the sky in deepening shades of orange, gold, and indigo.

He gestured toward a worn tapestry chair that faced the desk. "Please, have a seat. I will just be a moment."

Alexandra placed her candle on a small table and sat. As Longford finished some paperwork, she made a casual perusal of him. He'd changed from his worn gray suit into an embroidered green waistcoat and tweed frock coat. His short blond hair was neatly combed. He was so handsome, it made her ache. Her mind drifted, imagining what she'd do if he stood up, crossed to her, and took her in his arms.

A fire grew in her belly at the thought and she forced such thoughts away, taking the moment to glance around the room. Paintings of horses, dogs, and hunting scenes adorned the walls, which were covered in silk brocade that might have once been red, but had faded to salmon. She found the choice of artwork odd. Although she hadn't known Longford all that long, he'd shown no signs of being a hunting enthusiast.

After signing several pages, he set them aside and looked up. "Sorry to keep you waiting. What can I do for you?"

His expression and tone were so formal and aloof, it was like a blow to Alexandra's senses. He was regarding her as if they were total strangers, or at the very most, as merely employer and employee. Which, admittedly, they were. *But they had kissed.* Clearly, that kiss had meant far more to her than it had to him.

She recalled his words that night: *I should not have kissed you like that. It was unbelievably inappropriate. I hope we can forget my brief lack of self-control.* And finally: *That can never happen again.*

She'd taken that to mean that although he didn't make

a habit of kissing the serving staff, he'd felt something special for her; she'd been an anomaly. Maybe that wasn't
true. Maybe he'd "lost control" and kissed—or more than
kissed—lots of governesses and maids before she came along,
and felt guilty every time. The idea sent a stab of jealousy
spearing through her, a foreign feeling she didn't much like.

She swallowed hard and struggled to gather her thoughts.
"Your Lordship."

"Yes?"

"I was wondering . . . that is . . ." Why was she so tongue-
tied? She should get right to the points of her visit. Instead,
she blurted: "How long are you home for?" The question
sounded as if it were infused with hope, causing a blush to
rise to her cheeks. "I suppose this is a brief visit?" she added
quickly. "Did you take new portrait commissions while you
were in town?"

"I did not. As it happens, I gave up my rooms there, and
arranged for all my things to be sent home."

"Oh!" Alexandra's heart skipped a beat at the realization
that he would be staying on. "But why? What happened?"

His voice dropped slightly as he glanced at her, a look
that made her pulse race. "I find that I would rather be here
at present."

It was killing Thomas to sit there behind this wide expanse
of desk, to act as if nothing had passed between them. For a
solid week, he had thought of nothing but her. The minute
he had arrived at Polperran House, he had tossed his hat and

coat to Hutchens, then taken the stairs two at a time, and without quite planning it, had found himself at the door to the nursery. Where he had stood, drinking in the sight of her as she'd sat deeply engrossed in his sisters' performance, laughing with delight.

He had felt obliged to talk to the girls. It was awkward, but he had gotten through it, all the while wishing for a moment alone with Miss Watson. He hadn't had the nerve or the presence of mind to arrange it. Then, to his delight, she had suggested it herself.

Here they were at last. Together again. He wanted nothing more than to walk around this infernal, ancient piece of furniture, take her in his arms, and kiss her senseless. To reprise what they had started that night in the library. To see where it might lead.

Which of course, he couldn't.

He would have to take pleasure in the simple fact of their being in the same room.

Thomas cleared his throat. "Miss Watson. I am glad you came down. I wanted to say . . . I was impressed by what I saw in the nursery a little while ago. You seem to have come a long way with the girls in a short time. I am grateful."

"I'm glad you approve, my lord."

"Speaking of which, I have something for you." He retrieved a small stack of books from a nearby bureau and set them on the desk before her. "I bought these in town. Although it sounds now as though you might not need them."

Miss Watson picked up the volumes and glanced over the titles. They were schoolbooks in French, Mathematics, World History, Physical Science, and Italian. He had only been able to afford used editions, but hoped they were modern enough to be valuable.

"Thank you!" She appeared extremely pleased. "I can only go so far with lessons of my own devising. These will be wonderfully helpful."

"Good." Her enthusiasm made all his efforts worthwhile. He sat back in his chair, drinking her in. She was wearing a new dress, presumably the one she had ordered in London. She had been beautiful to him before, even in that severe black thing she always wore, but in this gown, prim and simple as it was, she looked radiant. The pale shade of blue complemented her eyes and sienna hair, and brought out the roses in her creamy complexion. "So. You said there was something you wished to speak to me about?"

"Yes." She leaned forward in her chair. "Three things, actually. First: I wonder if I could have the fire lit in my room on cold evenings, such as this one? I like to sit up for a while and read or do lesson plans, and it's freezing up there."

"Of course. But that is a question for Mrs. Mitchell."

"I asked her. She said that fires were only allowed when absolutely required, and with your permission."

His cheeks grew warm. He felt humiliated to have ever given such an edict, to be so short on funds that his staff was obliged to sit shivering in the dark. "Thank you for bringing this to my attention. I will take care of it."

"Thank you. And thank you again for the schoolbooks. I was hoping, though, to add one more subject to the curriculum. For that, I need a few more materials. Nothing expensive, I promise."

"What do you need?"

"Three sketchbooks and a box of pencils. A set of colored pencils would also be nice."

He frowned. "You want to teach drawing?"

"I do." From the pocket of her gown, Miss Watson produced a scrap of paper and slid it across the desk to him.

It was a pencil sketch of a fashionable woman, and rather well done. "Who did this?"

"Julia."

"Julia?" He was surprised.

"As you can see, she has real talent, and a particular interest in the subject."

He considered her request, but shook his head. "I wasted too much of my life on pencils, charcoal, watercolors, and oils, Miss Watson. I will not have my sisters repeat my mistake."

"How can you view that time of your life as a mistake?" She seemed troubled. "Art for its own sake is a reward. Even now, you earn an income from it."

"A miniscule income, Miss Watson, from something that gives me not an iota of pleasure." He handed her back the sketch. "I stopped my sisters' drawing lessons for good reason. It is a childish pursuit, which will be of no value to them in their future lives."

"I disagree. What difference does it make if they don't draw when they are grown? To have that opportunity *now* could make such a difference in their lives. Julia is struggling to find her place in the world, desperate to discover something she's good at. She's drawing in secret because she knows you disapprove. She'll continue to draw whether or not she's taught. And she's *good*. Very good. Only think what a difference a little guidance would make. It'd give her such a sense of self-confidence. And I think Lillie would enjoy it, too. She . . ."

She continued speaking. He was so distracted, however, by the pink glow of her cheeks and the way her eyes were sparkling, like the blue at the center of a flame, that the words no longer made an impression on his brain. She spoke with such fervor, it was as if she were lit from within. He loved that about her, hadn't seen passion like that since . . . well, since ever.

It made him want to give in, give her anything she desired. It made him fantasize about what she would be like in bed. All that fire, simmering beneath the surface—he had felt it ready to combust the night they had kissed.

He held up a hand, regretful that he had to stop her. "Miss Watson. I can see that you have deep feelings about this. But my mind is made up. You have a great deal to offer Julia and Lillie, beyond a subject as trivial as drawing."

"But—"

"There will be no further discussion on the matter."

Her face fell, all that passion and enthusiasm vanishing in an instant like a pricked balloon, as if he had deflated all her dearest hopes. He felt bad.

"Very well." She put the scrap of paper back in her pocket and paused, then said somberly, "On to my next inquiry, which I hope meets with more success. I wanted to discuss the quality of our meals in the nursery."

He had not expected that. "What is wrong with your meals?"

"Mrs. Mitchell is of the opinion that plain, wholesome food is all a child requires. We are thus served nothing but porridge for breakfast, boiled mutton and overcooked peas for lunch, and soup and bread for dinner."

"Precisely what I was fed at their age, and while at school."

"Did you like it?"

"I did not really think about it. I ate what I was given to eat."

"Do you feel differently now?"

"Now? You mean, do I care what I eat?"

"Yes."

"I look forward to a good meal as much as the next man."

"When did you begin to feel that way?"

He paused. "When I got to Oxford, I suppose."

"So, it wasn't until you were eighteen years old that you were introduced to the delights of other, more delicious foods? All your young life, the same boring, *wholesome* menu was forced upon you?"

"What are you saying, Miss Watson? That I should feed my sisters champagne and caviar?"

"No. But what about bacon and eggs? Apples? Strawberries? Cucumbers? Ham? Roast beef? Cookies? Cake?"

"By *cookies*, I presume you refer to biscuits? We have all those things, Miss Watson, on special occasions: birthdays, holidays, parties, and the like. I recall, as child, attending a strawberry-picking party once or twice."

"*Once or twice?*" Miss Watson shook her head in disbelief.

"I regret that you find your meals so unsatisfactory. If you like, I can ask Mrs. Nettle to send up something different for you, whatever she is dishing up in the servants' hall."

"This is not about me, Your Lordship. Yes, I find the food tiresome. But it's your sisters I worry about. I have studied nutrition. You are denying these children a proper, varied diet, which is essential to their growth and development."

"I believe British experts on the subject think differently."

"That doesn't make them right."

He sighed. "In any case, the menu at Polperran House is not my province. I defer that responsibility to Mrs. Mitchell."

"Mrs. Mitchell relies solely on Mrs. Beeton, a journalist, not a nutritionist. There are many excellent books on the subject. I beseech you to read them, and give the matter further consideration."

"I will take your suggestion under advisement, Miss Watson."

"The same advisement you gave to my request for sketchbooks and pencils?" She rose, upset. Before he could respond, she dropped a short, reluctant curtsy. "Thank you for your attention, my lord. I won't take up any more of your time. Good night."

She picked up her candle and swept from the room. He let out an irritated breath. The last thing he wanted was to argue with her. Why did she have to make things so difficult?

Alexandra stalked up the servants' staircase, greatly annoyed. How could Longford deny her requests? It wasn't as if she'd been asking for the moon. She might have understood if he'd claimed that he simply couldn't afford it. Although even on the smallest budget, he ought to have been able to spring for some paper and pencils, and a bit of variety in their meals!

But no. He'd denied her on grounds that her suggestions were contrary to his ideology. As if allowing his sisters to draw or to eat beef would somehow stoke a revolution! What backward-thinking, aristocratic nonsense. The man was a Neanderthal. How could she ever have imagined that she liked him?

Even though Martha brought up a basket of wood shortly thereafter, and laid a fire that kept Alexandra toasty, she couldn't forgive Longford's bullheadedness on the other issues. She spent half the night stewing about it before finally falling into a fitful asleep. The next morning, she awoke grouchy, with a headache.

She and the girls strode into the nursery almost at the same moment. The table was already laid with a white cloth, and Martha was setting out silver-domed-dishes at three place settings. To Alexandra's surprise, a new and delicious aroma was emanating from said dishes. Could it be . . . ?

Julia sniffed the air as she approached the table. "That smells like bacon."

Alexandra lifted the domed lid over her plate. It *was*

bacon, crisply fried. And scrambled eggs. Sautéed mush-rooms. A grilled half-tomato. And buttered toast.

Julia and Lillie lifted the lids covering their own plates to find the same delicious-looking feast.

"Bacon and eggs!" Lillie cried, ecstatic. "But we only get this at Christmas."

"Well, it's Christmas in May." Martha beamed as she set out cups and a pot of cocoa. "His Lordship come in early this mornin', he did, told Mrs. Nettle it was his wish that ye have the same breakfast he gets every day from now on. Not just breakfast, mind you. Luncheon and dinner, as well."

"Luncheon and dinner!" Julia's eyes widened. "What are they to be?"

"Ye'll have t' wait and see."

"But why?" Lillie asked.

"Who cares why? Let's eat!" Julia plunked into her chair and took a bite of bacon. Lillie followed suit. The expressions on the girls' faces as they chewed were akin to experiencing nirvana.

A smile tugged at Alexandra's lips as gratitude spread through her. So, Longford actually *had* listened to her. "It was very good of your brother to think of us." To Martha, she added, "Do you mind waiting a moment before you go? I'd like to write a quick thank-you note to His Lordship."

"Ye can write it, but he won't get it this mornin', Miss Watson."

A feeling of dread curled in Alexandra's stomach. "Why not?"

"On account of he left the house soon after breakfast."

"He left *again?*" Lillie cried sadly, through a mouthful of toast. "But he only just got home last night."

"He's not gone to London," Martha answered, "only rode off on his horse. Said he had business in St. Austell or might go as far as Bodmin, but would be back for supper."

Alexandra was relieved. "I'll write the note all the same. But as there's no hurry, I'll wait until after I've eaten."

They enjoyed breakfast immensely. As Alexandra ate, she wondered what business had taken Longford away so suddenly. While the girls worked on their French assignment, Alexandra wrote him a note:

> Your Lordship,
>   Breakfast was delicious and a treat beyond measure. Julia, Lillie, and I cannot thank you enough. If only you could have seen the expressions on their faces when they lifted the lids over their bacon and eggs, it would have been its own reward. It felt like Christmas morning.
>   With gratitude,
>   Miss Watson

It was the first time she'd ever signed her name as Miss Watson, and she keenly felt the lie behind it.

Luncheon proved to be another feast: ham, scalloped potatoes, cucumber salad, and a slice of lemon cake. The girls were thrilled. Longford had still not returned by dinnertime, which turned out to be individual baked pastries that Martha called Cornish pasties. They were similar to the beef pie Mrs. Gill had made in London, except in this case, a circle of dough had been folded in half, wrapping the filling of beef, turnip, onion, and potato with crimped edges to form a seal.

"This is my favorite food in the whole world," Lillie cried, savoring every mouthful, and Julia was equally appreciative.

After a day of interesting lessons and delectable meals, they were all three replete with satisfaction. That evening as Julia practiced piano, Lillie read, and Alexandra worked on the next day's lesson plans, John appeared in the nursery.

"Beggin' your pardon, miss." John placed a parcel wrapped in brown paper on the table. "His Lordship asked me to bring this up straightaway, and to tell you . . ." He paused, as if struggling to get the words right, "that it come from Bodmin, and he hopes it will suit."

Alexandra's only thought was: *Longford is home at last.*

"Who is it for?" Julia leapt up from the piano bench to stare at the package.

"All of you, I think. Miss Watson, Lady Julia, Miss Lillie." John backed out of the room with a bow.

It didn't escape Alexandra's notice that he'd called the youngest girl *Miss Lillie* instead of *Lady Lillie*. It didn't escape Lillie's notice either, for as the girl's eyes followed John's retreating figure, her shoulders sagged slightly.

Alexandra opened her mouth to call out a reprimand to the young man, but he was already gone. She turned to Lillie with a bright smile. "Lillie: would you like to open the package?"

"All right." Lillie untied the string and pulled away the paper covering. "Oh!" Her spirits instantly rose. "Sketchbooks and pencils! And colored pencils, too!"

Julia gasped with delight. "How did Thomas know, Miss Watson? You must have spoken to him."

"I did." Alexandra's heart turned over. So *this* is what Longford's mysterious errand had involved. He must have gone out specifically, against his own inclinations, to purchase these items for them. How good and kind that was.

"Did you talk to him about our meals as well?" Lillie asked. "Is *that* why we dined so magnificently today?"

"I did mention something about a more well-balanced diet."

"Thank you! Thank you!" Julia threw her arms around Alexandra.

"Yes, thank you, Miss Watson." Lillie also embraced Alexandra tightly, so that the threesome stood in each other's arms.

Alexandra smiled in wonder. It was the first expression of physical affection the girls had shown her. "Don't thank me," she said, returning the hug. "Thank your brother. All this was his doing."

Alexandra had just drifted off to sleep that night, when she was awakened by a sharp cry from the room next door. A low moan followed, and then the sound of weeping.

She got up, shivering. It was nearly midnight. The fire Martha laid earlier had died down to embers. Lighting a candle, Alexandra slipped through the connecting door into Lillie's room. The girl was sobbing into her pillow. Alexandra couldn't tell if Lillie was awake or crying in her sleep. Setting down the candle, she sat on the edge of the bed and gently caressed the girl's shoulder. "Lillie, sweetheart, it's okay. You're safe. Don't cry."

Lillie woke with a gasp and rolled to her back. After taking in her surroundings, she whimpered, "Oh Miss Watson!" Then she dissolved into tears again.

Alexandra affectionately brushed back a lock of brown hair from the girl's forehead. "What is it, Lillie? Can I help you?"

Lillie squeezed her eyes shut and silently shook her head.

"What were you dreaming about?"

Lillie wiped tears from her cheeks. "I don't know."

"I know you're unhappy about something. Whatever it is, you can tell me."

Lillie rolled to her side again, clutching the pillow. Her sweet young voice cracked as she whispered: "Nobody loves me. Nobody wants me here."

"That's not true."

"It *is* true. Miss Larsen said so."

Miss Larsen was their last governess. "What do you mean? What did Miss Larsen say?"

"She said I was not part of the family, that I did not deserve to live here, because I am a . . . a half-breed. What is a half-breed, Miss Watson?"

To hear such a statement and such a question from this beautiful young girl nearly broke Alexandra's heart. "It's something that you certainly are not, Lillie. You're a beautiful girl, and you belong at Polperran House just as much as anyone else. I don't want you to give another thought to anything Miss Larsen said."

"Yes, Miss Watson."

"When you go back to sleep, I want you to dream of something pleasant, like the drawing lesson we're going to have tomorrow morning. We'll go to the gardens and sketch the prettiest thing we find."

"Yes, Miss Watson," Lillie said again, closing her eyes.

"Sleep sweet," Alexandra crooned softly, as she bent to kiss the girl's brow. She massaged Lillie's back gently, until she felt the girl relax beneath her fingers. Just as the sound of Lillie's even breathing confirmed that she was asleep, the bedroom door slowly swung open.

Alexandra's gaze took in the tall figure who stood framed in the doorway, carrying a candle, and her heart jolted.

It was Lord Longford. His hair was in slight disarray. He wore black trousers, a white shirt that was half-unbuttoned from the neck down, and a dark red dressing gown, as if he'd been interrupted in the act of undressing for bed.

And he looked impossibly, irresistibly handsome.

CHAPTER SIXTEEN

Thomas had heard the crying from his bedroom down the hall.

Not that he hadn't heard such crying from Lillie's room before. He had, far too many times to count. He had never thought to investigate before. After all, what could he possibly do? Lillie sometimes had nightmares. She cried in her sleep. It was not something he had ever felt comfortable thinking about or dealing with. He had left that to the governesses, or to Mrs. Mitchell.

This time, though, he had felt compelled to look into it. Striding down the hall, he had told himself he was doing it for Lillie's sake, but he knew that was a lie. He had come because he'd guessed—hoped—that Miss Watson might be there. That it would provide an excuse to see her.

How right he had turned out to be.

She was sitting on the edge of his sister's bed, and as she glanced in his direction, he had to catch his breath. She had never looked more beautiful or more alluring. She was clad in just a thin white nightdress. The glow from a nearby candle bronzed her sienna hair, which fell in loose, billowing waves about her face.

Now that he was here, words failed him. Everything that came to mind—*How is she? Is she all right?*—sounded trite, particularly after a glance at the bed, which confirmed that Lillie was asleep. Well then, crisis averted. Of course Miss Watson had known what to do, what to say, to comfort his sister.

Not wishing to disturb the sleeping girl, he gestured to Miss Watson with a silent tilt of his head, inviting her to join him in the hall.

She stood and brought her candle with her. He shut the door, then led the way down the corridor to a spot around the corner, out of earshot, in case either of his sisters should wake again. He set his candlestick down on a low table as they paused and faced each other. Miss Watson, holding her own candlestick aloft, broke the silence.

"Thank you." She spoke just above a whisper.

Her remark puzzled him. "For what?" he responded with equal quietness.

"For the fires in my room." She smiled, her eyes bright. "The sketchbooks and pencils. And the delicious meals today."

"Oh. That." He'd been against the last two requests when she first made them, but upon further reflection, realized that she'd had a point. It was worth all the effort he'd gone to in search of those sketchbooks, just to see the smile on her face right now. "You are most welcome. But it is I who should thank you. For attending to my sister just now."

Moonlight from the nearby window bathed her in its glow. This, combined with the flickering flames of their candles, made him suddenly aware that she had nothing on beneath her nightgown. The thin white cotton molded itself around the firm roundness of her breasts, and the twin points of her nipples poked through the fabric. He could make out the indentation of her slender waist, and farther down, the shadow of her shapely legs and the apex where they met. The sight made his mouth go dry.

"That's the second time I've heard Lillie crying in the night." Miss Watson's distressed voice brought his gaze back up to where it belonged, on her face.

He nodded, swallowing hard. "Lillie has had bad dreams since she was an infant."

"I think it's more than a bad dream. She's very troubled."

"Troubled?" He forced himself to avert his glance, not to think about the fact that she was standing only two feet away, and nearly naked.

"Yes. Has she told you why?"

"I cannot say that we have spoken about the matter."

"Well, she thinks that no one loves her or wants her here."

That got his attention. He hesitated before replying. "Why does she think that?"

"She said that Miss Larsen, who sounds like a vile creature, told Lillie she wasn't part of your family. That she doesn't deserve to live at Polperran House. The woman told Lillie that she's a *half-breed*!" Miss Watson hissed the last two words. "Why on earth would your former governess have said something so cruel about Lillie?"

Thomas glanced away, deliberating. Well, sod it. It seemed that he had no alternative but to tell her. "You are right, Miss Watson. That was a very cruel remark. Had I known Miss Larsen ever uttered such a thing, I would have fired her on the spot. But I suppose she said it because . . ." He raised his eyes to hers again. "Lillie is not a Carlyle. She is my half sister."

Miss Watson stared at him. "Your half sister?"

"We had the same mother, but different fathers."

Her cheeks colored as she made the obvious and unhappy connection. "Oh."

"You might as well know the rest of it. It is a sordid tale, the shame of the house of Polperran." He let go a sigh, and keeping his voice low, went on: "I told you of my mother's unhappy life, due to my father's neglect and ill behavior?"

"Yes."

"Julia's birth sent her into an even deeper depression, from which she never seemed to recover. When Julia was nine months old, my mother left. With the medical man who had been attending her. We heard nothing more of her until a few years later, when we learned that she had died giving birth to a baby girl. Lillie."

"Oh no," Miss Watson cried.

"Her natural father, having lost his lover, wanted nothing to do with a bastard newborn, so Lillie was sent back to Polperran House. My father agreed to raise Lillie, even though she was no blood relation to him. But from the moment that baby arrived in this house, the stigma of her birth came with her. The servants . . ."

Understanding crept over Miss Watson's features. "That's why they don't call her Lady Lillie."

He nodded. "Because she is not my father's daughter, not of noble blood."

"Does Lillie know all this?"

"I don't think so. I hope not."

Her brows furrowed as she processed what he had told her. "Yet she seems to sense that she's different somehow."

He pressed his lips together in silent, troubled affirmation.

"What about you?" she asked. "Did you accept her?"

"I have tried. I am not sure I have succeeded very well."

When she glanced up at him again, her expression was filled with empathy. "Lillie was the visible reminder of your mother's infidelity and abandonment."

"Yes." He hoped, now that she knew, it would put an end to the subject. A moment of silence followed. Try as he might, Thomas couldn't prevent his treacherous gaze from drifting down once again to the shapely form of her breasts beneath her thin nightgown.

"Still," she countered, "what your mother did isn't Lillie's fault. It's shameful the way the staff treats her."

He shoved his hands in the pockets of his dressing gown, forced himself to keep his mind on the conversation at hand. "How does the staff treat her?"

"Haven't you noticed? They act like she's a second-class citizen, beneath their notice. When I arrived, Lillie was running around wild, and nobody cared." Miss Watson's voice grew increasingly animated. "She's an innocent, precious child, who should be accepted in her own right. She's every bit as worthy of their love and attention as Julia. And of yours, as well."

"I suppose that is true, Miss Watson," he responded, guilt spearing through him. "I have no doubt shirked my duty in that arena. But—"

"Which reminds me, there's something I've been wanting to ask: why don't you dine with your sisters?"

"I beg your pardon?"

"They're your *family*," she continued passionately. "The only family you have left. Why do you dine alone in your study, and leave them to take all their meals in the nursery?"

The question took him aback. "Where would you have them dine?"

"In the dining room. They're fifteen and twelve. Their table manners are perfect. Surely they're old enough now to join you for dinner?"

"I ate every meal in the nursery growing up, except tea. I didn't dine with my father until I was eighteen years old."

"Why?"

"Why? I don't know. It's what children do. The girls are not out yet."

"My mother and father were busy people, yet since we were girls, they dined with us whenever they could."

"I am their brother, not their father."

"But you're all they have in the way of a father. Or any parent, for that matter. Lillie and Julia love you and look up to you. Yet you ignore them." Blue fire blazed in her eyes as she glared up at him.

Thomas glared right back. She was brazen, this woman. Impudent. Opinionated. It irritated him no end. At the same time, it inflamed him. He couldn't take his eyes off her lips, which were full and rosy in the candlelight. The urge to take her in his arms and taste those lips again was so strong, it was all he could do to resist it. "You seem to forget: I am the master here. *You* are the governess. What gives you the right to speak to me this way?"

"I may not have the right, but I dare to say it anyway. Someone has to speak up on behalf of your sisters!" She gestured so dramatically that hot wax flew from her candle. She cried out, brushing off specks of wax that had singed her hand.

Without thinking, Thomas closed the gap between them in a single stride, removed her candlestick from her grasp, and set it aside on the corner table. Taking her injured hand in his, he brought it to his lips and kissed it softly. They stood but a hair's breadth away from each other. He could feel the heat from her body, could hear the way her respiration suddenly altered, matching his own jagged breaths.

"Be careful, Miss Watson. An unleashed passion can be dangerous, as you have just proved."

His words hung in the air. He could see, in her eyes, that she was just as aware of their double meaning as he was. Her cheeks grew pink. She slowly withdrew her hand from his and took half a step back. "I had better try to rein in my passions, then."

Thomas slid one arm around her waist and drew her against him. "I would rather you did not."

He paused, holding her. Waiting. Giving her a moment to push him away.

She did not. Her breasts and pelvis pressed against his

body, instantly arousing him. Through the thin fabric of their clothing, he could feel her heart pounding just as rapidly as his own.

Did she want this as much as he did? He felt her trembling, just as she had when they'd kissed in the library. What had happened to his firm resolutions about staying away from the serving staff, about keeping his hands to himself? He could not think about that now, not when they were alone in a moonlit hall, with her curvaceous body in perfect alignment with his.

"I have thought of nothing but you, every day, since the moment we met," he admitted huskily.

With his free hand he reached up and cupped her face, then gently tilted her head back to give him better access to her lips. *Just a few kisses*, he told himself. *It will be enough.* Softly, he pressed his mouth to hers. It was the tiniest of touches. A sweet flutter. Once, twice, three times. Absolutely lovely.

"You intoxicate me, Miss Watson." *And now you must stop.*

But he could not stop. As his lips connected with hers one more time, she moaned slightly. Her arms wound around him, as if trying to press him even closer. With that, all his reserve crumbled.

Thomas crushed her against him. He kissed her mouth, her cheeks, up and down the length of her throat, then back up to her mouth again. Her lips parted for him with a deep, jagged breath. He answered the invitation, sliding his tongue into her mouth. Time seemed to stand still as he kissed her.

He could think of nothing else other than his heated need for this intimate connection. And oh, how she responded. At first she was tentative, as if her mouth and tongue were learning, exploring. And then she began to match him, fire with fire. Passion unleashed.

He felt her rake one hand through his hair, while her other hand ran up and down his back. He stroked the side of her unfettered breast through her filmy gown, a curve so luscious it made him gasp with pleasure. Inching back ever so slightly, he slid his hand in between their bodies and cupped the roundness of her breast beneath his palm and fingers. He kneaded the soft globe gently, finding her nipple through the thin cotton and gently caressing it, an action which elicited another deep moan from her throat, and made him grow even harder with wanting.

Breaking free of her lips, he bent to lay kisses across that same perfect breast, holding it in his hand and dragging his tongue across the nipple through the thin cotton, until the fabric was so wet it was transparent. Taking the nipple in his mouth, he suckled until the bud grew tight. She gasped aloud, and he heard her breath skittering as hard and fast as his own.

Straightening, he returned to her mouth and kissed her and kissed her, drinking her in, feeling as if he could never get enough. He wanted more. So much more. His hand trailed down her body, found the inward curve of her waist, then slid lower, over her hip to massage her firm buttocks.

Her breath was uneven now as he gripped a handful of the fabric in his fingers, and then slid lower and gripped some more. He lifted her nightdress up and up, anticipating the moment when he could slide his hand beneath the garment's hem, and feel at last the softness of the naked flesh beneath.

His fingers had nearly reached their goal when an unwanted sound infiltrated Thomas's brain. *Plod. Plod. Plod.* What was that?

Bloody hell. It was the sound of approaching footsteps. From the servants' staircase.

They let go of each other at the same instant and stepped back, both struggling to catch their breath. Miss Watson's nightdress fell back into place as she crossed her arms over her chest, her face blooming bright red. As Thomas retied the belt of his dressing gown, rearranging the fabric to hide evidence of his arousal, he cursed whatever servant had chosen this inopportune moment to appear.

Mrs. Mitchell reached the top of the stairs and entered the hallway, carrying a candle. Catching sight of them, she stopped short, confused. "My lord? I thought I heard Lillie cry out earlier. And then I heard voices."

"Thank you for your concern, Mrs. Mitchell, but it is quite all right. Miss Watson saw to my sister, who is fast asleep. We were just discussing the matter of Lillie's nightmares."

Mrs. Mitchell stared at them for a moment, then dipped a curtsy. "Very good, my lord. Good night."

"Good night, Mrs. Mitchell," Thomas replied. Miss Watson said nothing.

The housekeeper returned from whence she came. As her footsteps died away, a sense of cold reality seemed to fill the darkened corridor. *What the hell was he doing?* was the primary thought running through Thomas's mind. *Had he taken leave of his senses?*

He turned back to Miss Watson.

She looked as rattled as he felt. "I should go now."

"Wait," Thomas said urgently.

She glanced up at him. In her heated gaze, he read confusion mingled with the aftermath of desire.

"I do not know what this is between us," Thomas began, "but . . ."

"I'd say it's pretty obvious what this is."

Her response was so direct and so unexpected, it caught him off-guard. A brief, uncomfortable laugh escaped him. "Perhaps, but . . . don't you think some things are better left unsaid?"

"Why?" Her cheeks were still stained red. "*You're* the one who said wait, who seemed eager to talk."

He blew out an exasperated breath. "Fine. Before we take leave of each other, let us clarify where we stand."

"Okay. Where do we stand?"

"Well," he said slowly, "clearly, I am attracted to you. And unless I am misinterpreting your response, I sense that you are attracted to me as well."

"I think we can agree on that."

"But . . ."

"But?"

Did she truly not understand this? Did he have to spell it out for her? "It is an attraction that is neither right nor proper."

"Because I work for you?"

"Yes, because you work for me!"

She nodded stiffly. "Of course. You're right."

"I took advantage of you, and I am sorry."

"Don't apologize. I was a party to this as well."

"I fear I have put you in a difficult position. I would not blame you if you chose to quit your post. I hope you will not."

She looked him squarely in the eye. "I have no intention of quitting."

Relief spiraled through him. "I am glad to hear it." He gave her a tight smile. "I hope this will not create any awkwardness between us. Going forward, I hope we can agree to meet in a more . . . professional capacity?"

"Of course," she said again, holding out her hand for a handshake. "My lord."

He took her hand and they shook on it. Without another word, she picked up her candlestick, relit it from his candle's flame, then slipped past him and strode off down the hall.

Alexandra climbed into bed, her mind spinning. It had all started out so innocently. First that heart-wrenching revelation about Lillie. Then she was just trying to talk to him about his sisters. And then . . .

The first time they'd kissed, in the library, it had been thrilling. Alexandra now knew *that* kiss was just a tiny taste of the kind of pleasure that could arise from an intimate encounter between a man and a woman.

This time, his kisses had been incendiary.

Shivering beneath the quilts, Alexandra relived the pleasure of being in Longford's arms. The fevered exchange of his lips on hers. His hands on her body. His mouth on her breasts. *Dear God.* As he'd kissed her and explored her with his touch and his tongue, he'd awakened unimagined sensations deep inside her belly, making her feel wet with inexplicable need in her most feminine of places. Even now, recalling the events in her mind gave rise to a sweet, unquenchable feeling of wanting.

She hugged her pillow to her chest, remembering Longford's words:

I have thought of nothing but you, every day, since the moment we met. . . . You intoxicate me.

She had felt the same. And he seemed just as unable to control his passions as she was. She'd felt the evidence of his desire when he'd pressed his body against hers. She might not know much about men, but she'd read enough risqué novels to know what *that* signified. The knowledge that she'd caused such a reaction in a man—in *him*—propelled her heart into a frenzied drumming.

Thank goodness Mrs. Mitchell had showed up when she did. Otherwise, Alexandra didn't know if she would have had the power to stop things from going further. The way things were proceeding, he might have ravished her right there, standing in the hallway.

Which she knew would have ruined her.

Did she want to be ruined? No, her reason told her, she didn't. But another side of her, a passionate side she'd never recognized before now, piped up from somewhere unknown and deep inside her and cried *yes yes yes, I want it. I want to feel, to live, to experience what it means to be a woman.* She didn't want that experience with just anyone. She wanted it with *him*.

Such thoughts were scandalous, even wanton. But it didn't matter, since they would never be acted upon. Thomas Carlyle, the seventh Earl of Longford, saw it as a cardinal rule to never have relations with a woman in his employ. She told herself that such deep principles were admirable. At the same time, she felt a nagging sense of loss. She was so much more than just a member of his staff.

If only, she thought for the thousandth time, *if only I could tell him: I'm an American woman of arguably equal status to yourself.* But that felt impossible. And the longer she waited, the harder it would be to say the words.

The morning dawned bright and blue. Alexandra rose blurry-eyed and splashed her face with cold water from the pitcher, bracing herself to meet the new day, determined to put the events of the previous night behind her.

Going forward, I hope we can agree to meet in a more . . . professional capacity?

Lord Longford's word rang in her ears. Well then. Going forward, she'd keep her wayward thoughts to herself, remain cordial in his presence. She could do it. She knew she could.

She opened the casement window and gazed out over the expanse of green that encompassed the Polperran House estate. It promised to be a beautiful day. She knew exactly what she wanted to do.

As soon as breakfast was finished, Alexandra and the girls gathered up their new sketchbooks and pencils, and set out from the house.

"What's your favorite spot on the grounds?" Alexandra asked, relishing the bright warmth of the sun on her face as they strode across the back lawn.

"The stables," Julia replied.

Alexandra laughed. "I was thinking of a more greenish sort of place, that would make a pretty picture."

"We could go to the fountain," Lillie suggested. She was in good spirits. Whether she didn't remember her episode from the night before, or simply didn't wish to discuss it, Alexandra couldn't determine, but she thought it best not to bring it up unless Lillie did.

"The fountain is dried up and dead." Julia made a face.

Alexandra was mulling over other possible sketching sites, when the sound of an axe splitting wood rent the air. *Whack. Whack. Whack.* They soon came upon the woodshed. Alexandra stopped, riveted.

The Earl of Longford was in the yard, chopping wood. He stood with his back to them, wearing an old pair of trousers and high black boots, and he was shirtless. Apparently unaware of their approach, he repeatedly raised the axe high above his head and smacked it down on the chopping block, splitting a succession of logs into smaller fragments with savage vehemence.

The morning sun shone on skin that was lightly tanned, picking up the gleam of perspiration. Alexandra's heart caught as she appreciated the splendid display of masculine flesh on view: his trim waist, the taut muscles of his back, the biceps and forearms that rippled and tightened with every heft of the axe.

The girls paused beside her, unaffected by their brother's half nakedness. Lillie was more interested in a tiny white flower she bent to pluck. "What kind of flower is this?" she asked Alexandra.

"I don't know."

Longford turned, noticing them now with surprise as he rested his axe on the chopping block and struggled to catch his breath. "That's a wood sorrel."

"A wood sorrel," Lillie repeated softly. "What a lovely name."

Longford darted Alexandra a nod in greeting. She dropped a quick curtsy.

"Out for a morning stroll?" His voice was matter-of-fact, impersonal. No one would ever suspect they'd shared an intimate interlude only the night before.

Well, Alexandra thought. He was a stronger person than she was. Or maybe he just cared less. "We're looking for a pretty spot to do some sketching."

He wiped his brow with a handkerchief from his pocket. "It's a fine day for it."

"Is there any place in particular you can suggest?" Alexandra asked.

He paused. "I can think of a few places."

"Will you show us?" Julia blurted.

He gestured to the pile of logs waiting to be split. "Sorry, I am already engaged."

Alexandra frowned. Once again, he was choosing to avoid his sisters. "Surely chopping wood is John's responsibility, not yours."

Longford met her gaze squarely across the expanse that divided them. "Perhaps I *like* chopping wood," he answered emphatically, as if daring her to contradict him again.

"Even so," Alexandra replied calmly, "you could consider doing it later. Your sisters would so enjoy your company."

"Please?" Julia said. "I am grateful for the sketchbook, Thomas. But I should be even more grateful if you would come with us."

"And show us the best place to draw," added Lillie.

Longford paused, glancing at his sisters, then his eye caught Alexandra's again. He let go a sigh, set down the axe, grabbed his shirt and waistcoat from where they lay nearby, and began to put them on. "Well, if all three of you are going to gang up on me, how can I say no?"

Chapter Seventeen

Longford led the way down a series of paths that went deeper and deeper into the woods, in a direction Alexandra had never explored.

As they walked, Alexandra smiled to herself, happy for his sisters' sake that he'd agreed to embark on this outing. As for herself, she'd just keep her distance from him as best she could, both physically and emotionally.

"Where are we going?" Julia asked, skipping to keep up with her brother's brisk pace.

"You shall see," was his only reply.

After they had walked for twenty minutes or so, the path wound down into a wide, sloping valley populated by beech and birch trees. Alexandra caught her breath, entranced by the beauty of the scene before them.

The trees, whose trunks were green with moss, thrust their leafy branches overhead like welcoming arms. Sunlight filtered down through gaps in the canopy, admitting glimpses of the blue sky above, while bathing the woodland floor in golden beams of light. On a rise about a hundred feet distant stood a small, slightly crumbling, grayish-white structure that could only be described as a Grecian temple.

A set of cut stone steps led up to its wide base, and four fluted columns held up a Doric pediment.

The most magical aspect of the setting, however—the thing that was so glorious, it overrode everything else—was the abundance of vibrant wildflowers that covered the ground like a dense, bluish-purple carpet, the endless blooms nodding on tall green stems in every direction.

"Bluebells!" Alexandra was mesmerized. The sight brought back vivid images of patches of similar flowers that she and her sisters used to come upon while wandering through the countryside. The sudden memory made her ache all over again for Madeleine and Kathryn, a longing she had to shake off with a firm, deep breath. She had Julia and Lillie, now; and she was beginning to love them almost like sisters. "They're a deeper color than the bluebells that grow in New York," she observed. "I've never seen so many in one place."

"It's the season for them," Longford commented.

"It's an enchanted bluebell forest!" Lillie beamed, dancing in a circle with her arms thrown wide.

"I forgot this place was here," Julia mused. She sat on a large tree stump and opened her sketchbook. "I'm going to draw the Grecian temple."

Longford hesitated, then asked: "May I sit with you?"

Julia's eyes grew wide with delight. "You may," was her proper reply.

He plunked down on the stump and watched in silence as Julia picked up her pencil and began to draw.

Lillie announced that she wished to draw the bluebells. She sat cross-legged on the woodland floor before a section of vibrant blooms, and Alexandra settled beside her, offering a few words of instruction.

For some time, the only sound that reached Alexandra's ears was the soft scratching of pencils on paper, and Longford's and Julia's quiet voices from across the way. Julia asked questions, which he answered. Alexandra could see the delight on the young lady's face as she eagerly listened, and drew. How wonderful, that he was sharing his knowledge with a sister who so dearly wished for the attention. Considering his current, self-professed aversion to all things art related, Alexandra knew it must cost him something to do this.

After a while, Longford came over to see how Lillie was faring. Wanting to give him private time with his sister, Alexandra got up and found a fallen log some distance away, where she began a sketch of her own.

Longford spent a good half hour helping Lillie with her sketch. As Alexandra watched, she could see that Lillie, although almost frozen with shyness at first, soon warmed up. After a while she was laughing and chatting as he gave her encouragement and feedback.

After checking on Julia again, Longford strode over to Alexandra and stood beside her, glancing down at what she was drawing. At his nearness, her heart began dancing to a different rhythm. She had to concentrate to retain her focus on her work: an overview of the valley with its trees and wildflowers, and the humans currently inhabiting it.

"Very nice," he commented with approval.

"It's very *rough*." She closed the sketchbook with a shrug.

"Yet it has potential. You have an aptitude for drawing.

So do the girls," he admitted. "Julia, in particular, has a real knack. As you so graciously pointed out to me the other day."

Her lips twitched. "Thank you again for listening. And for bringing us here."

"It is my pleasure." He held out a hand toward the sketch book. "May I?"

"Of course." She handed it to him, presuming that he wished to further study her drawing.

"The pencil as well. If I may."

She gave him the pencil. He sat down on a large rock a couple of yards away, facing her as he opened the sketchbook on his lap, turned to a blank page, and began drawing something.

Her heart twisted. She'd seen him paint, of course, even though he'd insisted it no longer gave him pleasure. But she'd never seen him draw. He was doing so now, voluntarily, gazing at some distant point behind her, and the ease with which his pencil flew indicated that the activity was like second nature to him.

"I used to come here to play as a boy," he commented as he drew, nodding toward the Grecian temple. "I always loved the folly."

"Why is it called a folly?"

"It is a rather useless structure, built on a whim by an ancestor of mine about a hundred and fifty years ago."

"I think it's lovely. Julia and Lillie are enjoying it here, too. I think it means a lot that you made time for them."

"Yet another thing which I would not have thought of, had you not pointed it out to me."

"Just doing my job, my lord."

"A job at which you seem to excel, Miss Watson." He pronounced the words with no more emotion than he might have said, *It looks like it is going to rain.* But his eyes, when he glanced at her, betrayed a greater depth of emotion he seemed to be struggling to hide. "What you said about the girls, last night," he added quickly. "You were right. They are both far more interesting and mature than I had expected. I suppose I should not be surprised that they are interested in art, considering that they grew up at Polperran House."

"Why do you say that?"

"Because everywhere you turn, there is an oil painting on the walls. As a boy, I would walk up and down the corridors, staring at the portraits of my ancestors. It amazed me to think that I was descended from this vast succession of people who I would never meet. At the same time, it was thrilling to note that they had been captured, often at the height of their youth and beauty, to live forever in oil on canvas. I decided that when I grew up, I would learn to paint like that."

His pencil continued to fly as he spoke, his attention focused on what he was creating. From the intensity of his expression, Alexandra saw that art for him was not a hobby, nor just a means to earn income, as he'd previously insisted. It was a passion and a compulsion.

"I envy you," Alexandra said.

"Envy me? Why?"

"Because you found something you loved at such a young age." She plucked a stalk of bluebell and twirled it in her fingers. "I understand that, as an earl, you aren't allowed to have a profession. But you have great talent."

"And you know this, how? Based on two paintings you saw at Mrs. Gill's?"

"More than that. Based on the paintings I saw in the attic."

His pencil paused. "What were you doing in the attic?"

"Mrs. Mitchell was loaning me this hat." She indicated the bonnet on her head. "I believe it was your mother's."

"It looks well on you. You may keep it."

"Thank you. But my lord, I've visited a lot of museums in the U.S. and abroad, and I've rarely seen works that evoke as much *feeling* as yours do."

"I appreciate—" he began, but she interjected:

"Your early work has merit in its own right. But your later work—it's easy to tell the difference—it's truly remarkable. There's one painting in particular I can't get out of my mind. It's a landscape of a garden with cypresses, flowers, a fountain, and a stone bench, overlooking a spectacular view of the distant hills. I'm guessing you painted it in Italy."

He nodded slightly. "I recall that painting."

"It's a masterpiece. It felt so *real*." Alexandra closed her eyes as she spoke, seeing the landscape once again in her mind. "As if I were actually *there* on that Italian hillside on that sunny day. I could feel the sun on my shoulders, smell the lavender. I longed to follow that gravel path to see what I might find beyond the edges of the painting. An ancient Tuscan house? A woman hanging laundry in her garden? A road leading deep into the countryside?"

She stopped to take a breath. Aware that he hadn't said anything, she opened her eyes to find him staring at her with a kind of hushed wonder. Her cheeks warmed. "I guess that's a long-winded way of saying how much I liked it."

"You do me honor, Miss Watson," he said softly, a new-found gleam in his brown eyes. "I have never heard anyone speak of my work as you do."

"Never?"

"Never. Not even my mother, God rest her, who was very free with her admiration when I was a child. She mainly just hung things on the wall and said, 'Very good, Thomas.' You, on the other hand, seem to understand what I was attempting to convey with that painting."

"It's all there, for anyone to observe. Surely the masters you studied with in Florence must have commented on your ability."

"They only pressured me to do better. All I could ever see were the flaws."

"That's so wrong! Everyone needs encouragement, my lord." She took a deep breath, gathering courage to ask the question that had been haunting her. "Is that why you gave up painting for pleasure? Because your masters in Florence were too hard on you?"

The light that had lit his face blinked out, as surely as if she'd doused a candle flame with water. "No," he said abruptly.

"Then what happened? Why are your best paintings gathering dust in the attic? Why don't you paint anymore, for yourself?"

His face darkened and he pressed his lips together. Just then Julia's voice rang out:

"Thomas! I need you. I cannot get these columns right."

Longford stood. "Pray, excuse me, Miss Watson." He handed her back the sketchbook and pencil, then returned to his sister's side.

Alexandra sighed in frustration, still no closer to learning what she wanted to know. Curious as to what he'd been drawing, she opened the sketchbook.

She gasped. It was a portrait of her, a close-up that captured her from the shoulders to the hat atop her head. It was so perfectly and meticulously done, she felt as if she were looking into a mirror.

Alexandra had no further opportunity to speak to Longford that day or the next. The girls were so disappointed when they'd had to quit sketching to return for lunch, Alexandra promised they'd come back soon to finish. However, a steady rain kept them inside at their lessons the following day, and the next day it was still too wet to go out.

When Alexandra joined the girls in the nursery after rest hour, although Lillie was happily reading, Julia was sunk down on the carpet, crying.

"Julia?" Alexandra crouched down beside her. "What is it? What's wrong?"

"I hate my brother!" Julia wiped away tears. "I hate him so much! He never lets us do anything."

"Just the other day, he took us sketching." Alexandra had

greatly enjoyed that morning. Not only for the beauty of the environs, but for the pleasure she'd had being in Longford's company, and the reminder it had brought of his skill as an artist. Since then, she'd opened her sketchbook countless times to sneak a look at the drawing he'd made of her, and felt a thrill of delight and awe at every viewing.

"But we sketched *here*. He never lets us go anywhere else."

"Where would you like to go?"

"She wants to go to the party," Lillie interjected.

"What party?"

Julia heaved a tearful sigh. "I saw the envelope on the tray by the front door. It was from Lord and Lady Trevelyan. It was addressed to Thomas, Lillie, and myself. I was afraid Thomas would throw it away, and my name *was* on the envelope. So I opened it."

"And?" Alexandra prompted.

"It was an invitation to a garden party at Trevelyan Manor next week. Oh, Miss Watson! It has been so long since I have seen Helen, or been to that house, or to any party whatsoever! I would give anything to go! But of course Thomas said no." She burst into tears again.

Alexandra glanced at Lillie. "Is this something you'd like to do, too?"

"Oh, yes!" Lillie gushed. "Anna was my best friend in the world. But I haven't seen her in so long, I've almost forgotten what she looks like."

"I'll speak to your brother, and see what I can do."

Julia looked at her doubtfully. "It will not do any good."

"We'll never know if I don't try."

After getting the girls started on their history assignment, Alexandra made her way downstairs. She found Longford at his desk in his study, a deep scowl on his face. He gestured for her to enter and sit.

"Miss Watson."

"My lord," she replied, taking a seat. "Is something wrong?"

"Isn't it always?" He blew out an unhappy breath. "A half dozen cottages in my village and three houses on outlying farms have broken windows and leaking roofs, which I cannot afford to fix. The Martin family—good people, salt of the earth—lost a child this morning to a fever. I blame myself. Their house was freezing. I sent over a cartload of firewood, but there is little else I can do. It frustrates me that my tenants are forced to live in such uncivilized conditions, and I am powerless to act."

"I'm so sorry to hear that." Alexandra was deeply moved by his sense of connection and devotion to his tenants. She felt bad for the Martin family and their lost child, felt bad about the financial situation in which Longford was mired.

The irony that *she* had exactly the kind of money he needed was not lost on her. It was what she'd been sent to England to do, after all: find a nobleman with a crumbling estate. Marry him. Exchange cash for a title. A purely business arrangement, a concept that still made Alexandra cringe. With Longford, though, would such an arrangement truly just be business?

"Hopefully, I can be of more service to you," Longford said. He set aside a stack of paperwork as he turned to her.

"I hope so." Alexandra blinked herself back to the matter at hand. "I wanted to ask about an invitation that arrived today from Trevelyan Manor. Julia said that she and Lillie haven't seen their dearest friends in years."

A frown took over his face. "I have said we will not go."

"Why is that, my lord?"

"I want nothing to do with that household."

"Why?"

"That is my business, Miss Watson, not yours."

"But the girls would so enjoy such an outing. Lillie and Julia are very isolated, with no company other than each other and myself. You said you hope they'll marry someday. How will they ever learn how to behave in society, if they spend all their growing-up years sheltered here? They need friends their own age."

"Let them find friends elsewhere," he growled, "but not at Trevelyan Manor."

"Where should they seek such friends? Lord and Lady Trevelyan are your closest neighbors. It seems to me that their daughters are Julia's and Lillie's only chance for company."

"I have already written a note refusing the invitation, and that is that."

"But *why*? Why are you so against anything to do with that family?"

"I have my reasons. And my decision is final."

"Does it have something to do with Lord Saunders?"

He looked at her sharply. "What do you know of Lord Saunders?"

"Only that he's the son of the Marquess of Trevelyan. And that you two were best friends until something happened that caused a breach between you."

"A breach? I suppose you could call it a *breach*." Longford let go a short, dark laugh. "What Saunders did to me was the most hideous kind of betrayal."

"What did he do, my lord?"

"I do not wish to discuss it, Miss Watson." His face clouded over like an impending storm.

"I'm just thinking of Julia and Lillie. If I understood what happened, maybe I could—"

"Maybe you could what?" he interrupted heatedly. "Fix things? Make the problem go away?" He laughed. "All right, I will tell you what Saunders did, if only to put an end to your ceaseless questioning." Longford's eyes flashed as he said through gritted teeth, "He stole the woman I loved."

CHAPTER EIGHTEEN

Alexandra waited with bated breath as Longford folded his arms across his chest, continuing grimly, "Saunders was my closest friend since childhood. As the only other son of a peer in this region, he was the only boy I was allowed to associate with. Our friendship continued while away at school, although we grew to be different in many ways. He was fascinated by science—he was always building some contraption or another—whereas I was interested in art. He seemed bored by country life, while I embraced it. When I was in Italy, he spent half his time in London. He developed quite a reputation with 'the ladies,' from what I hear. And then, as I told you, my father called me back from Italy against my will."

"He wanted you to marry."

"He wanted me to marry *money*. He had made a deal with a friend of his, a wealthy merchant from Cincinnati whom he had met in town, to bring over his daughter to be my bride. For days, we did nothing but argue, but when my father made clear how desperate was our financial situation, I felt I had no choice but to at least meet her. To my surprise, when the young lady came, I found I liked her."

"You did?" Alexandra hadn't expected that.

"Her name was Elise Townsend. Her father was prepared to settle a fortune on her upon her marriage. I knew the money would make my father happy, but it is not why I agreed to marry her. I fell in love with her. At least I *thought* I was in love, at the time. She seemed to share my passion for art, exulted over every one of my paintings on the walls, insisting I was a genius. I started painting a portrait of her, as a gift. The banns were read, and everything made ready for the wedding. But a week before the ceremony, Elise and Saunders ran off to America together."

"Oh!" Alexandra cried, aghast.

"I should have seen the signs. Elise spent barely two seconds with my father or my sisters. She just wanted to meet my friends. She did not like Polperran House, proclaiming it too shabby and too cold. In the end, she was no different from any of the other title-grubbing American heiresses who've been invading our shores, as unwelcome as the cheap American wheat that has ruined our agriculture. And she saw a better title in Saunders, a future marquess."

His harsh statement was uttered so bitterly it stung. A zing of guilt reverberated through Alexandra at the term *title-grubbing American heiresses*. But she couldn't think about that right now. She swallowed hard. "Did he and Elise marry?"

"They did not. Two months after sailing to America, I heard that Saunders was back at Trevelyan Manor, as single as the day he departed. I never heard a word from Elise again."

"Why didn't the marriage take place?"

"I do not know, and I do not care to know." He shook his head bitterly. "Can you imagine how foolish I felt, Miss Watson? Betrayed not just by the woman I loved, but by my best friend? After they left, I returned to painting, hoping to forget. But my heart was not it. With every stroke of the brush, I thought of Elise and all the impassioned conversations we'd had about art. Every one of my paintings at Polperran House brought back to mind her gushing comments, and reminded me of her unfaithfulness. Finally, I took them all down and stashed them away. I burned the portrait I had painted of her. Then I packed up my art supplies, I thought for good. If financial difficulties had not intervened, I daresay I never would have taken them out again."

The expression on Longford's face was so bleak, it wrenched at Alexandra's soul. "I'm so sorry," she said softly. "What Lord Saunders did was horrible. And Miss Townsend behaved in a cruel and heartless manner."

"You asked me, the day we met, what I had against Americans? Well, now you know."

"You can't hold all Americans in contempt based on the action of a single person."

"I try not to." He glanced at her with a tight smile. "I hired you, didn't I? And I am not sorry I did. Still, after what happened, it is hard not to harbor a certain prejudice against women from your country."

Alexandra's stomach tightened. "I hope you won't always feel that way. Just as I hope, someday, you can forgive the Earl of Saunders."

"Never."

"Never is a long time, my lord. Whatever happened in Cincinnati, Lord Saunders must have recognized his mistake. He came back unmarried. Did you know that last week, he stopped by, asking for you?"

"What of it?"

"I'm told he's been trying to speak to you for years, but you refuse to see him."

"I will never see nor speak to Saunders again, no matter how many times he comes calling with his hat in hand."

"Resentment and hatred are wounds that only fester as time goes by," she pointed out gently, "but they can be healed by forgiveness."

"Easy words to say, Miss Watson. Far more difficult to put into practice."

"Difficult, I agree. But not impossible. I understand why you ended your friendship with Lord Saunders. But he is just one member of the Grayson family. I'm deeply sorry for what you've gone through. But is it fair to make Julia and Lillie suffer for something that had nothing to do with them?"

Longford stared at her across the desk. "Are we back to that again?"

"You ought to—"

"Miss Watson," he interrupted heatedly, "you have an unpleasant habit of telling me what I *ought* to do. You demanded a new menu? I gave it to you. You requested sketchbooks? Done. You insisted that I spend time with my sisters? I did. Enough! I will hear no more on this subject." He gestured to the door. "You are dismissed. Please close the door on your way out."

At dinner that evening, Alexandra could barely appreciate the flavor of the roast pork Mrs. Nettle had prepared. Her mind was too full of all that she'd learned.

Her ruminations continued in the quiet hour that followed, while Lillie practiced at the piano and Julia continued to sulk and weep. Alexandra, on the other hand, at last understood the motive behind Longford's refusal to let his sisters go to Trevelyan Manor.

What a terrible blow he'd suffered, in losing both his fiancé and his best friend in one fell swoop. What a tragedy that his relationship with Miss Townsend had become so inexorably intertwined in his mind with art, that her betrayal destroyed his passion for the subject.

The point that rang closest to home for Alexandra, however, was the fact that the woman who broke his heart was American. *A title-grubbing American heiress.*

Another wave of guilt washed over her as she considered the great lie that still stood between them. Should she have told him the truth about her identity from the beginning? *No, no,* her instincts had been right all along. If she'd told him *then,* he would never have hired her. She would never have met his sisters, who she'd come to love, or come to Polperran House, which she'd grown to adore more with each passing day. She would have never gotten to know Lord Longford himself. A man who sometimes exasperated her, yet for whom, she could not deny, she had developed feelings.

He'd said those feelings could never go beyond a professional capacity. But what if they already had?

She'd hoped a time would come when she *would* be able to tell him the truth, without fear that he'd fire her on the spot. What would he think, if he discovered that she had the money he needed to save his estate? Was it possible they could be together? Was that something she even wanted? Would *he* want it? Would he want *her*?

His words came back again to haunt her, stabbing her in the gut like a knife:

She was no different from any of the other title-grubbing American heiresses who've been invading our shores, as unwelcome as the cheap American wheat that has ruined our agriculture.

How could she ever tell him the truth about herself now? If Longford ever learned who she was and her real reason for coming to England, wouldn't he despise her?

The crisp morning air invaded Thomas's lungs as he strode across the lawn to the stables. *Impossible woman*, he thought, his irritation growing with every step.

Miss Watson was constantly stirring up emotions that he had no desire to feel. One minute, he wanted nothing more than to take her in his arms. The next minute, she was provoking him beyond reason.

When she had cornered him in his study the afternoon before with that business about Lord and Lady Trevelyan's invitation, he had hoped to put an end to her inquiries by telling her the truth of the matter. Any reasonable human being should have been able to comprehend, after what had occurred, why he could not consider that family in any light other than revulsion.

Yet even when in possession of all the facts, she had still insisted that he allow the girls to attend that blasted party at Trevelyan Manor. What on earth did she think gave her, a *governess*, the right to tell *him* what he ought or ought not to do? He was the lord and master of this house. His word was law. He knew what was best for himself and for his family.

Despite the strength of these convictions, a tiny voice in the back of his mind responded with a comment she had made: *Is it fair to make Julia and Lillie suffer for something that had nothing to do with them?*

Perhaps not, he admitted with grim reluctance. But was it fair that he had been betrayed by the two people he had loved best in the world? Sometimes life wasn't fair. One simply had to deal with adversity as best one could.

He was nearly to the stable door, intending to ride out to inspect the fences along the northern edge of his property, when he heard a shout from behind him, and observed the very object of his reflections running toward him across the lawn.

"My lord!" Miss Watson cried, waving a hand at him.

He turned back to meet her. She was hatless and breathtakingly, infuriatingly beautiful. As he took in her worried expression, his annoyance vanished. "What is it, Miss Watson?"

She stopped before him, struggling to catch her breath. "Julia is missing."

The hairs raised on the back of his neck. "What do you mean, missing?"

"She didn't show up for breakfast or her morning lessons. I can find her nowhere. Martha says she glimpsed Julia walking this way early this morning. I thought she might have gone riding, and hoped she'd soon come back. But it's nearly eleven o'clock now, with no sign of her."

A quick check in the stables proved that Julia's horse was gone, and the stable boy admitted she had indeed left many hours earlier.

"Did she say where she was going?" Thomas asked the boy.

"No, my lord," answered the lad.

"It is not like her to go off without permission, or to stay away so long, is it?" Thomas inquired of Miss Watson.

"No," she agreed, "but Julia was very upset last night, over the matter of the invitation. She may have just gone out riding as a way to deal with her disappointment. But I think it likely that she had a specific destination in mind."

Thomas looked at her, catching her drift. "You think she went to Trevelyan Manor?"

"It's possible."

"Thank you for alerting me. I will go in search of her."

Thomas ordered his horse to be saddled, and took off in the direction of Trevelyan Manor. As he crossed his own property, he called out his sister's name, but received no response. What if she had been thrown? The idea that he might find her lying in a ditch, injured and in pain, filled him with dread. He prayed for the alternative: that she had in fact gone to Trevelyan Manor, and had arrived there safely.

That notion brought him no comfort either, however, for he had no wish to see the Graysons, or to visit that house.

He had just left his grounds and crested a hill, when he saw two riders on horseback not far off, heading his way: Julia on Windermere, looking, thankfully, unharmed, and on a mount beside her, Charles Grayson, the Earl of Saunders.

Thomas froze inwardly. He had successfully avoided all contact with Saunders for years. Now, such a meeting would be unavoidable. The bastard was directly in front of him, the same picture of health and good looks as the last time Thomas had seen him.

As he approached the two riders, Thomas silently cursed Julia for putting him in this unhappy position, determined to get this over with quickly. Julia's eyes widened with nervous surprise at the sight of him. When they came abreast of each other, all stopped, retaining their positions on their steeds.

"Longford?" Saunders stared at him. "I almost didn't recognize you."

Another reminder of how long it had been since they had seen each other. And why Thomas had grown a mustache, cut his hair. Without comment, he turned his attention to his sister. "Julia, where have you been?"

Her cheeks flamed and she stared at the ground. "I . . ." she began, then fell silent.

"Your sister paid us an unexpected visit this morning," Saunders cut in. "I did not think it safe or proper for her to ride all the way back to Polperran House on her own, so I have accompanied her."

Thomas would have thanked anyone else for the service, but not this man. "Let us go, Julia." He gestured to her to join him. As Julia silently trotted up, he added: "I am very disappointed in you. Miss Watson and I were greatly worried."

To his surprise her lips trembled, and tears formed in her eyes. "I am sorry."

He had expected defiance from her, not such a timid, emotional response. Uncertainly, he began to turn his horse around, when Saunders said, "Wait, Longford. Please do not leave."

Thomas responded with a silent glare.

"I beg you," Saunders continued. "Allow me one minute. For all the years that we were friends—"

"You are no friend of mine," Thomas insisted bitterly. "I am astonished that you have the temerity to even speak to me."

"One minute, that is all I ask. I hope it will be worth your while. If you do not agree, I promise to never make any attempts to speak to you in future."

Every molecule in Thomas's body urged him to refuse, to ride off that instant. But the image of Miss Watson suddenly popped into his brain, admonishing him: *He has been trying to speak to you for years, but you refuse to see him, and you really ought to reconsider. . . .*

If one minute of his time would get her off his back, and get this bastard to leave him alone forever, it would be worth it. "Fine. One minute." Whatever Saunders was about to say, though, he did not want his sister hearing it. "Julia, we are close enough to home now. You may go ahead on your own. Return directly to the stables, and then to the nursery. We will talk later."

"Very well." Her voice caught in her throat. "Thank you, Lord Saunders, for escorting me home."

"It was my pleasure, my lady," Saunders replied with a tip of his hat.

Julia dashed off without further comment, disappearing through the trees that bordered his estate. Saunders dismounted, so Thomas reluctantly did the same. After leading the horses to a patch of grass to graze, Thomas took out his pocket watch and turned to Saunders. "One minute. Go."

"You have every right to hate me, Longford," Saunders began quickly. "In your position, I would feel exactly the same. What I did was very wrong, and I am desperately sorry. But you do not know the whole story. For years I have tried to apologize and tell you what happened, and have been absolutely miserable that I could not."

Thomas made no comment, waiting.

"The thing is," Saunders went on, "I did not pursue Elise. She—"

"Oh please," Thomas interrupted. "Is that your defense? You are going to try to blame all this on her?"

"It is *my* one minute. You said you would listen."

"Go on."

"Elise was attractive and rich. I admit I was a little envious at first that you had made such a good catch. Even more envious, I think, that you had the freedom to choose your own wife, whereas I had long been expected to marry my cousin Sophie. But I saw how much you loved Elise, and wished only the best for you both." Saunders removed his hat and raked a hand distractedly through his wavy brown hair.

"However, I do not know if you are aware of this, Longford. Every time I saw Elise, whether it was at your house or mine, she made it her business to flirt with me. I have never been one to turn away from the attentions of an attractive woman. I saw no harm in it—she was your fiancé, and it was my aim to become friends. So I flirted right back."

Thomas's eyes narrowed. He had witnessed the flirting, but had just seen it as Saunders's and Elise's fun-loving, gregarious natures at play.

"She commented on the beauty of Trevelyan Manor, and several times mentioned how thrilling it was that a marquess was just one step beneath a duke. Then one night—do you remember the party we gave, when it was raining cats and dogs, and everyone stayed so late waiting out the storm? I'd had too much to drink, and had excused myself to go upstairs. Elise followed me to my bedroom. I insisted that she leave, but she undressed and threw herself at me. Before I knew it, things progressed, and we . . ."

Thomas was stunned. "Are you saying that *she* seduced *you*? You expect me to believe this?"

"It is the truth, as embarrassed as I am to admit it. I woke up the next morning with the world's worst hangover, and only the vaguest memory of what had happened. She called to remind me of it. She claimed that she had never been with a man before, which meant that she had never done it with you. Is that true?"

"Of course it is true. I think you know me well enough to realize *I* would never compromise such a woman."

"Well, I never meant to, either. But she insisted that she loved me, and that I was now obliged to marry her."

Thomas could see where this was going, and he didn't like it. He knew Elise had chosen Saunders over him to secure the title of marchioness, and he had hated her for it. He hated Saunders for stealing her away. But could it really be true that Elise had been so cold and calculating as to stoop to seducing his friend and *forcing* him into marriage? If so, although Saunders certainly wasn't blameless in the affair, it did remove a bit of the sting from it.

A memory from that summer three years ago surfaced in his mind: he was strolling on the beach along the cliffs below Trevelyan Manor, enjoying the wind in his face and the sight and sound of the crashing waves nearby. He had lost sight of Elise and Saunders. When he rounded a bend in the cliff, he saw Elise stroll up behind Saunders. He was seated on the rocks. She threw her arms around him. Saunders had immediately risen and backed away; even though he tried to laugh it off, his discomfort upon seeing Thomas had been immense.

It was there right in front of me, all along, he told himself. *But I was too blind to see it.*

"I felt like a total heel, Longford, but don't you see? After what happened—for all I knew, she might have been with child. I felt obligated to do the right thing. I didn't care about her money. I *was* attracted to her. I told myself that all is fair in love and war, that *I* was the woman's choice. All miserable excuses, I know."

"Why did you not tell me this at the time?"

"I wanted to, but I couldn't face you. I agreed to marry her, even knowing it would greatly disappoint my parents and my cousin." Saunders shook his head and let out a disgusted sigh. "I lived to regret it. On board the ship to America, I began to see that we were very different people who wanted different things from life. When we reached Cincinnati, this became even more clear. I understood, then, that she wanted the title of marchioness to improve the social standing of her family in that city, where she insisted she preferred to live, at least part of the time. I did not think much of her family, and was not fond of Ohio. I came to realize that if I married her, I would be a miserable wretch to my dying day. She also came to see that a union between us would be a mistake. When a month had passed, and it became certain that she was not carrying my heir, we amicably broke it off, and I came home. Ever since, I have been trying to explain and apologize, to no avail." The look of sincere contrition in Saunders's eyes was unmistakable. "Longford: I am more sorry than I can say."

Thomas processed all this for a long moment. He believed Saunders was telling the truth, but gave him a hard look. "I still think you are the biggest bastard who ever lived."

"I know I am. The question is, Can you forgive me?" Saunders's entire heart seemed to be contained in those few words.

With a tight smile, Thomas said, "I will try."

"That is all I can ask for."

The two men climbed into their respective saddles. Thomas was about to head off, when he suddenly heard Miss Watson's voice in his mind: *I hope, someday, you can forgive the Earl of Saunders. . . . Resentment and hatred are wounds that only fester as time goes by. But they can be healed by forgiveness.*

The pain of it all still seared him, and he had hated this man for so long. Was he ready to let go of that? He paused. That he could see even an inkling of anything remotely positive in this situation was almost unthinkable. And yet . . . "Saunders," he called out.

The man looked back at him.

"I am beginning to think," Thomas acknowledged slowly, "that you may have helped me dodge a bullet."

"I know *I* did. Indeed I hoped, prayed, that you would come to see it that way."

Thomas hesitated, then silently tipped his hat to his old friend.

Saunders's mouth widened into a smile as he returned the gesture, before the two men rode off in separate directions for home.

"I am so sorry, Miss Watson," Julia said through her tears.

"As you should be. Promise me you'll never disappear like that again."

"I promise," Julia vowed. "Thomas was so angry when he saw Lord Saunders. Do you think he will ever forgive me?"

"I'm sure he will."

Alexandra had been relieved when Julia returned to the nursery after her ride, but the stern reprimand on her lips had died at the sight of Julia's anguished face. Something, Alexandra thought, must have happened at Trevelyan Manor to upset the girl. Wanting a private moment with her, Alexandra gave Lillie permission to read in her favorite window seat in the gallery. Now, reaching across the nursery-room table to take Julia's hands, Alexandra added softly, "Do you want to tell me what happened?"

Julia burst into fresh tears and pulled her hands away, covering her face as if to hide her embarrassment. "Oh, Miss Watson! He hates me!"

Alexandra deduced that they were no longer discussing Longford or the Earl of Saunders. "Is this about Lord Saunders's younger brother? What did you say his name was?"

"James," Julia nodded tremulously.

"How old is James?"

"Sixteen."

A year older than Julia, then. "Is that why you rode to Trevelyan Manor? To see him?"

"No! Well, it is part of the reason. I had heard that he was home on leave from Eton. But I wanted to see Helen, too. I thought if I had to stay away from them a minute longer, I would die. And I was so angry that Thomas would not let us go to the party." Julia dried her eyes and took a breath. "So I decided to go first thing in the morning, before anyone could stop me."

"How were you received, arriving at such an hour?"

"Lady Trevelyan was so kind and gracious! She invited me to join them for breakfast. It was simply *heaven* to see Helen again. But although I smiled at James several times, he never *once* looked my way."

"Oh dear." Alexandra reminded herself that matters of the heart were deeply felt, no matter what one's age.

"Later, I went over to speak to him. But I could not think

of anything to say, except to compliment him on his boots. He just made the most awful face and ran away without a word!" Julia's mortification was obvious. "He hates me, Miss Watson!"

"I'm sure that's not true. I've heard it on good authority that sometimes, when a young man likes a girl, it makes him tongue-tied. So even though he is speechless or appears to be ignoring you, it may be that he secretly admires you."

Julia's cheeks grew pink, and her spirits visibly rose. "Do you think so?"

"It is entirely possible. In any case, I wouldn't worry. You're a smart, capable, and beautiful young lady. And you're still very young. When you come of age, you'll have any number of beaux on your arm."

"I hope so, Miss Watson."

For the rest of the evening, however, Julia's eyes kept darting worriedly to the nursery door, as if she expected Longford to appear there at any moment to reprove her. Alexandra also thought he might come. Although she didn't look forward to Julia being punished, Alexandra was curious to learn what had come of his encounter with Lord Saunders. But he stayed away.

They heard no more from him until the next morning, when Martha swept into the nursery with their breakfast.

"I'm sent with a message for you all from His Lordship," Martha announced as she laid the table.

Alexandra smiled as she removed the silver dome from her plate to reveal another delicious-looking meal of eggs and ham. "What message?"

"I'm to say that dinner won't be served in the nursery today like usual."

"Why not?" Julia and Lillie asked at the same moment.

"Because," Martha intoned, struggling to hide her own surprise over the matter, "you're all requested to join His Lordship in the dinin' room tonight, prompt-like at seven o'clock."

CHAPTER NINETEEN

"You must be mistaken, Martha," Alexandra observed.

Her heart warmed to think that she might take credit for this unusual invitation. But if she'd learned one thing since coming to Polperran House, it was that servants and governesses had their place. And under no circumstances did they ever dine with their master. "You must have misunderstood. His Lordship only means for Julia and Lillie to dine with him, not me."

"Beggin' yer pardon, miss, but he said all three of you are to come. Mrs. Mitchell asked about it especially. She said, 'Miss Watson as well?' all wide-eyed like, and he was most particular. 'Miss Watson as well,' says he."

Julia leapt up with delight the moment Martha left the room. "What shall we wear?"

"I'm going to wear my white dress with the yellow sash," Lillie decided, unable to contain her smile.

"I suppose it will have to be my green frock, it is the best after all," Julia mused. Turning to study Alexandra's dress, she added, "But you cannot wear *that*, Miss Watson."

Alexandra shrugged. Since she'd come to Polperran

House, she'd never been obliged to dress for dinner. Her mind drifted with a wistful pang to the dozens of spectacular Worth gowns she'd worn during the Season. She may have hated the way she'd been on display during those weeks, but she had to admit, she'd felt beautiful. In her current mode of dress, she felt dowdy. She'd feel dowdier still at a dinner table with Lord Longford.

"I have little choice, Julia. It's this dress or the black one. Take your pick."

"I have a better idea." Julia smiled. "Let us look in the attic."

At Julia's insistence, they applied to Mrs. Mitchell. Although the housekeeper's nose seemed out of joint, and she muttered about what she called "an unprecedented state of affairs," she agreed to let them forage in the attic and borrow whatever they liked.

Alexandra and the girls spent over an hour in the attic, looking through all the gowns on the racks. But they were old-fashioned, most had been made for women of a different size and shape than Alexandra, and many were moth-eaten. Eventually they had to give up the enterprise.

"It is too bad," Julia said with a sigh as they returned to the nursery.

Later that afternoon, however, while Alexandra was in the midst of a geography lesson in the schoolroom, John came in with a large box and said, "This just come fer ye, Miss Watson. Where shall I put it?"

"For me?" Alexandra couldn't imagine what it could be. "Set it on the table, John, and thank you."

"His Lordship sent this as well." John handed Alexandra a small envelope inscribed with her name, then left.

Perplexed, Alexandra removed the note from the envelope. It simply read:

> *Miss Watson,*
> > *For tonight.*
> > *With my best wishes,*
> > > *Longford*

Julia studied the label on the box and squealed, "Oh! It is from our dressmaker in London!"

"Open it!" Lillie cried.

Alexandra's heart began to dance as she opened the box and pushed aside the tissue paper. Within lay a new evening gown. As she withdrew it, she couldn't help but gasp. It was a confection of royal blue silk. Elaborate pin tucks decorated the skirts, the waist was cinched in by a brocade bodice, and tiny embroidered flowers in the same vivid shade of blue embellished the low, scooped neckline.

"Oh! How lovely!" Julia exclaimed.

Alexandra was flabbergasted. Longford must have ordered the gown some time ago. She could hardly believe that he'd bought an evening gown for her, a governess. He couldn't afford such extravagance. Still, she was thrilled beyond words.

None of them could concentrate on geography after that. They all went off to their rooms to dress. Since the new gown had been made by the seamstress who already had Alexandra's measurements, it fit perfectly. After Julia came in to help to fasten all the hooks in back, Alexandra couldn't help but do a twirl and then survey her reflection in her small looking glass. It was such a treat to wear something beautiful again. She liked it better than many of her gowns by Worth, most of which had been too ostentatious for her taste.

Over the past weeks, Alexandra had done the best she could with her hair, through time and practice eventually achieving a style she considered becoming. Still, even her best efforts weren't suitable for an evening gown like this one.

"What do you suggest?" The girls still wore their hair down and long, and there was no lady's maid at Polperran House.

"I have been studying the magazines and practicing on my hair since I was a girl," Julia announced, "and I know just what to do."

Bringing Alexandra into her own bedroom and sitting her down at the dressing table, Julia proceeded to curl and pin up Alexandra's tresses into a style almost as elegant as those the French hairdressers had achieved during the London Season.

"You're a wizard," Alexandra enthused when the make-over was complete. For the first time in weeks, Alexandra felt she looked like her old self. "Thank you, Julia." She clasped the girl's hand with affection.

Julia beamed, squeezing her hand in return. "No one would ever guess you to be a governess now, Miss Watson. You look like a queen."

Before going downstairs, Alexandra made sure the girls' sashes were adjusted just so, and that their hair had been brushed to its brightest sheen.

Now that the appointed hour was almost upon them, she was worried on Julia's behalf. Longford had yet to confront his sister about her misbehavior the day before. Alexandra knew the subject must come up this evening, and hoped he wouldn't be too hard on her.

She also felt a little awkward, recalling her conversation with Longford the evening before about Lord Saunders. She still believed that what she'd said was right, even if he hadn't wanted to hear it. But she got a sick feeling in her stomach every time she thought about the cause of his past heartbreak, the words *title-grubbing American heiress* still ringing in her ears.

How would he react, were he to discover that the stunning dress he'd just bought wasn't for a poor governess, but for one of the very heiresses he despised?

She would just have to make sure he didn't find out.

Thomas leaned close to the mirror and finished adjusting his white bow tie. The last time he'd actually dressed for dinner was at Christmas. What a dismal evening *that* had turned out to be. Tonight, he hoped, would be different.

"Which cuff links would you like, my lord?" Hutchens, who for years had been downgraded to play both valet and butler, offered him a choice of two sets in velvet-lined boxes.

"The gold ones, thank you." Thomas scooped up the links. As Hutchens returned the others to the dresser drawer, Thomas noted a frown on the servant's face. "What is it, Hutchens? Do you prefer the silver ones?"

"No, my lord. The gold ones are an excellent choice."

"Yet you seem displeased about something." Thomas inserted the gold links into the cuffs of his white dress shirt. "I thought you would be delighted to see me dress tonight, and to dine with my sisters."

"Indeed I am, my lord."

"Why do I not believe you? Is it because I invited Miss Watson?"

"You may invite whomever you like to dine with you, Your Lordship." Despite Hutchens's stoic words, there was an unmistakable hint of disapproval in his expression and tone.

"Yes I *may*. Have you forgotten what last Christmas was like? Or any one of Julia's and Lillie's birthdays? Every time I have ever sat down to a meal with my sisters, it has been the most damnable, awkward affair."

"Those occasions, regrettably, were not as pleasant as they could have been," Hutchens agreed, removing Thomas's black tailcoat from the hanger and holding it up to him.

"Not as pleasant?" Thomas shook his head in disbelief as he thrust his arms into the sleeves of the tailcoat and then buttoned it up. "Hutchens, they were horrific. The hour ticked by in miserable silence. It is why I have left them up in the nursery as a rule. Tonight, however, I have something in particular to say to Julia. I imagine things might get a bit prickly. She and Lillie seem to like the new governess a great deal. For that reason, I invited Miss Watson. I pray that her inclusion might help things along."

The memory of Miss Watson suddenly filled his mind. He felt no lingering bitterness over the manner in which she'd spoken to him about Saunders. In the end, she'd been right, and he admired her for speaking up. He enjoyed how animated she was, such a contrast to the prim English girls he'd known, who kept their opinions and emotions in reserve. He couldn't forget the way she had looked that morning, running up to him at the stables with roses in her cheeks. Or at the Grecian temple, her eyes the color of the bluebells that surrounded them.

That day had been a kind of exquisite torture for him. How he'd longed to be alone with her, to once again feel her body, to taste those honey lips. But that wasn't all he'd longed for—still longed for. He wanted her in his bed. He wanted to feel the passion he knew would erupt if they ever gave in to the feelings that simmered between them. Something which, damn it all, he knew could never happen.

Thinking about the gown he had ordered for her the day before he'd left town made him smile. Ever since he had painted Miss Watson in Mrs. Norton's white satin dress, he'd dreamt of seeing her in something similar. This new dress, he thought with satisfaction, was probably the most elegant thing she had worn in years, if ever.

He might not be able to touch her again, but he could look at her. And look at her he would.

"I am doing this for the girls," he told Hutchens emphatically. "To make them more comfortable. I know it breaks with all precedent and every rule of society to invite a governess to dinner. But since no one else will ever know, what difference does it make?"

Since her arrival at Polperran House, Alexandra had only glimpsed the dining room once in passing. As they entered, she paused a moment to take it in.

A magnificent green-and-white Wedgwood ceiling overlooked the large and airy room, its effect somewhat marred by a long crack and a water stain that bloomed from one corner. A fire burned in an ornately carved fireplace, and light danced from candles in the crystal chandelier, casting intricate shapes on walls papered in faded damask with a pattern of green leaves. An ancient hutch filled with china and glassware occupied one wall, a long sideboard the other. The immense table, elegantly set at one end with fine china, crystal, and silver for four, was surrounded by eighteen elegantly carved chairs upholstered in a fraying green-and-gold-striped fabric.

Despite the telltale signs of age and decay, it was a lovely and gracious room. Similar, Alexandra reflected, to the style of the dining room in their house in Poughkeepsie. Not ridiculously overdone like the palatial chamber her mother had built in their mansion in New York City, with its table to seat three dozen, its frescoed ceiling gilded in genuine gold leaf, and the wall-to-wall Numidian marble paneling.

The only other occupant of the room was John, acting

footman, who stood at attention, decked out in livery. He gaped at Alexandra as if in wonder when she entered, then clamped his mouth shut. Julia and Lillie moved to stand behind chairs opposite the head of the table, presumably their assigned seats. Alexandra moved to the chair beside Lillie. Hutchens now entered and took up his position beside the footman, darting the merest glance at Alexandra but displaying no reaction at all. Moments later, Lord Longford strode in.

Alexandra caught her breath.

He was dressed in white tie and tails. Although it was routine evening attire, she'd never seen Longford so elegantly dressed. With his neatly combed short blond hair, his gleaming brown eyes, and his trim mustache in an otherwise clean-shaven face, he looked unbelievably handsome.

Her heart seemed to skip several beats. She suddenly wished that they were alone together, not flanked by servants and two impressionable young ladies. She wished she could cross to his side and touch him, had to force herself to remain rooted to the spot by her chair.

He moved briskly to the head of the table. His gaze immediately found Alexandra's and he paused a long moment, taking her in, his expression so filled with undisguised approval, she felt a frisson of pleasure ripple through her.

He cleared his throat, turning his glance on his sisters. "You are looking well this evening, girls." They beamed in answer as he nodded toward Alexandra, adding in a slightly gruffer tone, "As are you, Miss Watson."

"Thank you." *You are looking well yourself,* she wanted to

add. "Thank you for the gown, my lord. It was most unexpected and very thoughtful."

"It was my pleasure."

Hutchens pulled out Longford's chair. His Lordship sat. Then Hutchens and John helped each of the female members of the party to sit, with Alexandra the last to be accommodated. It felt divine to be in a proper dining room again, to be waited upon. Alexandra hadn't realized how much she'd missed it.

As she took her seat, Alexandra darted another glance at Longford, and held back a smile. The idea that he'd invited them all to dine, and had gone to the effort of dressing for the occasion, filled her with admiration. Even more than she'd felt the day he took them sketching, an event which had happened by accident and mild coercion. He'd arranged *this* evening on his own. She had never liked him so well as at that moment.

Longford unfolded his napkin on his lap. The girls and Alexandra followed suit. She was pleased to see the young ladies displaying their best table manners. Sitting with them in this formal setting, Alexandra couldn't help but recall the many thousands of times she'd dined in similar fashion with her own family, her father at the head of the table, her mother seated imperiously at the foot. The mood had been very different, however. Her mother had constantly criticized everyone and everything, including the food and the staff. Her father had often shared the news of the day and asked challenging questions, while she and her sisters had exchanged an almost constant barrage of lively chatter.

An awareness came over her of how special those intimate mealtimes had been, how precious was the essence of family, even an imperfect family. How dearly she missed them all.

"You may pour the wine, Hutchens." Longford's voice broke into her thoughts.

Alexandra had to swallow hard over a suddenly constricted throat. Taking in the faces around her, she reminded herself that she was part of a new family now, even if she was an outsider and her inclusion was temporary. And she was happy to be here.

As the butler filled Longford's glass from a bottle of red, the earl glanced at Alexandra. "Miss Watson? Would you care for some wine?"

"Yes, thank you." It was the first time she'd been offered the beverage since her arrival at Polperran House. She took a sip, appreciating its robust flavor. "Mmmm. A Chateau Lafite Rothschild, if I'm not mistaken?"

Longford's eyebrows lifted, as if surprised she'd recognized it. "Indeed. It is from our own cellar, which my father kept very well stocked."

Alexandra felt her cheeks grow warm. From his expression, it was clear he thought it strange that a governess would be familiar with such an expensive wine. "I've only had the pleasure of tasting it once," she said quickly, "some years ago. But I've never forgotten it."

Longford responded with a comprehending nod.

John and Hutchens backed away to stand at attention by the wall. Some minutes ensued as the girls gazed expectantly at their brother. Longford tapped his fingers on the tabletop, looking uncomfortable, as if unsure how to begin.

Hoping to ease the tension, Alexandra said: "It was a wonderful surprise, my lord, to receive your generous invitation to dine this evening."

"Ah, yes. As to that." Longford cleared his throat, glancing briefly at the girls. "You may be wondering why you are here, as it is not one of our usual special occasions. I simply thought, as you girls are getting older now, instead of taking all your meals in the nursery, it might be nice to dine together occasionally." He darted Alexandra a glance, his eyes silently acknowledging that this had been *her* idea. "And, as you are accustomed to dining with your governess, I thought I would include Miss Watson as well."

"Thank you," exclaimed Julia. Lillie's smile also conveyed her delight.

"Keep in mind, I said *occasionally*. Do not expect this to be a daily event."

"Again, it was a thoughtful gesture," Alexandra put in. "We are all happy and grateful to be here."

"I hope that will still be the case, when you hear what I have to say next." He gave Julia a look.

All color drained from Julia's face. Before Longford could say more, Martha and Susan entered with the first course. Fragrant bowls of soup were distributed, and the maids left. Longford took a spoonful of the broth, then said, "We need to speak about what happened yesterday, Julia."

Julia stared into her bowl, as if she'd lost her appetite.

Although Alexandra had anticipated that this was coming, she felt sympathy for her young charge.

"Do you realize the kind of trouble you might have gotten into, Julia, riding off to Trevelyan Manor all on your own, without telling anyone where you were going?"

Julia shook her head bleakly.

"A stranger might have accosted you. Your horse might have thrown you, and left you broken and bleeding. Not to mention the lack of propriety in making an unannounced visit at such an ungodly hour. What must Lord and Lady Trevelyan think of us?"

"I know what I did was wrong." Julia's voice wavered. "I am *so* sorry."

"You flagrantly disobeyed a rule. I feel it my duty to punish you for this offense. Perhaps I ought to forbid you from riding Windermere for several weeks, or a month altogether."

"Oh, *please* don't!" cried Julia anxiously. "Please!"

Alexandra rushed to the young lady's defense. "Isn't that a bit harsh? If this is the first time she's ever—"

Longford held up a hand to silence her. "However," he continued matter-of-factly, "as Miss Watson is so keen to point out, it is your first offense of this kind. Of any kind, for that matter. Yesterday, when I found you, I noted that you were sorry. I have therefore decided to let you off without a penalty."

"You have?" Julia nearly sagged with relief.

"Should you ever transgress in this manner again, rest assured that your riding privileges will indeed be revoked, for a period of some duration."

"I understand. *Thank you*, Thomas. Thank you."

Alexandra, greatly pleased by the good sense and kind-heartedness of Longford's decision, lifted her gaze to his. In his eyes she read a question, as if he were seeking her approval. Flattered to think that her opinion mattered to him, she smiled and lifted her wineglass in silent salute.

He returned her smile, then sipped his own glass of wine. Everyone ate their soup. In a spirited voice, Longford said: "Now, I have another piece of good news."

"What?" Lillie asked.

"I have written to accept the invitation to Lord and Lady Trevelyan's garden party on Tuesday."

Shouts of excitement burst forth from both girls.

"What made you change your mind, my lord?" Alexandra asked, although she was beginning to suspect the answer.

"Well, thanks to my sister's unauthorized adventure yesterday, I was obliged to talk to Lord Saunders. And our former, friendly relations have been restored."

Alexandra knew there was a great deal in that statement that had been left unsaid. "I'm glad."

"Does this mean I can see Helen anytime I want?" asked Julia.

"And *I* can see Anna anytime?" interjected Lillie.

"Within reason," Longford replied.

The girls could barely contain their happiness, and immediately began chatting across the table. The main course was soon served, roast beef with all the trimmings. As they began to eat, Longford looked to be searching for a new topic of conversation. It was Julia who broke the silence.

"Tell us about New York, Miss Watson."

Alexandra tensed. "New York?"

"An excellent notion, Julia." Longford turned his gaze on Alexandra. "You attended Vassar College, I recall, but I know very little else about you."

Since arriving at Polperran House, for obvious reasons, Alexandra had spoken as little about herself as possible. But now all three were looking at her, expectant and waiting. If she were careful, she decided, she could answer the question honestly. "Well, I was born and grew up in Poughkeepsie."

"Poughkeepsie?" Lillie repeated. "What a strange name."

"It's a small city on the Hudson River, north of New York City, distinguished by the fact that it was New York's second capital shortly after the American Revolution. The name comes from an American Indian word meaning, 'reed-covered lodge by the little-water place.'"

The girls laughed.

"I think you mentioned that your father was a banker?" Longford remarked.

Alexandra nodded, keeping her expression even. "We had a nice two-story house, painted white. Nothing like Polperran House, of course. But I loved it dearly. It had a wide front porch and a small garden in the back where I used to play with my sisters."

"You have sisters?" Julia said, her fork halfway to her mouth.

"I have two: Madeleine and Kathryn."

"Are they older or younger?" Lillie asked.

"I'm the eldest. We're a year apart in age. Some of the

games you and I have played the past few weeks are pastimes that my sisters and I enjoyed at your age."

"No wonder they're so much fun," Julia observed.

"I'm so glad you enjoy them." Alexandra felt Longford's eyes on her, and noticed he was smiling.

A plaintive note filled Lillie's voice as she asked quietly: "Did you have a mother?"

Alexandra's heart caught. "Yes. I still do."

Julia looked interested. "Do you ever get to see her?"

"I haven't seen her in a while."

"Do you miss her?" Lillie asked softly.

"Sometimes," Alexandra replied carefully, "I think that being parted from your mother only makes you stronger."

Another silence fell, as everyone focused on eating their meal. A few moments later, Julia asked: "Miss Watson, did you ever have a beau?"

Alexandra stifled a smile. It was just the sort of question Julia would ask. "A beau? Not really, no."

"So, you never received a proposal of marriage?" pressed Julia.

"I didn't say that. Actually, I received two offers, but I turned them—" Alexandra broke off, cursing herself. That can of worms was better left unopened.

"Why did you turn them down?" Lillie asked.

"The men did not suit me." Again, Alexandra felt Longford's eyes on her, and her heart skittered.

"I hope you *never* marry," Lillie insisted. "I hope you stay here *forever*."

"She can't stay here forever," Julia pointed out reasonably.

"*We* will marry one day, and have no need for a governess. Although," she added, darting a glance at Alexandra, "I am glad you are here *now*, Miss Watson."

"Thank you, Julia. So am I."

Thomas sipped his coffee, listening to Miss Watson's and the girls' amiable chatter as they finished their plum cake.

Things had gone rather well tonight.

It had been a stroke of genius to invite Miss Watson to dine with them. An even bigger stroke of genius to buy her the new gown. Even in that black dress of hers that screamed *governess* with every stitch, she was more beautiful than any woman he had ever met. But in this new royal blue silk creation, which showed off her creamy skin and décolletage to perfection, she was breathtaking. All evening long, it had been a pleasure not only to listen to her, but to sit and look at her.

It had, of course, been frustrating as well. He would have far preferred to dine with her alone. An intimate evening, just the two of them conversing about literature and art, followed by . . . further intimacies. As it was, he'd found his mind constantly wandering to the things he *wished* he was doing with her upstairs in his bedroom.

He gave himself a mental shake, returning his thoughts to the proper channel.

All of his instincts for the evening had proved right. Miss Watson's presence here had made everything less awkward. She had been helpful—indispensable, really—in getting the conversation going. He'd been obliged to reprimand Julia, but he'd taken care of it in a way that seemed to fill his sister with relief, and appeared to have met with Miss Watson's approval.

Not that he was required to satisfy Miss Watson in such things. But it gratified him to think that she *had* been pleased. After the difficult part was gotten over, and Miss Watson had talked a bit about herself, things had progressed in such a cheerful and congenial manner. He had truly enjoyed himself, and believed that Julia and Lillie had as well.

A fact which was verified some minutes later, after he nodded good night to the girls and they sped out of the room, promising to go to bed straightaway.

The table was being cleared, leaving himself and Miss Watson briefly alone.

"Thank you," she said in a low voice, coming up to him as they both rose from their chairs.

"For what?" His heart quickened as he gazed down into her blue eyes. She really was absolutely stunning, and in that low-cut gown. . . .

"For dinner. For the gown. For being so lenient with Julia. She was dreading what you might say or do. Her visit to Trevelyan Manor yesterday was actually a rather heartbreaking experience for her."

"Oh? Why is that?"

"Julia has a crush on James Grayson, which is apparently unrequited."

"Ah. So that explains why she looked so unhappy when I encountered her. I wondered."

"I did my best to comfort her afterward, but there were a great many tears."

"I appreciate you being there for her." Thomas was touched by her sensitivity, and knew that he would have been useless at such a task.

They moved to the door and said their good nights. He was sorry to see the evening end. She was about to go, but turned back and said: "I'm so glad to hear that you mended fences with Lord Saunders."

"So am I."

She looked up at him then, a thousand questions in her eyes.

At that moment, Hutchens returned. Thomas felt it best to keep the details of that matter to himself. "Suffice it to say," he replied with a smile, "that I have a new perspective on the matter."

CHAPTER TWENTY

The morning sun shone through the mullioned windows of Thomas's study, bathing the room in natural light.

As he ate breakfast, Thomas realized that, for the first time in years, he felt no pain over Saunders's betrayal and Elise's desertion. Quite the reverse, in fact. It was as if a great weight had been lifted from his shoulders. Since Saunders's revelations, Thomas had become increasingly convinced that he had escaped what would have been a calamitous marriage.

If anything, he felt he owed Saunders a debt of gratitude for bringing to light his former fiancée's true nature.

Glancing about the room as he drank his coffee, it suddenly struck Thomas how gloomy his study was. He couldn't do anything about the faded furnishings and decaying fabric on the walls. The pictures, however—the hideous hunting scenes, and the paintings of horses and dogs—they had all been hung there by former masters of the house. Perhaps it was time to change them.

He thought about the paintings he had completed in Italy, then banished to the attic in a fit of . . . what? Temper? Self-pity? Perhaps both. Well, those feelings were gone.

He stood, filled with a sudden yearning to see those works of art again.

He dashed up the grand staircase, then up the steps to the attic, emerging into that dusty space for the first time in years. Bending low beneath the sloping ceiling, he found his canvases lined up against the wall exactly where he had left them. Locating an old rag, he wiped grime from the inside of the nearby windows, letting a bit more light into the cluttered space. Then he crouched down and looked through the paintings, some of which he had forgotten entirely. Others were like coming upon long lost friends.

He set aside the works of his youth that, although favorites of his departed mother, deserved no better fate than to evoke fond memories upon future attic viewings. A half dozen others, however, from his Italian period, he determined to be quite good. These he would enjoy seeing again on the walls of his home.

One painting in particular stood out as being head and shoulders above the rest. It was the landscape of the Italian garden that Miss Watson had mentioned. She had called it a masterpiece, comparable to the paintings she had admired in the museums of New York City and Europe. He couldn't say if it truly fell into that caliber. But he had to admit, it was one of his better works.

Thomas picked up the painting and set it atop a trunk, where it caught the light from the window. As he stepped back to study it, he was reminded of the pleasure he'd had in painting it. The sense of accomplishment he had felt when he'd finished.

Except that he'd never felt as though it *was* quite finished. Somehow, he'd always sensed that something was missing from this particular painting.

As he stared at it, Thomas suddenly realized what was missing. And he knew precisely how to rectify the matter.

Alexandra paused in her tracks. Three days had passed since she and the girls had dined with Lord Longford, one of the most pleasant evenings she'd spent in years. The invitation had not been repeated, but since then, Longford had stopped by the nursery on two separate occasions to say hello. Once, she had even spied him from afar in the garden, sitting on a bench, and was almost positive she'd seen a sketchbook in his lap and a pencil in his hand.

Now, having just left the nursery, intending to fetch a book from the schoolroom, Alexandra was distracted by a faint aroma coming from further along the corridor.

The unmistakable smell of oil paint.

A smile worked at her lips. Could this mean what she hoped it did? Alexandra followed her nose down the hall and around the corner to a distant part of the house she had not yet seen. The further she went, the stronger the smell became. When she came to an open doorway from which the scent seemed to emanate, she stopped, peering around the doorjamb.

Afternoon sun flooded the room with light. The room appeared not to have been used in a long time. What little furniture it contained was covered by white sheets, all except for a small table, upon which were spread the familiar tools of an oil painter's trade. In the center of the room, the Earl of Longford stood at an easel, deep in concentration as he worked on a canvas.

Although curious to see what he was working on, Alexandra had no wish to disturb him. Silently, she withdrew and retraced her steps back to her own region of the house, warmth radiating through her.

The day soon arrived for the garden party at Trevelyan Manor.

As Alexandra looked the girls over to make sure they were tidy and neat, Julia said, "Do not forget your bonnet, Miss Watson."

"My bonnet? But surely I am not to attend the party."

"Of course you are." Julia eyed Alexandra as if that were something even a simpleton should know. "We could not go without you. Governesses are expected to watch over all the children. Not that *we* require any looking after," she added with an impish smile.

Alexandra received this news with mixed feelings. Since her arrival in Cornwall, the only place she'd been beyond the perimeter of Polperran estate was Longford village. Trevelyan Manor was in the other direction, fives miles away on the coast, which she was very interested to see.

On the other hand, she wasn't keen on the idea of attending a party. She'd had her fill of them in London. She worried that at a social event like this, she might be recognized, but then decided that was unlikely. The people she'd met in town were still *in town*, for the Season. This was to be a relatively small gathering, attended, she'd been told, only by the social elite of this remote part of Cornwall.

Unfortunately, she had nothing to wear other than her blue day dress, for the new silk gown was far too elegant for an afternoon outing. There was nothing for it, however; she double-checked with Longford, who insisted that she was not only expected, but he relied upon her to go.

The June sun had painted the sky a bright, cloudless blue. Longford rode alongside on horseback while John drove the coach carrying Alexandra and girls. For some time, they rumbled past endless fields. Eventually they crested a hill, opening up a new vista, and Alexandra drew in an appreciative breath.

A vast green valley stretched before them. Boulders of various shapes and sizes lay scattered willy-nilly, as if tossed about by giants. The road wound down through the valley like a ribbon, ending at an enormous great house of granite and gray slate, surrounded by vast gardens.

"There it is." Julia's eyes were glued to the window. "Trevelyan Manor."

As impressive-looking as the manor house was, the most spectacular aspect of the scene was the backdrop. Less than a quarter mile beyond, a stretch of low, green cliffs undulated around a curve of azure bay, where the sea spewed white foam as it crashed onto blackened rocks and a golden sand beach.

Alexandra drank in its beauty as the carriage made its approach. Longford trotted up to the house and dismounted from his steed as they all arrived.

Their party was kindly received in the front drawing room, which was in many ways similar to the one at Polperran House, except that here, the furnishings appeared to be new and well maintained. Lord and Lady Trevelyan, a beautifully dressed middle-aged couple, professed their delight in receiving Lord Longford and his sisters, making no reference to the gap of years since their last such encounter.

"Where is Saunders?" Longford asked, glancing around.

"Sorry, old chap," Lord Trevelyan replied. "Charles left for London yesterday. Or was it Truro? You know how he is, itchy feet, always dashing off somewhere, not content to remain at home for more than a week or two at a time."

"You will find the rest of the family in the garden, however, along with the other guests," Lady Trevelyan remarked. "I do hope you enjoy yourselves."

Longford bowed, while Alexandra and the girls curtsied their thanks.

They were quickly ushered outside. A wide green lawn wound down past formal gardens, overlooking low cliffs with a superb view of a dark rocky cove and beyond that, the sparkling blue sea. Alexandra inhaled, relishing the tang of salt in the crisp air and the sight and sounds of distant swooping seagulls. Several long tables were set up for a meal to be served later in the afternoon. Well-dressed people strolled the grounds, chatting, while children of various ages played lawn games.

It was a lovely scene, evoking memories of similar parties Alexandra had attended over the years with her family. She was beginning to think this might prove to be a pleasant afternoon after all, when Longford directed, "It looks like the children's table is over there." He indicated a table a little distance away from the main activity, where a handful of women in drab dresses and nanny uniforms were pushing infants in perambulators or supervising young children. Alexandra understood this was where she was meant to position herself.

"I see, thank you."

A red-haired gentleman who looked to be Longford's age strode up to him with a hearty greeting.

"Wexham! It has been an age." Longford glanced at his sisters. "Behave yourselves, girls. Whatever Miss Watson says, goes."

The girls nodded their promise. The two men walked off, conversing. Lillie spotted her friend Anna, and gaining Alexandra's permission, ran off to greet her. "Stay in sight," Alexandra called out.

"Oh no," Julia said suddenly, under her breath.

Alexandra followed the direction of Julia's gaze. A congenial-looking youth with brown wavy hair was engaged in a game of lawn bowling. "Is that James Grayson?" she whispered.

Julia nodded, her cheeks crimson.

"Remember what we discussed. You don't need his attention or approval, or that of any young man. Just be yourself, find your friend, and have a good time."

Julia pressed her lips together with determination. "I will."

At that moment, another young lady strode up, attired in a stylish gown of deep rose sprigged muslin, her soft brown ringlets perfectly arranged beneath her matching bonnet. "Julia," she murmured solemnly. "I thought you would never come."

After the girls exchanged embraces, Julia turned to Alexandra. "Allow me to introduce my friend, Lady Helen Grayson. Helen, this is my governess, Miss Watson."

"It's a pleasure to make your acquaintance," Alexandra said with a smile.

Helen merely nodded with quiet dignity, her intelligent eyes briefly assessing Alexandra, before glancing at her feet.

After gaining Alexandra's permission to stroll through the formal gardens and return in an hour, Julia dashed off happily with her friend. Alexandra stood still for a moment, taking in the scene.

At nearly all the parties and balls she'd attended over the years, other than the weeks of the London Season, she'd been in the warm and welcome company of her sisters. As heiresses, they'd been feted and sought out by many of the men at the affair. It felt strange to be so alone, in a sea of people where no one even gave her a second look. She felt unnecessary, unwanted, invisible.

Well, she reminded herself, this is who she was now. And it wasn't forever.

The reminder that her time in Cornwall would eventually end gave Alexandra a sharp, unexpected pang. So much had happened, it was hard to believe she'd only been here a little over three weeks. She'd never imagined that she'd be a governess in England or anywhere else, but she had to admit, there were many aspects of the occupation she enjoyed.

When it came time to leave, she realized with surprise, she would miss the feeling of usefulness she'd discovered as a teacher, the daily interaction with her pupils, the satisfaction of imparting knowledge, of a job well done. She would dearly miss the girls themselves. Not just the girls. She would miss . . .

Alexandra drew a mental curtain over any further thoughts in that vein. In about two months, she'd have the money she needed to sail home. Back to her own family. Back to Vassar College. Where she belonged.

Although she longed to wander down to the beach, Alexandra felt that would be irresponsible. She was here to watch over the girls, and needed to remain where they could find her. Instead, she made her way to the area Longford had pointed out.

Amidst the group of nannies and governesses, a plump woman in a gray gown was seated on a chair not far from the children's table. She looked to be in her mid-forties, had a pinched face, and appeared content to watch the proceedings with no immediate responsibilities.

Alexandra took possession of the chair beside the woman and extended her hand. "Hello. I'm Lexie Watson."

"Harriet Berry," the woman responded in a clipped tone, surprised by Alexandra's proffered hand, but shaking it nonetheless. "I'm Lord and Lady Trevelyan's governess. You must be the new American governess at Polperran House?"

"I am."

"You've come a long way to watch other people's children."

The abrupt statement took Alexandra off guard. The less she offered on that score, the better. "I suppose I have."

"How are you getting along?"

"Okay, I think."

"From what I heard, those girls are a handful, with new governesses coming and going."

"Actually, they are lovely young ladies. I think they just needed someone who understands them."

"Is that so? I hope for your sake that's true. Our jobs are hard and lonely enough, without our charges plaguing the life out of us every day."

Alexandra glanced at her. "Are Helen and Anna difficult?"

"Not at all, they're very well behaved. I have it easy *here*, and on occasions such as this, practically nothing to do. But my previous positions were not so amiable. Let us not dwell, however, on the inequities of life. It's a party, and we have the ideal vantage point from which to view the proceedings. I don't suppose you know anyone?"

"No."

"Allow me to give you a running commentary."

Miss Berry pointed out a fine-looking man in clerical garb. "That's Mr. Curtis, the new vicar of Trevelyan, and a nicer young man you couldn't hope to meet. Word has it that he's looking for a wife, but three trips to Bath have so far not proven fruitful. And that," she added, indicating an attractive, dark-haired fellow in a tweed suit, who looked to be about thirty years of age, "is Dr. Hancock, the new physician in this part of the county. Lady Trevelyan is so taken with him, she won't have any other doctor treat herself or the children."

Miss Berry filled the next half hour by pointing out a great many of the people assembled around them, both male and female, giving Alexandra their names, places of residence, occupations if any, and the recent gossip she'd heard about them. They were mainly members of the gentry class, and although Alexandra found it impossible to retain all the information provided, it was an enjoyable way to pass the time.

A bevy of servants began bringing out the afternoon meal, laying the tables with platters of ham, cold chicken, cheese, bread, salads, bowls of strawberries, and an assortment of pies, tarts, and cakes.

As Alexandra observed this activity, she became aware of three women who stood nearby, conversing. One of them was a heavyset woman with a bulldog face, who might have been about fifty. She wore an extravagant white gown, an enormous plumed hat, and an expression of extreme haughtiness. This, Miss Berry had earlier explained, was Mrs. Gordon. Her husband was among the wealthiest landowners in the county. Beside her were her two daughters: young ladies splendidly dressed in summer gowns with matching bonnets and parasols.

"Look at all the nannies," commented the first young lady with a sneer. "Can you imagine being obliged to care for a crying infant at a party?"

"Why people insist on bringing children and their servants to these affairs is beyond me," declared Mrs. Gordon with a sniff. "They are far better left at home, where they belong."

"Those two must be *governesses*," observed the second young lady. "They look so dried up and poor. I thank God we are old enough now to be free of such creatures."

Alexandra felt her blood rise at these comments. Miss Berry had overhead it, too, for her face went ashen.

"Do you remember the tricks we played on our governesses?" The first young lady tittered. "When we put boot polish inside Mrs. Landers's black hat? And castor oil in Miss Ray's tea?"

"Or the time we found Miss Dickerson's private diary, stayed up all night reading it, and then threw it in the lake?" replied her sister. They both laughed.

"I never had so much trouble in my life," insisted Mrs. Gordon, "as I did searching for a suitable governess. They are a troublesome race. I sometimes think it a wonder that you girls received any education at all."

Alexandra could take no more. She rose, strode directly up to the three women, and said, "It is indeed a wonder, madam, that your daughters received any education, if you all treated their governesses in such a callous and unfeeling manner."

The matriarch gasped her outrage. "I beg your pardon?"

"Did you ever stop to think," Alexandra went on heatedly, "how lucky you were, to employ a governess to teach your children?" To the young ladies, she added: "Or how fortunate *you* both were, to have been taught at home by a woman whose sole job was to attend to your daily needs, who did her best to nurture and care for you, while coordinating your studies? There's a good reason why your mother never sent you to school, with thirty or more children in a classroom governed by a single teacher! How do you think you would have fared in *that* environment?"

The young ladies were affronted. "How dare you speak to us like this?" cried the first.

"I dare because you need to hear it!" Alexandra responded vehemently. "You complain that governesses are poor and a troublesome race. Yes: many are poor, but they are the educated daughters of the clergy and the gentry class—your own *race*, as you call it—who through some misfortune not of their own making, require a home and a means of support. How can you despise them? Have you no heart at all? One tiny twist of fate might have put you in their shoes."

"I will not stand here and be thus insulted," cried Mrs. Gordon. "Girls: let us go."

"If you would treat your governesses as human beings," Alexandra threw at the three ladies as they stalked off, "you might discover that they are interesting people in their own right!"

Alexandra's pulse pounded as she stared at the backs of the retreating ladies. She couldn't remember when she had ever felt so angry. She was glad she'd said what she did, even though it hadn't seemed to make any impression at all.

She suddenly became aware that it had grown quiet around her. Miss Berry was staring at her hands. Alexandra realized that a great many people were staring at *her*, including Julia, Lillie, and their friends. *Dear God. Had all these people been listening?*

That's when Alexandra caught sight of Lord Longford, standing nearby. From his expression, it appeared that he had heard every word.

Chapter Twenty-One

"I still cannot *believe* you said all that to Mrs. Gordon!" Julia cried, seated across from Alexandra in the carriage as they made their way home. Julia was biting her lip to keep from laughing.

"I shouldn't have." Alexandra blushed anew at the reminder of what she'd done.

After her rant, she'd kept her head down and remained in the children's area, speaking to no one other than Julia, Lillie, and Miss Berry, who'd quietly congratulated her for voicing aloud what she'd never had the nerve to say. Alexandra wasn't sure, however, that having the nerve had been a good thing, since Lord Longford had not approached her the rest of the day.

"I'm glad you did!" Lillie gushed. "You are so brave."

"I have never liked Mrs. Gordon or her daughters," Julia admitted. "They are like stuffed pigs."

"Stuffed pigs with parasols," Lillie agreed.

Despite her worries, Alexandra had to laugh at this description. For a moment, general merriment rang inside the carriage. "It isn't funny," Alexandra finally insisted, wiping tears of mirth from her eyes. "Your brother could dismiss me for speaking out like that."

"He would not dare," Julia said. "And if he does, I will insist that you stay."

"So will I," Lillie promised.

After they returned to the house, the girls raced upstairs. Lord Longford stopped Alexandra in the hallway as she was heading for the servants' staircase.

"Miss Watson." His expression was unreadable. "Might I have a word?"

Alexandra's blood froze. Did he intend to let her go? She dropped a curtsy. "Certainly, Your Lordship."

"I overheard what you said to Mrs. Gorgon today."

She hesitated. "I believe her name is *Gordon*, my lord, not *gorgon*."

"I think my term more appropriate." His lips now twitched, and a hint of humor glimmered in his eyes.

Alexandra's spirits lifted as she waited for him to go on.

"I have some history with Mrs. Gordon. We attended a gathering at their house when I was a boy, where Saunders and I climbed one of their apples trees and enjoyed some of its fruit. Her daughters caught us in the act and told their mother, who expressed her displeasure by forbidding us from having ice cream when it was later served. I have never quite forgiven them."

A laugh escaped Alexandra's lips, then she covered her mouth with regret. "I'm sorry. I shouldn't have laughed. That's a terrible punishment for a boy."

"It is quite all right. Although I was devastated at the time, I can laugh about it now, because someone—*you*—finally put that horrid woman and her daughters in their place." He looked at her directly. "What you said may be hard for people like Mrs. Gordon and myself to hear, but every word was true."

"And here I was afraid you were going to let me go."

"It would take a far greater offense than that, Miss Watson," he said, smiling, "for me to let you go."

The following afternoon, while Longford and Julia were out riding, Lillie asked Alexandra, "Would you like to see my secret hideaway?"

Although Lillie had kept her promise to spend her time under the eye of her governess over the past weeks, and seemed quite happy to do so, Alexandra still wondered where the girl used to disappear to. "If you'd like to show it to me."

Lillie led the way up the stairs to the attics, this time to an area Alexandra had never seen, at the far end of a distant wing. There, in a musty corner surrounded by grimy windows, a collection of boxes, old furniture, ancient rugs, and other discarded belongings had been arranged to resemble a cozy sort of room. Old toys were neatly arranged on a set of shelves, and various dolls sat or reclined on makeshift chairs and beds.

"Did you set all this up yourself?"

Lillie nodded. "It is my house."

A house, Alexandra thought, where the little girl could escape and feel that she belonged, where no one would judge her for being different. "It's lovely," Alexandra said, tears studding her eyes.

"I used to come here every day." Lille glanced around at the haven she'd built, then gave a little shrug. "But I don't really need it now."

Alexandra drew Lillie into her arms and hugged her tightly. "I'm glad, Lillie. I'm so glad."

Since the day Alexandra had spied Longford painting in the room down the hall, she'd been intensely curious to know what he had been working on. She didn't venture there, however, hoping that when he was ready, he would show the results of his efforts.

One morning, she stopped in his study to ask him a question, but he wasn't there. Turning to leave, she noticed a new painting hanging on the wall above the fireplace. It was the Italian landscape she'd seen in the attic and had so admired. How lovely, she thought, that he'd finally hung it up where he could see it and enjoy it.

There was something different about the painting, though. She realized that he'd added a small figure to it. Beneath the jasmine bower, on the stone bench that had formerly been empty, sat a young woman in a blue gown and hat. Alexandra gave the painting an even closer inspection and inhaled in surprise. The resemblance was unmistakable. The figure in the painting was *her*.

Her heart flipped over. Longford had painted *her* into that beautiful landscape. What an honor! But then an inner voice piped up: *Don't flatter yourself. So, he added a figure to the painting. It could have been anyone.*

Even so, as she left the room, she couldn't suppress a smile.

The ensuing ten days were among the happiest of Alexandra's life.

Longford spent a part of each day with her and the girls, either riding with Julia, walking with them all in the gardens, or giving sketching lessons both inside and out of doors, where he taught some tricks for creating depth and perspective with charcoal and pencils.

At Alexandra's suggestion, the girls rehearsed and gave a piano recital for Longford and the house servants, which was well received, particularly by Mr. Hutchens, who avowed a deep interest in music.

Lillie was now behaving like a proper young lady, and so the servants were beginning to treat her with more kindness and respect. As the days went by, Alexandra noticed, too, that Mr. Hutchens seemed to have let go of his former reserve toward *her*, and accepted her as a valued fixture at Polperran House.

Longford brought down half a dozen more of his paintings from the attic, and asked for Alexandra's advice as to where to hang them. They spent a rainy afternoon and evening enjoyably taking down family artworks he'd never liked and replacing them with works of his own. He invited Alexandra and the girls to dine with him on two more occasions, evenings which rang with laughter and the pleasure of amiable conversation.

Every night, as Alexandra climbed into bed, she went over the events of the day in her mind, reliving each happy moment, yet painfully aware of how precious and fleeting they were. The idea of parting from them always brought the threat of tears to her eyes.

Although she wanted to go home, Alexandra was torn by an equal desire to extend her stay at Polperran House, conflicting feelings that confused her. She still missed her own sisters with a fierce, ever-expanding ache, but she'd grown so close to Julia and Lillie, she'd come to think of them as family as well. She'd come to regard Longford as the most remarkable man she'd ever known. She enjoyed every moment spent in his company. When she wasn't with him, she was thinking about him, and looking forward to the time when she'd see him again.

Never far from her thoughts were the memories of the two times they'd kissed. During those interludes, she'd felt both an intimate connection and a kind of physical pleasure that she'd never imagined could exist. She longed to feel that way again, with him. When she slept, her dreams were often carnal in nature. Longford came to her bed and took her in his arms, kissing her urgently, making her body feel as if it were on fire. She always woke up with a frantically beating heart, yearning for more.

She knew it was impossible. Yet that didn't prevent her from wanting it. At the same time, she was plagued by an ever-present sense of guilt. She was dreaming about making love to a man who didn't know who she really was. She'd given him a false name, and allowed him to hire her as his sisters' governess, a job for which she'd had not an iota of experience. She felt awful about the deception she'd been perpetrating, longed to tell him the truth about herself.

But after all this time, after so many weeks of lying, how could she?

Thomas rolled over to find the lithe, naked form of a woman warming his bed. His heart leapt with pleasure and excitement. Moonlight filtered down through the window, shining on Miss Watson's beautiful, sleeping face, and illuminating her curves. His hand reached up to cover one perfect breast, and he instantly became aroused. Then he was on top of her, his mouth on hers. Beneath him, he felt her body respond as she—

With a start, Thomas awoke, breathing hard, his heart hammering. He blinked at the darkness, cursing himself and his errant brain. Every night, it was the same dream, over and over. Only the details changed. Sometimes he encountered her in the library, as he had that night so many weeks ago. Sometimes it was the hallway, where she fell into his arms, wearing nothing but a thin nightdress that he tore off until she stood naked before him. Once, it had happened in the dining room, where he'd made love to her on the table, heedlessly knocking crystal and china to the floor.

Sometimes, as tonight, the lovemaking was interrupted at the very start. Other times, it had veered close to its inevitable conclusion. He had dreamt that he was thrusting inside her as she moaned beneath him, every movement bringing them both closer to the release they sought, and he always awakened hard and aching, feeling as if he might explode with need.

Closing his eyes, Thomas fought to regain control over his body. These dreams . . . this incessant *wanting* . . . it was driving him to distraction.

And it would not do.

"How thrilling!" Julia cried.

"Please say that we can go, Thomas!" exclaimed Lillie.

Alexandra glanced at Longford, who was rather comically crammed into one of the small benches in the schoolroom, his long legs stretched out before him. He'd interrupted their studies to deliver a letter that had just arrived from Trevelyan Manor.

It was an invitation solely for the girls, to join Lord and Lady Trevelyan and their daughters on an impromptu holiday to Penzance, at the most southwesterly end of Cornwall, where they intended to stay for a week to take in the sights. Their sons Charles and James would not be among the company. Miss Watson need not go, as their own governess, Miss Berry, would watch over all four girls.

Alexandra wondered if she were deliberately being excluded because of her verbal tirade at the garden party. Even if that were so, she didn't mind. This was a wonderful opportunity for the girls, and she welcomed the respite it would give her. Although she enjoyed her job, she'd only had a single day off since coming to Cornwall, and she'd spent the better part of it preparing lesson plans.

"Well," Longford said, his eyes twinkling, "I do not know. Penzance is an infamous pirate town. I am not certain it is entirely safe for you to visit there."

"Thomas!" Lillie punched him in the shoulder. "Do not be silly."

Julia swatted him with her notebook. "There are no pirates anymore."

"Truce! Truce!" Longford raised his hands in concession. "I give in. You may go. On one condition."

"What condition?" Julia asked.

"That you return safe and sound in a week, as this letter promises."

"Hurray!" Lillie threw herself onto Longford's lap and hugged him. He hugged her back.

"Thank you!" Julia planted a kiss on his cheek. To Alexandra, she added with enthusiasm, "We have to pack. Will you help us, Miss Watson?"

The next two days were devoted to preparation. The girls were too excited about their upcoming holiday to attend to their studies, so Alexandra read up and spoke to them about Penzance instead, to give them a history of the area they'd be visiting. They decided to bring their sketchbooks and pencils, promising to capture what they could of the scenic vistas on paper.

Lord and Lady Trevelyan and their daughters pulled up early on the morning of departure to pick up Lillie and Julia on the way to the train station. The girls hugged their brother and Alexandra, waved to the assembled servants, and then jumped into the waiting conveyance.

"Good-bye!" Lillie cried, waving again through the window of the departing carriage.

As she watched the vehicles vanish around a bend in the drive, Alexandra felt as if she were saying good-bye to her own sisters. Even knowing it was only for a week, her heart was heavy.

Alexandra returned upstairs. With the girls gone, she'd have a lot of time on her hands. She hadn't made any plans for the day, and wondered what she ought to do. She began by organizing her teaching materials, a task which was accomplished by the time luncheon was served. It felt strange to eat in the nursery all by herself. When she'd finished her meal, it was such a beautiful day, she decided to take a walk to her favorite spot and read.

In the library, she found a particular book that had been on her mind. After donning her hat, she folded up one of the old quilts from her bed, tucked it under her arm, and left the house. Winding her way through the overgrown garden, she soon found herself at the blue door.

The path wound through the familiar thicket of overhanging tropical trees and ferns, finally ending at the quiet pond, where the only sounds were the rustle of the breeze in the branches and the lazy buzz of insects.

Spreading out her quilt beneath a tree, Alexandra sank down happily, opened her book, and soon lost herself in its pages.

Thomas's pace was persistent as he strode across the lawn.

He had spent the morning wading through the outstanding bills and other correspondence on his desk, struggling to pay attention to the letters of inquiry he had received in response to his advertisements in the London papers. They were all from seemingly qualified young ladies. He had less than two months to find Miss Watson's replacement, yet his eyes had glazed over as he perused the letters. He did not have an ounce of interest in any of them.

His mind had kept wandering to thoughts of the governess now in his employ.

Knowing that Miss Watson was somewhere on the premises, not involved in caring for his sisters, but actually free and available, was driving him mad. With her work ethic, she was probably in the nursery or schoolroom at that very moment, writing up a geography exam or preparing a mathematics lesson. His feet itched to take himself there, to that private sanctuary now free of pupils, where he would find her alone. Just the two of them. He would shut the door, walk up to her, and . . . and . . . he refused to allow his thoughts to go any further.

He'd known he had to get out of the house, as far away from her, and the temptation of her, as he could. It was too nice a day, in any case, to spend cooped up inside.

And so here he was, heading out to the gardens, his portable easel and a blank canvas under one arm, and a leather satchel in the other, containing drawing and painting supplies and a bottle of Mrs. Nettle's lemonade.

He followed a path that wound through the garden, the sun warming his shoulders where it filtered down through the trees. As he stepped over roots and pushed aside branches threatening to overtake the walkway, he couldn't help but frown, wishing for the thousandth time that he could afford to maintain his grounds as they deserved. But that was not going to happen in his lifetime. He pushed the worry from his mind. He needed a reprieve—an afternoon in a peaceful spot where he could relax and paint.

It was so warm, Alexandra had taken off her shoes and stockings and removed her hat. The tree above her was heavy with green leaves, the shaded area below dappled by the sun. She leaned back against the trunk, reading, lulled by the sounds of this tropical hideaway and the sweet scent of the multicolored lilies that crowded the water's edge.

The sound of approaching footsteps caught her attention. How strange. She'd come here at least half a dozen times, and she'd always had the place to herself. Looking up from her book, she saw Lord Longford emerge from the tree-lined path.

Alexandra's heart skipped a beat as she inhaled in surprise.

He caught sight of her and stopped. "Miss Watson."

His expression and tone confirmed that he was equally surprised to see her. He was more casually dressed than he'd been that morning, wearing the same dark trousers and white shirt, but minus the frock coat, waistcoat, hat, and tie.

Under one arm, he carried a small blank canvas and what looked like a portable folding easel. Over his shoulder was a leather satchel.

She rose, her bare feet digging into the mossy ground. "My lord." They stared at each other awkwardly.

"Forgive me. I had no idea you were here."

She raised the book in her hand. "I came to read."

He gestured with the items he carried. "I came to paint."

"I can see that." It was thrilling to know that his passion for art had returned.

"Well. I will leave you to your solitude." He turned to go.

"No, wait," she called out abruptly, making him pause. "This is your secret garden, my lord."

"My *secret garden?*"

"That's what I call it. Anyway, it's yours. If you wish to paint here, it's your right. I'll go."

"I won't hear of it. You were here first. I shall find another spot."

"That isn't necessary." Gesturing toward the mossy bank around her, she added: "There's no reason why we can't both be here." No reason, except that it wasn't entirely proper for them to be alone in such a secluded spot. She shoved the thought to the furthest corner of her mind. They'd been here together before, hadn't they? "You can paint while I read. There's plenty of space."

He hesitated. "Are you certain you do not mind? I would not wish to intrude."

"I'd welcome the company, actually. I've become so used to being with the girls every minute, it feels strange to be on my own."

"Well, then." He strode toward her with a smile. "It would be my pleasure to join you."

Chapter Twenty-Two

When Thomas had caught sight of her, sitting a few yards from the water's edge beneath that tree, barefoot and bareheaded like some water sprite, his heart had almost stopped.

He had known that spending another minute in this remote spot with her was a dangerous idea. But she had asked him to stay. Now, wild horses could not drag him away.

Thomas set up his easel and canvas not far from where she sat, then took out a pencil. "What are you reading?"

She held up her book. It was *Great Expectations*.

Thomas grinned. "A day for old favorites?"

She nodded.

"For me as well. I have painted this pond many times." He could feel her eyes on him, watching him draw as she settled back against the tree trunk.

"Do you always begin in pencil?"

"I do. I find it invaluable to sketch out the basics before I begin filling in with paint, which easily covers over it."

"Interesting."

He struggled to concentrate as he sketched out an overview of the scene before them.

"I love this spot," she commented, her tone languid. "I often come here in the afternoons to read."

"Do you? I had no idea. This was my favorite place to read in spring and autumn, and to swim in summer."

"You swim in the pond?" The notion appeared to delight her.

"It is quite refreshing this time of year. If you do not mind the lily pads."

She laughed. "My parents used to rent a cottage on a lake every summer when I was a girl. It was deep in the woods. My sisters and I loved it there. To swim beneath a cobalt sky, surrounded by fresh green pines, is my idea of heaven."

He glanced at her. A dreamy expression crossed her face. Her cheeks glowed, dark eyelashes fringed her blue eyes, and several tendrils of sienna hair had come loose from their pins. It was all Thomas could do to restrain himself from crossing to her, dropping to his knees, and taking her in his arms.

Instead, he forced his attention back to his drawing. "You are very close to your sisters, are you not?"

"We have our squabbles, as all siblings do, I imagine. But we are so close in age, we depend upon each other. Even when we fight, we always make up quickly."

"It must be difficult, being so far away from them."

"It is."

She said nothing more, and he didn't want to press the point. "You are lucky to have such a history with your siblings. I was an only child for so long. All the years I was growing up, really. My only friend was Saunders, but he lives five miles away. Most of the time, I had to make my own, solitary amusements."

"That sounds lonely."

"It was, rather."

"I was never lonely when I was young. But I had such grand plans for my myself," she added with a sigh.

"What plans?"

"I could never settle on one thing in particular. When I was very little, I wanted to be an actress on the stage. Later, I thought I might become a doctor."

"A doctor?"

"We have a few women doctors in the U.S. now, just as you do in England. As I grew older, though, I became more fascinated by what my father did." She broke off, and seemed to choose her words carefully as she proceeded. "He was involved in banking, but he would never explain any of it to me. He said I was a girl, and didn't need to 'bother my pretty head about such things.' I promised myself that I would go to college and learn all there was to know. But in some ways, it only made things harder. Every subject I studied was of interest to me. All I know for certain now is that I want to do something important with my life."

He gave her a smile. "I think you have found your profession, Miss Watson. And you acquit it most admirably."

She blushed, but did not reply.

"You seem embarrassed. Why? I merely complimented your work, as you have so often complimented mine. That is one of the things I value most about our friendship, Miss Watson. That we have always told each other the truth." His thoughts veered to Elise, who had duped and betrayed him. Something he knew the decent, principled woman sitting beside him would never do. "There are no secrets between us, no surprises. When you tell me something, I know I can trust you."

Miss Watson's cheeks flushed even redder now. She lowered her eyes, and seemed to be searching for a reply. "I'm glad you feel me worthy of your confidence," she murmured at length. For some reason, she seemed incapable of going any further.

"I am honored that you chose to share yours."

Quiet stretched out between them. Finally, she said: "What about you? Your ambitions? Did you have other dreams, in addition to painting?"

He continued sketching, reluctant to reply. "I did have another dream, as a boy. It was foolish, though."

"What dream?"

"To have my artwork recognized by the Academy of British Artists. To have a painting of mine hang in one of their exhibitions. And to be invited to become a member."

"Why is that foolish?"

"Because," he explained patiently, "members of the aristocracy cannot become members of the academy."

"Because art is a trade?"

He nodded.

"You could break tradition. You could be the first peer to join the academy. You could change things."

"I am afraid it does not work that way."

"But it should! Even if it's true that a nobleman can't be a *member* of that academy, surely anyone can submit a painting for consideration to hang in one of their exhibitions. If you—"

"*No,*" he interjected.

"Why not?"

"It simply is not done, Miss Watson."

"All your rules, don't they seem a bit ridiculous to you? In the U.S., it doesn't matter who you are. If you have talent and work hard, you can usually get ahead and be recognized and appreciated for your achievements. Whereas here, you're not allowed to even try."

"Your country is still new. It is an experiment, with no proof of how it will turn out. This is England. We have done things the same way for centuries, and we like it that way."

"Couldn't you pull a few strings, due to your title, to get your work shown?"

"If I did—*if* that even worked—that would take away all meaning from the achievement. I only want to earn a place at the table, so to speak, due to the value of the art itself, not my rank." He shrugged. "And now, even if I wished to do such a thing, it is impossible. If I went public as an artist, I could never sell a painting again. My one, surreptitious opportunity to earn income would go up in smoke."

Miss Watson blew out a frustrated breath. "Well, it's too bad. Because you deserve to hang in exhibitions and to have your work seen."

"It pleases me that you think so."

"*Thinking* gets you nowhere. *Action* is required."

"I thank you for your interest and concern. But—" He put down his pencil, wiped his perspiring forehead with the back of his forearm. "It is so bloody hot. The only action I can contemplate at this moment is a long, cold drink."

"You can say that again."

He grinned, then reached into his satchel and removed the bottle he had brought.

Her eyes widened. "Is that lemonade?"

"I stole it from the icebox. I am afraid it is not cold anymore, and I neglected to bring glasses. But if you are not averse to drinking straight from the bottle—"

"Please. I'm a Yankee. Drinking straight from the bottle runs in my blood."

Thomas laughed. He moved to sit down beside her on her blanket. Unstoppering the bottle, he handed it to her. As she took the bottle, her fingertips grazed his, sending a zinging sensation up the length of his arm that made him catch his breath. Their gazes met briefly. In her eyes, he read uncertainty, and a reflection of the burgeoning desire he was feeling.

She held the bottle up to her lips, tipped her head back, closed her eyes, and took a long drink.

He watched, his eyes riveted to her face. His heart began to beat double time. She was sitting just a few inches away. As she drank, a drop of liquid escaped from the bottle and trickled down her chin, then ran the length of her throat, before disappearing into the neckline of her gown. He wanted, with every fiber of his being, to reach out and trace the path of that errant moisture.

But he knew he couldn't. Shouldn't. That's all it would take: one touch, and he would be lost.

"Ahh, delicious. Thank you." Alexandra's heart pounded like a drum as she opened her eyes and offered Longford the bottle.

He took it, drank, then stoppered it and set it aside.

He was no longer making eye contact with her. She could guess why. From the moment he'd sat beside her, the moment their hands had touched, she'd wanted nothing more than to fling the bottle aside and fold herself into his arms. She wanted it still. She sensed that he wanted it as well, but was too much of a gentleman to act on it. His sense of honor was holding him back.

Honor? she thought fiercely. Was there any place for honor in this relationship?

If she'd had any honor, she wouldn't have taken this position in the first place, wouldn't have hidden her real identity behind a lie. When he'd made that comment about honesty, Alexandra had wanted to die from shame. She'd been so tempted to tell him everything then and there, but he'd looked into her eyes with such openness and trust that she'd lost her nerve.

No, it was too late to care about honor. But feelings were another thing.

A deep, visceral sensation raced through her body and she acknowledged with sudden force what she had been unable to see until now: She loved this man.

She loved him.

She didn't know the precise moment when the emotion had taken hold of her heart, only knew that it had. For the feeling to be this strong, she must have loved him for quite some time.

Inching closer to him on the blanket, she rose up on her knees, placed her hands on his shoulders, and planted her lips firmly on his.

She felt him stiffen briefly, sensed his surprise. But seconds later, he responded, his mouth moving against hers. Then his arms swept around her, and she tumbled into his lap.

His mouth devoured hers. She pulled him closer until her breasts were pressed against his chest. He kissed her and kissed her, his lips moving back and forth across her own. She loved the way his small, soft mustache gently prickled against her mouth. Then his tongue parted her lips and found its way inside, colliding with exquisite intimacy against hers. The kiss was everything she'd been dreaming about, and more.

Her hands roamed across his back. Every muscle and sinew beneath her fingers only made her hungry to feel more. His own hands wound up into her hair, caressing and smoothing it back from her face as the kiss continued, until she was so breathless she had to break off and gasp for air.

He paused, too, inhaling great gulps into his lungs as their eyes met, the fevered need she saw there matching her own. She was still sitting on his lap, their arms wrapped around each other as they both struggled to catch their breath.

He said nothing; nor did she. But she didn't need words. They were communicating in another manner now. She could sense the way he felt and what he wanted, for she felt and wanted exactly the same.

He cupped the back of her head with one hand and drew her face closer, until her mouth was just inches from his. With the gentlest of movements, he touched his lips to hers again. He kissed her once, twice, three times, then moved sideways to kiss her cheeks, up to kiss the bridge of her nose, her forehead, back to her lips again. Moving down to her neck, he peppered it with a series of delectably soft kisses that made her tremble, sending sparks like electricity shooting through her every vein.

She heard him moan low in his throat, and suddenly he was rolling over with her clasped in his arms until she lay beneath him. His body covered her own as his mouth came down intensely on hers. Through the fabric of her gown and petticoat, she could feel a rigid shaft against her thigh, and knew it was evidence of his own fevered need. She returned his kisses with all the fervor that was in her heart, wanting him to know how she felt, that she wanted this, wanted him.

His hand caressed her waist, then rose up to cover her breast. But too many layers of clothing separated his hand from her flesh. She wished her clothing to be gone, to be naked beneath him.

Before she could further that thought, all of a sudden, to her extreme disappointment, he stopped. She could see the hard evidence of his arousal straining against his trousers as, with a groan, he rolled off of her onto his side and lay there unmoving.

"We cannot," he said, deep regret etched in those two simple words.

What he did next took her by surprise. In a few swift movements, Longford yanked off his boots and stockings. Leaping to his feet, he strode to the edge of the pond, unbuttoning his shirt as he went. Throwing his shirt onto the bank, he walked determinedly into the water, then dove beneath its depths.

Alexandra sat up, catching her breath as she watched him

swim away. *We cannot.* She sensed that it had taken all of his strength to break away from her. She understood why; her own body was aflame, and she wanted more.

Alexandra stood.

The future that lay before her was murky, but she knew one thing for certain: she loved him. She may never feel this way about a man again, might stay single for the rest of her life. But they were here together now. Alone. This moment might never come again. If anything more was going to happen, she was going to have to make it happen herself.

She unhooked the bodice of her gown, took it off, and tossed it aside. Then she unfastened her skirt and stepped out of its folds.

With each article of clothing she removed, Alexandra knew that she was playing with fire. Her knowledge of love-making was limited to the embraces she and Longford had shared. But she was ready and eager for its mysteries to be revealed to her, as long as it could be *with him.* And she was reasonably certain that if she walked into that water half naked, his resistance would crumble.

A tiny voice in the back of her mind struggled to be heard, warning her that there might be repercussions. Repercussions which could change the course of her entire life. But she forced the voice away.

He was swimming away from her, unaware of her actions. She undid the hooks on the front of her corset and divested herself of it. Then she took off her petticoat. She was now down to nothing but her thin chemise and drawers. Despite the warmth of the sun on her bare arms and shoulders, she trembled, resisting the urge to cover herself. If she were going to do this, she had to give herself to it, body and soul.

Holding her head high, Alexandra crossed the mossy bank and walked into the pond. Her toes contracted as they touched the soft, muddy bottom. The water at the edge of the pool felt as warm as a bath, but grew refreshingly cooler as she plunged forward.

The water was just lapping at Alexandra's thighs when Longford turned and caught sight of her.

CHAPTER TWENTY-THREE

*D*ear God.

She was walking into the pond. And she was nearly naked.

Thomas wanted to call out *What are you doing?* But the words stuck in his throat.

He told himself that she just intended to swim. Overheated by their amorous encounter, she needed to cool off, as he did. But that did not account for the determined look in her eyes, or the fact that she was swimming straight toward him.

He touched bottom, his shoulders just above the surface of the water. Moments later, she was there, wrapping her arms around him, her face just inches from his. He was still desperately aroused, but felt himself grow harder yet as her breasts and slippery body came into contact with his.

"We should not . . ." he began, placing his hands on her upper arms, but he couldn't bring himself to push her away.

"I want to," she whispered. "Don't you?"

"Of course," he admitted, his voice so low, it was practically inaudible to his own ears. "But . . ."

In answer, she pressed her lips ever so softly against his.

Thomas almost lost control at that. But he steeled himself as he gripped her arms and broke off the kiss. "I do not think you understand what you are asking for." Swallowing hard, he looked directly into her blue eyes. "Have you ever . . . ?"

She shook her head, her eyes never leaving his. "But I want this. I want it. With you." She kissed him again. Harder this time.

He could resist no further. He gave in to her lips, returning her kiss with all the passion he'd been restraining. His tongue plunged into her mouth. He slid his arms around her, pressing her to him.

With one hand he stroked the length of her back, then cupped her firm derriere. As if by instinct, she lifted her legs and wrapped them around his waist until he could feel, through their wet clothing beneath the water, the apex of her femininity pressed up against his rigid shaft. He heard her breath catch in surprise, as if the contact had evoked some unexpected sensation. He held her there, pressing her tightly against him, as his other hand roved over her back, then up between them to capture one of her breasts in his palm.

He massaged her breast as he deepened the kiss, their wet slippery bodies moving against each other. All that separated his hand from her flesh was a thin layer of drenched cotton, yet even that was too much. He wanted to feel her naked flesh, wanted no barrier between them.

Without a word, he scooped her up in his arms and carried her out of the pool, up onto the mossy bank, to the tree beneath which her blanket was spread. Kneeling down, he set her gently on the quilt. Her chemise and drawers were so wet, they were transparent. He could see her rosy areolas and pink nipples poking through the fabric, as well as the dark triangle between her legs, a sight which made his breath come hard and fast.

He wanted her more than he had ever wanted anything in his life. But he had to be careful. He would not, he promised himself, take this beyond a certain point. Grabbing hold of the hem of her chemise, he said, "I want to see you. All of you." She raised her arms, helping him as he pulled the sodden garment over her head.

"Beautiful," he murmured, gazing at her bare breasts. "You are so beautiful."

She untied the string at the waist of her drawers, and he quickly peeled them down the length of her legs, until she lay completely naked to his view. His trousers were the only barrier between them that remained, but he didn't dare remove them. He stretched out beside her, rolling her into his embrace again until they were no longer two bodies but one, with mouths, arms, and legs firmly entangled.

His hands and lips were everywhere. Touching. Massaging. Caressing. It was all Alexandra could do not to cry out from the pleasure of it. His mouth nuzzled her breasts, first one, then the other, licking and sucking at her nipples, sending little electric shocks zinging throughout her body.

Her heart pounded. Her breath became ragged. She thought nothing could feel more wonderful. And then . . .

Then his hand found its way to her most intimate place. With his fingers, he began doing things to her there that she had never imagined, things that made her gasp with shock and pleasure and an undefined yearning that burned deep beneath her belly. Expertly, he manipulated the flesh of her feminine folds, paying special attention to a spot she hadn't known existed, a nub that was so sensitive, it seemed to leap to life and vibrate against his touch.

"Oh," she cried. She couldn't say more, for with every pressure of his fingers, she felt a storm of intense pleasure rising deep within her feminine core. She panted as the feeling built and built, every muscle in that region seeming to tighten as if seeking some kind of inexplicable release, until the feeling became everything there was.

She cried out again as it suddenly overtook her, as if her body was exploding into a million fragments of pleasure and light.

Slowly, slowly, she came back to herself. Through a groggy haze, she saw him smiling down at her, a kind of satisfaction in his eyes. But when he rolled on top of her again, and his mouth once more came down possessively on hers, she was reminded that *he* had not yet been satisfied. She could still feel the evidence of his need, a shaft of steel pressed against that part of her which had just been awakened to heavenly bliss.

Breaking their kiss, she gripped the waistband of his trousers and said quietly: "Take these off."

Thomas paused. He was painfully erect, aching for completion, cradled against the very cove of her femininity. Every impulse urged him to remove the final barrier that separated them, to free himself and plunge into her again and again, to relieve the sweet, desperate tension that had been building inside him for weeks.

Instead, he took a long, deep breath and shook his head, touching his forehead to hers. "I do not dare."

Her blue eyes widened with confusion. "But how else can we . . ."

He silenced her with another, brief kiss. "My darling, I know my limits. I am only trying to protect you."

"But . . ."

"Trust me when I say that we have taken this as far as we can go. Any further, and I could no longer restrain myself. If I were to even . . ." He broke off, then shook his head. "The consequences could be too serious. I do not want to ruin you."

Her face clouded with disappointment and guilt. "A single coupling does not always end in . . ." She did not finish the statement.

"But it can. Therefore, it is too great a risk."

"But what about you?"

"I gained my pleasure in giving *you* pleasure. That is all the gratification I can, or will, allow myself." He reached up to smooth her wet hair back from her face. "You are so lovely, Lexie." It was the first and only time he had allowed himself to call her by her given name. It sounded strange yet wonder-

ful on his lips, and seemed to startle her, as well. He kissed
her again. "So lovely."

Lexie. He'd called her Lexie.

Hearing that name, spoken with such affection for the
first time in so many months, by a man she adored, caused
Alexandra's eyes to fill with tears.

Longford said it would be best if they returned to the
house separately. Alexandra nodded, although the suggestion brought a rush of heat to her cheeks. She wasn't at all
ashamed of what they'd done, but understood why it was important to him that they keep it a secret.

They dressed and gathered their belongings. She left first,
her hair dripping and her heart pounding as she made her
way through the gardens to the house. Making love with
Longford had been glorious, thrilling, electrifying. Under
the tender ministrations of his hands and mouth, her entire
body had felt as though it were on fire. He'd brought her to a
point of explosive pleasure that had surpassed anything she'd
ever conjured in her wildest imagination.

Now that her own physical needs had been satisfied and
she could think coherently again, she realized that she'd behaved very recklessly. If things had progressed any further,
she might well have conceived a child. She was grateful that
he'd had the presence of mind to exercise such restraint.

At the same time, Alexandra sensed that in stopping
when they had, they'd missed out on the most important
part of the act. That as intimate as the experience had been,

an essential connection had not been made. And she felt guilty that he'd been left wanting.

The evening passed in oppressive solitude. Dinner was brought up, and Alexandra ate alone.

She paced back and forth in the nursery, her thoughts turning to the days ahead. She had to work here seven more weeks to earn the money for her passage home. She wondered what would happen when the girls returned from their holiday. Would Longford continue to invite them all to dine with him occasionally? Or, now that they'd broken his rule and made love, would he find it too uncomfortable to be around her? She hated to think that those evenings with him which had brought her so much pleasure might be at an end, all because she had insisted on taking things . . . where she'd taken them.

A sleepless night ensued, in which Alexandra mentally examined the events that had brought her to this moment. From the day she'd escaped her awful fate in London, she'd been increasingly drawn to the man who'd rescued her, even when she'd believed him to be a poverty-stricken artist. Since coming to Cornwall, she'd gotten to know him intimately. And she'd fallen in love with him.

The Earl of Longford was different from the other English lords she'd met. He didn't simply complain about his problems, he did something about them. He worked on his own lands. He'd found a way to earn an income to help support his family and estate. She admired him for that.

She admired him for so many other things as well: his artistic talent. His love for literature. His concern for his staff and his tenants. His newfound interest in and devotion to his sisters. His kindness to *her*. He was sensitive. He was thoughtful. And he was a man of principle. All the reasons why she loved him.

All the reasons why, she realized, the notion hitting her with the force of a tidal wave, she could never leave him.

For weeks on end, she'd wanted to go home, to finish her education. Now, her wishes were very different. With all her heart, she loved Lord Longford. She wanted to spend the rest of her life with him. She'd often told herself she wanted to do something important with her life. Well, what could be more important than rescuing Polperran House from ruin and saving it for future generations? There could be no more honorable use for her father's wealth, she thought, than to bring this impoverished community back to life.

If they married, she'd be partnering herself with a man she adored and respected. A man whose children she'd like to have. A man she could love to the end of her days.

She wasn't sure, however, how *he* felt. If he would want *her*.

Alexandra rolled over in bed, her stomach clenching in desperate worry. He'd been so deeply hurt in the past, he'd insisted that true love didn't exist, that he would never marry. She had no idea if she could persuade him otherwise.

She knew he felt great affection for her. After what happened at the pond, there could be no doubt about it. But although everything that had passed between them felt as real and true to her as her own heart, in fact, it was based on a lie.

The comment he'd made weeks ago, about the fiancée who'd betrayed him, again came back to haunt her: *She was*

no different from any of the other title-grubbing American heir-
esses who've been invading our shores.

Alexandra had been so afraid to admit the truth. But the
charade had gone on long enough. Whatever the outcome,
she now had no choice. If they were to have any possibility of
a future together, she had to tell him.

Thomas strode the entire length of the gallery and back,
then repeated the process all over again. If he kept this up, he
feared he would burn a hole in the carpets. But never in his
life had he felt so unsettled and restless.

The night had come and gone. Outside, dawn had long
since broken. But all those hours of pacing hadn't brought
him any clarity or peace of mind.

He could think of nothing but Miss Watson. Her wet
body in his arms. Her naked breasts in his hands, his mouth.
The sound of her moans as his fingers brought her to climax.
The passion in her eyes. The intensity of feeling that had
washed over him as she lay beneath him in perfect nudity,
willing to give herself to him.

It had taken every reserve of his strength and honor to
stop things when he had. Could he trust himself to do so
another time? He wasn't certain.

Did he want there to be another time? Yes. For the love
of God, *yes*, he did.

He knew that in the weeks ahead it would be difficult—
perhaps impossible—to stay away from her. His mind leapt
to the time beyond that. Three months, she had said. That

was the longest she could stay. Which meant only seven weeks remained. As soon as she'd earned her fare back to New York, she'd be gone.

The idea of her leaving hit him like a physical blow. The past weeks had been among the sweetest he had ever experienced. Julia and Lillie were happier than he had ever seen them. Miss Watson had broadened the girls' minds, taught them things they never would have learned under anyone else's tutelage. He was beginning to enjoy his sisters' company so much, he could hardly credit the distance that had once existed between them.

He and Saunders were friends again. Good relations had been restored between Polperran House and Trevelyan Manor. He had even started painting again. All changes that were due to Miss Watson. Without him even being aware of it, she had changed everything.

He tried to imagine what life would be like without her. The days stretched before him like an endless void. The girls would miss her. But the girls would recover. Would he?

He shook his head. No. No. He didn't want her to go. He wanted more of the conversations they'd shared. He felt he could talk to her about anything, and she would always listen, understand, and challenge him in unexpected ways. He wanted to sleep with her every night and wake up beside her every morning. He wanted to share all the best moments of life with her. Because he loved her.

Dear God. He loved her.

He didn't want to admit it to himself, but there it was. He had told himself that he would never love again, that love was a fairy tale. Women broke your heart. They left. They were treacherous, not to be trusted.

But perhaps not all women were untrustworthy. He trusted *her*. Trusted her so much that he had lost his heart. He had fallen in love.

With a governess.

What on earth was he going to do? He couldn't marry a governess, could he?

The scene he'd witnessed at the garden party at Trevelyan Manor came to mind. The horror on people's faces as they had stared at Miss Watson during her tirade. Every word had rung true, and he had admired her for saying them. Yet those very people who had been offended were his neighbors. It was not an issue for him to marry an American; that was done all the time now.

But he was uncertain if they would accept a *governess* as his wife, his countess.

Uncertain if his children, should they be so lucky as to have any, would be accepted if their mother was of such lowly status.

With her fierce intelligence, fine education, and sympathetic heart, he knew Miss Watson would make him a fine companion, a wife of whom he could be proud. He did not know, however, if others would see it that way.

It was a conundrum he had no answer for. He required input from someone of his own class, a friend whose opinion he respected.

Then he realized he had such a friend.

Thomas made his way to the stables, intending to saddle

up Merlin and ride to Trevelyan Manor. Saunders had sent a note the day before, saying he was returned from London. But as Thomas reached the outbuilding, he heard approaching hoofbeats and seconds later, Saunders himself appeared on horseback out of the trees.

"Longford!" His friend reined to a halt before him. "You are out and about early."

"As are you. What brings you here at this hour?"

"I had a sudden urge to ride. Before I knew it, I found myself at your gate, so I thought I would drop in."

"I am pleased. I was going to come see you," Thomas admitted.

"Oh?"

"I am in a quandary and need your advice. Can we walk?"

"Certainly." Saunders dismounted and handed his reins to the waiting groom.

Thomas gestured toward a path leading into his gardens, and Saunders accompanied him as they strode in that direction.

"What seems to be the trouble?"

"A woman."

Saunders's eyebrows raised in surprise. "You would ask *my* advice about a woman?"

"It seems I have no one else to turn to."

"Well, I am honored, and happy to help if I can. I had no idea you were involved with anyone."

"Nor did I. But it appears that I am."

"Are you in love?"

"Yes. I love her."

Saunders smiled. "This is wonderful news. Who is this paragon of virtue, who has captured your affections?"

Thomas looked Saunders in the eye. "Miss Watson, my sisters' governess."

Saunders's smile disappeared. He let go a long breath. "I see your dilemma. I pray that you will start from the beginning, and tell me everything."

Alexandra paced back and forth in the nursery, her mind in a whirl.

All night long, she'd tossed and turned, trying to conjure the words for the admission she needed to make. She still had no idea how to begin. But she had to tell him, and let the chips fall where they may. She just prayed he would understand and forgive her.

Glancing out the window, she thought she glimpsed Longford in the distance, vanishing into the trees. Suddenly, she couldn't wait another minute to speak to him. Grabbing her hat and shawl, she raced down the back stairs.

As they walked up one path and down another, Thomas told Saunders the whole story, beginning with the day Miss Watson raced out of that alley in London, and up through the preceding weeks, in which she had become so dear to him.

"I can tell she adores Julia and Lillie. They love her. And I love her as well." He made no mention of their sexual liaisons, preferring to keep that private. Saunders listened with attention, giving the matter the gravity it was due. "What should I do? Would you marry a governess?"

"Probably not. But it is not my decision. It is yours."

"That helps me not at all, I am afraid," Thomas said with a light laugh.

"Perhaps it is not such a difficult decision after all," Saunders mused. "Miss Watson is an educated woman, is she not?"

"Indeed. She has attended college in New York."

"What class would you say she is from?"

"Her family was apparently well-off, until her father lost his fortune by some means or another."

"The American equivalent of the gentry class, then, am I right?"

"It would appear so."

"So it is not as though you want to marry the chambermaid."

Thomas frowned. "But what will people think?"

"Do you really care what people think?"

"Don't you?"

"I do not know. I suppose we do care, because it has been drilled into us all our lives that we must."

"We have to live with those people, Saunders. Without their approval, we would lead a very reclusive life. You must have heard what happened at the garden party at your house. Miss Watson defended women of her station in the most direct and conspicuous manner. She has thoughts and opinions, is not content to sit quietly in the background, as Englishwomen do."

"A common trait among Americans."

"Yes."

"And yet, forgive me if I am wrong, but I suspect that is what you like about her."

Thomas opened his mouth to refute this, but found he could not. Another realization hit him. Glumly, he said: "It is a moot point, in any case. I do not know why I am even bothering you about this. I cannot afford to keep a wife. I am barely managing to keep my head above water as it is."

"Is it as bad as that, Longford?"

"I am afraid it is."

"I am sorry to hear it. Can I help? Father keeps a tight rein on the purse strings, and I am on a rather strict budget. But if there is anything I can do . . ."

"No thank you. I would not dream of it. I will get by. But how can I ask a wife to join me under such circumstances? To live in a house that is falling to pieces?"

"Perhaps it will not matter to her. She has lived there for a while now. From what you said, she is not a stranger to financial difficulties."

"True."

"Do you truly love her, Longford?"

"I do."

"Do you imagine that you would be happy, sharing your life with her?"

"Very much so."

"Then you have to ask yourself: what is more important, the approval of society, or your own personal happiness? Do not forget, we are peers of the realm. Your wife will be a countess, no matter who she was before. By virtue of her title alone, people will be obliged to look up to her. If she is a worthy woman, I believe she will win people's respect. Regardless of their mothers' origins, your children will be lords and ladies, and I believe they will be accepted as well."

Thomas turned that over in his mind. "A fair point."

"You are lucky, you know. You have it far easier than I do, when it comes to planning your future."

"Why is that?"

"Because you may *choose* whom you marry. You do not need anyone's permission. My parents nearly flayed me alive over the Miss Townsend affair. I had to give my solemn vow never to repeat such a mistake. My fate is sealed now."

Thomas looked at him. "You will marry your cousin Sophie, then?"

"I have not made her an official offer. I will, in time." Saunders sighed heavily. "But you! You have no one looking over your shoulder, insisting that you do your duty. You are already the Earl of Longford. You can marry anyone you like, and thumb your nose at the world."

"I suppose I can." Thomas realized he was smiling. "Thank you. You have been a great help after all."

Saunders clapped him on the back. "Are you going to propose to her, then?"

"Yes." Happiness shot through Thomas like a ray of sunshine. "I believe I will." He would not waste any time about it, either. He would return to the house this instant and find her, unburden his heart to her.

At that moment, they emerged from the cover of the trees onto the lawn, and Thomas stopped short.

The woman who had made up the subject of their entire conversation stood but a few yards before them.

Alexandra had just crossed the lawn and was heading for a path that led into the gardens, when Longford emerged from the trees. Another gentleman was with him. He looked vaguely familiar. She wondered if this was the Earl of Saunders, who she'd once spied from the nursery window, but had yet to meet.

Longford looked particularly happy. Alexandra was about to say good morning, but before she could utter the words, she noticed the other gentleman staring at her in absolute astonishment.

"Miss Atherton!" he exclaimed in consternation. "It *is* you, is it not? Miss Alexandra Atherton, of New York? Good Lord! What are you doing in Cornwall?"

CHAPTER TWENTY-FOUR

Alexandra froze, too shocked to speak.

"Forgive me," the gentleman continued, coming forward with a small bow. "I am Charles Grayson, the Earl of Saunders. We met only briefly in town in April, at Mrs. Dawlish's soirée. You were the belle of the ball that evening, so it is no surprise that you have no recollection of me. But I own, I am very surprised to see you here. I had no idea you were visiting Polperran House."

"You are mistaken, my friend," Longford interjected with a short laugh. "This is not—what did you call her? Miss Atherton?"

"But it must be. There cannot be two such women in the world." To Alexandra, Saunders added: "The newspapers were full of your disappearance some weeks ago. 'American Heiress Leaves Country,' I believe the headlines read?"

Confusion reigned in Longford's eyes as he stared at Alexandra. "American heiress?"

"Everyone presumed you had left England and returned to New York," Saunders went on, oblivious to the maelstrom his observations were causing, "but then I think there was some other story about Switzerland and your health? I hope you are recovered now, Miss Atherton? You appear to be in the bloom of health to me."

Alexandra's body pulsed with alarm. She was so consumed by mortification, she couldn't utter a word, could hardly breathe.

A dawning sense of horror and understanding registered on Longford's face as he took all this in, perhaps recalling the newspaper articles in question. "Is this true? Are you Alexandra Atherton? The missing heiress?"

Alexandra met his gaze, hoping he could tell how desperately embarrassed and sorry she was. But all she saw on his face was a rising sense of consternation, hurt, and anger.

"What is it? What have I said? Surely Miss Atherton is a guest of yours, Longford?"

"She is no guest." Longford's building rancor was evident in every syllable. "She is my sisters' *governess*."

"Their governess? But that is impossible. Miss Atherton is heiress to—" Lord Saunders broke off, glancing from her to Longford. Then, with a gasp: "Dear Lord. Do not tell me *this* is the Miss Watson you have been going on about?"

"It is."

A tense silence fell. The blood drained from Saunders's face. Alexandra finally found her voice.

"My lord," she began quietly, addressing Longford, "I was planning to tell you. That was my purpose in coming to find you just now. I was *going* to tell you."

"Going to tell me *what?*" Longford's eyes were like flint. "That for weeks now, since the day we met, you have been deceiving me? Living under a false name? Playing me for the fool?"

"I didn't—"

"Pray, forgive me," Saunders interjected. "I see that I have spoken out of turn. I regret any distress I may have caused you both, and I will now take my leave. Good day, Longford. Miss Atherton." With a brief tip of his hat, he sped off in the direction of the stables.

Leaving Alexandra and Longford standing on the lawn, staring at each other.

"My lord, I had a reason for—" Alexandra began.

"I am sure you did," Longford spat out. "Tell me: what was the purpose of your little game?"

Alexandra had planned to ease into the truth. Now that it had been blurted out by someone else, she had no alternative but to defend herself. "It was no game."

"You've never taught children in your life, have you? I should have known. You Yanks are all alike. You lied through your teeth, and like an idiot, I was completely taken in, allowed you to lead me along like a dog on a leash."

"It wasn't like that," Alexandra cried, but he went on.

"I believed you were a poor governess. How you must have laughed, insisting that I pay for your new clothes, pretending to be thrilled by that new evening gown, when you must have trunks full of far more elegant gowns. What were you after in coming here? My title? Did you, somehow, become privy to my antipathy to heiresses? Did you think to worm your way into my affections in this backhand manner, and then reveal all, hoping to become my countess?"

"No! I knew nothing about you, I swear it. If you will only let me explain."

"Pray, do go on, *Miss Atherton*," he retorted acidly. "What can you have hoped to gain with this charade?"

"All I hoped to gain was my fare to New York."

"You expect me to believe that one of the richest heiresses in America requires ten pounds from me to board a sailing vessel?"

"Yes!"

"Forgive me if I find that to be utterly ludicrous."

"It's the truth." Alexandra took a deep breath and plunged on. "I came to London for the Season with my mother. She was forcing me to marry a man I couldn't stand. I had to get away. The day we met, I was just trying to go home. I escaped from Brown's Hotel, and from there, it's exactly as I told you: my bag was stolen at Euston station, I had no ticket, no money. I was lost, then I ran into you and fell in the street."

"If it is true what you say, you must have made friends during the Season, had dozens of money-hungry men at your feet. Why did you not seek help from one of them?"

"I made no true friends, and didn't trust any of the people I did meet not to send me back to my mother."

"When you came to Mrs. Gill's house, why did you not simply tell us who you were?"

"For the same reason. I was a stranger to you, a burden. Why should you go out of your way to shelter me, a wealthy woman who had a suite of rooms at one of the best hotels in London? You have no idea what my mother is like. She'd have locked me in my room and kept me there until I gave in and married that horrible viscount. I couldn't go back!"

"And you did not trust me to do the right thing?"

"It wasn't a matter of trust, it was—"

"I beg to differ. This was all about trust. From the very beginning, you did not bring me into your confidence because you did not trust me. You made up a name for yourself, you invented a story about being a governess—"

"The only thing I lied about was my last name. My nickname *is* Lexie. As for the rest—it just happened. Mrs. Gill made assumptions about me and I went along with them. It seemed safest to let you think I was a governess. I didn't expect to be in your company more than a day or two. I just wanted to go home. But I had nothing, not a penny."

"You could not ask your father? A man with all the money in the world?"

"It would have taken days to hear back from him, and knowing my father, he would have said no, and betrayed my whereabouts to my mother."

"So instead, you betrayed *me*." Fury burned in Longford's eyes. "When we came to Cornwall, hundreds of miles away from your mother, why did you not tell me then?"

"I wanted to. But I was so afraid you'd fire me. Then I saw how disgusted you were by people like me. Title grubbers, you called us. I know what I did was wrong—"

"Wrong? I am afraid *wrong* does not begin to cover it, *Miss Atherton*." His shook his head, eyeing her with loathing. "As of this moment, you are discharged from your duties. I want you gone from this house today."

"*Today?*" Alexandra's voice broke. "But where will I go?"

"I will have my carriage made ready at eleven o'clock to take you to the station for the afternoon train to London.

Where you go and what you do after that is not my concern."

With that, Longford spun on his heel and strode rapidly away.

Tears streamed down Alexandra's face as she gazed out her bedroom window at the green lawns and gardens beyond. All this time, she'd been afraid to tell Longford the truth, yet she'd never imagined the result would be as calamitous as this.

Yesterday, he'd been such a tender lover. Today, he'd looked at her with hatred and disgust. She knew she'd brought this on herself. She was ashamed, and absolutely devastated. There was so much more she'd wanted to tell him, how sorry she was, all the feelings she held in her heart, but she'd never gotten a chance to say the words.

The fact that she'd never see Julia and Lillie again spurred a fresh burst of tears. What would they think when they came home from their holiday, only to find her gone? Alexandra had left a note for each of them, expressing her regret that she had to leave so unexpectedly. She worried that Longford might confiscate the notes, but she had to try.

Wiping her cheeks, Alexandra checked her hat in the mirror, the one she'd borrowed from Mrs. Gill. She was leaving in the clothes she'd arrived in, keeping only the handbag Mrs. Mitchell had found for her in the attic. She didn't feel comfortable keeping the blue day dress, the silk gown, or any of the other things Longford had paid for. In any case, she had no luggage in which to carry them.

Alexandra made her way down the back stairs and said good-bye to the servants. Martha, with tears in her eyes, gave her a fond hug. "I'm so sad ye're leaving us, Miss Watson. I hope yer family emergency is nought too serious."

The maid's words surprised her. Apparently, Longford hadn't revealed the truth about Alexandra, or why she was leaving. Was it meant as a kind gesture? Or simply to hide his own embarrassment?

"I'm sad to leave, too, Martha. More than you know."

Mrs. Mitchell was waiting in the inner hall with a sealed envelope and an unhappy expression. "I'm very sorry to see you go, Miss Watson. Here are your wages."

"Thank you."

"If you give me your address, I'll have your things sent to you."

"There's no need. I hope you can find some use for the clothes. Perhaps give them to the poor."

Mrs. Mitchell nodded. "There's one thing more. His Lordship asked me to give you this." She gestured to a parcel leaning against the wall.

Alexandra's brow furrowed. The rectangular-shaped parcel, wrapped in brown paper and tied with string, was about two feet by three feet in size. "What is it?"

"I believe it's one of his paintings."

Alexandra wondered why Longford would give her a painting. But she was too distressed to think about it. "Good-bye, Mrs. Mitchell. It has been a pleasure working beside you."

"And you, Miss Watson."

Woodenly, Alexandra picked up the wrapped parcel. Hutchens was waiting at the front door. "Have a safe journey, Miss Watson." Although he maintained his usual outer reserve, she detected genuine regret in his eyes at her departure.

"Thank you, Hutchens. Be well." Alexandra exited the house and moved to the waiting carriage.

Pausing at the carriage step, she glanced back at the house. To think that she'd never see Longford again, to leave in this way . . . her heart was so heavy with sorrow she thought it might burst. A movement from one of the gallery windows caught her eye. She noticed Longford briefly glance out, then turn away.

Her heart twisted. This was wrong, wrong, wrong. She couldn't leave, couldn't let it end like this. *She loved him.* Somehow, she had to let him know how she felt, make him understand.

Handing the parcel to John, Alexandra dashed back to the house, slipping in past an astonished Hutchens just as he was closing the front door. She darted up the main stairs, down the long corridor, past the library, and around the corner to the gallery, where she raced in to find Longford at the far end, pacing.

"Lord Longford."

He turned to face her, scowling. "Please go, Miss Atherton."

She paused a dozen feet away, tears blurring her vision as she caught her breath. "I can't. Not like this. Not until I've told you how sorry I am."

"You're *sorry.*"

"Yes! I'm so very, very sorry. I understand why you're angry. I should have had the courage to tell you the truth a long time ago. Especially when things between us became so . . . so . . ." She gulped, felt her cheeks growing hot as she moved closer. "But it can't be over! If you could just try to understand and forgive this one thing—"

"*This one thing* taints everything. Do you not see that?" He stepped back, maintaining the distance between them. "You deliberately deceived me. I could never trust you again."

"You can. What happened between us was real."

"Real?" he scoffed. "How can I ever know what is *real* where you are concerned?"

"My feelings for you are real. I love you. I have loved you for a long time."

"You dare to speak of *love*?"

"I do. I love you. Yesterday, I felt that you might feel the same way about me. If that's true, I'm still the same person you were with on the bank of that pool."

"I do not even know who that woman was."

"It's still *me*! The only thing that's different is my last name. Everything else I've told you is true. My father has a great deal of money, yes. And I'm due to receive a portion of it when I marry. But why can't that be a good thing? If we marry, I can help bring your estates back to life for you! For *us*."

"There is no *us*, Miss Atherton." Longford took two steps back, holding up his hands as if to ward her away. "Do you actually imagine I could ever conceive of *marrying you* after this? I want nothing to do with your money. And I want no more to do with you. Go now, Miss Atherton. Or you'll miss your train."

The tiny local train station at Bolton was deserted. Alexandra sat on the hard wooden bench, awaiting the next locomotive, her heart broken in two.

The envelope with her wages contained eleven pounds. It was far more than she'd legitimately earned for five weeks of service, a very generous sum. Ten pounds was exactly the amount required for a second-class steamship ticket to New York, and the rest would pay for train fare, facts of which she suspected Longford was well aware.

She wiped the tears that seemed impossible to stem, struggling to focus on her journey. Instead of going to London, should she change trains en route and travel straight to Liverpool? From a discarded newspaper, she learned that the next steamship for New York didn't leave for another three days.

Three days. She needed every penny she now possessed to cover travel expenses. Which left virtually nothing to pay for three nights' lodging. She couldn't go to Liverpool, friendless and alone. She'd put that off until the day the ship sailed, and go to London after all. But where would she stay?

Briefly, she considered going to Brown's Hotel. The last newspaper article she'd seen about herself had mentioned that her mother still resided there, and that Madeleine had joined her. How Alexandra longed to be in her sister's company! They'd been apart for so many months.

Returning to her mother's bosom, so to speak, would give

Alexandra the sanctuary she so desperately needed. She'd have to beg her mother's forgiveness, of course. Her mother would be absolutely furious at Alexandra's desertion. But perhaps she'd also be relieved to see her safe and still eminently marriageable.

Another thought came on the heels of that one: of herself at the pond with Longford. A hot blush rose to Alexandra's face. Although she'd behaved wantonly that day, thanks to Longford's restraint, she was still a virgin. She wouldn't put it past her mother to have a doctor check that status.

This sobering notion gave Alexandra pause. She knew her mother's aim would still be the same: to marry off each of her daughters to a title. There was the slight possibility that, if Madeleine found a husband, their mother might allow Alexandra to remain unattached. But it seemed a vain hope. It was far more likely that she'd lock Alexandra up again and try to force her into the same kind of horrific marriage as before, if not to Viscount Shrewsbury, then someone just like him. Or worse.

Alexandra shook her head. No. She couldn't take that chance, couldn't even think of revealing herself to her mother, unless she could control the time and place.

Another idea presented itself: she could go to Mrs. Gill's. The landlady had been so kind in the past. She might be willing to take Alexandra in for a few days. If not, Alexandra would just have to pay for a place and figure out the rest tomorrow.

Blowing out a long breath, Alexandra dried her eyes and glanced around the empty train station, her attention settling on the wrapped parcel leaning against the bench beside her. Curiosity overtook her. Carefully, she untied and unwrapped it to reveal what lay beneath.

It was Longford's painting of the Italian landscape, the one she'd so dearly admired. The one in which he'd added a figure that resembled *her*. Like his other works, it was signed *T. Carlyle*.

She stared at the painting in confusion. It was one of his best works, a veritable masterpiece. Why had he given it to her? She wondered if it was a parting gift, because he knew how much she loved it.

Then another idea occurred to her, an idea so painful it nearly closed her throat with aching sadness: that it was meant as a slap in the face. That he felt he'd ruined the painting by adding her to it, and wanted it gone, just as he never wanted to see her again.

CHAPTER TWENTY-FIVE

"That's quite a story, Miss Atherton." Mrs. Gill regarded Alexandra over her teacup with wonder. "I can't get over it. Here I thought you were as poor as a church mouse, but all this time, you had a fortune fit for a queen."

"I'm so sorry to have deceived you, Mrs. Gill," Alexandra replied. "But at the time, I felt I had no choice."

She'd arrived at Mrs. Gill's lodging house at half past ten. The landlady had quickly recovered from her surprise and warmly invited in her unexpected guest. They'd been chatting for over an hour. Alexandra, disinclined to break Longford's cover in case he should ever return to this house, continued to refer to him as Mr. Carlyle, and she hadn't said a word about their thwarted romantic relationship.

Alexandra had told Mrs. Gill all about herself: why she came to England, her mother's insistence that she marry the viscount, and her escape from the hotel weeks ago. To explain her sudden appearance now, Alexandra had simply stated that she wanted to go home, but found herself short of funds. "Unfortunately, I cannot go back to my mother, as I'm sure you understand."

"Oh no, dearie, you couldn't do that. Forgive me for saying so, but your mother sounds like a selfish, dreadful woman."

"At the moment, I fear her judgment is clouded. I admit, though, I feel a little guilty that I've been out of touch for so long. I *am* her daughter. She must be worried about me."

"Be that as it may, I'm glad you came to *me*. I still say, it's a shame you have to go back to America. But I understand you being homesick. It was very good of Mr. Carlyle to give you steamship fare."

"And it's good of you to let me stay here. I'll send you the sum to cover my lodgings when I get home."

"Oh, don't you worry about that, dearie." Mrs. Gill waved her hand. "I only wish there were some other way I could help." Nodding toward the rewrapped parcel Alexandra had brought with her, she added: "Now are you ever going to tell me what that is?"

W hen Alexandra awoke the next morning and found herself in her old room upstairs, her thoughts drifted to Longford, and tears welled in her eyes.

She could live a hundred years and never meet another man like him, a man she so completely adored, and with whom she felt so perfectly matched. If only she could go back in time, she'd do things differently. But it was too late now.

Although she knew it was over between them, she couldn't simply turn off the workings of her heart. She loved him. She would always love him. And Lillie and Julia! It pained her to know that she was cut off from them forever, a pain all the more acute from the knowledge that she had no one to blame but herself.

Alexandra rolled over in bed, pondering her uncertain future. If she couldn't marry Longford, she decided, she would never marry at all. But somehow, she had to find a way to make some *good* out of this horrible situation. For a long while, she lay there, thinking, until an idea began to take shape in her brain. Yes, she thought, as the details of the plan became increasingly clear to her. *Yes.* She knew exactly what she wanted to do. What she *must* do.

That morning, at a travel agency, she purchased a ticket for the next steamship to New York, departing from Liverpool in two days. The rest of the day was taken up by her newfound errand. As she walked back to Mrs. Gill's house after completing her task, navigating the smoky, noisy, dusty London streets—this time with a map to guide her—Alexandra smiled to herself in satisfaction. She knew she had done the right thing, and prayed for the best.

On her second and last day in town, Alexandra became determined to discover what she could about her mother's and sister's circumstances, and to affect a visit if it were safe. She enlisted Mrs. Gill's aid, and the two women went to Brown's Hotel. While Alexandra waited outside, lest she be recognized by the hotel staff, Mrs. Gill made enquiries about Mrs. Atherton and her daughter.

"Well!" Mrs. Gill said in a huff when she came out some time later. "The man at the desk wouldn't tell me a single thing, but I found a chambermaid who was helpful. There is indeed a Mrs. Josephine Atherton staying here with her daughter Madeleine, in just the rooms you mentioned. And you'll never guess where they are at this very moment! Why, they're just a few blocks away, having tea at the Mayfair Café."

Alexandra's heart skittered. Her sister was so close! "Oh, Mrs. Gill. What should I do?"

"You're longing to see your sister, aren't you? To say goodbye?"

"Yes. But at the same time, I'm afraid. My mother will be so angry with me, there's no telling what she might do."

"Unless your mother is an officer of the law, I don't see what she can do to you in a public place like the Mayfair Café."

"You're right, Mrs. Gill. Thank you." Screwing up her courage, Alexandra said: "Lead the way, please."

A ten minutes' walk brought them to the designated spot, a redbrick building with white awnings and a magnificent set of etched-glass doors. Alexandra's heart pounded as she paused outside, gathering her courage to go in.

"I'll wait for you out here," Mrs. Gill encouraged. "Be of stout heart, Miss Atherton. Give that mother of yours a piece of your mind!"

"I will," Alexandra promised.

The café was abuzz with the sounds of conversation and tinkling silverware, as ladies in fashionable dress sipped tea and ate finger sandwiches at tables draped in white linen. Scanning the crowd, Alexandra saw her mother and Madeleine seated halfway down the room. Her mother's elegant white lace blouse and mulberry-colored jacket strained across her full bosom, as she barked at her daughter across the table.

At the sight of her sister, Alexandra's heart turned over. Madeleine, her chestnut hair twisted up beneath a midnight-blue hat, frowned silently as she stirred her tea, looking paler and thinner than the last time Alexandra had seen her.

Alexandra quickly made her way to their table, steeling herself for battle. "Hello, Mother. Hello, Maddie."

The two women stared at Alexandra, stunned into momentary silence.

"Alexandra!" her mother cried at last. "How . . . what . . . well! Well!" Her eyes darkened with anger and her jaw tightened. "So. You've come back at last."

"Lexie!" Madeleine leapt up and threw her arms around Alexandra. "Oh, Lexie! How I've missed you."

"I've missed you too, Maddie. So much." Alexandra returned the embrace with fervor, then pulled back to study her sister. "Let me look at you. You're as beautiful as ever, but far too pale. Are you enjoying the Season?"

Madeleine shrugged. "Not at first. I didn't want to come, didn't want to leave Vassar before the end of term. I felt I had no right to be here, it was your place, your clothes. But . . ." Madeleine paused, then rushed on: "But where have you *been*? We've been so worried about you!"

"Yes, where have you been all these weeks, Alexandra?" her mother demanded.

"Apparently, I've been in Switzerland. For my health."

Her mother frowned haughtily. "I had to give *some* explanation to the press." Indicating an empty chair at the table, she commanded, "Sit down."

"I'd rather stand, Mother. I have a friend waiting. I won't be long."

"What? After all this time, you think you can just say hello and leave? I won't hear of it. You will sit down and tell me exactly where you've been and who you've been with."

"I'll do no such thing."

"You will, and you'll do it now." Her eyes were calculating. "There's not a moment to waste. The Season will be over in six weeks, but if people believe the Switzerland story, you still have a chance to find a match. Viscount Shrewsbury is out of the running, unfortunately—he chose that dull cow from San Francisco. But he's only one fish in the sea."

"Mother," Alexandra said forcefully, "let me make one thing absolutely clear: I am not marrying anybody. I only came here to let you see for yourself that I am alive and in one piece, and to say good-bye to Maddie."

"Good-bye?" Madeleine repeated sadly. "Where are you going?"

"Home."

"*Home*," her mother scoffed, as she rose abruptly. "You will come back to the hotel with us, now, where we'll discuss your future in a civilized manner." Waving her hand, she cried to one of the servers, "Boy! You there! Bring us the bill at once!"

The server scuttled off to the back. Alexandra shook her head, turning her full gaze on her mother.

"I would have gone home weeks ago, if I'd had the money. But I have it now. I've already bought my ticket, and I leave tomorrow."

"This is absurd." Her mother was incensed. "Why are you so set on going home? What do you mean to do when you get there?"

"I hope to go back to Vassar. After that, I'll find a job."

"A job?" Her mother was horrified.

"Yes, a job."

"Lexie!" Madeleine's eyes shone. "How thrilling."

"This is unheard of. You're the daughter of a *multimillionaire*. You're an *heiress*. You will not embarrass me by *working* for a living."

"I'm sorry if that embarrasses you, Mother. But the truth is, I've been working to earn my living the entire time that I've been gone."

Her mother looked aghast. "Doing what? And where?"

"I was a governess at a country estate."

"Dear Lord," her mother exclaimed with disdain, fanning herself with her hand. "A *governess*."

"For the first time in my life, I found something I'm really *good* at, that I enjoy. I want to do something meaningful with my life, Mother, and teaching seems to me an excellent way to accomplish that. I want to get my degree if I can, and then I intend to seek a position as a teacher or perhaps a headmistress at a school in New York."

"You are talking nonsense, Alexandra. I won't allow you to throw your life away in this fashion. You will do as we planned. I will announce that you're back from Switzerland, your health fully restored. You will immerse yourself in the final weeks of the Season, and we'll find a titled man for you. Otherwise—and hear me now, for I won't repeat myself: I will speak to your father and see to it that you are disinherited. You won't get a single penny from either one of us, and we will never see you again."

Madeleine gasped in dismay. "Mother! You wouldn't do such a thing."

"I can, and I will."

Alexandra let go a sigh. "If that's the way you want it, Mother, so be it. I know what it's like now to be without Father's name and money to provide for me, and you know what I discovered? Being poor is not the end of the world. I was forced to support myself. And I rather liked it."

"You'll be a poverty-stricken spinster, then? You would willingly give up your inheritance and the joys of marriage and motherhood, for what? To be indentured to teach the brattish offspring of total strangers for the rest of your life?"

"If I could do it all—if I could marry a man I love, raise a family, and find a way to do something else with my talents and abilities beyond being a wife and mother—I would. That would make me very happy. But I won't marry just for the sake of a title, or to make *you* happy."

"You are a foolish, foolish girl, Alexandra," her mother snapped.

"Maybe so. But I'd rather be foolish and content, than miserable and married to the wrong man."

"Hear hear!" Madeleine cried, taking Alexandra's hands in her own and squeezing them.

"Madeleine Atherton! Sit down this minute."

Madeleine flushed but remained standing, and continued to hold on to Alexandra's hands.

"Maddie," Alexandra said softly, "do you want to come home with me? If you have ten pounds in your purse, we can travel together."

"Don't put stupid ideas into your sister's head. I have control over Madeleine's money. Don't think I didn't learn my lesson with you. If she knows what's good for her, she'll stay exactly where she is."

A moment passed. Then Madeleine said, "I'm sorry, Lexie. I know how much this means to Mother, and I don't mind *trying*. Just last night, I met someone." Her blush deepened.

"Oh. I see."

"I doubt anything will come of it," Madeleine quickly added. "We barely exchanged two words. But . . ."

"Well, Maddie darling," Alexandra replied with a warm smile. "If he's a man of any sense, he'll recognize what a prize he's found in you. I just hope he's worthy of you." She wrapped her arms around her sister and held her tightly. "I love you, and wish you all the happiness in the world."

"You too, Lexie," Madeleine whispered in Alexandra's ear. "Be safe. Be happy. And please write."

"I will," Alexandra promised.

Chapter Twenty-Six

Thomas dug in his heels, pushing Merlin as fast as the horse would go across the meadow. The wind whipped cold and fierce against his cheeks as he galloped along, trying to lose himself in the pure rush of speed.

He'd been riding like this every morning for two days straight. Hoping it would help him get past his fury, help him forget.

But he couldn't forget. She was hundreds of miles away now, he'd never see her again, yet he saw her every single moment in his mind. He couldn't forget the sweetness of her laugh. The deep huskiness of her voice. Her unique turn of phrase. The way she looked with the sun shining on her hair, surrounded by a field of bluebells that matched her eyes. The tenderness on her face as she read to his sisters. Her smile. The soft wantonness of her mouth as she'd returned his kisses. The way she'd felt, her body nestled against his, when he'd made love to her. An act they'd come very close to completing.

He had tried to rid his mind of these memories, but he could not. For the past two days, he'd found himself wandering the hallways of Polperran House, his pulse quickening at the sound of every footstep, wishing that it were hers. In her room, he'd found all the clothes he'd bought her hanging in the wardrobe, a visible reminder of her former presence there.

Her sketchbook was on the dressing table, and he'd turned to the drawing he'd made of her. A likeness that seemed so real, it almost felt as if she might leap off the page. He'd buried the sketchbook in a drawer, then had sneaked back in the dead of night to reclaim it, setting it on the dresser in his own room, where he could gaze at it whenever the mood struck.

The mood struck far too often.

How could he still think of her with any kind of affection, after what she did? Was he deluded? She had lived in his house for weeks, pretending to be a poor governess, while all that time she was the daughter of one of the wealthiest men in America. How could he have been so blind as not to notice? How could he have been so foolish?

He galloped up the rise in the road, arriving at the crest of the hill in view of Trevelyan Manor and the coastline beyond. He wondered if Saunders were home. Thomas hadn't spoken to his friend in two days, since that awkward moment when they had encountered Miss Watson . . . *no, Miss Atherton* . . . on the lawn, and Saunders had made it clear who she really was.

Suddenly, Thomas felt desperate to speak to someone about his torment. Perhaps Saunders could help lay the situation to rest.

Upon reaching the manor house, Thomas handed his

reins to a groom and was soon admitted inside. Saunders greeted him with a firm handshake and led him to a quiet room at the back of the house.

"I am so sorry about the other day," Saunders said, pouring Thomas a brandy before they both sat down. "I fear I opened Pandora's box."

"So you did, and not a moment too soon."

"I have been hoping to hear some word from you. What is the result? Did you and Miss Atherton come to an understanding?"

"An understanding? I should say not. I sent her packing."

"You sent her away?" Saunders stared at Thomas in dismay.

"On the next train to London."

"But why? You said you love her."

"She lied to me, Saunders."

"Yes, but did she explain why she did it?"

"She claimed her mother was set on marrying her off to some viscount in London, and she had to escape. She found herself with no money, she said, but did not tell me her real name for fear I would send her back to her mother. She accepted my offer of employment to earn her fare to America."

"Who is the viscount?"

"I have no idea."

"Wait. I read about it the papers. What was his name?" Saunders thought for a minute, then gave a gasp of disgust. "*Dear God.* I remember now. It was Viscount Shrewsbury. I thought it an odd choice for a woman like her. I have met Shrewsbury. If Miss Atherton was about to be wed against her will to that bastard, I do not blame her for running away."

Thomas tried not to let Saunders's reaction sway him. "That does not excuse her giving me a false name, and pretending to be a governess to my sisters."

"Is that what she did, Longford? Did she really *pretend* to be a governess?"

"Yes. She—"

"From what you told me, she performed the job rather expertly. 'Best governess my sisters have ever had,' I believe you said. She loves your sisters, you explained, and your sisters love her."

"What is your point?"

"My point is, Is what she did really so terrible? It seems to me that she started out desperate and got caught up in a lie which was difficult to undo. She was probably afraid to tell you. And no wonder: look how you reacted when you found out."

Thomas took a swallow of brandy and frowned. "Why are you sticking up for her? After pretending all that time to be someone else, do I really even know her? She betrayed my trust, as surely as Elise Townsend betrayed it."

"Now hold on, you cannot compare her with Elise Townsend. I do not know Miss Atherton as you do, but the word in town was that she was a class act, an intelligent, fascinating woman. Elise was the antithesis of that. She was—pardon my French—a self-centered, scheming bitch. Miss Atherton had a reason for keeping her identity a secret. Maybe she took it too far, but . . . did she say she was sorry?"

"Yes." An uncomfortable heat rose to Thomas's throat and he tugged at his necktie, wishing he could pull it off.

"Did she say she loves you?"

Thomas nodded, his eyes on the carpet.

"Do you believe her?"

"*Yes.*" The admission erupted from somewhere deep in his belly, like a soft, hoarse cry. "She said she hoped to marry me. To use her father's fortune to help restore Polperran House and Longford village."

"And you have a problem with that?" Saunders asked in disbelief.

"What do you expect me to do? Forgive her?"

Saunders's eyebrows lifted as he darted Thomas a sharp look filled with meaning. "Haven't you ever told a falsehood to anyone, Longford? Haven't you ever, even once, *lied just a little*—even if by omission—to attain something you dearly needed or wanted?"

Thomas froze, the question hitting him straight in the gut. He realized, suddenly, that he had indeed done such a thing, many times over. To every client to whom he had sold a painting as *T. Carlyle*, and every day he'd stayed under the roof of his good landlady, Mrs. Gill. For two years now, he had been perpetrating a fraud. Was it really that much different from what Miss Atherton had done? Of course, he told himself, he'd had good reason to do so. But then, hadn't she?

Saunders was shaking his head, his expression making it clear that he'd read the answer to his question on Thomas's face. "Who are you to cast the first stone, Longford?"

Thomas swallowed hard. "But I promised myself never

to marry for money. I will not stoop to accepting a handout from some American millionaire, just because I have fallen for his daughter. . . ." His voice trailed off. The old excuses sounded absurd even to his own ears.

"You. Are. An idiot."

"I am beginning to think I am," Thomas said slowly. He reminded himself again how different his life was since Lexie had come on the scene. His newfound relationship with Julia and Lillie. His friendship with Saunders restored. The joy Thomas had found in painting again. It was all because of her.

"It is obvious to anyone with half a brain that you are head over heels in love with her. Would you like to know what I would do, in your shoes?"

"I think you have made it pretty clear what you would do."

"I will say it, nonetheless, since you seem to need to hear it. I would get your arse up out of that chair and take the next train to London. Follow your heart, Longford! Give up all these stupid prejudices and be happy. Marry for love." Saunders sighed. "It is more than I expect to do for myself."

Thomas called for his carriage and packed a bag in ten minutes flat, determined to make it to the Bolton station for the one-o'clock train to London. To his frustration, he arrived just as the train was leaving in a cloud of smoke and steam.

The next train was not due for another two hours, and it didn't go direct to London. It was the milk run. He would have to change trains several times. Thomas considered going home and trying again tomorrow, but worried that might be too late. Instead, he sent John home with the carriage and waited.

As he paced back and forth at the station, impatiently biding his time, Thomas worked on his plan. Somehow, he had to win her back. Find the proper words to let her know how desperately he regretted everything he had said and done, and how much he loved her.

But first, he had to find her. He had to take it on faith that she'd actually gone to London. He had given her enough money to pay for her fare back to America, which she had made clear from the beginning was her desired destination. He purchased a newspaper, and learned that a ship was due to depart Liverpool harbor for New York the very next evening. Would she be on it? There was no way of knowing. How would he even find her, at such a busy port of call? He shook his head, deciding to try London first, take his chances that she was in fact there and had not yet left town.

The train was infernally late, causing him to miss his next connection. The train after that broke down, causing another interminable delay. And so it went, making it the journey from hell. The trains stopped running when he reached Basingstoke, and he was obliged to take shelter in a filthy inn, taking the first train out early the next day. By the time he finally reached London, it was half past seven in the morning.

In a city of this size, where to begin looking for her?

She was an heiress. She must know dozens of well-heeled people with whom she could stay. But, he reminded himself, if she did not go to any of them weeks ago in her first distress, why would she turn to them now? He recalled her saying that she had stayed with her mother at Brown's Hotel. But no; under no circumstances would she have gone to her mother. Instinct told him that if she *was* in town, she would have gone to one of the few people she felt she could trust: Mrs. Gill.

He grabbed a cab and went straight to Mrs. Gill's house. Arriving there, he knocked loudly, but received no response. He pounded on the door, calling out. Still nothing. What the devil? He checked his pocket watch. It was just after eight. Mrs. Gill rarely left the premises at such an early hour. Was she out of town? And what of the kitchen maid, Mary? Why was she not in? If Miss Atherton had stayed at this house, Mary would know all about it.

He suddenly remembered that Mary sometimes went out early to buy fish and produce at the street market a few blocks away. It was worth a try.

Alexandra sighed heavily as she and Mrs. Gill moved through the crowds at Euston Station, her thoughts drifting to the last time she'd been here, intending to make this same journey.

That morning, so many weeks ago, she'd been alone, relieved to be leaving London, worried that there might not be a room available aboard the ship, and filled with anxiety lest something else should go wrong. Today, circumstances couldn't be more different. She already had her steamship ticket in her possession, which she was ready to guard with her life. She had Mrs. Gill to see her safely off. And she wasn't exactly relieved to be leaving.

"What is that sigh for?" asked Mrs. Gill as they headed toward the platform for the Liverpool train. "I thought you were happy to be going home."

"I am happy. But I'm sad, too, at the thought of leaving England. And saying good-bye to you." Alexandra managed a smile for her friend, as she touched her bonnet. "Thank you again, Mrs. Gill, for letting me keep the hat. It's a long way to New York, and I'll feel better with something on my head."

"You're most welcome, dearie. Anyway, it looks better on you than it ever did on me." Mrs. Gill cast her a sidelong glance then, commenting, "You know, when you told me about your time in Cornwall, you said a great deal about the girls you cared for, but nary a word about Mr. Carlyle."

"Didn't I?" Alexandra felt herself blush as an errant tear infiltrated her eye. She quickly wiped it away.

Mrs. Gill tucked one of her arms beneath Alexandra's and drew her close as they walked. "Did you lose your heart to him, dearie?"

A little sound escaped Alexandra's lips, halfway between a laugh and a sob. "I fear I did, Mrs. Gill. But he didn't want it."

"Ah, child. The ways of love are never easy. I suppose he thought you were too good for him, rich as you are, and him just a country painter."

Alexandra shook her head, her voice cracking as she replied: "I don't think that was the problem."

"Well, dearie. It seems to me that a young lady in your position will have dozens of worthy men to choose from. And I always say, if something is meant to be, it will be."

The street market was a noisy, dirty affair with red-faced vendors hawking everything from fruits and vegetables to live poultry and sides of beef. Thomas moved quickly through the throngs, straw and grime from the cobblestones sticking to his boots as he searched every face for the one he sought.

At last, he spotted Mrs. Gill's kitchen maid, Mary, looking over the turnips and potatoes at a nearby stall. "Mary?"

The maid turned to him in surprise and dipped a quick curtsy. "Good morning, sir."

"Good morning. Mary: I have only just arrived in town, and I . . ." If Miss Atherton *had* gone to Mrs. Gill's, he was uncertain what name she would have used. "Can you tell me, Has Miss Watson been to the house of late?"

"Miss Watson?" Mary's eyebrows raised. "Did ye not know then, Mr. Carlyle, sir? Her name's nay Miss Watson, but Miss *Atherton*." Confidentially, she added, "She's an *heiress*."

So she *had* been there. And she had told them who she was. But apparently, she had not divulged his own true identity. "Yes. Just so, has *Miss Atherton* been staying at Mrs. Gill's?"

"She has, sir. Came to us three nights ago."

"It is vital that I see her, but I found no one at home. Do you know where she might be?"

"I do, sir. She and Mrs. Gill left over an hour ago for Euston Station."

"Euston Station!"

Mary nodded. "Miss Atherton's on her way back to New York, sir, on the first boat train."

Bloody hell. There truly was not a moment to lose. Thomas thanked the girl, dashed back through the marketplace, and hailed a cab.

As the vehicle crawled along through the London streets, Thomas cursed the morning traffic. The journey seemed to take forever. Upon arrival, he paid the cabbie and dashed through the grand portal into the station, then checked the board to learn from which platform the Liverpool train was embarking. It was due to leave in ten minutes.

Ten minutes!

Thomas's heart pounded as he raced the full length of one platform, then another, pushing his way through the crowd, heedless of the grunts of complaint from the people he was affronting. At last, he reached his destination. The crowds were immense, couples embracing by the waiting locomotive, from whose smokestack a gray plume was already shooting upward. He rushed toward the train, dashing around piles of luggage, then paused, gasping, frantically searching for a glimpse of Miss Atherton.

And then he saw her.

She was standing by the door to a waiting third-class passenger car, wearing the same black dress she had worn when he'd first found her, and she was in the arms of another woman. Mrs. Gill. They were hugging good-bye.

Thomas broke into a run. The embrace between the two women ended. Mrs. Gill waved and disappeared into the crowd, unaware of his approach. Miss Atherton turned and climbed up the steps into the waiting car.

"Wait!" he gasped. "Miss Atherton! Wait!"

She whirled around on the landing of the passenger car doorway, her face registering her astonishment upon seeing him. He hurried over and stopped immediately below the car's steps, struggling to catch his breath as he gazed up at her. He had prepared a speech in the cab, but now that they stood nearly face to face, he could not recall a single word of it.

"Please. You cannot leave," is what came out of his mouth.

Her brow furrowed as she looked down at him. "As you see, I am."

"I pray that you will change your mind. Please, Miss Atherton. Please get off that train."

"Why?"

"Because I have been a fool."

She went still at that. He didn't wait for her reply, but rushed on:

"When I learned who you really are, I should have embraced it. I should have understood that only extraordinary circumstances could have propelled you to act as you did. Instead, all I could see was my own hurt and wounded pride. But how can I blame you, when you did nothing I had not already done myself, many times over? I am so sorry. So deeply, deeply sorry."

"I appreciate your apology." She seemed to be struggling for calm. The train whistle blew, signaling its imminent departure. "But you still haven't given me a reason to get off this train."

"I give you this reason: you cannot go because it will take you away from me. I love you, Miss Atherton. I love you with all my heart. You are the best thing that has ever happened to me, and I cannot imagine my life without you in it. I want to spend the rest of my days with you, if you will have me. Will you marry me? Will you do me the honor of returning to Cornwall with me, and be my wife?"

To the end of his days, Thomas knew he would never forget the surge of relief and joy he felt when Miss Atherton's mouth curved into a smile, and she stepped down from the train.

Her blue eyes sparkled with emotion as she wrapped her arms around his neck. "Yes," she said firmly, as their lips met in a fiery kiss. "Yes, I will marry you. You big fool."

CHAPTER TWENTY-SEVEN

The wedding took place two months later at St. Perran's Church in Longford Parish. Alexandra wore a spectacular gown of white Belgian lace created for her, of course, by Worth in Paris. Her four bridesmaids, the sisters of the bride and groom, looked beautiful in their own white lace dresses. The Earl of Longford and his best man, the Earl of Saunders, were resplendent in their morning coats.

"Alexandra," her father said, before he walked her down the aisle, "I'm so proud of you."

"Are you, Father?"

"How can you doubt it? I still shudder to think of all you went through. I would never have disowned you, my dear, no matter what your mother might say."

Moisture gathered in Alexandra's eyes. "Thank you, Father."

When the service was over, Alexandra was delighted by the welcome she received from the community, and particularly satisfied by the humble curtsy offered by Mrs. Gordon.

Mrs. Gill, beaming with pride and happiness, gave her an

especially warm hug. "To think I had an earl living under my roof for months, and had no idea! I'm so happy for you both, dearie."

"I can never thank you enough, Mrs. Gill. For everything."

Kathryn was thrilled to be in England again, and happy to see her sister marry a man of whom she had immediately approved.

"He is so divinely handsome," Kathryn whispered in Alexandra's ear when the service was over, and family and friends were gathered in the long gallery at Polperran House for an elaborate afternoon tea reception. "It's no wonder you fell for him like a ton of bricks. If only he had a brother."

"Be careful what you wish for," Alexandra warned her sister. "You know that *this* has only inflamed Mother's plans for you and Maddie."

They both glanced across the room, to where their middle sister was laughing with Lillie and Julia. Madeleine was still unattached, having pronounced herself to be incompatible with the man who'd briefly attracted her interest earlier in town. She'd formed an immediate bond, however, with Julia and Lillie, who were thrilled when their favorite governess became their brother's bride.

"I am aware," replied Kathryn with a smile. "But I'm on my guard. After what you've been through, there's not a chance on earth I'd let Mother pick out my husband."

Mrs. Atherton was all delight that her daughter had married an earl. Although she'd tried without success to push Madeleine into the arms of several eligible men that season, Mrs. Atherton hadn't dared to repeat her histrionics or try to force the issue, not with Lord Longford looking over her shoulder.

"Now that Alexandra is a countess, I fully expect an invitation to Mrs. Astor's next winter ball," Alexandra overheard her mother saying with satisfaction to her father some time later, as the guests began to disperse. With a smile she added, "Isn't this a grand old house?"

"Very grand indeed," Colis Atherton replied, curling his handlebar mustache with his fingertips as he glanced around the room, which was festooned with flowers paid for out of his own pocket. "But I must say, Alexandra and her new husband will need every penny of her fortune to get this place into shape."

"When they're through, it will be a showplace, my dear," his wife answered. "A delightful country retreat, suitable for entertaining other peers of the realm. You understand that this is just the beginning. This season may be over, but there is always next year—and we will be back. I can hardly wait to see Mrs. Astor's face the day she learns that *all* my daughters have married men with titles."

"Well," Colis Atherton responded with a nod, "you have certainly made a good start."

Alexandra turned to Longford, who was seizing two glasses of champagne from a passing tray. "Did you hear that?"

Her husband nodded, handing her a glass with a smile. "I did, my love. But I do not mind. I have come to admire your mother."

"Admire her? Why?"

"For her quest that you marry a titled man. Because it brought you to me."

Alexandra smiled up at him. "I could not agree more." They clinked glasses and drank. "In the same vein, I hope you'll look more kindly on *your* father."

"My father?" he repeated, surprised.

"I don't blame you for being angry with him. But he paid for your education in Italy, which he couldn't afford. And far more than that: he took in Lillie, which was a kind and generous thing to do."

Thomas nodded slowly as he gazed down at her. "You are a wise woman. No wonder I fell in love with you." Setting aside their glasses, he took her in his embrace and kissed her. "Thank you for marrying me."

"Thank you for asking."

"There's something I feel bad about, though. I keep thinking about what you had to give up to be with me."

"What did I give up?"

"Your return to Vassar. Your college degree. I know how much your studies mattered to you."

"I'm not at all sorry," Alexandra replied, gazing into the eyes of the man she adored. "I learned a great deal in college. But if I've learned anything in life, it's to know when it's time to accept that you've achieved enough in one arena, and be willing to move on to the next. What matters to me now is the man standing before me, and the life we're going to build together."

Later that night, when Alexandra and Thomas were at last alone together in his bedroom, she felt shy in his presence for the first time in weeks. Since their engagement, they'd kissed at length and spent many long evenings in the library, talking about the future. But they'd never again repeated the intimacies they'd shared that afternoon at the pond.

Now they were married. She stood before him in a white silk nightdress that clung to her body, accentuating her curves. Her hair, relieved of its pins, cascaded around her shoulders. A fire burned in the grate, infusing the room with warmth. Thomas came to her, naked from the waist up.

"My love," he whispered. "You are a vision. I cannot tell you how long I have dreamed of this moment."

"So have I," she admitted. "I just hope I'll know what to do. We only got so far before."

He kissed her, his gentleness conveying both reassurance and the depth of his affection. "Fear not, my lovely wife. Whatever happens, it is just you and me now, expressing our love for each other."

He pulled her against him until their lips and bodies met and clung. She loved the feel of his male torso, the way it fit so perfectly against her own. Her hands slid around him, exploring the length of his back, curling into his silky hair as they kissed. Then, drawing back slightly, he lifted her night-gown over her head.

She trembled slightly, self-conscious in her nudity, but his warm brown eyes gleamed with appreciation as he took her in. She could see that he found her beautiful. In one swift movement, he divested himself of his trousers and took her in his arms again. She felt his naked manhood, pressed hard and insistent against her. The kiss that followed was every bit as thrilling and sensuous as their very first kiss, yet now it was even more wondrous and meaningful, for it was infused with the deep love they felt for each other.

Moving to the bed, they melted into each other's embrace again, hands everywhere, mouths meeting with such passion, it left them both breathless.

His lips and tongue paid tribute to the sensitive tips of her breasts, until she heard herself moan. Hot desire curled in her belly as he traveled lower, covering her stomach with kisses, and then lower still, until he reached the V between her legs and parted them with his hands.

She hadn't expected this. "What . . . are you doing?" she asked softly.

"Hoping to bring you bliss," was his reply.

She inhaled sharply as his mouth and tongue began lapping at her most private of places. She wanted to voice her consternation and surprise, but was suddenly incapable of thought, much less speech. His ministrations continued until she felt a tide of yearning rising inside her, as it had once before when he'd touched her there with his fingers.

This time the feelings were even more intense, wrapping her in a sensation that built and built inside her womb until she thought she might die from the pleasure of it, until finally her body ignited with white-hot sensation, as if flying off a precipice into pure joy.

It took a long moment to find her voice. "Dear God," she said breathily, her legs still reverberating as he made his way up her body again with moist kisses.

He settled himself atop her, and she felt the hard length of his desire once again trapped between their bodies. Cupping her face tenderly with one hand, he whispered, "Did you like that, Lady Longford?"

"I more than *liked* it, my lord. I *loved* it." She smiled, smoothing one hand down the length of his back. "And now, it's your turn. I want—"

"Wait." He readjusted himself so that he lay beside her, then took one of her hands in his. "Will you touch me first?" he whispered.

He placed her hand around his naked male member. It felt hard as steel. He silently guided her to move her hand up and down along its length. She loved the way it felt, the way her touch affected him, the way his stomach contracted and his respiration altered, as if he were working hard to control himself. Finally, he stayed her hand with his own and kissed her fervently.

Reaching down, he pleasured her again with his hand, in that place which was now hot and wet, but felt empty somehow. Soon, the sweet tension built inside her again and she was aching once more for release.

"Please," was all she could think to say.

Moving back atop her, he brushed his lips against hers and said, "This might hurt at first, my darling, as it is your first time. But I hope the pain will be fleeting." With gentle slowness, he guided himself inside her. It did hurt a bit, and at her intake of breath he paused, gazing down at her questioningly. "My love?"

"I'm all right. Keep going."

He nestled further, until the space that had felt void and wanting was suddenly filled. He began to move, and as she instinctively moved with him, the initial pain began to fade, until it was overtaken by a sensation that redefined the very word pleasure.

Her hands gripped him, holding him close. She wanted to tell him how wonderful it felt to be in his arms with their bodies joined, as close as two people possibly could be. But words failed her; her mind spun. With each rocking thrust, she felt her own body tensing and coiling again as it reached for the now-familiar precipice.

They were both breathing hard and fast. She matched his tempo, reveling in the pure joy of this union that was so much more than she ever could have imagined. Then she crashed over the edge again. Seconds later, she heard his own deep moan of pleasure, felt the rapid pulse of his manhood inside her, and she knew that he'd found his own release.

Afterward, they lay in each other's arms, holding each other close, foreheads touching.

"I thought I had a pretty good imagination," she said softly, gazing into his brown eyes, "but I never knew that *this . . .* could be like *that.*"

His eyes were filled with affection as he tenderly stroked her cheek. "Neither did I," he admitted roughly. "Neither did I."

"Do you think . . . we could do it again?"

He chuckled deep in his throat. "As my lady commands." Then his mouth took possession of hers once more.

Alexandra lay on the sofa in the private sitting room off the master bedroom, clad in a diaphanous peach-colored Grecian gown that revealed more than it hid. A fire burned in the hearth, warming the room, a complement to the glow of happiness she felt as the wife of Thomas Carlyle, the Earl of Longford.

Ten weeks had passed since their marriage. She and Thomas had honeymooned for a month in Italy, an unforgettable trip generously paid for by her father. They had then returned home to resume their wedded bliss at Polperran House, where Lillie and Julia now enjoyed the attentions of a wonderful new governess.

Alexandra had so adored her own time teaching the girls, however, that she spent part of each day working with them herself. She was also working directly with the headmaster of the local school in the village to add more varied subjects to the curriculum. She volunteered there, two afternoons a week, teaching geography and literature, and Thomas offered his time giving art lessons to the children.

She kept in touch with her sisters via weekly correspondence, letters that she read and reread with great pleasure, while looking forward to visits from them in the future. Kathryn and Madeleine were both back at Vassar, although Madeleine had promised their mother another London Season next year, after she graduated.

With some coaxing, Alexandra had finally persuaded her new husband to accept help in the way of her fortune, to revitalize Polperran House—if not for himself, she insisted, then to preserve it for future generations. He seemed pleased with the improvements so far. In the past two months alone, the roof had been repaired and dozens of windows had been replaced. Improvements were underway to update the plumbing and install gas lighting. They'd ordered new furnishings, and more than two dozen new carpets had been installed. To Alexandra's delight, six new gardeners had been employed, and work had begun to restore the gardens to their former glory.

The residents of Longford village were excited about changes under way, including roof repairs and other structural improvements to their cottages. Alexandra and her husband had also purchased new farm machinery for their tenants and brought in experts to discuss the possibility of growing crops other than wheat, which might bring in more income.

Thomas, his interest in painting already revived, had been further inspired by the works of art in the great museums of Florence and Rome. Although he no longer had to paint portraits for hire, he'd admitted that there was one portrait he'd been dreaming of painting for some time now, the one which was currently in progress: a portrait of Alexandra as the goddess Aphrodite.

"I have been wondering," Thomas remarked, dabbing at the palette with his brush, "since I no longer worry about being recognized in town, What would you think if I shave off my mustache?"

"I hope you won't. I fell in love with you wearing that mustache. And I love the way it feels when you kiss me."

"When I kiss you where?" His eyes glittered.

"Everywhere," she answered, and they both laughed.

"It just occurred to me," he mused, returning to work on the canvas, "you never told me what happened to that painting I gave you all those months ago, the day that I . . ." He paused, a guilty look crossing his face.

"The day you threw me out of the house?" Alexandra asked calmly. At the time, it was the most bitter and painful moment of her life. Now that they were happily married, and he'd spent months expressing his love for her and his regret over what happened, she could look back on it with equanimity.

He dared a glance at her. "Have you forgiven me?"

"With all my heart."

He sighed with relief. "Well, then. What about the painting—that Italian landscape? As I remember, you were quite fond of it."

"I was. I still consider it one of your best works." It was interesting timing, she thought, that he was asking about that painting today, of all days.

"What did you do with it? Did you sell it?"

"Sell it? Of course not." The idea had never even occurred to her.

"Well, then?"

"What did you hope I'd do with it?" she teased. "You never said why you gave it to me." She'd always wondered why, but considering what she'd done with the painting, she'd thought it best not to bring up the subject.

"I gave it to you because you said you loved it. I suppose, deep down, even in the throes of my anger that day, I knew it was wrong to make you leave, and thought the painting could somehow make up for it."

"I thought it might be something else. That you couldn't bear to look at it anymore because you'd added me to the scene."

"What? No! Not at all. I just wanted you to have it. I hoped it would make you happy."

She smiled, gratified by this discovery. "Well, I hope, when you learn of its fate, it will make *you* happy."

"Its fate?" He paused, brush in hand. "That sounds ominous."

She got up from the sofa. "I have something to show you. A letter arrived for you today. I'm not sure if it's good or bad news, so I was waiting to give it to you at dinner. But this seems as good a time as any." She moved into the adjoining room, retrieved the envelope from her bureau drawer, then returned and offered it to him.

He put down his paintbrush and studied the envelope. "It's from the Academy of British Artists." He glanced at her in confusion. "Why are they writing to me?"

"Open it and find out."

He removed the letter from the envelope and read it aloud.

The Academy of British Artists
Suffolk St., Pall Mall East, London
Attn: Mr. T. Carlyle
c/o Polperran House, Longford, Cornwall

Dear Mr. Carlyle:
Thank you for submitting your painting, Italian Rhapsody, for our consideration. It is our great pleasure to inform you that Italian Rhapsody has been accepted into our winter exhibition as a work of merit, to hang in the main gallery.

In recognition of your achievement, and as a gesture of our regard for your exceptional work, we would like to extend to you an invitation to become a member of the Academy of British Artists. Another letter will be forthcoming explaining the means by which you may be instated as a member. It will also contain further details about the winter exhibition, which is due to run January 10–March 14.

In the meantime, thank you again for your submission and your interest in our organization. We look forward to a future association which we hope will benefit all concerned.

> *With all best wishes,*
> *G. Somerset, Supervising Director*
> *The Academy of British Artists*

Alexandra exclaimed with delight and clasped her hands, waiting eagerly for his response.

Thomas stared at the missive. "My submission? Lexie, what have you done? You *gave* them my painting?"

"I didn't give it. I *submitted* it."

"When?"

"The day after you fired me, when I returned to London."

He winced at her words, then glanced at her, dumbfounded. "How? Do you know someone on the board?"

"Not a soul. But I managed to find the person in charge. I told him I'd been engaged to submit a work of art for a friend. The summer exhibition was already in full swing, but once he saw the painting, he said I could enter it in the competition for the winter exhibition. I used the name T. Carlyle, knowing you preferred to be incognito. And your address only suggests that you live here, with no hint that you're an earl. The man said it'd be months before they announced their decisions. I didn't want to say anything, in case they didn't accept it."

Thomas shook his head, amazed. "I do not know what to say."

"Are you pleased?" she asked carefully, gazing up at him.

"Of course I am."

She let out a relieved breath. "I'm so glad. When I dropped off the painting, I never expected to see it, or you, ever again. But I hoped . . . I *dreamed* of making *your* dream come true, Thomas."

"Even though," he said ruefully, "the day before, I'd behaved in the most cruel and insensitive manner."

"You're a wonderful painter, Thomas. Your work has a right to be seen. I predict there will be many more paintings as marvelous as *Italian Rhapsody*. But for now, it'll hang in a place of honor at the academy, just as you wished. And they've invited you to be a member."

"A great honor. But how can I possibly accept?"

"How can you not? You don't have to paint for a living now. There's no reason for you to keep your ability a secret. Stir things up, Thomas! Be known by your own name for the talent that you are. What can it hurt when they find out you're an earl?"

"They could refuse to accept the painting. They could rescind their offer to join the academy."

"Maybe. But I doubt it. Just because a member of the nobility has never applied, it doesn't mean they wouldn't accept him if he did. There must be other peers who are dying to have their work recognized. You could pave the way for the rest. It's always hardest to be the first to challenge old ideas, to break new ground. But it's the American way."

He nodded thoughtfully. "And you are quite the American girl, aren't you?" he said, echoing a statement he'd made months ago. Only this time, he said it with admiration and love.

"And proud of it," she replied with a smile.

Still gripping the letter, he drew her into his arms. "I do not deserve you, Lady Longford."

She threaded her fingers up through his silky blond hair. "There are just as many times when I think I do not deserve you."

"Have I told you lately that I love you?"

"Not in the last five minutes."

"Well, it is a sentiment that bears repeating." His eyes glowed with affection as he gazed down at her. "I love you, Alexandra Carlyle, my Countess of Longford."

"And I love you, Thomas Carlyle, my earl."

They kissed each other then, a long and lovely kiss filled with all the promise of the future, and all the love in their hearts.

ACKNOWLEDGMENTS

Many thanks to my agent Tamar Rydzinski for her encouragement to write historical romance, her many thoughtful readings of the book in progress, and for finding it a home at Avon. Huge thanks to my beta readers Claudine Pepe, Meredith Esparza, and Bill James.

I am indebted to Gail MacColl and Carol McD. Wallace for their detailed work To Marry An English Lord, and to Sally Mitchell for her Daily Life in Victorian England, which served as resources for this novel.

Thanks to my editor, Carolyn Coons, for shepherding this book through the publication and design process. A big thanks to Guido Caroti for the awesome cover, copy editor extraordinaire Ellen Leach, and the entire team at Avon. I wish to especially thank Lucia Macro for her support of my work through decades and countless books. I loved writing this novel, and am having such fun with the series!

Biggest thanks of all to my darling husband Bill for being so loving and supportive of my need to tell stories, even though it requires so many long hours and weeks and months at the computer away from you. Thank you for enthusiastically accompanying me on all the research trips to England, boldly driving on the "wrong" side of the road, and sharing my delight as we scouted ancient great houses and wandered through endless fields of bluebells. You are my rock and my strength, and I adore and appreciate you.

ABOUT THE AUTHOR

SYRIE JAMES is a bestselling author whose critically acclaimed novels have been translated into eighteen languages. Syrie loves writing books set in nineteenth century England, where she believes she must have lived in another life. Her books have been Library Journal Editor's Picks and won numerous awards including the Audiobook Association Audie for Romance, Women's National Book Association Great Group Read, B&N Romantic Read of the Week, Best Snowbound Romance (Bookbub), Best of the Year (Suspense Magazine and Romance Reviews), and Best First Novel (Library Journal). Syrie lives in Los Angeles and is a member of the Writers Guild of America. She has addressed audiences as a keynote speaker across America and England, and has written, directed, and performed in numerous theatrical productions for the Jane Austen Society of North America.

Discover great authors, exclusive offers, and more at hc.com.